The Living and the Dead

By Christoffer Carlsson

Blaze Me a Sun
Under the Storm
The Living and the Dead

The Living and the Dead

CHRISTOFFER CARLSSON

Translated from the Swedish by
RACHEL WILLSON-BROYLES

PENGUIN MICHAEL JOSEPH

UK | USA | Canada | Ireland | Australia
India | New Zealand | South Africa

Penguin Michael Joseph is part of the Penguin Random House group of companies whose addresses can be found at global.penguinrandomhouse.com

Penguin Random House UK,
One Embassy Gardens, 8 Viaduct Gardens, London SW11 7BW

penguin.co.uk

First published in Sweden as *Levande och dödaby* by Albert Bonniers Forlag 2023
First published in the United States of America by Hogarth,
an imprint of Penguin Random House LLC 2025
First published in Great Britain by Penguin Michael Joseph 2025

001

Copyright © Christoffer Carlsson, 2023
Translation copyright © Rachel Willson-Broyles, 2025

The moral right of the author has been asserted

Penguin Random House values and supports copyright. Copyright fuels creativity, encourages diverse voices, promotes freedom of expression and supports a vibrant culture. Thank you for purchasing an authorized edition of this book and for respecting intellectual property laws by not reproducing, scanning or distributing any part of it by any means without permission. You are supporting authors and enabling Penguin Random House to continue to publish books for everyone. No part of this book may be used or reproduced in any manner for the purpose of training artificial intelligence technologies or systems. In accordance with Article 4(3) of the DSM Directive 2019/790, Penguin Random House expressly reserves this work from the text and data mining exception

Set in 13.5/16pt Garamond MT Std
Typeset by Six Red Marbles UK, Thetford, Norfolk
Printed and bound in Great Britain by Clays Ltd, Elcograf S.p.A.

The authorized representative in the EEA is Penguin Random House Ireland,
Morrison Chambers, 32 Nassau Street, Dublin D02 YH68

A CIP catalogue record for this book is available from the British Library

HARDBACK ISBN: 978–0–241–77308–6
TRADE PAPERBACK ISBN: 978–0–241–77309–3

Penguin Random House is committed to a sustainable future
for our business, our readers and our planet. This book is made from
Forest Stewardship Council® certified paper.

To Stig

For coming to me, and
for existing, and for being
the brightest and most beautiful
light in my life

Is there no line drawn
Between the living and the dead?
Do the dead wash up
Onto the shore
Do the living drift out like timber
Hardly moving?
          — KERSTIN EKMAN

Characters

THE BOYS AND GIRLS FROM SKAVBÖKE

Sander Eriksson: An eighteen-year-old boy; Killian's best friend
Killian Persson: An eighteen-year-old boy; Sander's best friend
Mikael Söderström: An eighteen-year-old boy; the oldest son of the wealthiest family in the community
Filip Söderström: Mikael's younger brother
Pierre Bäck: A friend of Sander and Killian
Jakob Lindell: One of the boys from Skavböke
Felicia Grenberg: An eighteen-year-old girl

THE PARENTS

Madeleine Grenberg: Felicia's mother; widow
Linda and Sten Persson: Killian's divorced parents
Lillemor and Karl-Henrik Söderström: The parents of Mikael and Filip
Inga-Lill and Bengt Lindell: Jakob's parents
Eva and Erik Eriksson: Sander's parents

OTHER CHARACTERS

Kjell Östholm: Widower; local farmer; dog owner
Bill: A very good dog
Hampus Olsson: An eighteen-year-old juvenile delinquent
Isidor Enoksson: The local priest

THE POLICE

Gerd Pettersson: Head of the local police department
Siri Bengtsson: The new colleague
Vidar Jörgensson: Police officer
Adrian Al-Hadid: Vidar's younger colleague
Markus Danielsson: Vidar's and Adrian's chief

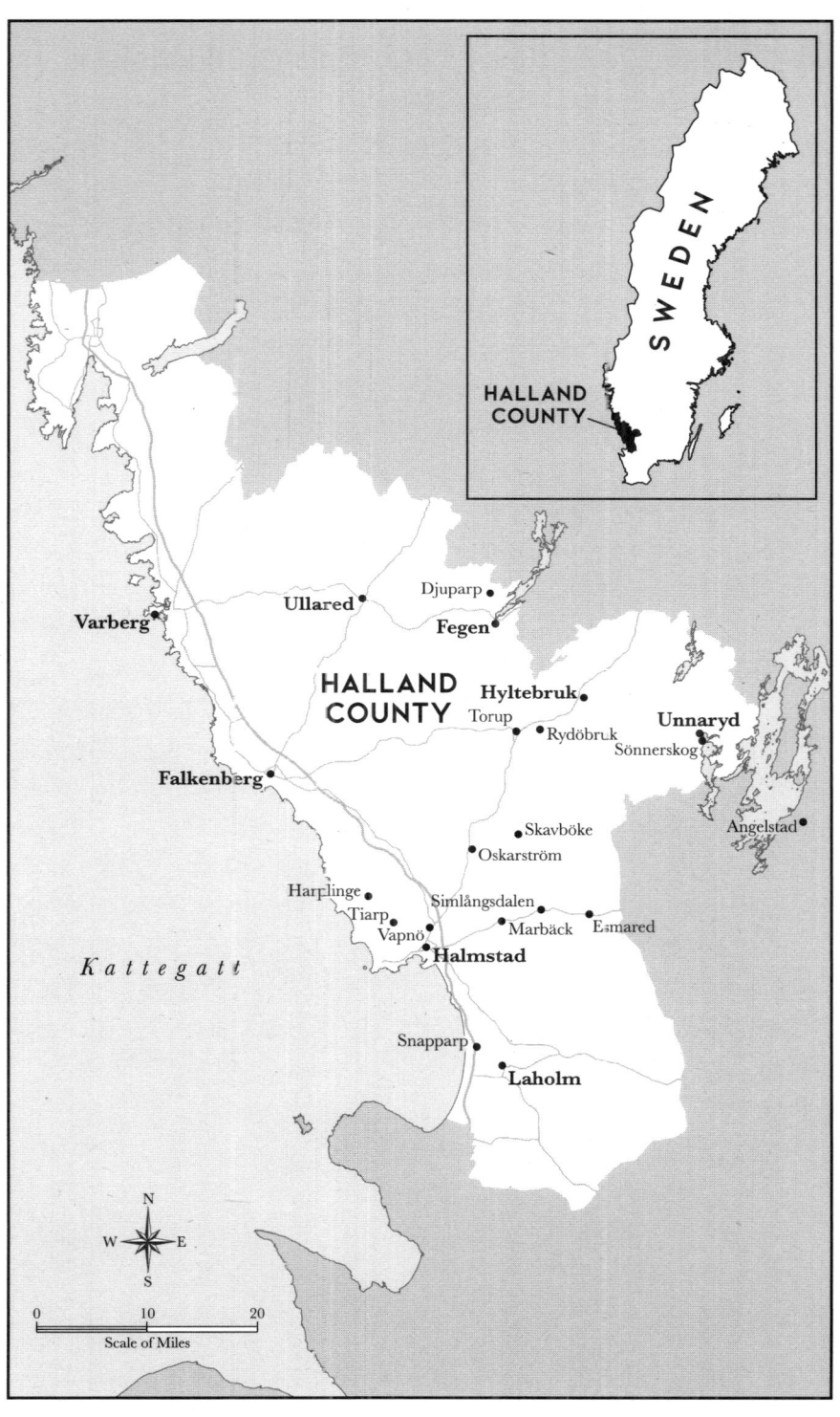

PART ONE

In Halland, the Paths Lead Anywhere

I

She believed in the truth, possibly the truth at any price.

It was this belief that guided her toward a career in law enforcement, and that, in turn, had brought her to Skavböke. This seemed like the best way to look at it. Some things in life are just that simple.

Others can be considerably more complex.

Perhaps it's telling: on that cold morning in December 1999, when it all began, she was almost lost. Although she had caught a glimpse of the house through the trees just a little while before, it was hard to find her way to it. Skavböke was intricate, its paths far too thorny, its woods too deep. No vast open fields to navigate by, just myriad small farms and terrain, damp forest and dim clearings.

But then it appeared before her, the Eriksson family home: two stories built on a small open patch surrounded by thick old oaks and birches.

The son of the house opened the door, his hair damp, wearing sweatpants and a T-shirt. Eighteen years old and thin, almost sinewy, he stood with one hand on the doorframe and an intelligent gleam in his alert eyes.

'Hello,' she said. 'My name is Siri Bengtsson. I'm with the police. May I come in?'

'My parents aren't home.'

'You're actually the one I want to talk to. Sander, right?'

'What is this all about?'

If he knew, he hid it well.

'I'd like to sit down and talk about it.'

As he showed her into the kitchen, she saw scratches on his forearms.

The house felt smaller than it was. The ceiling was low, and heavy furniture lined the walls. Advent candelabras shone in the windows, and shiny red Christmas ornaments hung gleaming in front of the curtains. When Siri sat down on the creaky kitchen bench, she felt a cold draft from the window.

Across the table from her, Sander kept his hands in his lap as though he'd been sent to the principal's office for a talking-to. His gaze was open and full of genuine curiosity. But the rest of his face suggested hesitation, and she knew the type: over the years, Sander Eriksson's face would become harder before softening again.

She took a notepad from her pocket and clicked a pen. 'To start, may I have your name and personal identity number?'

He told her, and waited as she jotted it down.

'And who lives here, besides you?'

'My parents.'

'No siblings?'

He shook his head tentatively.

'We're investigating an incident that occurred near here last night. Perhaps you've already heard about it?'

'No, what happened?'

'A young person has been found dead. And so I need to ask you a few questions about your whereabouts yesterday.'

Sander's eyes grew large.

'Dead? Here? Who is it?'

'I'll try to answer your questions as best I can if you'll answer mine first. Does that sound okay?'

He nodded, likely realizing that he didn't have much choice.

'So,' Siri said. 'Yesterday.'

'It was a normal Friday, I guess.'

'And what does that entail?'

'School during the day. Party at night. That's about it. I also went to a friend's house, in between.'

'And who's that friend?'

'Killian, is his name. With a *K* – Killian Persson.'

Siri took this down.

'Thanks. And Mikael Söderström,' she said, more slowly. 'Is that a name you're familiar with?'

When Sander finally spoke, it was as though he were standing on a frozen lake, scared he might fall through the ice.

'Is he the one who died?'

'Do you know each other?'

'We're in the same class, and he lives pretty close by. I've known Mikael forever . . . not super well, I guess, but since we're both from here, you know . . . We went to the same school, had the same friends, we played soccer together when we were little.'

'In Oskarström?'

'No, Sennan. You don't play in Oskarström if you come from Skavböke.'

'He's your same age, eighteen?'

'Yes, that's right.'

'Who would you say Mikael's friends are?'

He thought for a moment, or appeared to be thinking.

'I mean, like, everyone. I don't know.'

'Who does he spend a lot of time with?'

'Oh, some of the guys who were at the party, of course. So, Jakob Lindell. Pierre too. Pierre Bäck. The party was at his house.'

'Pierre's house?'

Sander nodded.

'And you saw Mikael there last night?'

'Yeah, sure.'

'Did you go there together?'

'I went with Killian. Mikael was already there when we arrived, I think. Yeah, he was, because I saw his coat in the hall when we came in. Filip too. Filip is Mikael's little brother.'

'How old is Filip?'

'Sixteen. Um, so is Mikael dead?'

The question sounded childish, and he must have heard it too, because he blushed. Siri held off on telling him. She was trying to get a sense of who this person sitting across from her was. Impossible to say, at this point. Maybe he was just a worried friend and classmate. Most people were no more than that.

'I know this is difficult, but we have to get through my questions first. How long were you all there, at the party?'

'Until around one. Killian got a little too drunk, I guess, and so did I, so we decided to walk home.'

'Do you remember what order people left in?'

Sander squinted, as if to see his memories more clearly.

'Mikael's brother, Filip, left early, with a girl. They were almost the first. A little while later, Mikael left. Jakob too. And then me and Killian.'

'And that was at one o'clock?'

'There's a clock on the wall in the front hall at Pierre's. It said it was one when we left.'

'Which way did you go?'

Siri wished she had a map as Sander explained.

'And your friend?' she asked when he was finally finished.

'Killian?'

'What about him?'

'Which way did he go?'

'Didn't you talk to him?'

'We're going to interview basically everyone around here, but right now I'd like to focus on what you have to say.'

'Okay, well, we left together. And when we said goodbye he kept going. So I guess it would have taken him a while after that to get home. He lives a little farther on.'

'But you're sure he went home?'

'Yes.'

'Okay. How?'

'How what?'

'I'm sorry, I'm not being clear.' Siri shifted in her seat. She was getting too warm in her uniform. 'What I meant was, how can you be sure he went home?'

'Well, because he said so. Where else would he have gone? He was super drunk.'

'You sounded so certain, as though you walked him all the way there. But you're saying that's not the case?'

'Killian is my best friend,' Sander said, as though he needed to defend himself. 'If he was going to do something else, he would have said so. But obviously something could have happened along the way, like he ran into someone and decided to spend the night somewhere else. But it was the middle of the night, so who would he have run into?'

Siri waited, as if she found the question more intriguing than rhetorical.

'Do you two typically walk home?'

'Depends on where we've been. But there's no bus up here, so you have to get home from Oskarström on your own. Either on foot, or by bike, or on a moped, you know? Or by car.'

'And what did you do when you arrived home?'

'Nothing. I fell asleep and then I woke up about an hour ago.'

'How much did you have to drink at the party?'

'I had some beers. Six or seven, maybe.'

'I was wondering, this route you say you took home from the party.' She tapped her pen on the notepad. 'It doesn't sound like you went through the forest. Am I understanding that correctly?'

'No, we didn't, really. We mostly followed the road and the trails.'

'So you might have walked through the forest as well?'

'Huh?'

'You said you *mostly* followed the trails.'

'Oh, no. No, we didn't go through the forest. What happened to Mikael?' Sander asked again.

This time, Siri saw no reason not to tell him.

'He's in a car about two kilometers from here, beaten to death.'

Sander didn't move a muscle; his eyes were perfectly blank.

'What?' he whispered.

'What do you think about that?'

'What . . . what do I think about that? I mean . . . I think it's terrible, obviously. Do you know who did it?'

'That's what we're trying to find out. Was anyone angry at him?'

'No. Not that I know of.'

'Nothing you've heard about? At the party, for instance. Was there anyone who wanted to hurt him, anything like that? No arguments or fights or stuff like that?'

'Yeah. No, yeah, there was. The kind of stuff that happens at parties, but nothing serious.'

'But Mikael was involved in this fight?'

'Yes. With Jakob.'

Siri flipped through her notepad. 'Jakob Lindell?'

'It was just, they're having a tough time right now. I know his dad needed to borrow some money from Mikael's dad once. I don't know if he got it. Yesterday I heard Mikael, like . . . oh, I don't really know. But we were sitting on the couch talking and Mikael brought up something about money. Later there was a fight up there, upstairs. But like I said, nothing serious or anything.'

'Did you see them together at any other point during the evening, Jakob and Mikael?'

All the color had drained from Sander's face.

'Yeah, sure. A bunch of times.'

'What was the mood between them those times?'

'They were just talking. Or that's what it looked like. I didn't hear what they were saying. But look, Jakob is a really nice guy, he's incredibly laid-back, he would never . . .'

Siri nodded. 'I understand. How about those?'

Sander followed her gaze and looked at his forearms, at the scratches there. He tried to hide them with his hands as though he'd been found out somehow, but then he stopped himself and sat still.

'What about them?' he asked quietly.

'How did you get them?'

'It was when I was helping Killian with his cabin yesterday. We were hauling a bunch of debris and I scratched myself.'

Back in the car, Siri studied her notepad, the brief notes she had taken. Then she wrote one more word and circled it, as if to indicate a working theory of sorts:

lying

2

Later, when the course of events was known and people in the village tried to understand how it could have happened, lots of them thought back to this very meeting. There, around the kitchen table at Sander's house, in Siri's interview with him on the morning of December 18, 1999, they saw some sort of beginning.

Each story needs a designated starting point. In some cases, we can all agree on an unambiguous inciting incident, as if it were possible to travel back in time and finally say: here. This is the precise moment when the hands of the clock begin to move.

But here, that isn't so. In order to uncover what happened to the boys from Skavböke, each of us must settle on a vantage point from which the events can be observed.

Perhaps that vantage point wasn't with Sander or Killian, or even Jakob Lindell, but with the brothers, Mikael and Filip. Or Madeleine, or even Felicia. After all, someone must be the guilty party.

Or is it all of them? The whole village, in fact. Small towns sometimes have a voice of their own. Perhaps a town can also destroy itself, if worse comes to worst.

The people who move in and out of the pages of this story muddle the picture, disrupt thoughts. That's what they're meant to do, even though we might wish they wouldn't. The story doesn't care about wishes or ideas, none of that. Instead, it offers a cast of folks who speak and act, who give witness statements both false and true, who reject and elevate one another. Some withdraw and don't want to be seen, yet continue to operate in silence. Their actions, in turn, recur as ripples in the lives of completely different people.

Yes, so it seems.

Might as well start with the interrogation, then, as we've done.

Or possibly: somewhere entirely different.

Perhaps at what seems like the outskirts of it all.

Indeed, that too is a beginning. To begin with a missing teenage boy and how Siri Bengtsson, three years after the incident in Skavböke, left the police force.

3

It all started with a raid on a homeless encampment. They've always been around, dotted here and there throughout the country in forgotten, out-of-the-way places. By the late '90s, and the start of the new millennium, they had grown in size and number.

No one in the encampments actually wanted to cause much fuss, but still, given the clientele, violence and addiction were common issues. This was the place for those whom modern society had chewed up and spit out: the evicted and ostracized, the sick and poor, addicts and aging petty thieves. If they bothered average citizens, the media and the police heard about it.

This particular encampment was located deep inside Halland, between Fegen and Djuparp, and had long been left to its own devices since only those who were lost would ever end up there. One hot August morning in 2002, Siri was summoned there, along with a dozen colleagues from Halmstad and Falkenberg.

Their task was simple: shoo the poor bastards away and tear it all down. If any of the officers found purpose or pleasure in the assignment, it wasn't obvious.

They could see glimpses of the encampment between the trees. Trash and litter lined the path through the woods: syringes and old socks, blankets, paper bags, and rotting cardboard boxes. They could smell the dank stench of piss and shit. Low murmurs in the distance blended with the buzz of the late-summer insects.

'Fun's over,' one of Siri's colleagues said joylessly.

Living in the camp were about a hundred people, men and women, young and old. Some resisted; a few even lashed out, but most of them acquiesced willingly. They gathered their belongings and scattered, sad and ashamed.

A young man was watching Siri from across the area. He was hovering along the edges of the encampment as he put on a shirt; perhaps he'd just washed up. When their eyes met, he grabbed a backpack and headed into the woods.

As if he'd been prepared. No one tried to stop him.

Siri saw his back vanish among the trees and had the strong sense she'd seen him before. But he was quite far already, about fifty paces through the forest, in her estimation, and she couldn't be sure.

'Do you know who that was?' she asked several of the residents. 'The guy with the backpack, who ran off?'

Hardly anyone responded. Those who did speak up didn't have much to say.

'He's not very old, that one,' someone said. 'Just a boy.'

'He was new,' said another. 'Hadn't been here very long. But he was helpful. Strong, he was, and he shared what he had. You say he took off? I'll be damned.'

Siri jotted down some inconsequential notes. The encampment was damp and stuffy, the air still. It smelled so sour that she felt ill; she began to sweat and her palms grew slick. They worked in the woods until darkness fell and the moon shone lonely and full up in the treetops.

When she arrived home, she took a long shower, then sat down at the kitchen table and stared out at the late-summer night, lost in thought.

That autumn she began to search the records of known disappearances. There was something about him, the young man in the forest. Maybe it was his age, or that he'd looked healthier than the others, more alert – at least from a distance. And maybe it was how confidently he had fled, without hesitation. As though he didn't quite belong in the encampment, as though he had something worse to hide than everyone else.

The missing-persons cases in Halland were plentiful, with the very young and old starkly overrepresented. The vast majority were found within a day or so, and almost everyone else shortly thereafter, most often alive. A few were found dead, and a small number of unfortunate souls remained missing, as though time had simply decided to swallow them up.

One of those was Hampus Olsson.

Siri remembered him. It was his face she'd seen on the front pages just as Skavböke's fifteen minutes of unwanted fame began to abate. Skavböke. That was how she thought of it all, she realized. It had been three years now; had so much time really passed? She read the old reports about Hampus Olsson, her stomach slowly turning to ice.

He came from Rydöbruk, about forty kilometers outside Halmstad, and had been seventeen that Christmas. He was a smart kid who liked hockey and cars but had been on a downslide since high school, was seldom home and hardly ever showed up to school. Instead, he spent much of his time with a group of similar types from around the area. On Christmas Eve of 1999, he had tried to make it through the holiday within the walls of his house, since his mother, a welfare case from Knäred, had begged and pleaded with him to stay home.

At last, apparently, he could stand it no longer. According to his mother, it was around seven o'clock when he grabbed a mostly full bottle of Zaranoff vodka from the counter and headed into the dark, and that was the last anyone had seen of him.

He had been wearing baggy black jeans, a large navy-blue hoodie, and a black puffer coat. On his head, as always, he wore a burgundy Colorado Avalanche cap – his favorite team. Witness statements suggested he'd hitchhiked out of Torup; someone had seen a guy standing at the side of the road with his thumb out, but no one had been able to confirm it.

Given that Hampus was who he was, the search lasted for a long time, and the assumptions about what had happened grew increasingly pessimistic. *I'm sure he's lying dead somewhere*, one of Siri's colleagues in town said in a dull voice when she called to check on the case.

Seventeen when he disappeared, which would make him about twenty now, if that was Hampus Olsson she'd seen in the woods. Maybe. Yeah. She was pretty damn sure it was him.

Siri put everything aside and moved on; she had stressed-out bosses and piles of cases to deal with. The days progressed as usual, but at night that figure at the edge of the forest came back to her. She considered taking the matter to a superior but decided against it.

Instead, she moved forward in silence, as though she were searching for an answer she didn't really want to find. She tracked down Hampus's old high-school teachers at Kattegat School and let them describe what kind of student Hampus had been, the few times he showed up.

'I always thought it would have been better for him to attend a different school,' said John Lundström, who'd had Hampus in Swedish. 'Considering he lived so far from here, I mean. I suggested it to him more than once, to try to get him to cut class less. For a guy like Hampus there was, how to put it, so much temptation along the way to school. But neither he nor his mother did anything about it, so nothing happened. Which was too bad; he wasn't a dumb kid. But he had a lot of bad luck.'

Bad luck, indeed. Siri visited his home village of Rydöbruk, met his mother at a treatment home outside Falkenberg, and spoke to Hampus's old friends, the ones who could still be located.

Siri just wanted to find him. That was all. She thought he deserved to be found. If you're seventeen and you go missing, there has to be someone to look for you, and everyone else seemed to have given up.

She studied maps to figure out which roads he might have taken. After work she often kept her uniform on and, instead of going home, headed out to the forests of Halland. She would park her car out of sight so no one would wonder why she wasn't driving a patrol car. She knocked on doors and showed people photographs, asked questions. Folks shook their heads and apologized, sorry they couldn't be of more help.

She took short naps in her car, then drove on.

He must have left an impression somewhere. There always is one, if you know what you're looking for.

At last, she found it.

One month later, she quit.

4

The inspector from the Environmental Protection Agency was a conscientious man. He was in the habit of collecting even the tiniest pieces of litter in a bag and tossing it all at the trash station behind Vallås on his way home, but he knew he should turn in the empty shell he'd just happened across in an out-of-the-way part of Långhultamyren Nature Reserve. He put the shell in the bag and drove straight to the police station.

There the bag with the empty shell made its way to a young officer who was working with Siri out in Oskarström that week. They'd both been in Halmstad to drop a wino off at lockup and were now discussing Sweden's new import: Halloween. It seemed to have really taken off up in Stockholm in recent years, and soon it would probably reach Halland too.

'Imagine having to chase after drunks dressed like Spider-Man, the *Scream* killer, and Gandalf,' said Siri. 'Jesus.'

'Who's Gandalf?' asked the young officer.

'*Lord of the Rings*? A wizard?'

The officer looked bewildered. A colleague stuck his head in to ask if they had any time to spare.

'There's someone out here who wants to turn in a spent shell,' he said. 'I'm sure it's just from hunting, but I can't deal with it, I'm full up.'

Siri got to her feet. 'We're on it.'

The young officer trailed her like an anxious puppy.

'I found this,' the inspector said hurriedly. He'd had to wait for a long time for anyone to help him. 'You can toss the rest, it's just trash. Bye.'

Siri opened the bag and froze. 'Hey. Listen – Hey, wait.'

The inspector looked back. Siri cautiously lifted a threadbare burgundy cap from the bag. The Colorado Avalanche logo, the faded burgundy *A*, and the swoop of snow crashing over it to make a *C*.

'Where did you say you found this?'

The inspector had nodded at his feet and recommended rubber boots, but Siri didn't have any. Soon she was out in the forest, her feet wet, shivering in the cold. She was shown the exact spot and examined the area closely.

They were on a small trail that wound its way through the forest.

'How far would this path lead you?'

'No idea,' said the inspector. 'Far.'

'To Rydöbruk?'

'Sure, eventually. In Halland the paths lead anywhere, if you walk far enough.' The inspector took a map from the large pocket of his coat and consulted it along with a compass. 'Yes, that's basically straight north of here. But it would take a day or so, on foot.'

It was Hampus Olsson's cap, there was no doubt about that, but Rydöbruk was a long way for a teenager. Maybe he really had hitchhiked, as witness statements suggested.

Another kilometer or so down the path, Siri found a bottle of Zaranoff brand vodka. When she gingerly picked it up, there was a vibration in her chest as though she were in the presence of a ghost.

She felt called upon to continue; the trail would fade if she stopped, she was convinced of it. But it would take more feet on the ground – ones with rubber boots and thick socks, for instance. She could no longer feel her toes.

When Siri returned to Halmstad and reported what she

had found, she asked to put together a search party. The human chain they formed turned out to be large and sprawling, but together they worked doggedly for over a week. Even the inspector from the Environmental Protection Agency, who knew the land well and turned out to be a helpful guy, took part.

After a few days they reached the area around Mjäla, where the forest opened into vast fields and farmland that was about to go dormant for the winter. In the distance she could make out a farm. Siri stopped the human chain, let them rest and deliberate about how to proceed, while she went to talk to the farmer. She was gone for almost an hour and when she returned, those in the chain said later, she wasn't the same. Suddenly withdrawn and distracted, she held a piece of paper in her hands and seemed hesitant to get the chain moving again.

At last someone pointed out that it was getting late and they had only about an hour of daylight left; perhaps it would be better to pick back up tomorrow.

'Yes,' Siri said stiffly. 'Yes, let's do that.'

'Did he have anything to say?' asked the inspector from the Environmental Protection Agency, nodding at Siri's hands.

She folded the paper and stuffed it in her pocket. 'Who?'

'You know, the farmer. Did he see anything?'

'Oh.' Siri shook her head. 'No, nothing. Hampus was never here, according to him, but I suppose we'll have to see for ourselves. We've got permission to go wherever we like on his land, he said, as long as we're careful. We'll meet up again tomorrow.'

The search was never resumed.

PART TWO

The Boy on the Bridge

5

Those who knew Sander Eriksson and Killian Persson back then always said they were inseparable.

Each was so clearly an only child – and maybe it was that simple. Here came Sander, walking through Skavböke, with Killian at his side. Killian was practically his best friend's opposite, tall and burly and blond as he was, with clumsy hands and a kind but mildly perplexed gaze. They made an odd pair, but at the same time they made sense together. It wasn't hard to understand what they saw in one another.

Killian. The *K* pronounced like 'shh': Sheel-yan. The name has deep roots in Halland, yet it started out as Irish, or maybe Scottish. Long ago it came to Sweden, was passed down from father to son, and given to a husky boy from Skavböke. In the winter of 1999, he was eighteen years old.

His father, Sten, had moved out, so these days Killian lived with his mother, Linda, on the outskirts of the community. They, like Sander's family, had never been farmers.

'Some folks aren't even poor farmers,' as the saying went. 'They're just poor.'

Killian only ever spent time in the house to eat or sleep. There was an old workshop on the property, and six months ago Killian had decided to tear it down and build a new one. He would live in it, he said, and he called the concept 'the cabin.'

Sander helped. All they kept of the old shop was its stone foundation; they began to demolish the rest with sledgehammers under a blazing July sun. Splinters and sawdust sailed.

It was cathartic to destroy something that had started out whole.

But it did take a hell of a long time, and both of them grew exhausted. That evening, they regarded the half-razed shop with beers in hand.

'There must be an easier way to do this,' Sander said.

They grabbed a few beers and set off through the village. Soon they were standing behind a barn over on Kjell Östholm's farm, gazing longingly at his old tractor.

'Do you know how to drive it?' Killian asked.

'No, do you?'

'Almost. I think. It's just that there's so many levers.' Killian drained his beer and looked around. 'So, is he here?'

'His car is gone.'

'Shit, let's try it, right? What's the worst that can happen?'

They climbed into the driver's seat. Sander was getting drunk by this point and spilled beer on the engine. When Killian turned the key, the tractor did nothing but give a weary sigh. He tried again. The tractor sputtered and briefly woke up, only to doze off again.

Killian looked at the beer can in Sander's hand.

'Maybe it's thirsty. Try giving it a little more.'

Sander leaned out of the cab and dumped the beer onto the engine. Killian tried to start it again and the engine coughed, faltered, and creaked grumpily, but then roared to life, awake and ready.

Sander and Killian reached for the sky, a silent gesture of triumph.

At first there were a lot of fits and leaps, but soon they were driving smoothly through the village, through the warm summer evening. The sound of a chugging tractor was as natural, in Skavböke, as the birds and the cows. As they turned into Killian's driveway, they lowered the bucket.

Killian closed one eye and aimed for the remains of the shop with its half a roof and leaning walls.

'I'm thinking we just scoop it up. Can you grab me another beer?'

'But . . .' Sander said as he hopped back into the cab with two fresh cans. 'I don't think it's exactly like scooping up sand with a shovel.'

'Not exactly,' Killian said, taking a big gulp of his beer. 'But almost.'

He worked the levers and the tractor leapt forward again.

They rumbled across the yard and the massive tires left deep brown tracks in the grass. They ran straight into the shop, their determination in the lead and the bucket right behind.

In the sudden collision Killian dropped his beer, and frothy Carlsberg streamed over the floor of the cab. With a disappointed groan, he let go of the wheel and reached to right the can.

'Killian, the wheel!'

Sander leaned over Killian and tried to keep the tractor steady as the bucket began to crunch through the shop.

Through — or over. It was like the machine couldn't quite get its teeth into the structure; instead it began to scrabble up it, like a dog trying to leap over a log that's too high. The engine growled and they began to rear back.

'Let off the gas!' Sander yelped; he had to hold tight to keep from falling off.

'What?' Killian shouted. He'd finally recovered his beer and was trying to see if there was any left.

The wooden wall of the shop cracked. The tractor hissed and everything began to lean weirdly. They were about to roll over.

'You have to let off the gas —'

A ceiling beam gave way under the weight of the tractor, and the engine gave one last, deep cough. With a heavy thud, the tractor tipped onto its side like a wounded animal, and Sander and Killian tumbled out of the cab. The ground shook and a big clump of soil flew into the air as one corner of the cab plowed into the grass. The engine died.

Killian was on his back. Sander too. They were still holding their beers. Killian craned his neck and tossed his empty can away, then looked at Sander.

'Well, that went great.'

'Almost like scooping up sand with a shovel,' Sander said.

'Maybe we should have put a forklift on the tractor instead.'

'Yeah, I'm sure that was the issue.'

It had taken time, lots of hot summer days and chilly fall mornings, but when winter rolled around almost six months later, there was a tidy new cabin where the old shop had once stood. It smelled just like it had in their dreams: fresh, clean lumber and oil. They had built it themselves, erecting walls and trying to figure out how insulation worked; they had laid a floor and installed a ceiling and decorated the place as best they could. They had even built a little hatch in the floor, no bigger or deeper than a shoebox. They called it the Hidey-Hole, a stash for beer.

Now as Sander arrived in the cold December dusk, he saw Killian hauling something across the lawn, something that looked like a big creature of metal.

'What's that?'

Killian straightened up. Despite the chill, he looked hot.

'A generator. It's so fucking cold out now. I got it from Frans; he said it doesn't work, but I think he's wrong. Wanna try?'

Sander put down the bag of beer he'd brought and got a grip on the generator.

'Shit, it's heavy.'

'Here,' Killian said. 'This'll be good. I made a little hole in the wall here.'

From the ceiling inside the cabin dangled a single lightbulb. Killian tried to slip the cord through the hole in the wall to hook up the generator.

'It'd be perfect if I can get it working before we go to Pierre's. That way I can sleep out here tonight, when I get home. If I manage to bring a bottle or two back, it'll go into the Hidey-Hole.' Then, as if he'd just remembered something, he looked up from the floor. 'By the way. How'd it go, what did he say? I noticed the two of you went off to talk.'

Yes, they had.

6

Sander had met with a man from Stockholm with sparkling blue eyes. Ardelius, his name was, and when Sander looked at him it was as though a gap appeared in the curtains, and through that gap he could see the real life that awaited him out in the world.

It took some effort, or maybe keen perception, to see it that way. From a distance, Ardelius appeared ordinary, almost meek. His brown jacket drooped on his shoulders and his wrists were wrinkly and thin; the skin of his cheeks was pale and spotty like the walls of a waiting room. But his eyes revealed something unusual about him. Maybe that's the way people's eyes look, in Stockholm.

And his voice. It was low and pleasant, melodic but steady. He sat still, too, no fidgeting, as though he had all the time in the world. Leaning back with his legs crossed and his fingers laced around his knee, his gaze calm and curious as he looked at Sander over the table.

He had Lundström to thank for being here. Lundström's first name was John, but no one called him that. He was just Lundström. He came from Åled and was said to have been one of the best chess players in Halland as a teenager. He had made it all the way to Stockholm, and after he put away the chessboard to focus on other problems, he ended up at the university. And there he stayed. Philosophy, apparently. He eventually returned to Halland, but who knew why.

Last fall, Sander's class had him as a mentor and teacher

of religion and Swedish, and Lundström had taken them to a lecture at the college. The lecture, which was on ethics and the law, was given by Magnus Ardelius, head of the Department of Law up in Stockholm and an old classmate of Lundström's. The short man with bright blue eyes spoke about maxims and systems of belief, of golden rules old and new.

'The law,' he said, 'functions as the barrier along the brink of society's cliff. It demarcates the outermost point. Everything up to this point is negotiable, but past it . . .' He paused for effect. 'Nothing. Right and wrong can be determined in an instant.'

A barrier, a limit. That was appealing. When Ardelius was finished, Lundström leaned toward Sander, who was in the row in front of him, and said, 'You just wrote an essay about law and justice. You should go down there and talk to him.'

'About what?'

'Just about what you had to say.'

Sander shook his head, but Lundström pulled him down to the front and suddenly he was in front of Ardelius, Lundström at his side.

'This is Sander, one of my students. He'd love to talk to you a bit more.'

Ardelius, looking friendly, studied him.

Now here they sat, at a café close to the big auditorium. Sander had just finished explaining his essay.

'That sounds like an interesting topic. And I'm so glad to learn John has such gifted students. Are you interested in the law?'

'Yes, I guess so.'

'You're graduating next summer, aren't you? What do you plan to do after that?'

'I don't know. But my grades are pretty good.'

The man took a thick catalog from his briefcase. On the front it said STOCKHOLM UNIVERSITY. He opened it, found the right page, and dog-eared it before closing the catalog and placing it in front of Sander.

'In case this is of interest to you.' He smiled faintly. 'Sweden is a big country. It has many faces. Stockholm is only one of them, and maybe, like John, you wouldn't want to be there forever. But it's not so bad for a little while.'

Sander blinked.

'What you said during your lecture, about the edge of the cliff. Or brink, you said the brink of the cliff.'

Ardelius raised a curious eyebrow.

'Yes?'

'You were saying that the legal system, or the law, is like a boundary for us. Or did I misunderstand you?'

'No, that's more or less what I meant. The law marks an outer limit for human behavior.'

'But people break the law all the time. What's beyond that boundary?'

Ardelius smiled.

'A very good question. But,' he added, 'I'm afraid I have to go. My train.' He offered his hand. 'You can bring that question to us in the fall, if you like.'

'Thank you,' Sander said. 'I look forward to it. Very much.'

'Then we should be the ones thanking you for your trust. Many happy returns for the season.'

Many happy returns. Language Sander wasn't used to. He wasn't used to any of this. Ardelius was an important man, busy doing things so great and complicated that you probably had to be from Stockholm to comprehend them. Sander wished that the professor would remain in that chair. Would stay. Just for a little while longer, Sander wanted to experience that sense of gazing through a new window, of thinking new thoughts.

But everything must come to an end. Here he was, Sander Eriksson, in December of 1999. Here, perhaps, he would remain.

Ardelius had discreetly, almost silently, risen from the chair. He turned to Sander again and gave him a quick wink, as though from now on the two of them shared a secret.

7

'What was it called again?'

'The law school at Stockholm University is called Juridicum. That's the place to go, if you want to major in law.'

A *major* at university, as opposed to a *track* in high school. Tracks were narrow and meandering, could fade away at any time. A major was something greater, more robust. Someone who was accepted into a major must be special, Sander imagined.

Killian shaped his mouth to say *Juridicum*, and although he had just heard it out loud twice, he seemed to waver on its pronunciation.

'Cool,' he said, going back to the cord and the generator.

'I haven't made up my mind. I'm going to spend some time thinking about it. Applications aren't due until after New Year's and then we'll see if I get in.'

'I'm sure you will.'

'You could come, too, if you want. The two of us could go. Maybe you don't want to go to college, I get that, but it's *Stockholm*. There would for sure be a job for you there too. Tons of jobs. And good bars and clubs. Girls. I mean, you should see the ones in the catalog he gave me, I'll show you.'

That didn't come out the way he'd meant it to. Sander had planned it just as he planned everything; words and strategies were fingers that could pick apart tricky knots. But this time he spoke too fast and stumbled over syllables, perhaps because he was nervous or unsure if what he was saying was true.

'Yeah,' Killian said, as though he wasn't particularly interested, or simply didn't want to let on that the idea bummed him out. 'Maybe.'

He looked around with an odd expression on his face.

'Look, you know how getting out of here is, like, your dream? Isn't it?'

'Part of it, anyway.'

'This is mine.'

'What is?'

'Building a home of my own, kind of. Maybe with more rooms than this, when I can afford it. A bigger beer bunker.' He chuckled, but quickly grew serious again. 'Getting a job somewhere nearby. Having a family. Cars to tinker with and all that. I like it here. I don't need much else.'

'That's because you've never thought about it.'

'But I *have*. You talk about leaving all the time, which means I've thought about it too . . . but I don't think it's for me.'

Sander didn't know what to say to that. The cabin they'd built suddenly seemed like a monument of sorts, a symbol of what he would be leaving behind.

'Okay.' Killian stood up. 'Let's test it out. Turn on the switch.'

They had installed it a few weeks ago. The button was in the right spot, just a little crooked. Sander pressed it. The lightbulb flickered and crackled, but then a loud bang came from behind the cabin. The generator.

'Shit. Maybe it is broken after all.'

Killian went out to see what had gone wrong. The cold winter night swept in, and Sander shivered.

A few dozen miles from the coast, just where the Nissan River curves away to reveal all the beauty Halland has to offer. That's where you will find little Skavböke, and all the kids had turned eighteen that year, all but Filip. The days still passed as unnoticed as before. The farmers struggled on, cars left homes in the morning and returned at dusk, children played soccer on the gravel road and went ice-skating on the lake; they watched the combines during the harvest, how they moved across the field toward a deep forest and clear sky.

But a change was drawing near: the '90s were almost over. So much had changed in this country, their parents said, that some days it barely felt familiar anymore. Hard to know what it meant to live in Sweden nowadays, what it meant to be Swedish. The greater world had come whooshing in, and there were signs of it everywhere. Stores were given new names when the old ones failed, names that you'd only ever seen on TV before. These days, capital moved faster than ever and wherever it went it left ruins in its wake. So said a politician on TV.

There were winners and losers, and it was clear that Skavböke was the latter, but exactly how this had happened was difficult to figure. The whole country was supposed to thrive. The politicians said this too. But jobs that used to demand workers' hands had long since been done by machines, and soon computers would take over.

Maybe there was no limit to how superfluous humans could become.

Cash was in short supply, but other things seemed to exist in excess: salt and sugar, corn and wheat and oats, potatoes and pigs, and of course milk. Tons of milk. It was called 'white silver'. Once upon a time, Halland cows gave more milk than all the other cows in the country combined. Until just a few years ago, the Söderström farm in Skavböke had several hundred dairy cattle. Now there were much fewer, and it was hard to say where the money had gone. To liquor, maybe, and other comforts it took to get through life.

Why were farmers made stewards of the land? That's just the way it is, probably, but it still bears considering.

Oh, to be eighteen in Skavböke. All you thought about was money, sex, and freedom. It's not easy to say which events were important or insignificant; even something that seemed trivial could feel pivotal: putting on a new shirt or jacket, perhaps. Catching someone's eye. Lighting a cigarette and speaking in a low, serious voice. There was no way to know.

'There.' Killian came back inside and eyed the lightbulb that dangled from the ceiling. 'Try one more time. Then we'll head to Pierre's.'

Sander did as he said. The lightbulb flickered again, but then it settled down to a bright, warm glow. Sander looked at Killian and they smiled.

A moment in the heart of Halland, at the very end of a century.

8

The murder was committed in the night, after the party at Pierre's house. Sander and Killian had been there, no doubt about it. They arrived at the house in Årnilt together and left together, too, another not-insignificant observation.

In many respects, it was a party like any other. A visitor in the home that evening would have caught scraps of conversation, music, the occasional argument. Someone had just bought an expensive cell phone, and no one had a clue why. There was no coverage out here, because the closest tower was way over in Amböke. Cell phones were useless in Skavböke and would stay that way for several years.

There were flashes from a disposable camera a couple kids had brought; glasses clinked and the music streaming from the speakers got louder and louder. Sander and Killian discussed the upcoming match between Oskarström and Breared. Things didn't look good for Oskarström, they agreed. But miracles had happened before, although God rarely interfered with anything as profane as the Oskarström soccer team.

No one knew where Felicia was, whether she had come to the party, was she somewhere in that house? Sander didn't know what he would do if he saw her. Maybe nothing. That seemed like the safest bet, given what happened last time.

It had been a warm night last summer, late August, and they were standing alone in the kitchen at Alice Fredriksson's house. For some reason, the rest of the party had moved to the lawn. Sander described the episode with the tractor and the shop, only a few weeks old at that point, and it made Felicia laugh and call him and Killian idiots. But her eyes sparkled as she said so. Encouraged, Sander went on to explain the Beer Bunker, which was just an idea at the time, or maybe you could say it was a *vision*. She laughed again, just as Sander hoped.

Then they kissed.

She'd mentioned his name in passing earlier that evening, and it felt like the first time he'd heard it. Brain buzzing with alcohol, he was enchanted by how 'Sander' sounded when it came from Felicia Grenberg's lips, gliding so softly over the consonants, kind of like a song.

The kiss ended when she had to turn away to puke in the sink. Sander simply stood there, unsure whether they would keep going once she was done vomiting.

She'd had too much to drink, she said without looking at him, and apologized. Felicia's disappointment was perhaps not as fervent as Sander's. As though her body's reflexes had interrupted something she wasn't all that interested in.

Now Sander was drinking his beer on Pierre's parents' leather sofa. Just as well if she didn't show up. She would be staying here in the area like everyone else, and he was already on his way out.

Sander thought of Ardelius's wink, a detail so minor it could mean anything. Even so, it stuck with him, like a promise soon to be fulfilled. When he returned to school after that conversation, he heard the rustling of the dead trees bordering the Kattegat School parking lot on Skepparegatan, and the pavement was covered in slush. Everything was brick and cramped classrooms, winter coats and afternoon math; everything was the same yet different. He carried the course catalog in his backpack and the world took on a new luster. A particular shimmer appears around the edges of places and people when you start to realize that they can be left behind.

Pierre settled onto the armrest. His voice slurring, he complained that there were too many people there, although hardly anyone had arrived yet.

A Christmas star glowed from the window, peaceful and warm. In the corner was a fresh, plump spruce tree covered in tinsel and red ornaments. It was the last Friday before Christmastime, with two weeks left of the century. It would be an unusual New Year's Eve: at home on their farms, and in their homes, people would sit in front of their TVs, tense and anxious, ready to hurry down to the basement if the end of the world arrived. Rumor had it that computer systems were programmed to crash and the banks would collapse; satellites would fall from the sky and the power would go out for good. Their parents had been talking about it nonstop. Not everyone believed these rumors, but some did. Others decided it was better to be safe than sorry.

'At first Dad didn't believe it at all, but now he's taking it a little too seriously,' said Jakob Lindell. 'He withdrew all our money before he and Mom left yesterday, because he'd heard that's what Kjell Östholm had done. So now we've got basically everything we own in cash. For real.'

'How much is that, a thousand kronor?' Mikael Söderström asked acidly.

'More or less.' Jakob laughed, the kind of hollow sound an empty keg makes if you hit it, and spilled his drink on his pants. 'Yeah. I don't know. It's definitely not much, but there's some.'

'Enough to pay off your TV.'

Jakob stared at Mikael's half-drunk grin.

'Oh, lay off.'

'Oops. Is that a sore spot?'

'Stop it, Mikael,' Pierre said softly.

'But it's true.'

'Just because it's true doesn't mean you have to say it,' Sander said, taking a sip of beer.

Jakob's father used to repair trucks, but he'd been laid off a year or so ago. These days he was trying to get the old family farm up and running again, but they didn't have much: a couple chickens, a pig or two, some cropland to work. He'd once asked Mikael's father for money, but neither Mikael nor Jakob knew if he'd actually borrowed any. They were neighbors, more or less, the Söderströms and the Lindells, and around here you either loved or hated your neighbor. Jakob had once confided in Sander that his parents had come close, on more than one occasion, to selling the farm and moving to an apartment in Oskarström.

'So, like, where is he keeping it?' Killian asked, gazing around for another beer. 'The money, I mean.'

'In a cushion on the kitchen bench, basically. Just like Kjell. I think he's going to move it when he and Mom get home. Anyway, fuck it. Let's talk about something else.'

'You're the one who brought it up,' Mikael said.

Jakob glared at him. 'Shouldn't you be keeping an eye on your little brother or something?'

Mikael laughed harshly. 'Wow, what a comeback.'

'Can you all just quit it?' Pierre said.

Filip, Mikael's little brother, was two years younger than the rest of them. Everyone knew he puked the second he drank any wine, and that Mikael usually had to haul him home. Filip had said he was coming to the party, but no one had spotted him yet.

Killian rose unsteadily from the sofa and went to the bathroom. Sander meandered to the front hall and asked if anyone had seen Felicia. No one heard him. On the wall there was a large, ornate pendulum clock, made of wood. It was quarter past eleven. The face of the clock was an old map of Sweden. Sander examined it as though it were a riddle.

A big country with many faces. That's what Ardelius had said.

Soon Sander would be far away from here. The thought felt good, like a release.

9

Some goings-on at the party weren't very visible, or else they were visible but no one thought much about them. Later, Siri and her colleagues would spend a very long time trying to bring clarity to events no one had thought mattered.

Glass and porcelain shattered. Sander found Filip sitting on the floor of the kitchen and told him that his older brother was around somewhere and was definitely looking for him. Filip clumsily unscrewed the cap of his plastic bottle.

'He was being a total asshole to Jakob just now,' Sander went on.

'No surprise there,' Filip muttered.

'Oh?'

'He thinks Felicia Grenberg likes Jakob. Or that Jakob likes her, hell if I know.'

'He does?'

'This is my brother's way of dealing with it. Being a dick and acting all, what's the word, superior.' His gaze flickered over Sander. 'Believe me, I know.'

'Dealing with what? Does Mikael like Felicia?'

Filip laughed as though the answer were obvious.

Filip was short and lanky and kept his head shaved. He had sharp, angular features, with a pointy nose and thin lips, a blunt chin that formed a *W*. His complexion was darker than his brother's, and his disposition was grimmer. He'd been like that since they were little. Filip had fewer friends and a tougher time at school; counselors had been involved more than once. But he was also funny and intense and you never quite knew what he was up to, whether he was messing with you.

Filip dropped the cap, which skittered across the floor. 'Shit. I hate when that happens.'

Sander bent down to pick it up.

'Is she here?' Sander asked.

'Who?'

'Felicia?'

'No clue. Fuck, you ask a lot of questions.' Filip took the cap from him. 'Thanks.'

'Does she like him?'

'How the fuck should I know? But my brother usually gets what he wants, one way or another.'

Sander stayed put as Filip stumbled off. Another crack in the world. Surely she wouldn't even notice if he left. When he pictured Mikael and Felicia Grenberg all entwined in some secret corner of the house, a hot, sharp stab of rage flamed up in his chest.

Loud voices from upstairs. A scuffle. Something else broke.

'Hey!' Pierre shouted. 'Stop it! Jesus, just stop! Calm down.'

People's fuses were too short. Too much going on in their hands and not enough in their heads.

Sander went back to the leather sofa in the living room and sat down next to Killian. When Pierre came down a few minutes later, he sank to the floor, exhausted, and lay down on his back.

'I'm never having a party ever again.'

'What happened?' Sander asked.

'Jakob and Mikael got into a fight, is all.'

'Who won?'

'It's fine now. I broke it up.'

So Mikael wasn't with Felicia, at least. The first piece of

good news tonight. Sander looked around for her again. Killian leaned toward him to be heard over the music. He was starting to slur his words.

'Madeleine hurt herself today. So I think Felicia's staying home with her.'

'Hurt how?'

'I guess she fell off the roof. I heard Alice and Isabelle talking about it when I was in the bathroom.'

'Oh. Okay, sure.'

Killian lowered his voice a notch. 'I wonder how much money it actually is.'

'What?' Sander was slurring now too. 'What do you mean?'

'You know, in Jakob's kitchen bench.'

'No one here probably has much, really.'

'Yeah, but still.'

'Hardly anything.'

Sander's words made something between them shift.

'Why do you say stuff like that?' Killian asked.

'Like what?'

'Like you look down on other people.'

'I do not.'

'Well, it sounds like you do.'

'Fine, but I don't.'

Pierre roused himself from the floor.

'Well, time for another beer. Or maybe the hard stuff, shit, I think there's vodka in the fridge.'

Some people went to the kitchen, others to the yard; some went upstairs to try to have sex or smoke weed. A picture was broken and soon Pierre himself was walking around with the frame around his neck, speaking in a snobby voice, holding a newfound bottle of vodka in his hand and proclaiming, 'Heeeere comes a reeeeal connoisseuuuur! Riiiight from the arrrrsehole of Sssstaaahhhckholm!' Spit flew from his lips and he stumbled on the hall rug and hit the wall. The Sweden clock fell from its hook onto Pierre, and he laughed and said, 'Myyyyy, wassssn't *that* a tiiiiimely misssstake!' Pierre kept chuckling to himself while Sander helped him put the clock back up. A camera flashed.

Shortly after this climax, the party began to wind down. People were too drunk and getting tired; they had to get home so they could sneak in before their parents woke up. Filip had vomited and headed out hand-in-hand with a girl, into the winter night. A little while later, Sander and Killian stood in the front hall, Killian wobbly and holding a cigarette. There was a chilly draft from the open door.

Killian stepped out onto the stairs. 'I know you're not going to stay. I'm not stupid. I get it. And I get why you want to go. What you said before, inside, it's true, isn't it? That's how you feel.'

'Not about you.'

'I don't mean about me, I mean . . .' Killian appeared to be thinking it over. 'Everything.'

'I'll come back to visit and all that. And maybe I'll move back home after a while. But I don't know, I just need . . . you can come with.'

But Killian shook his head. 'It's your brain that's taking you away from here. Your grades. I don't have those.'

'C'mon, you're smart.'

'Not like you.' He exhaled as he stood on the stoop, straightened up, and gazed out at the darkness, at the forest over past Årniltsvägen. 'No, I'm going to end up here. But that's what I want, so I'll be just fine. Have you told your parents?'

'No. But I'm sure they'll understand.'

He wasn't nearly as sure as he made it sound.

Killian rested a heavy hand on Sander's shoulder. 'Wanna go home?'

Sander looked at his friend's feet. 'But you're not wearing any shoes.'

As if this were news to him, Killian raised his eyebrows at the icy steps.

'You seem to be right. Guess I'm kind of drunk after all.'

The camera flashed behind them, from the living room, capturing for posterity a kid who had dozed off on the sofa and was drooling onto the armrest. Sander blinked. For an instant he saw two Killians.

'Me too, I think.'

Sander and Killian left Pierre's party together. It was one in the morning. Everyone agreed on that.

What happened after that has remained a mystery for over twenty years.

10

Kjell Östholm was the first one to spot the car, and it was really all thanks to Bill.

Bill was almost two, but he hadn't been with Kjell for more than a few months, so the German shepherd hadn't completely adjusted to life on the farm. Sometimes Bill woke up hours before dawn.

It was a different story in the past, of course; Kjell remembered the years when his wife was still alive, and he kept a dairy herd, as the happiest of his life. Back then, the alarm clock rang at quarter past three and Greta would pat Kjell gently on the chest to get him up.

These days, Bill woke Kjell. This morning, he'd slunk into the bedroom just before five, placed his front paws on the edge of the bed, and grunted.

Kjell took his time getting up. As he got on in age, his thighs and back gave him trouble and his balance was temperamental. It was past five by the time they were wandering across the property in the cold.

When Bill began to act strange, Kjell wondered what was going on but let him be. They went across the field, toward the fence on the other side.

Down on the road was a car, an old gray Volvo 240 with its back gate open. Kjell stopped.

'So I said to Bill, I said,' he explained in the police interview, 'we'll have to check that out. So we climbed over the fence and approached the car. And I looked into the back, of course, because the dog was leaping around something awful and I had to see what it was. Then I screamed and ran home as fast as my legs would carry me and called it in.'

Gerd Pettersson was leaning against the wall outside an apartment on Odengatan in Oskarström, fervently wishing that the new colleague from the city she'd been promised had been scheduled to start their first shift at midnight. This kind of call was so exhausting and took forever to get through alone.

'Well, help me!' she heard from inside the apartment. 'Don't just stand there.'

The order was followed by thuds and bangs.

'Hasse, I want you to unlock the door and take a few steps back into the hall. Can you do that?'

Gerd's words became round and tinny in the cramped stairwell.

'I can't,' Hasse bellowed.

'You're upsetting the neighbors, you know.'

'I don't give a damn! Go get the machine.'

'What machine?'

'The computer machine.'

'What would we do with one of those?'

'On New Year's Eve all the machines are going to explode in midair. They know all about it. If you put out a computer machine they won't dare to radiate you anymore.'

It was almost five thirty in the morning. One of the neighbors had called to complain about old Hasse Ek, who lived on the top floor. He'd been on a roll since midnight, the caller reported, shouting and ranting, banging on walls and doors and keeping the whole building up.

'Can't you help me?' Hasse howled.

It's so odd, Gerd thought. *The tinfoil-hatters always manage to sound both enraged and pitiful.*

You'd never know it now, but Hasse had once been one of the most promising harness-racing drivers in the county of Halland. Gerd herself had cheered him on at the Halmstad racetrack one summer when he took the Sprintermästare title. Everyone was there, even Isidor Enoksson, the village priest. Everyone placed bets, the priest included, and after a beer or two up in the stands they got him to confess what he really believed in: Hasse Ek. And God. Two entities which were, at that particular moment – according to Isidor – one and the same.

Maybe the priest should have believed in liquor as well, because it was stronger than Hasse and as the years went by, it slowly conquered him. After a few stints at the rehab clinic, the old man sobered up, but the hard life had taken its toll and he began to rant about electromagnetic rays. He did have children, two of them, but they'd flown the nest long ago. They didn't have the energy to deal with him. His ex-wife lived with a banker in Halmstad.

'Hasse,' Gerd pleaded.

The microphone on her uniform crackled to life and the call echoed off the walls.

'What was that you said? Skavböke? Now?'

11

The police station in Oskarström was on Brogatan, right next to the Nissan River. Once upon a time it had housed no fewer than five valiant officers of the law. Now, at the dawn of the new millennium, reallocation of resources and the centralization of authority had reduced these representatives to two, and, on this particular late-December morning, one. One single police officer for five thousand residents. When the new day dawned, there would be two once more, doubling the manpower, according to those math whizzes in Halmstad. The newcomer was called Siri, and she had some common last name. Karlsson, Bäck, something like that. She was coming from the city.

But for a little while longer, Gerd Pettersson was on her own. Some in the area were afraid of her, but lots of people liked the tall woman with frizzy hair that fell past her shoulders, and her gruff, loud laugh. She was approaching sixty and had been a police officer for her entire adult life.

Gerd started the car, crossed the bridge over the Nissan, and headed out of Oskarström and up to Skavböke, in the dark.

Kjell's farm was quiet, the night thick as oil. Bill began to bark as she stepped out of the car, and a white light blinded her.

Kjell was sitting on a chair at the base of the steps, his dog and shotgun next to him, a flashlight in hand.

'Do you have a license for that, Kjell?' Gerd asked.

'Damn straight I do.'

It took a moment for him to get to his feet. He had been waiting for almost an hour, hadn't dared to do anything else in the meantime. You couldn't be sure of anything anymore. Not these days. The world was changing too fast. Everything said 'Made in China', little punks stole diesel and equipment from honest, hardworking folks, and people were saying that in a week, on New Year's Eve, all the clocks would stop. And now this – a night that seemed to be twisting its dark claws around him. The scene that awaited down on the road.

He took in the sight of Gerd in the sharp beam of the flashlight, as if she were a disappointment.

'Did you lose everyone else along the way?'

'I'm the only officer on duty right now.'

'I guess I'll hold on to the gun, then.'

'Sure, but Kjell, that light.' Gerd squinted. 'Aim it at the ground, would you?'

She blinked and saw white spots.

As they crossed the frozen field, Bill walked loyally and silently at Kjell's side, as though he'd known him for years. He could probably tell that something was wrong. They climbed over the fence and there, on the road that formed the border between Kjell's land and Söderström's, was the Volvo. Gerd turned on her own flashlight and told Kjell to stay back.

She approached the trunk to peer inside and lingered there for quite some time.

'Well,' she said when she returned. 'I think I'm gonna have to call this in.'

12

The light over the fields and meadows was pale and chilly as quicksilver that morning. It gradually gathered strength and people woke with a strange feeling in their bodies, something *kymig* – uneasy, eerie. As though the whole village had dreamed the same uncanny dream during the night.

Blue-and-white police tape fluttered around the Volvo. A large van had pulled up there, and people in uniforms and dark-blue coveralls went back and forth from its open back doors. Hands covered in lavender vinyl gloves held cameras, notepads, pens. The activity proceeded solemnly, quietly; any discoveries were disclosed with great discretion.

Kjell stood outside the tape with Bill, who was visible, and recognizable, from a distance thanks to his pale coat. Many people noticed the dog first. Next, presumably, they noticed the stranger. That was how she was described, Gerd Pettersson's new colleague, who had the bad luck of starting her new position at the Oskarström police station on that particular morning.

Siri Bengtsson had arrived early and seemed unbothered by the fierce cold. According to her contract, she wasn't due to start until Monday, but she had personally contacted Gerd at the Oskarström office to suggest she come by over the weekend to become familiar with her new workplace.

If she regretted that choice, she didn't show it. She was skinny as a young birch tree, everyone thought, not least Gerd. She barely filled out her uniform, and she wasn't much older than such a tree either, with aloof features and intense brown eyes that seemed bottomless. Most people assumed she had roots in China or maybe Thailand.

Gerd tried to make up her mind about what she was seeing. It looked like an accident, yet something was off. The Grenbergs' Volvo had crashed into a tree down on the road that ran between the Östholm and Söderström properties. The back gate of the car was open.

There were visible tire tracks in the slush behind the car, as though the Volvo had skidded and yawed before the driver lost control and sailed right into one of the big old trees that lined the road. If you walked around and stood by the driver's-side door, you could see blood on the steering wheel, and there were more dark-red stains, alongside some footprints left by large, rugged shoes.

And there, in the cargo area, a boy. Two blows to the head, it looked like. One at his temple and one on the back of his neck. Blows from what? Gerd and Siri leaned over the body of Mikael Söderström. No smell yet. That was because of the cold, according to the medical examiner on duty, who had been summoned to Skavböke. He was of the sullen, cautious sort and didn't say much more. The fatal blows to the head, though – anyone could see those.

'And,' the medical examiner said after a great deal of observing, 'last night, sometime.'

'What's that?'

'The time of death.'

'Right, we knew that. Could you be a little more specific?'

'Not really. Not yet.'

Gerd glanced wearily at Siri. 'Okay. But if you had to guess?'

'I don't like guessing.'

'For Christ's sake. One o'clock? Three o'clock?'

He shrugged and looked at the body. 'Sometime between one and two.'

'So, one thirty?'

The medical examiner pursed his lips. 'Maybe.'

When Gerd leaned down once more, she noticed flakes of rust in the boy's hair.

'A hammer?' she suggested.

'Or a shovel,' Siri said. 'Something like that.'

It really was *kymig*. Not just that Mikael was the one lying there – it was the car, too, the fact that it belonged to Madeleine Grenberg. She had bought it for herself and her daughter, Felicia, after Göran died and they could no longer make payments on their big Ford.

Madeleine herself had called the police this morning when she woke up and made her way, on her crutches, to the kitchen to brew coffee. She had looked out the kitchen window and wondered where on earth her car had gone.

Madeleine's injury was also a well-known fact, even though no one in the village had witnessed her fall from the roof yesterday. Several people had heard her calls for help as she lay on the ground, though; among them was Frans Ljunggren, a mechanic, who came to her rescue and drove her to the hospital. Her left leg was X-rayed, examined, and placed in a cast up to her knee. Now she needed crutches to get around, and Felicia was sticking around their house to help her out.

At the moment, Madeleine was near the scene, tippy and unsteady on the crutches; apparently she hadn't gotten used to them yet. The two officers made their way over to her. Madeleine looked fragile and shaken; her handshake was chilly and slack.

'Hi,' Siri said. 'My name is Siri. I'm new.'

'I don't understand what happened,' she said. 'Is it really Mikael?'

'Yes,' Gerd said. 'I'm afraid it is. How did your car end up here?'

'No idea. I have no idea.' She repeated the words mechanically, tonelessly. 'It was in its usual spot at our place when we went to bed last night.'

'And when was that?'

'Oh, a little before eleven, maybe.' She nodded at her cast. 'They prescribed pills to help me sleep. Once those kicked in, I slept like the dead. Felicia went to bed at the same time. The car was gone when I got up this morning, but I was still all groggy from the pills, so it took a while for me to realize something was wrong.'

It wasn't uncommon for people to borrow the car, especially young people in the village who didn't have cars of their own yet, but they always asked first. After checking with her daughter, Madeleine felt she had no choice but to call the police and report it stolen.

'Your daughter thought you should call,' Siri said, more as a statement than a question. 'What time did she go to bed, again?'

'At the same time as me.'

'And did you see her during the night?'

'No, it, I . . . The pills, like I mentioned. Why?'

'We have to ask, Madeleine,' said Gerd, as though she were speaking to a friend, nodding toward the car. 'Given that it's your car, and the keys are in the ignition, that means whoever took it had access to the keys. And there's the fact of Mikael. Felicia knows him, obviously.'

'Yeah. Of course.' She nodded, her gaze vacant, and wobbled on her crutches. 'I'm happy to help. You know, sometimes I just leave the keys in the car, because who's going to steal it out here? And on occasion I forget to take them out of the ignition.'

A moment later, Madeleine hopped stiffly away on her crutches.

'Listen, Gerd,' Siri said. 'What she said about leaving the keys in the car. Can that really be true?'

'Welcome to the sticks,' Gerd said.

She crossed her arms and studied the vehicles that had begun to gather outside the cordoned area. Old Kjell was still there with his dog. He was giving a loud and dramatic account of his morning walk and the discovery of the car to anyone who would listen.

Gerd clicked on her radio and called the station.

'Where are we at with the dogs?'

'The closest team is in Gothenburg. It's going to take all day to get them here.'

Gerd shook her head. 'Thanks, I guess,' she said, and clicked off.

It was good to have Siri, at least, although it was a disadvantage that she didn't know the area. Another disadvantage was her miniature size, and the fact that she probably had to hold tight to a sturdy object if a breeze kicked up, and her lack of experience in general was a third. But even so, Gerd found it was nice to have someone at her side on a morning like this, at the very start of an investigation that already didn't bode well.

Siri approached the police tape and addressed Kjell.

'I don't suppose he's a hunting dog, is he?'

Kjell lit up. 'Why, yes he is. Smart as a whip.'

'Do you think he can track blood?'

Well, look at that, Gerd thought. *Never judge a book by its cover.* Maybe there was a real police officer in that tiny body after all. A small one, at least anatomically speaking, but even so.

13

Soon Kjell and Bill were being led in a broad circle around the car. Evidence on the ground was marked with numbered black flags.

'Here.' Gerd slowly lowered a creaking knee to the ground next to a few bloodstains the size of one-krona coins. 'We'll start here.'

Kjell blanched. 'Is that Mikael's?'

'We don't know, but we'd like to find out.' Gerd waved over the dog, who wagged his big tail eagerly. 'Shall we try it?'

'If there's blood to track, Bill will find it,' Kjell said, instantly behaving as though he were at the center of the investigation.

Soon the two officers were trailing the old man and his dog, who kept his nose to the cold ground. His tail in the air, a flag of concentration.

'Here.' Kjell pointed at the slope. 'We need to go up into this grove.'

There had been a thaw about a week earlier and most of the snow had melted, but then the cold returned. Here and there, the forest protected a patch of white; hard, crusty slabs.

'Keep your eyes peeled,' Kjell said. 'There've been wild boar around recently. Do you hunt?'

'I don't,' Gerd said. 'But my husband used to.'

'I do,' Siri said. 'But it's been a while.'

Gerd and Kjell stared at her in surprise. Maybe she was kidding; Siri didn't offer any more information. Instead she stopped next to a patch of snow the size of a dinner plate. In it was a footprint.

'What size shoes do you wear, Kjell?'

'Forty-one.'

'This one is a forty-three, at least. Larger, I'd say.' Siri compared it to her own boot. 'Whoever was walking here has gigantic feet, compared to mine.'

Who doesn't? Gerd thought, sticking another black evidence flag in the ground. Not far away, in a smaller patch of snow, they found an identical print.

'By the way, Kjell, what did you decide to do?' Gerd asked. 'About the money, I mean.'

'I withdrew it all last week, and so did Frans Ljunggren. And Bengt Lindell too.'

'That must be an awful lot of money.'

'Oh yes, quite a bit.'

'I don't want to know where you're keeping it. But I hope it's under lock and key, at least —'

'I've got a double lock on my front door, and I sleep with the shotgun next to my bed,' Kjell interrupted.

'. . . in a safe, for instance,' Gerd concluded wearily.

'With a shotgun around, it's perfectly fine in the mattress.'

Siri kept her mouth shut.

The forest gave way to a crop field, and Bill stepped out into the frozen clearing nose-first, but then he returned to the edge of the woods and sat down with an excited gleam in his big eyes. A cold wind blew in over the land.

'All right. End of the line. The trail probably keeps going a ways into the field, but Bill can't follow it any farther. And if he can't do it, it must be pretty hard.'

Bill waited for a signal. When none came, he stood up and looked pleadingly back and forth between Gerd and Kjell, his tail wagging gently.

'What were you doing between twelve thirty and two thirty last night?' Gerd asked.

'Me?' Kjell raised an eyebrow. 'I was sleeping, obviously.'

'Gerd.' Siri was staring at the ground a few meters away. 'Here. More prints. But they're going in the other direction. From the car he goes down there, then comes up here. Then he goes back to the car. And he's not alone. Look at that, the print next to it. It's smaller. See?'

Gerd nodded. She squinted across the field again. 'There.' She pointed. 'That house, over there. On the other side of this field. That must be where he was headed. To the Erikssons' house. And then he comes back.'

'What's their son's name again?' Siri asked.

'Sander,' Gerd said. 'Sander Eriksson.' She paused. 'Maybe you could talk to them.'

'We have company,' Kjell informed them, sounding almost amused.

Reporters. They parked alongside the cordons and climbed out, hungry, cameras and microphones in hand. One of them dropped his notebook. The wind caught it and it sailed across the field. The reporter ran after it and the man with the camera followed. It looked like he was laughing.

14

Sander's mother, Eva, was sitting at the kitchen table and warming her hands on her cup of coffee as she listened to the radio. A couple of teenagers had tried to knock over the Christmas tree on Stora Torg in Halmstad overnight. They gave up when one of them hurt his hand badly enough to seek medical attention. A man had been caught breaking into an electronics store at the Eurostop shopping center in Stenalyckan. According to the police, he had been trying to unplug all the appliances so they wouldn't explode on New Year's Eve. The man had been carted off to the psychiatric ward under loud protestation. New budget cuts for the municipality. Preparations under way for Christmas celebrations at county nursing homes. And now, the weather.

That was all. Sander opened the fridge, poured a glass of milk, and sat down beside his mother, yawning. The night before throbbed in his temples.

'How are you?' She drank her coffee. 'Late night?'

'Where's Dad?'

'He's off checking something on my car. It didn't sound so good when I started it yesterday, so he said he'd take it into the shop. Since it's the weekend and all. Would you have wanted to go too?'

'No.'

'You always used to want to go with him when he ran errands. I think he misses that a little bit.'

Sander drank his milk but didn't comment.

'Speaking of which,' she said, 'where did you two go last night?'

'Pierre's. We had to walk home, so, yeah, it did end up being a little late.'

'A little late?' Eva stood up and went to the sink to pour out the dregs of her coffee. 'I'd say the middle of the night is more than a *little* late.'

'Quit with the nitpicking already.'

'Nitpicking? I don't care if you are eighteen now, as long as you're living under my roof I get to ask where you spend your time.' She grinned and turned off the radio. 'Guess I'll head out now. There's a crashed car over by Kjell Östholm's farm, I don't know what the hell is up but I thought I'd go by and see if I can help at all.'

Sander looked perplexed. 'What, did someone get hurt?'

'I don't know, but I saw emergency lights this morning. Listen, I folded your laundry downstairs. Bring it up and clean your room. It's a pigsty in there.'

'Hey, Mom.'

'What?'

Sander breathed, silence. 'Never mind.'

She raised an eyebrow. 'Are you sure?'

'Yeah, it was nothing. We can talk about it tonight or whatever.'

'Lean down.'

She was small and dark-haired, half a head shorter than her son, so he bent down just like he used to do. She pressed her lips to his forehead, her soft hand on the back of his neck, and Sander thought: *Stay. Don't go.*

After his mom left, he turned on the faucet in the bathroom. The pipes creaked and hammered as he showered.

When he stepped out, there was someone outside, on the other side of the front door. A knock. He could see their shadow moving but couldn't tell who it was. Sander dressed quickly and went to answer the door. He caught a glimpse of the visitor through the window: a short, dark-haired woman with Asian features and a mouth like a small line on her face. Sander had time to notice the word POLIS on her shoulder.

15

What could be expected of a boy like Killian? Not much. It had been said many times: he came from a family of men with violence in their bones.

With a big head comes big dreams, and out here a head was something you could do without, if you had to. A body was enough. A guy without a head, that was Killian, who let himself be guided by what his hands and his thighs could do, by what he had between his legs. It was just that it was hard to carry everything around just in your body. Secrets, lies, and fears – other people had brains for that stuff. When it ended up in your hands or your dick, watch out.

It really didn't have anything to do with his parents, Sten and Linda, even if it appeared that way. They had slipped out of love once upon a time and never managed to claw their way back. They were fond of one another, but that wasn't enough.

Killian, at least, had stopped hoping. It was easier that way. You could imagine any number of outcomes: If his father had stayed, he would be a kind and solicitous dad, giving Killian rides to and from practice back when he was on the soccer team. Just like other dads, he would have asked about Killian's day at school and then helped Mom with dinner, dishes, and laundry. He would have kept the car and the house in good working order, not to mention the workshop and their small yard. He would have worked but always made time for Killian, to sit with him as he did homework or maybe even go to parent-teacher conferences, where he would ask the teachers good questions and defend his kid if they were unfair, but he would also firmly correct Killian if he made a mistake. He would listen to Killian and understand him.

If he hadn't left. That was probably how he would have been. You can imagine anything at all. Saying it out loud is another matter, so he seldom spoke about his father with anyone.

But Killian seemed to have been saved from his fate. Was that the right way to put it? The Lord had sent his only begotten son to Earth to save the world, as Isidor Enoksson taught them during confirmation class a few years ago. Maybe God also performed considerably more modest acts of mercy, because Killian's mother liked to say that since her son never had any siblings he was given Sander instead. It was like they had been bestowed upon one another.

Now that Sander kept talking about leaving, maybe Killian would turn out the way everyone feared. Sooner or later. It was only a matter of time.

A bolt of lightning. A storm. An icy rain; hail falling so fiercely it hurt. This is what roiled inside Killian when he imagined what life would be like without Sander. Like a hole in his chest.

When he went downstairs for breakfast, his mother was waiting.

'Didn't you sleep in the cabin?' she asked.

'No, I slept in here after all. It was so late, and I was cold.'

'Wait. What happened to your nose?'

He had a hand on the door of the fridge. 'I fell down.'

'Where?'

'On the way home. It was slippery. I was still holding my last beer and I didn't want to spill it.'

'What, so you caught yourself with your face instead?'

'Basically, yeah.' Killian tried to smile. The bridge of his nose was throbbing angrily. 'But I'm fine.'

He opened the fridge. It had broken twice this winter and was almost bare.

'You're acting weird,' he said, closing the fridge again. 'What's going on?'

'When I went to buy a Christmas tree, I saw Madeleine's car all roped off and surrounded by cops down on Kjell's road. When I got home just now there was a patrol car outside Erik and Eva's too. I guess Madeleine's car got stolen.'

Erik and Eva. Sander's parents.

'Stolen? Out here?'

'I heard they filed a police report, Madeleine called it in this morning.'

'Then what were they doing at Sander's place?'

'I don't know, but it's roped off, too, over by Kjell's field. I was going to go see if something else happened. If someone is hurt.' She eyed his nose. 'Do you want to come?'

'I need to work on the cabin. Just gotta hit the john first.'

In the bathroom he applied a plaster to his nose. It was too small and hardly covered the wound, but it was better than nothing. Then he headed out in a hurry, almost as though he were running away, even though he wasn't.

Outside, he could hear the cozy, dull hum of the generator. He watched through the window as his mother got in the car and drove off. Only a few minutes had passed when he heard a car coming back, and he suspected she had returned to get something. She often forgot her wallet at home.

But it wasn't her.

16

Dark algae covered the foundation. The battered wooden siding looked sick and emaciated, as if something were consuming it from the inside. Siri rang the doorbell. It rang crossly in the front hall. Nothing inside, no movement at all. She looked around.

It turned out the people she'd spoken to hadn't been misleading her. Killian Persson really did live in a cabin. Or rather, something that was meant to be a cabin someday, when it was finished. It had been built at the edge of the small yard and still hadn't been painted; its bare wood made it look stiff and clumsy. Two small windows watched her like dark eyes. A generator hummed rhythmically nearby, and the door was closed. Just as she was about to knock, she heard something moving very close by, as if someone had been waiting for her.

Suddenly he was right there, Killian Persson, tall and blond and with messy hair. He looked like he'd just woken up, and his eyes were red and blank. His nose was swollen, inflamed, and he had put on a small plaster that had no hope of concealing the nasty wound there. She introduced herself and waited for him to say something. When he didn't, she asked, 'Are you all right?'

'Oh, yeah.' Killian snuffled. 'It's just, I hurt myself yesterday and every time I bend down it throbs like hell.'

'How did you get hurt?'

'I fell down on the way home, is all. I'm fine.'

'On the way home from what?'

'A party.'

It was warmer inside the cabin. Must be because of him, his large body moving around in there, working. It appeared he had been trying to get the power to work. In one corner were two chairs and a table, old patio furniture that had been hauled in. Tools were scattered on the table, switches and cables, rolled up wires and cords.

'Something happened,' he said after a moment. 'Didn't it.'

'What makes you say that?'

He shrugged. 'Feels like it.'

Siri pulled out a chair and sat down. It was even more uncomfortable than it looked. 'How do you mean?'

He'd been examining the light switch on the wall. It was a little crooked. Now he leaned against the wall instead and crossed his arms.

'My mom mentioned something about it before she left. And then you showed up.'

'Right,' Siri said, observing the swelling of his nose under the plaster. 'Maybe you should get that checked out at the hospital. It looks awfully swollen. Where did you fall?'

'I tripped on a branch or a root or something, I couldn't see in the dark. We had been drinking some at the party, so I didn't have time to catch myself.'

'What kind of party was it?'

What followed was the same description Siri had heard less than an hour before. That time it had come from Sander Eriksson's lips, and was longer and more coherent, fuller in detail, but fundamentally the story was identical. He mentioned Jakob Lindell, the fight with Mikael, and that it had ended when Pierre Bäck stepped in to intervene.

'But what do you think they were fighting about?'

'Money, would be my guess. Anyway, that's what they were

hassling each other about in the living room, where we were. But I don't know, could have been something else.'

'Would Jakob be capable of hurting Mikael?'

'Why would he do that?'

'Because they were fighting over money, for instance.'

'But it all worked out.' He shook his head. 'No, no. Jakob is a nice guy.'

Something didn't add up here. Siri closed her notepad and tucked it back in her pocket.

'Who would you say is your best friend?'

'You know, the guy I was talking about. Sander.'

'Do you think *he* would be capable of hurting Mikael?'

Killian looked uncertain. 'What? Why would he do that?'

'Could he, do you think?'

'Sander's never been able to fight, he's too nice.'

'But what if he got mad?'

'If there was something going on between him and Mikael, they would have talked about it.'

Siri nodded and looked around thoughtfully. 'He's the one who helped you build this cabin, right?'

'Yeah, totally.'

'So he's a helpful guy?'

'Well, yeah, of course. We're friends.'

'Do you help him too?'

Killian hesitated. 'Sure.'

'Did you and Sander run into Mikael on your way home from the party?'

'No, it was just me and him, until we split off.'

'Did you run into Mikael on your own, then? Did something happen between you?'

'Uh, no. Like I just said, I didn't see anyone on the way home.'

There was something there inside him, but it was out of her reach; she couldn't quite get there. He may have been eighteen, but despite his adult size he was just a boy, and he wasn't formally a suspect for any reason. At last she gave up and simply wrote in her notepad:

hiding something

17

Siri returned to the scene of the crime with Sander and Killian's lies buzzing in her head.

I fell down.

We were hauling a bunch of debris.

The hell they were. But she couldn't get any further.

She heard a beckoning whistle. It was Gerd, who had been inspecting the area around the Volvo, where work had abruptly stopped. Now she was crouching to examine something in the snow.

'What is it?'

More prints.

'Aren't these another set?' Gerd said. 'They're different from the two we found up there. The sole is wrong. These came from someone else.'

Siri leaned down to get a closer look. 'Yes. They're different.'

Size 39, maybe 40. Not a boot. Some kind of athletic shoe. But the print wasn't very clear; they couldn't make out the brand.

'And look at this,' Gerd said. 'From here you have a perfect view of the scene – both the road he's coming down and the crash itself.'

She stood up, her knees creaking, and gazed across the village. More reporters were arriving. They parked their cars and got out. A band of black birds shot into the milky-white sky.

'Somewhere,' Gerd said, 'we have a witness.'

18

Growing up here, the people were as much a given as the roads and the paths, the old stone walls and the houses. Everything around you had always been there and would always remain. There was endless daylight, innumerable black nights, never-ending bus rides to and from Oskarström. When the bills were paid new ones came around, just like summers did. Animals died; new ones were born. Summers came and went. Winters, too, and Christmas Eve, Christmas Day, Boxing Day, New Year's, January, February, all the months of the year, and then it was Christmas Eve again; they had tons of Christmas Eves, Christmas Eves to the end of eternity, moments that would never stop coming around again. There *was* no end, and it was impossible for anyone or anything to cease to exist one day, to be erased from this life.

Then death took Mikael, and everything changed.

The first time Sander tried to comprehend that Mikael no longer existed, the thought dissolved like smoke in the air before him. It didn't work. Mikael could be dead while life here went on just like always? No, he couldn't. His locker was still there in the hallway at school, his bike was there. If Sander went to his house he would see all of Mikael's clothes and shoes, his desk. They *belonged* to him. Of course he was still around.

When they were little, Mikael played forward for Sennans IF soccer team, and these days he and Sander were the two top students in their year at Kattegat. Mikael was tall and slim, but he had broad shoulders, the body of a swimmer, and an angular face with gentle, pale-blue eyes.

To celebrate Mikael's birthday when they were younger, all the friends would gather around a long table in the yard behind his big house, under a line of colorful umbrellas to block the sun. They drank soda and ate hamburgers, played games on the lawn. One of the best games was 'sniper'. Mikael's dad, Karl-Henrik, would line up the empty soda cans on sawhorses, count the right number of paces, and place the air gun on a piece of plywood. The championship could begin, and when it was all over, they selected a winner, who would enjoy the eternal honor of victory, and, for one year, possession of the Söderström Shooting Trophy. Karl-Henrik himself had made it: it was a large cup carved from wood, to which he had attached a heavy marble base. The winner got to hoist it over his head and, perhaps even better, have the first pick of ice cream. During the championship, Mikael's mother set up a whole dessert buffet in a shady corner of the yard.

Mikael was one of the first to start driving a moped and an EPA tractor; he snuck the occasional cigarette but nothing harder, and he liked to party, but not too much. He was just *Mikael,* and everyone liked him. It was hard to imagine that he had any secrets, especially the kind that could kill you.

That evening, on the national news, everyone watched the prime minister call for a summit following a meeting of the NATO countries' foreign ministers in Brussels. A healthcare scandal in Malmö, a big strike notice at a sawmill in northern Sweden. Then, before anyone could prepare themselves, the viewers were tossed into Skavböke, here, home, and the whole village saw its own reflection in a dark pool.

Words and images described something unfamiliar – different people, a place that wasn't like theirs but gloomier and colder. A camera panned across Kjell Östholm's field and across the Söderström land before the segment showed images of the blue-and-white police tape fluttering ominously in the foreground. And beyond it, the police themselves.

It felt as though all of them were suddenly extras in a movie, and despite the gravity of the situation, Sander couldn't help but feel important, as though he were onstage in a play. Overnight, someone in Skavböke had become a killer.

'They were here, filming?' Sander's mother looked almost affronted from her spot on the sofa, as though this were an inappropriate intrusion. 'When did that happen?'

She sought protection in Erik's arms.

Sander was reminded of the riddle Isidor Enoksson had once presented to them during a school field trip to the chapel. Sander, Killian, and the others were only little then, maybe eight or nine. The riddle was short, and in the form of a question: When the boy jumped off the bridge, where was he?

After a long silence, Killian replied: 'In the air.'

But Sander shook his head. 'By the time you're in the air, you've already jumped. You have to be somewhere else before that. Right?'

The old priest nodded.

'But that means he has to be standing on the bridge,' Killian said. 'Or the railing.'

'No,' Isidor said. 'That's where he is *before* he jumps.'

Slowly, the implication of the riddle became clear. But the answer didn't. It seemed to reveal a truth about life around them: some things you saw might not have a name. Some things here in the world were both evident and impossible, perfectly obvious yet incomprehensible at the same time.

That was where Mikael was now. In the riddle about the boy on the bridge.

19

The police station in Oskarström consisted of a few small office rooms next to a larger space that could function as a conference room or a base of operations. Gerd couldn't remember the last time they'd used it for anything other than storage, she said. They had a small kitchen, a bathroom with a shower, and a changing room with lockers Gerd had once scored from an abandoned boxing gym in Sennan. The only thing in the office that had been manufactured on this side of the '90s was the gun safe. They'd gotten a new one a few years ago.

'Cozy,' said Siri.

'Nope,' said Gerd. 'I wouldn't go that far. But this one here's my office. You can do whatever you want with the adjoining room. It's been empty ever since I ended up on my own here.'

Siri's office was a cubbyhole with plain furniture, and it smelled like someone had forgotten to empty the coffee-pot there. She opened a window, then returned to Gerd and searched her notepad for a blank page.

'So, what do you think of your office?'

'Well.' She sat down. 'I'm sure I'll do just fine there with a few plants in the window.'

Gerd laughed. 'Okay then. Shall we begin?'

There was a dull buzz in Siri's fingertips, as though everything she touched had a current of electricity. She had never been part of a homicide investigation before, and she had only followed a few of them at a distance, since they were – thank God – rare in this county. Maybe that was where all this energy had come from, a first-time experience, the fear of missing some crucial bit of information.

The physical evidence was painfully thin. They had Mikael's body, of course, and an autopsy was scheduled for the next day. They had the blood on the steering wheel and the footprints in the snow, leading away from the car toward the Erikssons' place and back again.

Possibly a witness, who, in the best-case scenario, would come forward on their own.

'But if that was going to happen, they would have been in touch by now,' Siri said.

Gerd nodded grimly.

That was all, and it meant that for the time being they had to rely on interviews with people who had known Mikael. And that seemed to be practically everyone. Some interviews had been conducted by Halmstad, the formal home of the investigation, but most had been performed by either Gerd or Siri.

They'd been at it all day, and this was their first chance to review their notes. It was past midnight by the time they were done, and Siri's hands were shaking from too much caffeine.

She looked at her notepad and read: *The Söderströms. Erikssons. Grenbergs, Perssons, Lindells, Bäcks.* It was hard to make sense of it, remember who was who. During the day, she had noted:

Karl-Henrik and Lillemor Söderström: large farm. rich by comparison. two sons, Mikael 18 and Filip 16. both boys at party.

Bengt and Inga-Lill Lindell: former blue-collar, trying to get family farm off ground not far from scene. neighbors of Söderströms. one son, Jakob 18, argued with Mikael at party.

Siri had been a little cautious with Jakob Lindell. Instead of visiting him at home she had spoken to him on the phone, an information-gathering interview. If suspicion against him increased, they would bring him to the station instead. That was how she had dealt with teenagers in other cases, and it was often a successful tactic. It was easier to lie over the phone, and if they were lying they were in a bad way. But when she spoke with Jakob, he described the party, the argument, and the ensuing scuffle in a simple and straightforward manner. He, too, was distraught to hear about Mikael's death. He sounded genuine, and Siri had begun to doubt her initial suspicions.

'Yoo-hoo,' said Gerd. 'Did you fall asleep?'

'I'm thinking.'

'What about?'

'Do you know them? Sander Eriksson and Killian Persson?'

'It's more like I know their parents. But sure, I know of them. Two local eighteen-year-olds, one much brighter than the other. Practically joined at the hip since they were little. What about them?'

Siri gazed at her notes.

Erik and Eva Eriksson: blue-collar, live quite a ways from the scene, up on the hill. one son, Sander 18, at the party. scratches on arms. lying.

Linda and Sten Persson: poverty, divorced. one child, Killian 18, who lives in a shack on the property. best friends with Sander. serious injury to nose. hiding something.

'I'm pretty sure they haven't told me the whole story.'

'About what?'

'About what they got up to after the party. Sander Eriksson has scratch marks on his hands and arms. Like he had run through the forest. And those prints we saw in the snow.

In the front hall at Sander's house I saw three pairs of shoes that belonged to him. Athletic shoes – Nikes, I think – sturdy boots, and a pair of Converse. Black ones, as I recall. And in Killian Persson's cabin, there were a pair of athletic shoes in a much larger size. That would match the print in the snow up there. Killian also has quite the gash over the bridge of his nose, and quite the shiner too. He claims he fell down on his way home, but how do you fall on your nose? The blood on the wheel of the Volvo is likely from the driver being injured in the crash. What's more, the two of them told me identical stories. And then there's the Volvo. It belongs to Madeleine Grenberg, who reported it stolen. We don't know exactly when it was taken, but I'd be willing to bet it was around the same time when Eriksson and Persson were in the vicinity.'

'Which was what time?'

'They left the party around one.'

Gerd made a face and stretched. 'I'm too old for this, being out in the cold all day, oof. But that's a good start. Well done. Anything else?'

Siri's cheeks were warm as she turned the page of her notepad and read *Madeleine Grenberg*. Notes: *husband deceased. trouble making ends meet. works on Söderströms' farm, lives in a house on the property. one daughter, Felicia 18, who knows the others but wasn't at the party. car stolen by sp?*

Gerd glanced at Siri's notes.

'"SP"?'

'Just an abbreviation for suspect.'

'Is that the kind of stuff they teach you at the academy nowadays?'

'Among other things.'

'Madeleine and Felicia do indeed live in a house on the property, just as you note. But that property is huge,' she corrected, 'so it might not be the way you're picturing it – the houses aren't exactly right next door. Have you been there?'

'It got to be too late, I wanted to be considerate. Thought I'd start with that first thing tomorrow.'

Gerd nodded in understanding. 'And what about you?'

Siri raised an eyebrow. 'Me?'

'Yeah, how's your living situation?'

Siri gave a curt laugh and tidied a stack of papers.

'Fantastic,' she said.

'No husband or anything?'

'Not that I'm aware of, no.'

In the winter of 1999, all she had in her apartment was furniture. Everything else would have to come later, if at all. Lots of people she'd graduated with a decade ago had children now; they had bought houses and gotten married. Sometimes, when Siri thought about it or ran into one of them in town, pushing a stroller or carrying bags of groceries, she felt a pang of envy in her chest, but that happened less and less often these days.

'How about you?' Siri asked.

Gerd shook her head.

'Just the memories,' she said. 'Shall we move on?'

Just the memories. Siri wondered what was hiding behind those words, but she didn't ask.

'That blood on the wheel,' Gerd said. 'A blood sample from Killian Persson would be just the ticket. That would nail it down.'

'We can't get one, though.'

They would need a warrant from the prosecutor, and there wasn't sufficient evidence. Killian Persson was eighteen. Of legal age, sure, but barely.

'Yet,' Gerd said. 'We can't get one *yet*.'

Instead they turned to the crime scene techs' photographs

from the house where the party had taken place. These photos had been taken just a few hours ago. Today's technology meant that everything moved at astonishing speeds.

Unfortunately for the investigators, Pierre Bäck, host of the party, had cleaned up before passing out on the floor. He'd hung up what had fallen down and fixed what had broken, or at least he had tried his best. He'd gotten the big wall clock in the hall going again just before he fell asleep, but all he could do for the framed picture that had crashed down during Mikael and Jakob's scuffle was to piece it back together with duct tape, and Pierre was still pretty smashed when he did it, so the results were worse than they otherwise might have been.

When Saturday rolled around, his parents woke him up close to lunchtime. They had just returned from Friday's fiftieth-birthday celebration and wondered what on earth was going on in the village, with all these cops and journalists all over the place. A few hours later, a tech was meticulously documenting every nook and cranny of their home while Siri and Gerd interviewed the parents.

'I was thinking,' Siri said. 'The telephone line at the Bäcks' place.'

'What about it?'

'The tech asked if we had checked on it. Have we? To see if any calls were made during the party?'

'We haven't had time,' Gerd said, without looking up from her notes. 'You can put a request in tomorrow.'

'We need to track down those cameras too. I know there were disposable cameras around.'

It took about half an hour to walk from the party house to Skavböke. Mikael had been there, and so had his brother, Filip; Jakob; Sander; Killian; and about two dozen others. Filip had taken off first, in the company of Elina Jönsson.

Elina was in Filip's class; she lived nearby and he claimed he had spent a few hours with her. Gerd had called the girl, who immediately corroborated this information.

Mikael went on his way soon after, and Jakob left soon after that. Then a few more people took off, with Sander and Killian among the last to go. All of them, except for Filip of course, claimed to have gone straight home and to bed, just like after any other party.

Which really left only two alternatives.

'Either our guy wasn't at the party . . .' Gerd said.

'Or someone is lying,' Siri said, her eyes going to Sander's and Killian's names in her notepad.

Gerd didn't say anything for a moment. Then: 'Maybe there's a third option as well, but I hope not.'

'What's that?'

Gerd suddenly looked exhausted. 'They're all lying.'

20

Sander lay awake, paging through the course catalog Ardelius had given him. It smelled like it looked, like the future; it was a portal that almost transported him there. STOCKHOLM UNIVERSITY, it read on the front, next to a lovely seal: a torch wrapped in an olive branch, with three crowns alongside. This felt important somehow. He paged through the catalog, reading about majors and courses, but more than anything else he was drawn to the pictures.

There was nothing remarkable about them, really; they depicted students around tables full of books, paper, and pens; students strolling side by side across a lawn and laughing; students socializing over coffee in a big café; young people who looked a lot like him but in a packed auditorium the size of the main stage at the theater in Halmstad. Photographs of the university library captured shelves upon shelves of books, infinite books.

He turned the page. In less than a year he could be sitting right there, at that same table, living that very same life.

Sander would be going away. *Away*, that was the word for all of this.

No point wasting time on them, on Mikael and Felicia, Jakob and Felicia. Felicia. Who did she like, really? Maybe none of them, probably that was the case. But she had kissed Sander. Did that mean anything?

Probably not. Girls were unfathomable; there was no understanding them.

Away.

Sander found the section of the catalog about the major in legal studies: *The law school at Stockholm University is the largest legal studies program in the country, both in terms of researchers and students.*

The phone on the nightstand rang. When Sander answered, there was only silence on the other end.

'Hello?' Sander said, sitting up straight, his heart racing. 'Killian?'

It wasn't perfect silence. No one spoke, but he heard movement.

'No,' a voice began. 'This is Jakob. Hi. How are things at your place?'

'Fine.' Sander changed his mind. 'Or, you know . . . we're okay. You?'

'Mom and Dad are out of town, I mentioned that yesterday, didn't I? So they keep calling to check on me. I can't even deal with picking up the phone anymore. But I'm okay too. Or, you know, I don't know, that's why I was calling. You were there yesterday, when we were on the sofa chatting. Remember how I said Dad withdrew our money?'

'Yeah, sure.'

'Okay. Because I . . . Fuck, I don't know what I'm gonna do, I know this is peanuts given everything else, really, compared with Mikael. But it's not good.' He lowered his voice. 'The thing is, someone was here. I'm sure of it.'

'What? When?'

'Like, last night, after the party. The money – it's gone. Someone took it.'

21

There's a chapel in Skavböke, built by the community under leadership of vicar Teodor Lindqvist almost a hundred years ago. They had collected twenty-three thousand kronor. It was enough, but just barely.

Inside the chapel is a mural depicting the Creation, with the Fall of Man facing the chancel. It's a strange construction, almost as though it revealed a truth about humankind.

You can't see one without a glimpse of the other.

Maybe the same is true of justice. In the end, you can't look away; you must face it all.

Isidor Enoksson had been leading services at Skavböke Chapel since 1967. Before him had been Hugo Edman, and before that was Teodor Lindqvist himself, a theological lineage Isidor was very proud of.

Early in the morning on the fourth Sunday of Advent, in this blessed year of 1999, he stepped onto the street in Oskarström after paying a visit to Hasse Ek, the ill-fated old harness driver. It wasn't so hard to do the Lord's work, not really. That was what traditions and psalms were for. They bound earthly life to the next and helped us understand the great moments of human existence. Now, more than ever, it was important to gather around light and hope, but Isidor had a feeling his words wouldn't be heard in the usual way today, that he would be addressing a different audience than he was used to.

Isidor needed to worship as much as anyone right now. He always found himself feeling uneasy as he sat with the old tin-hatter in his apartment. For Isidor, conversations with

Hasse Ek weren't only an opportunity to practice the duties of pastoral work; they were also a key to a part of him no one else knew about.

'I used to bet every last krona on you,' Isidor once confessed. 'Out at the track. Even when it wasn't my own money.'

He had come very close to ruination. Gambling was under his skin; he could feel it still today, a prickly sensation when he passed a horse trailer on the county roads, when he saw an ad on TV or walked past the gambling machines during an occasional lunch at Ida's Bar and Grill.

Not that the priesthood had saved him either, not at all, even though one might assume that's what had happened. He had started conveying God's mercy to mankind through the church much earlier. If a little cash turned up missing from the coffers, he expected God would notice but let it be. After all, the Lord had more important matters to see to. These days, when Isidor visited Hasse Ek, it was like getting closer to a part of himself that was otherwise difficult to reach, yet all the more important to remember for that very reason. It's so easy to forget your weaknesses.

With a heavy heart, he got in his car and turned the key. Karl-Henrik and Lillemor Söderström up there on the farm, and Filip, the younger brother who was suddenly his parents' only son. Isidor couldn't even imagine what that must be like. He should probably go over there and check in on them. Filip especially – this couldn't be easy for him.

Today, on the second day after the murder, almost everything was about the Söderströms. The initial shock had moved through the village, and the eerie calm that remained gave rise to questions. Some of them would be answered during the very service Isidor himself would lead in a few hours, although perhaps it wouldn't be the ones folks might have guessed.

22

Gerd Pettersson lived in a snug little house in Oskarström, and when Siri parked on the street she caught a glimpse of her new colleague's frizzy hair in the kitchen window. Despite the early hour, she seemed nimble and alert, full of focus. She swiftly downed the last bite of her sandwich.

A house. Yes, maybe it was about time to get one. Siri had grown up in a series of apartments in the central neighborhoods of Halmstad. In her memory, the furniture was always the same, which made the rooms it stood in look identical even though the apartments weren't. She remembered early mornings before Dad left for work as a foreman at Pilkington Glass, quiet moments at the kitchen table with Mom before they had to get ready for school. Autumn weekends, going along to hunt with Dad and being supplied with activity books to keep her from pestering during the long hours outside.

The passenger door flew open.

'Good morning,' Gerd said, plopping heavily into the seat. 'Aren't you an early bird.'

'Always have been.'

'Did you get any sleep?'

Siri had left Oskarström very late, worn out from a first day full of too many intense impressions. Despite her exhaustion, she had lain awake for a long time in the quiet apartment, trying to organize those impressions, put them in order and study them, as though they were objects she could scrutinize and comb for something she'd missed.

'A few hours. You?'

'I'll make it. Didn't you bring anything?'

'I did, but I didn't have time to stop and buy it.'

Siri reached into the backseat and fumbled for the thermos and the two plastic mugs next to it.

Gerd took them. 'This is better anyway. Home-brewed coffee, damn, that's nice. You drive, I'll pour.'

The clock on the dashboard read 9:30. They drove to the office and changed into their uniforms, then headed to Skavböke with plenty of time to spare. Gerd poured coffee into a plastic mug and set it in Siri's cupholder before filling her own.

'I need to call the prosecutor and Violent Crimes in Halmstad later,' Gerd said. 'Can you remind me? They'll want an update.'

'Have any of them even been out here yet?'

'They came out yesterday afternoon, apparently. Stood around staring and offering opinions for a while before they declared they were freezing their asses off and took off again.' Gerd scoffed. 'I'm sure they have their own stuff to deal with in town and all, but damn, I've never gotten along with them. These days we stay out of each other's way as best we can. Hopefully you won't have to deal with them much either. City people.'

Gerd said 'city people' as though it were a curse. It probably was.

'I didn't mean . . .' Gerd rushed to say, glancing at Siri. 'I mean, there are some good folks there too. I've heard.'

Siri laughed. 'I'll do my best.'

'Has it been a challenge?'

'What do you mean?'

'Well, you know, just, you're kind of small. And, um, a little unusual.'

Siri changed gears. Her response made it clear that she'd

gotten this question before. 'I worked in Correctional Care one summer. When I met officers, they often said they needed people like me on the force. I didn't really know what that meant, but since I had no idea what I wanted to do I decided to apply. That's the gist of it. It hasn't been too much of a challenge.'

That probably wasn't the whole truth, but maybe it was part of it. If you asked her dad, it had all started with the activity books, thin volumes full of riddles and puzzles to think about. Was it even possible to trace a career so far back in a life? Sure, maybe. Sometimes. She would sit with those books for hours, until she had solved every one and felt a certain relief: now the world made sense.

'How about you?'

'Not that different from you, maybe,' Gerd said. 'I needed a job.'

She slurped as she drank.

'You've been an officer for a long time, haven't you?' Siri asked.

'Since 1965.'

'You must have been an early one. As a woman, I mean.'

'You better believe it. I was one of the first to emerge from those doors up in Stockholm, once they started accepting women into the academy. God knows, I might have only been the second or third woman with the Halland Police. Those were different times. I used to say I had a dog with me. When I was chasing after hooligans I pretended to let this dog loose on them.'

'What?'

'When we got the new uniforms, Christ, they were so heavy, and there was this burglary on Klammerdammsgatan in Halmstad where the thief leapt out an open window and ran off. I had never run in that uniform before, of course, only in lightweight workout gear, you know. That was how we trained. We should have done it all in uniform, to get used to them. Anyway, this bastard was getting away from me. I don't even remember who it was now. *Woof!* I barked. *Woof!* Stop, or I'll release the dog! *Woof-woof!*'

'Did it work?'

'Hell no. I didn't sound anything like a dog.'

Siri burst out laughing.

'I never tried to sound like a dog,' she admitted, 'but my first chase on foot was in town, too, down Brogatan. A pursesnatcher. It happened in the middle of the square. I ran after him as fast as I could, but like you say, we still don't practice running or obstacle courses in uniform even today. So,' she said, gesturing, 'I threw my baton at him.'

Gerd laughed so hard it turned into a cough. 'Did you get him?'

'Not by a long shot. But of course, I was running after him, heading for the bus bridge, so when I reached the baton I picked it up and tried again. But no luck. Another miss. So I was just as unprepared as you, in one way.'

'In one way,' Gerd echoed, raising her mug, 'it's a whole different world, being a female police officer in 1999 as opposed to 1965. But in another way, it's really not. Cheers to that. And Merry Christmas.'

'Cheers, Gerd.'

A brief silence. She had mentioned a husband, Siri recalled, a husband who'd been a hunter. 'You didn't live alone in your house, did you? Originally, I mean.'

'No, that's right. My husband died ten years ago. Thomas.'

'I'm sorry.'

'Thank you.'

Neither of them spoke again until they turned off the road and parked next to the chapel.

23

The service went poorly. Everyone was on the same page about that, in hindsight. What no one could agree on was the exact point at which it began to go south. Some said they could sense it in the air the moment they stepped into the chapel. Others claimed it was when Sander and, especially, Killian arrived, given Killian's appearance.

Some people claimed it all started with the police. They walked in in their uniforms, both Gerd and Siri, and took seats in the back.

According to Isidor himself, it was when the Söderström family, or what was left of it, arrived. People had already been talking about them in the pews, of course, wondering if they would attend, but no one had actually expected them to. Yet there they were: Karl-Henrik, Lillemor, and Filip, with the ghost of Mikael a cold, dark absence trailing after them.

This Sunday, attendance at the chapel was better than it had been in years, probably on account of Friday night's tragic incident. A small choir, among them Sander's and Killian's mothers, would stand outside in the chilly air to sing after the service, and mulled wine and gingerbread cookies would be served. Isidor waited up in the chancel, surrounded by Christmas decorations. Two Christmas trees with warm lights and deep-red ornaments glowed alongside candles in a variety of holders.

It looked peaceful, but Isidor felt doubt and the itch of gambling grow within his hands. It was where he always felt the expectations of the motley congregation as they waited to hear him speak.

Everyone was thinking of Mikael. Where was he now? Was he listening? Who knows what really happens to the dead? Several times over the weekend, folks had experienced a shimmer in the air, a sudden will-o'-the-wisp. Could have been an illusion, light reflecting off a closing door somewhere nearby or a truck passing on the road.

Maybe not. It almost felt like he was still around.

The world of Skavböke was no longer solid. It had begun to shift like melting ice.

Killian's father, Sten, arrived late and last of all. He stepped in like a larger, more haggard version of his son and glanced at Linda, who turned to stare stubbornly at the windows. Sten strode up to Isidor and shook his hand.

'It's been a while since I was last here,' he said to the pastor. 'But I felt like . . . I thought I ought to . . . you know.'

Isidor smiled and nodded kindly.

Madeleine sat on the other side of the center aisle, her crutches leaning against the pew, busy trying to keep her injured leg straight. When she and Sten noticed each other, their gazes lingered.

This was the first time many of the young folks had seen each other since the party. That was why some were only now noticing Killian's nose. People tried to keep from staring.

'Do you know what happened?' Jakob whispered to Sander, who was sitting closest to him.

As Sander briefly recounted the accident, Jakob looked perplexed.

'He fell on his nose?'

'That's what he said. I don't know, I wasn't there.'

The service began and Isidor spoke about them, about the village and the terrible thing that had happened. Gathering here, all together, was one way to find strength in one another. So far so good, but suddenly he seemed clueless about what to say next, if only that they should start to search for that strength, without detailed instructions of how to begin.

'On the fourth Sunday of Advent, the angel Gabriel appeared to Mary and told her she would give birth to the son of God,' he said tentatively.

Then he spoke about the Lord, who was tender, slow to wrath, and full of love. Gracious to all, benevolent toward his creation. In response to the tribulations of earthly life he offers a single comfort: mercy.

Isidor tried to choose his words carefully, and this was certainly obvious, but it still seemed as though he kept slipping up. Afraid of missing the important words, he said far too many.

He reached for a hymnal and opened it.

During the hymn, which was sung without accompaniment, Sander leaned toward Jakob and whispered, 'Did you talk to them?'

Jakob shook his head.

He had come home after the party to find the house unusually chilly. Someone had broken a pane of the glass door in the back, facing the yard, and had stuck in their hand to turn the lock.

'You should tell them,' Sander whispered, nodding discreetly back at the rear of the chapel, where the cops sat. 'Since they're here.'

Jakob shrank back as though Sander had demanded he confess his sins, and shook his head. The hymn faded and a sense of emptiness trickled into the pews. Someone coughed.

'Why not?' Killian said, and when Jakob looked confused,

he added, 'Your parents are going to figure it out when they see the hole in the glass. They're going to ask questions.'

'Yeah.' Jakob looked helpless. 'I know. They're not home yet; they'll be here after lunch. But we argued, you know? Me and Mikael. First the crap when we were on the sofa, and then, even worse, what happened upstairs. When the police called me yesterday, and I told them about it, I could tell it made them suspicious. If I take this to them now, they'll ask why I didn't tell them right away.'

People sitting nearby heard them whispering and glared. Isidor had begun to read from the Gospels.

'They only called you?' Sander whispered harshly in surprise. 'They came to my house.'

'Mine too,' Killian said.

'They just called. But I could tell it made them react.' He gave a pointed look. 'When I told them about the fight. And now, with this theft, what if they come arrest me or something, what the fuck am I going to say then?'

But it wasn't all that unusual – fights happened at parties, they just didn't typically end in someone's death. The cops knew that. Besides, it was better for Jakob to tell them about the stolen money. They would find out eventually anyway and wonder why he'd tried to hide it, and it would –

Karl-Henrik Söderström whipped his head around as though someone had suddenly grabbed him by the hair on his nape. His face was red and puffy, his eyes shiny as he stared the guys down.

'Shut the hell up, for Christ's sake,' he said, so loudly that Isidor fell silent up at the front.

The words ricocheted around the chapel.

Karl-Henrik's gaze slid away, trying to find something to focus on. The two cops watched attentively from their seats.

'To all generations,' Isidor began anew, but he stopped when he saw Karl-Henrik struggling to rise from the pew.

'Can you explain it to me?' He stepped into the aisle, resting one hand on the back of the pew for support, gazing unsteadily at Madeleine and Felicia. 'Huh? Everyone knows. Doesn't it matter?' His voice was thick. 'Everyone knows he was in your car.'

Up in the chancel, Isidor said, more to the police in the back than to Karl-Henrik: 'Please allow me to continue.'

'Karl-Henrik, please,' Lillemor tried, trying to grab his hand, but Karl-Henrik waved it away and pointed at Felicia.

'You and Mikael,' he said, his voice losing its strength. 'Right, the two of you were –'

Karl-Henrik's eyes darted. Felicia opened her mouth, but nothing came out. Gerd had already stood up. She was standing in the center aisle, perfectly calm, as though everyone weren't following her every move. She rested a hand on the bereaved father's shoulder.

'I think we should go get some air, Karl-Henrik.'

Siri came to stand on his other side, and he followed them to the exit without any fuss.

Lillemor was left behind. She put her arm around Filip, who was slumped in the pew. Afterward, everyone tried to remember if he had moved at all during his father's outburst, but no one could say for certain; it seemed he had been completely paralyzed. Then, suddenly, Lillemor stood up and pulled Filip with her. They left the chapel, a listless son and a mother breathless, like she was trying to keep panic at bay.

Isidor cleared his throat. It was probably a moment for him to speak, but in retrospect no one could reproduce his words. The choir arranged themselves outside, dutiful but rather bewildered, and the mulled wine and gingerbread cookies were served. *O, come, all ye faithful, joyful and triumphant,* they sang, their voices bright and fragile, as Sander and Killian looked around, worried that something else – what, they didn't know – might happen.

The extent of what had happened didn't become clear until the next day, when everyone learned that Inger Nilsson, an old newshound at *Hallandsposten*, had managed to infiltrate and witness the whole spectacle.

24

Away, Sander thought again that Sunday. That's the word for all this, simple as that.

In fact, maybe it had been there inside him for a long time.

When he was little, he often liked to go outside and pretend that, just as all grown-ups feared, war had come. One day he made his way out of Skavböke on the narrow forest paths, headed down to Årnilt, crossed the bridge into Oskarström. It was summer, hot outside, and the sun was high in the sky when he finally dared to emerge from the forest and approach the road. No soldiers here. The coast was clear. He looked up at the sky: no mushroom clouds either. There was still time.

And suddenly, someone was looking at Sander from across the road, a boy with a big shock of blond hair that moved gently in the breeze. He was wearing filthy clothes, with holes in the knees of his pants, and when Sander walked toward him he could tell the boy smelled a little funny.

'What are you doing?' the boy wondered, gazing uncertainly at Sander's rifle, a smooth branch he held in both hands.

'There's a war,' Sander said. 'Didn't you know?'

The boy's eyes grew wide. 'No. There is? Here?'

'How old are you?'

'Seven.'

Hard to believe. The boy in front of Sander was already a head taller than him, and he was as wide as a whole motorcycle. But he looked strong too. Probably good to have around in a war, no matter how old he was.

'What's your name?'
'Killian.'
'What?'
'Killian.'

Sander had never heard a name like that before, but then again, no one else shared his name either.

'Do you want to join? We need more valiant soldiers.'
'What does "valiant" mean?'

Sander had to think about it. 'That you're brave, sort of. All heroes are valiant.' He crouched down and peered around, like a soldier would do. 'We just need to find you a gun.'

Killian turned his head to look at a large bush nearby. From it he snapped off his own branch, and once he pinched off the little twigs, it looked almost exactly like Sander's, just a little flimsier.

'Will this work?'
'It can be a Kalashnikov.'
'What's a —'
'Look out, they're coming!'

After a moment, the bus to Halmstad arrived, chugging and sighing. When Sander saw it, there was a tingle in his belly and he turned to his brother-in-arms. 'Do you have any money?'

Killian's eyes were huge as he gazed at Sander. 'No.'
'You need money so you can pay.'

Sander dug deep in his pocket and took out two ten-kronor bills.

'Here.'

The bus driver took their money and they sat in the way back. While the world was going by outside, Killian worried about what he would say if his mother boarded the bus, what would happen if the driver threw them off, if they would be able to find their way home again, if some grown-up would help them, if there were strangers on the bus or in town who wanted to hurt them, if –

'Killian.' Sander touched his arm. 'Relax. It's fine. We're just riding the bus.'

'But I'm worried, though. How will we get home again?'

'You can ride back on the same ticket, of course. And no one will notice that we're gone.'

With every intersection, red light, and curve they passed, Killian's concerns were drowned out by curiosity. Soon they both had their faces pressed to the window, as though neither of them had ever seen the city before. It seemed brand-new.

They got off at Stora Torg, which was bustling with movement and energy. People walked by with grocery bags or briefcases or suitcases in hand; buses drove by and birds flocked around the big fountain. They saw different cars from the ones at home, smelled different smells and heard different voices. When they passed cafés, they overheard what people were talking about, how they laughed.

Sander saw bus stops for lines with destinations he'd never heard of, and he wondered where they were. He observed the city people, how they were dressed and how they behaved, where they looked when they walked. He tried to move like them, because if he could do that, he thought, he would be one of them.

Killian stopped at each shop window, had a look, and moved to the next. He said things like 'Hey, those shoes are super nice, I want ones like that' and 'Weird how they're selling winter clothes right now, it's summer' and 'Wow, princess cake!'

Sander secretly watched him, this new comrade, and tried to figure out who he was. He was big and friendly, but sometimes he almost seemed a little dumb, as though the world were a question and he had no answer.

'How many pieces of princess cake can you eat?' Sander asked.

'I don't know. Two, maybe.'

'I once ate almost one and a half, all but the marzipan. I bet you could eat three, if you really wanted to. At least three, because you're so big.'

'Yeah, I probably could,' Killian said, 'but I've never had more than one piece.'

They passed a shop that sold women's underwear and stopped in front of it. For a long time afterward, they didn't say anything.

'That was weird,' said Killian.

'Yeah,' Sander agreed.

Soon they took the bus back up to Oskarström. They went their separate ways in Skavböke, at the fork in the road.

Sander suspected that his new friend didn't have an easy life. Maybe that was why he was so big, Killian, so he could protect himself. The same way lizards grow a protective layer of scales against the world, Killian had grown husky and tall.

Sander walked home, and soon he was sitting at the table with Mom and Dad, eating spaghetti and meat sauce, the same dish he had read on the menu outside one of the restaurants in town just a few hours ago. He and Killian, the two valiant soldiers, had been there. They had visited the toy store Lekcenter, had stood outside the department store Åhléns, had gone to the shoe store and the bakery. And Mom and Dad had no idea.

It was almost scary, how crafty he was.

That evening, he lay in bed and closed his eyes, tried to stitch the many images in his memory into a whole, like a movie he could watch over and over.

He couldn't quite put it into words at the time, but a sort of undercurrent had formed, a promise and a question: How could he leave this life behind for something greater?

25

Mikael Söderström's autopsy was performed on the morning of Sunday, December 19, and the results were clear but, given the situation, hardly illuminating. At around one thirty on Saturday morning, he had died outdoors as a result of blunt trauma to his temple and the back of his head. Then he had been tossed into the cargo area of Madeleine Grenberg's car and left there.

They could not be sure of the scene of the crime. Nor of the murder weapon, but it was probably a large tool, such as a shovel. And presumably an old one – flakes of rust were found in Mikael's hair. There had been alcohol in his blood, but not very much. Whatever good that information might do – after all, he'd just been at a party.

Mikael Söderström, eighteen. Just a boy, his whole life ahead of him. His father had been led out of the chapel during the Advent service, an incident Siri and Gerd documented after the fact and included in the investigation materials. That was the easy part – discerning what it meant was a different matter. They had tried to interview the family again, especially Karl-Henrik, but all they got out of them was information they already knew.

'He was so much like me,' Karl-Henrik said, over and over. 'He was so much like me.'

As though a part of his very being had been torn from the world, and wasn't that the truth?

'He addressed Felicia Grenberg in the chapel,' Siri said now that she and Gerd were alone in the office. 'She's the one he targeted, as if she and Mikael were together somehow. Is that so, do you know? Did they have a relationship?'

Gerd shook her head. 'I've heard rumors, of course, but nothing that concrete.'

'Rumors about what?'

Gerd made a face. 'That he forced himself on her at some party, I think. But there was never any proof, and we're not a gossip mill. We're no Majken Gustafsson. The hairdresser,' Gerd clarified when Siri raised an eyebrow. 'Before she closed down her salon a few years ago. She used to sing in the choir, by the way, you know – the one that sang today. So did I.'

'You did?' Siri couldn't disguise her amazement.

'Yes, back in the day. I thought it was nice around Christmastime. I like to sing, but not by myself.'

Siri examined a note in front of her. It had to do with the fight between Jakob Lindell and Mikael. It seemed money was the root of the argument.

'They could have been fighting about Felicia as well,' she mused.

At that moment, a visitor turned up on their doorstep. They feared it was somebody from the Violent Crimes Unit in Halmstad, or worse, journalists, but no: it was Bengt and Inga-Lill Lindell. Between them stood none other than their son Jakob.

'We need to report a theft,' Bengt said.

They went out together, Siri and Gerd, and given the circumstances they performed a thorough investigation of the scene. Gerd photographed the broken glass on the stained parquet, and the bench where Bengt had secreted the family's savings. Siri noted half an impression of a shoe on the floor just inside the door. Presumably the perpetrator had taken off their shoes after leaving that print.

She studied the impression at close range.

'Too smeared to lift,' Gerd said, taking a picture with the camera. 'But we'll document it anyway.'

Then she dutifully photographed the door, both from a distance and close up, with the broken pane like an open wound. Almost the whole house fit into the frame.

Meanwhile, Siri spoke to Jakob, who stood with his arms wrapped around himself as though he were freezing, looking like his whole world had fallen apart.

'It's okay, Jakob,' she said softly. 'This kind of thing can happen to anyone.' Siri almost wanted to touch him. 'How are you holding up? It must have been a difficult weekend.'

'I'm okay. I just want the money back.'

'How bad was this fight you had with Mikael at the party?'

'What do you mean, how bad?'

'Was it about Felicia?'

Jakob's eyes got big. 'Felicia? No, no. It was just about money and stuff, that kind of crap.'

'But you like Felicia?'

'As a friend, sure. But that's all.'

'But did Mikael think you did? He liked her, right?'

'No, I don't know. Who told you that?'

'I just wondered. Did Mikael like Felicia?'

'Everyone likes Felicia. But if there was something more going on between them, I didn't know about it. I guess you'd have to ask her.'

'What about after the party, what did you do?'

'I went home, obviously.'

'Straight home?'

Jakob looked perplexed. 'Yeah, of course.'

Siri waited. So did Jakob.

'Okay,' said Gerd. 'I'm all done.'

*

Back at the station, they sat in Gerd's office, Gerd at her cluttered desk and Siri on one of the wooden chairs. All Siri had added to her own office so far was a new notepad, a set of empty binders, and a few random mugs. It still smelled like old coffee in there.

'According to the autopsy, Mikael dies at around one thirty in the morning,' Siri said. 'Ten minutes later, around twenty to two, Jakob arrives home.'

By that point, the pane of the door was already broken, and someone had taken the money – over fifty thousand kronor – out of the kitchen bench and vanished. No evidence beyond the smeared footprint had been found in the house; the burglar had taken one step inside, stopped to remove their shoes, and then continued. This burglar was either experienced or clever.

'Lots of money,' Siri said. 'Poor bastards.'

'Yes. But if you're stupid enough to withdraw your savings, hide it carelessly in your home, and let your son go to a party where he blabs about it, you have only yourself to blame.'

'Who does, the son or the parents?'

Gerd only muttered in response, and went to the bathroom.

26

Almost everyone at school had read or heard about Inger Nilsson's article and what had happened during the Advent service out in Skavböke. The piece used astonishingly thoughtless language to describe the drama that played out in the center aisle as Karl-Henrik Söderström stood up on shaky legs and, after flinging accusations, was led out of the chapel by the two police officers.

No names were given, and certain details were left out, but everyone knew who it was. All of Skavböke was ashamed, as though they had not previously realized that the world could stare right in at them when they were at their most vulnerable.

Lundström, the Swedish teacher, was the only one who appeared to ignore it all. He and Sander had first met late last summer. That day, Lundström stood at the lectern he had just inherited and introduced himself to the class in a businesslike manner, as though it were a formality and nothing more.

The first assignment he gave them was to write a poem. They were encouraged to take their time and think carefully about what they wanted to say. Sander, true to form, forgot all about the assignment and composed his poem on the bus from Oskarström the morning it was due. He titled it 'Autumn Comes to Skavböke, Halland.'

When he dropped it on the desk, Lundström was at the chalkboard, writing out the day's lesson plan. From the corner of his eye, he saw the sloppily torn-out paper land on top of the pile. He cast a hasty glance at it and turned back to the board. One more glance, and he picked up the poem. He read it slowly.

'Did you write this?' he said.

'Yes.'

'You're . . . Sander, right?'

'Yes.'

Lundström nodded. There was a sparkle of curiosity in his eyes.

That autumn, something happened with Sander, and not even Killian understood what it was, at first. Sander began to hang around school a little longer, often reading stuff he didn't have to read, and he appeared to be trying harder to prepare for tests and essays.

Now it was almost Christmas vacation. The teachers were putting in their last bursts of effort for the year; maybe the students were too. Everyone wanted to go home. The radio in the cafeteria was playing Christmas music. After break, while the others were stashing last period's books in their lockers and taking out new ones, Lundström waited for Sander in the doorway of his office and nervously clicked a ballpoint pen.

'Hi. How are you doing? You look pale.'

'I had trouble sleeping this weekend.'

'I can imagine. Us teachers found out this morning. We'd heard about the incident itself, of course, and we read the newspaper too. But we just learned that it was Mikael.'

Away, Sander thought again. That was the word burning inside him. Because . . . it wasn't *escape,* was it?

'I want to do it. I'm going to apply.'

Lundström smiled and tucked the pen into his breast pocket. 'That's great.'

'You're from Åled originally, right? Why did you come back? From Stockholm, I mean. Like, back to us farmers?'

'There's nothing wrong with farmers.' Then Lundström paused, as though the answer wasn't obvious. 'I fell in love.'

'In love?'

'Yes.' He smiled, looking chagrined. 'Isn't that reason enough?'

That same day, Sander saw Felicia.

Her locker was in the same hallway as his, but it was close to one of the big windows. Outside, a heavy snow was falling. She stood alone by the window, her hands thrust into the deep pockets of her down coat, as though she were trying to get a look at something down in the schoolyard. A large leather bag, its gold color flaking, sat on a chair next to her.

'Hi,' Sander said, as casually as he could, heading for his locker. 'You're still here?'

'I'm about to head home, just waiting for the snow to let up. I forgot to grab my umbrella this morning.'

'I don't think I even own an umbrella,' Sander said.

'So you just get wet when it's like this?'

'Why not, I'm waterproof.'

She laughed. Felicia had a unique laugh. It was loud and shrill and it made her nose crinkle irresistibly, almost like an invitation to join in.

'You know,' he said, as if she had asked him a question, 'I'm going to leave here. I'm moving away after this summer.'

'Where to?'

'Stockholm.'

'What are you going to do there?'

'Go to school.' He smiled. 'Live. Live my life. Maybe I'll even get an umbrella.'

'What are you going to study?'

'Law. At Stockholm University. Juridicum, it's called. Then

I want to travel. Like, as a corporate lawyer, probably. For a big company.'

'What, like IKEA?'

'Oh hell no. Not IKEA.'

Walking across the schoolyard, through the falling snow, they saw Filip. He had big headphones on. In his hands he held a notebook, and he was scribbling frantically in it even as he tried to protect it from the moisture.

'It's so awful,' Felicia said softly. 'Did you see the paper today?'

'Yeah. Did they come talk to you all? The police, I mean?'

'For hours, both yesterday and on Saturday. It was our car, after all.'

Sander felt he should say something, but no words would come out – all he could think about was touching her. Her straight brown hair fell over her shoulders. It looked so soft.

One day, long after he left Skavböke and became a different person, years after he met someone and had a kid or two, maybe they would meet again in town, during one of his visits to Halland, and he would think: it could have been the two of us. A little sentimental and, what was the word, bittersweet. Things would work out for him, and all of this, stuff that meant so much right now, would seem childish and silly.

At last, the question fell from his lips: 'How were things between you and Mikael?'

'Between us? Oh, fine, I guess. What do you mean?'

He opened his mouth and wished an answer would come as easily as the question had. But nothing happened.

'I don't know,' he said. 'I was just thinking.'

Felicia looked at him intently. 'What were you thinking?'

'I had the idea that he liked you. I mean, *like*-liked you.'

'Did he?' A furrow appeared in the smooth, soft skin between Felicia's eyebrows. 'If he did, I never knew it.'

'Maybe it was only a rumor.'

'Was it a good party?' she said, a weird question in this context, but he understood what she meant.

'Yeah, it was good. We had a fun time; too bad it ended the way it did.'

That sounded weird too. All the words were strange now, as though what had happened over the weekend had twisted them, making it hard to speak without slipping and falling.

'I wanted to go, but I had to stay home with Mom.'

'Yeah, I heard. Lucky you did, in the end.'

'By the way, I'm sorry.'

Her gaze was sincere, as though she expected him to know what she was referring to.

'For what?'

'Well, maybe it's no big deal, but I've been thinking about it a lot. I mean, last summer. When we . . .' She giggled nervously. 'I mean, I was so fucking drunk.'

'Oh, right.' Red spots bloomed on Sander's cheeks, and he began to dig through his locker in the hopes that Felicia wouldn't notice. 'It's totally fine. I wasn't exactly sober myself.'

He tried to laugh, too, but it sounded fake even to his ears.

'I'm heading out now,' Sander said. 'Want to come?'

She looked out the window again. Filip was gone, as though the snow had devoured him.

'I think I'll wait a bit and see if it stops snowing.'

'Do you like the movies?'

Felicia looked nonplussed. 'The movies?'

'Like, going to the movie theater. To watch a movie.'

'I know what movies are.' She tucked a strand of hair behind her ear. 'Sure, I guess so.'

'Maybe you'd like to go. Sometime. With me, I mean.'

'I guess you should ask me.'

'Maybe I will, then.'

She went back to watching the snow fall. Felicia was like money: only too much of her was good enough. Sander slowly locked his locker. He felt confused and his temples were throbbing, but somehow he felt oddly hopeful.

27

What the hell had Filip even been doing at school the Monday after his brother was murdered? Acting as if nothing had happened, or like he didn't even care? Maybe, someone said, Filip had only gone to school to get away from home, which seemed to be explanation enough. And who can say how any of the rest of them would have reacted?

Whatever his motivation, he'd left something behind at the end of the day. That evening, Killian called Sander to say that Filip's teacher had come down the hallway holding Filip's backpack.

'Filip just forgot it, apparently, guess he had other things on his mind. Gunilla asked if I could bring it to him.'

'And you said yes?' Sander asked.

'What the hell else could I say? He's got homework for over vacation and shit in there.'

'As if he's going to do any of that now,' Sander muttered.

'Can you come with me? I'm not about to visit that fucking house by myself.'

Given how things had gone in the chapel on Sunday, it probably was a good idea for Sander to go with him.

They met up in the dark and reluctantly headed for the Söderströms' place, Killian with Filip's backpack slung over his shoulder, and Sander with a strange, tense feeling in his body.

'I asked Felicia if she wanted to go to the movies with me,' he said after a long silence.

Killian turned his head. 'What did she say?'

'It sounded like she wanted to.'

'What, did she say so?'

'She said I can ask her, and we'll see.' Now, saying it out loud, he could tell that it didn't really sound as if Felicia wanted to go to the movies with him. 'I mean, that's not how she said it; or, that *is* what she said, but it was more like *how* she said it. You know.'

Killian walked on, his gaze on the ground. His shoes left deep tracks in the snow.

'Okay,' he said.

'What?'

'Nothing, I'm happy for you. I just don't want her to, how do I put it, disappoint you again.'

'I wasn't disappointed last summer.'

'Right, okay.'

'I *wasn't*.'

'Okay. Great.'

They kept walking. At last, Sander said: 'And I'm not going to be disappointed this time either. After all, I'm moving away. And she knows that, too, I told her today.'

There was a flash in Killian's eyes. 'But if she did want to be with you, would you stay?'

'Killian, I don't know. If anything happens between us, I suppose it'll just be like a short-term thing.'

Killian seemed to be considering the implications of all this. 'Have you told your parents? That you're moving away?'

'Not yet. But I will.'

'What is it you think you're going to find in Stockholm?' All of a sudden, Killian sounded exasperated. 'What do you think is there that isn't good enough for you here?'

'I don't exactly know. I think I can learn something about who I am.'

'What do you mean, *who you are*? Don't you know?'

'Sure, but not like that.'

'What? I don't get it.'

Sander sighed. Killian was so dense sometimes.

No one here gets it, he thought, but he didn't say it. Instead, as if to change the subject, he stopped mid-step and said: 'Did you look inside his backpack?'

'No.'

'We saw him today, at school, me and Felicia. Don't you want to see what's in there?'

'But it's Filip's.'

Sander opened the zipper while Killian watched. Inside, they found an old cap, some textbooks, some loose-leaf paper, and a notebook. He took out the notebook and handed the backpack to Killian as he began to page through it.

'What are you doing?'

'Filip was walking along and writing in a notebook.'

He found the right page, and his eyes scanned the text that had been so hastily scribbled down, intense and uneven, scrawling.

A car came down the road, headlights bright white. Sander turned his back to it and ripped out the page.

'What was it? What does it say?'

'It's a crib sheet, for a test. He can't have that in the notebook; if anyone finds out he'll get in trouble.'

'But you can't just rip it out.'

Sander folded the paper and tucked it into his pocket. Down the road, the Söderströms' house was a dangerous tower, big and dark and secluded.

'Come on,' Sander said in a low voice. 'Let's get this over with.'

28

The Söderströms' place was waiting for them like a haunted house.

'Let's make this quick,' Killian said, looking at the front door.

'Yeah,' said Sander. 'Super quick.'

They rang the bell and waited. Nothing happened. Sander tried the door.

It was unlocked. They cautiously stepped inside, breathing in the silence.

'Hello?' Sander called.

A shotgun was leaning against the wall in the front hall.

Flowers on a table, tons of bouquets. Sander recognized the one his mother had purchased. A *condolence gift*, she had called it. In the living room was a Christmas tree, decorated and lit up, on a preprogrammed timer. If you walked by at the right moment, you could see it turn on or off while no one was there. The vacuum cleaner was sleeping in a corner. Coats hung from pegs and leftovers were shriveling on the stove in the kitchen.

Someone, probably Karl-Henrik, was moving around in the basement. He didn't seem to have heard them.

It wasn't perfectly silent. The sound of clinking bottles leaked faintly through the floorboards, and from above they heard the dull murmur of a television.

'Hello?' Sander called, louder this time.

No response.

They went upstairs. Sander avoided looking into Mikael's room, even though part of him really wanted to. She had said they were just friends, so surely it was true. Or was it? Was she lying, had Felicia ever been in there? Recently, maybe? He pictured a shirt that didn't belong, a forgotten hair tie, lip gloss on Mikael's nightstand.

'What's wrong?' Killian asked.

'Nothing.'

The door to Filip's room was closed, but they could hear music from the other side, loud music coming through headphones, and it sounded like he was typing furiously at his computer.

'I –' came a voice from the stairs, startling Sander.

It was Karl-Henrik. Sander didn't understand how he could possibly have snuck up behind them without a sound. There had always been something frightening about him, as if a smoldering fuse always trailed behind him. Now, as he leaned against the wall at the top of the stairs, blinking blearily, it felt like Karl-Henrik might detonate at any second.

'You,' he said, when he realized it was Killian. 'What the hell are you doing here?'

Killian gulped. 'We were just bringing Filip his backpack. He left it at school.'

Karl-Henrik grabbed the wall so he could stand up straight and stared icily at Killian. 'How the fuck do you have the balls to come here? After what you did?'

'He didn't do anything.'

Karl-Henrik's head cocked in surprise, as though he hadn't registered that there were two of them until Sander spoke.

'Oh no?'

Karl-Henrik took a step toward them. He stank of alcohol, stale and sour. Slowly he brought a hand to Sander's shoulder. It was heavy as a brick as he rested it there.

'You better watch yourself.'

Sander tried to get away from that hand, but Karl-Henrik

was strong, and he suddenly squeezed Sander's shoulder hard, like he was trying to wring water from a sponge. Sander hissed and tried to free himself.

'What the fuck are you doing?' Killian said, about to intervene, but just then something happened.

The door to Filip's room swung open and there stood Filip, looking like he always did, wearing baggy jeans and a gray hoodie. His gaze wandered, his eyes struggling to stitch the scene into a comprehensible whole: Floor. Dad. Backpack. Hand on shoulder. Wall. Door. Sander. Killian. Wall again. Distant point.

'You have company,' said Karl-Henrik.

He had let go of Sander. He turned around and staggered back to the staircase, where he grabbed the railing and went back downstairs without another word.

29

Filip stared vacantly at them. Behind him were plates full of uneaten frozen pizzas and a pile of empty soda cans. The floor was strewn with clothing, and the bed was unmade. A TV was on, showing the end of a movie.

'Did he say anything?' Filip asked in a flat tone.

Killian opened his mouth, but Sander cut in: 'No. Nothing.'

'What are you doing here?'

Killian hesitantly held up Filip's backpack.

'You forgot this,' he said.

'Oh, right.' Filip took it from him. 'Where, uh . . . where did I leave it?'

'At school.'

'Okay.'

A change: previously, there had been a picture of Filip and Mikael on the wall, a family picture taken on vacation. In it, Mikael and Filip stood in bright sunlight, arms around one another. Sander and Killian had both seen it before. The nail was still there, but the frame was gone.

'Did you see the shotgun in the hall?' Filip asked.

'Yes.'

'Dad keeps taking the car out at night to search for whoever did it. I asked if I could come with, but he says no.'

His gaze had clouded over. It was hard to say whether he was speaking to them. He wasn't looking at Sander or Killian. His fingernails were dirty. Filip had started shaving only a few months before, and his chin and cheeks were covered in downy stubble.

Sander gently laid a hand on Filip's bony shoulder. 'Hey, I just wanted to . . . Take it easy, okay?'

Filip looked like he had just been startled awake after dozing off. The movie on the TV ended. The tape began to rewind automatically.

'I don't want anyone to find out,' he said. 'But I have to tell someone.'

'You know,' Killian jumped in, 'if you want – we finished the cabin, it's got power and everything. If you need somewhere else to sleep. Or just somewhere to, like, be.'

'Yeah,' Sander agreed, adding emphatically, 'or if anything else is going on.'

The videotape clicked. It was back at the beginning. Filip pressed Play on the same movie again. *American Graffiti*.

Killian shot an inquiring look at Sander, looking for a signal: what should happen next? Sander took his hand from Filip's shoulder, unsure if he'd even noticed that someone had touched him.

On the way home, it stopped snowing. Sander and Killian walked side by side, sticking close, down the road. They spoke quietly about nothing in particular until the words seemed to run out, and then they continued in silence. They were almost home now. To Killian's. They could see the cabin in the distance, pale and cold under a white Halland sky, the same piece of sky they'd lived their whole lives under. In Sander's pocket was the page he'd torn from Filip's notebook. He wondered if Filip would notice it was missing.

'Damn, he's creepy,' Killian said. 'When he grabbed you like that, I almost thought he was going to punch you.'

'Me too. Maybe he was going to.'

'Have you seen him? Out with the shotgun? Like Filip was saying.'

'No, have you?'

'I thought I saw a car yesterday. But I don't know, maybe it wasn't him. When he brought up the shotgun, I thought about the last time we were there. I felt so fucking sorry for Mikael that time. Remember?'

Something stirred within Sander. The memories and events, the notebook page in his pocket. A thought was beginning to take shape inside him.

'Maybe it's connected?' he said. 'All of it.'

What had happened? Sander thought of glass, transparent and cold, glimpses of events on the other side. He couldn't make up his mind. Did the memory mean nothing at all, or was it the other way around – maybe they were brushing up against the deepest of undercurrents.

30

It happened sometime in October. They were walking by the farm on their way home from school and saw Karl-Henrik and Mikael coming out of the house. They were all bundled up in outdoor gear, and each was carrying a shotgun. Karl-Henrik was first to notice someone by the gate. He brought up a hand to shade his eyes against the cold October sun, and when he recognized Sander and Killian, he waved wildly.

'Why, hello, you two!'

Sander eyed the *L* of the open shotgun in Karl-Henrik's hands. 'Are you going hunting?'

Karl-Henrik pointed at a grove of trees across the field. 'We've got wild boar tracks over there. Thought we'd settle down and see if we can take out some of the bastards. I don't want them here. Mikael's coming with, he needs to learn.'

He turned to his son and tousled his hair. Mikael looked uncomfortable.

'Would you like to join us?' Karl-Henrik went on. 'I've got two extra guns in the car – you can both shoot, can't you?'

Sander and Killian exchanged glances. Soon they were sitting in a filthy Range Rover that smelled like dust and smoke, heading down one of the gravel roads that wound through the area.

As Karl-Henrik drove, he talked about the wild boar, where they'd been spotted, how many there were, how big they were, the risks of letting them roam. Sander and Killian were holding unfamiliar shotguns, and in front of them were the backs of Mikael and Karl-Henrik's heads. They looked the same from behind. In some folks, that was where the heredity showed.

There was a darkness to Karl-Henrik that was hard to put your finger on, and it made Sander uneasy. He smiled quite a bit, and spoke in a soft, gentle voice; he didn't treat them quite like adults but not like children either. Maybe that was just it — it was hard to tell how he saw you.

They parked by the grove. It seemed larger up close, the treetops swaying way up high, their trunks close together. You couldn't see through to the other side. Karl-Henrik climbed out and fed two shells into the chamber. Under his watchful eye the others followed suit.

'The lever's a little stiff,' Mikael said.

'You just need to press harder. Have you got a bum thumb or something, boy?'

Mikael gritted his teeth. The lever gave way and the shotgun popped open. One cartridge went in. Two. They headed for a nearby log and sat down. Karl-Henrik had borrowed Filip's school backpack, and from it he took a Thermos of coffee and some cups.

'Relax. Are you trying to strangle that gun?'

Mikael had been squeezing the barrel so hard that his knuckles went white and his hands red. He loosened his grip.

When they heard a rustle nearby, they got ready and held their breath.

'Not a boar,' said Karl-Henrik. 'Just a hare.'

Mikael exhaled. Sander turned his head. In the distance, he could see the roof of Madeleine and Felicia Grenberg's house. 'How long does it take to walk over there?'

Karl-Henrik poured himself more coffee. 'Ten minutes or so. Maybe fifteen.'

'You have a lot of land.'

'Yes. But considering Madeleine shows up late every morning, you'd think she had three times as far to walk.' He shook his head. 'Those two are a mess. I shouldn't let them stay on the farm, really, but they've had it rough since Göran died. So I let them live over there.'

Mikael didn't say anything. To Sander, the mossy ridge of Felicia's roof appeared tempting, lovely and warm.

'I try to be a nice guy, but, you know, we have a farm to run here. We're not in the business of handouts. And they have trouble making rent.' Karl-Henrik's gaze wandered over the tree trunks again, where the wild boar should be. 'But Mikael likes Felicia, anyway. Don't you?'

Mikael blushed.

'No, I don't,' he mumbled.

'Do too.'

'Dad, stop it.'

Another rustle, farther away. Sander and Killian slowly raised their shotguns.

A big, black creature emerged. It rooted at the ground. Sander and Killian took a breath, but a meaty arm came down over their barrels. Karl-Henrik silently gestured at them to wait, and he nodded at Mikael, who closed one eye, aimed, and pressed his finger to the trigger.

Mikael took a deep breath. The boar stopped and looked at them with deep black eyes.

Mikael fired. The beast leapt and ran off.

He fired again, frantic now. The boar's large backside vanished into the grove, while Mikael, trembling, tried to grab more cartridges from the box on the ground.

'Don't bother.' Karl-Henrik thundered. 'It's too late. You missed. He's gone.' And he slapped Mikael on the back of the head with an open palm. 'You're worthless. Almost worse than your brother.'

The contempt in Karl-Henrik's voice made Sander wish he could do something, maybe touch Mikael, who suddenly looked so alone. But he couldn't do that, so he did nothing.

31

It was Wednesday, two days before Christmas Eve, and Siri and Gerd were leaning toward the speakerphone to hear what the prosecutor in Halmstad had to say. He had finished delivering his formal report, but he had one last holiday message to convey:

'Okay, so, I'm going home now. Try to let Halmstad handle this until Monday. I'll be back in then. And please stop bothering the people at Telia. I know you want those phone records, but it's Christmas.'

Siri took a bite of a gingerbread cookie and shot a questioning look at Gerd.

'Absolutely,' Gerd said grimly.

Seconds of silence on the other end. 'Merry Chr –'

Gerd slammed the receiver home and stood up. 'Stay there, I'm going to grab something.'

Siri looked at the phone, which still seemed to be recovering from its harsh treatment. She would have liked to do the same thing to it. Instead, she turned to the report from Telia they had printed out. After a call from Gerd earlier today, the phone company had moved their request to the top of their to-do list.

The local phone towers had crackled to life at seventeen minutes past eleven on the night of December 17, when a call was placed from one of the telephones in Pierre Bäck's house in the middle of the party.

Someone had called Madeleine and Felicia's house. Whether the call was subsequently answered was not evident.

Could Jakob Lindell have made the call? If he had, did that make him their suspect? Siri thought of the blood on the steering wheel in the car, of Killian Persson and the gash on his nose. They really did need to get a blood sample.

Jakob had a motive of sorts, but there was nothing to put him at the scene of the crime. Killian might have had a link to the scene, but he had no motive. Were both Jakob and Killian lying? Or was neither of them involved?

She couldn't make it make sense.

Instead, Siri studied the results of the database search that glowed on the screen.

There was a computer in the office, but Gerd said she never used it. If she needed to find information, she did it in the real world instead. Siri found the real world unnecessarily tiresome and liked new technology, so she tried to start up the old dinosaur. It beeped, hummed, and sputtered for a good long time, but after that it was usable.

She had noticed something just before the prosecutor called, a report that had been filed with the Halmstad police one evening last autumn. It had to do with an assault at one of the bars on Brogatan. The bar owner himself called it in. He wanted to advise law enforcement of a fistfight, that two men had flown at one another until one was knocked out by a punch and the other stormed off. Names were included: Killian Persson's father, Sten, and Mikael Söderström's father, Karl-Henrik. Both from Skavböke.

Siri tried to follow up on the matter, but there wasn't much to find beyond the initial interview with the bar owner and an attempt to get both Sten and Karl-Henrik to account for what had happened. When neither of them wanted to talk, much less pursue any action, the matter was left to wilt away and that was that.

'Merry Christmas,' came Gerd's cheerful voice, and she walked in with a wrapped present in hand.

It was a perky little houseplant. A handwritten note read: *Hi! I'm an elephant ear, and I'm easy to care for. Water me once a week and don't expose me to too much sunlight, and I'm sure we'll get along.*

Siri recognized Gerd's handwriting. 'Thank you so much.'

When she gave her a prolonged hug, Gerd grew awkward.

'I just thought it would help cozy the place up, is all,' she muttered, nodding at the computer screen. 'What have you got there?'

'An assault.'

Gerd read it.

'I'll be damned. I didn't know about that.' She squinted at the screen. 'How did you find this?'

'I thought about the looks I saw Sten Persson and Madeleine Grenberg exchanging in the chapel this past weekend, and I thought there might be something to it. So I performed a few searches, is all.'

'What a genius idea. He was at Madeleine and Felicia's house today, did I mention that? His car was parked there when I drove by. It looked like they were having coffee.' Gerd brought a finger to the screen. 'This appears to have happened in Halmstad. No investigation opened.' She stood up straight and put her hands on her hips. 'Well, that explains why I don't have any memory of it. But,' she added, 'the question is, what does it mean? If anything. It's not exactly out of the ordinary for two area men to land in a drunken fight. When was this?'

'A year ago.'

Gerd pursed her lips. 'Well, who knows.'

Just then, the desk phone rang. Gerd brought the receiver to her ear and listened. Her eyebrows shot up, adding extra wrinkles to her already furrowed brow.

'Oh? And what would that be?' She checked her watch. 'Sure, of course. That's fine. Good, see you soon.' She hung up and aimed a suggestive nod at the computer. 'Speak of the devil.'

32

'These gingerbread cookies aren't very good,' Siri said, pushing the plate across the table. 'But help yourself.'

'Coffee's fine,' he said.

Sten Persson selected two Christmas pigs and took a sip of the black coffee. Sten was so large that he made the spindly wooden chair look unnaturally tiny. They were in the station's break room. The lighting was warmer here, and the furniture more comfortable; the walls were done in floral '60s wallpaper. They were adorned with maps, dated checklists, and lists of phone numbers that didn't go anywhere anymore, things to browse while you waited by the stove or the coffeemaker. Siri wondered who had put it all up – she doubted it was Gerd.

'How are things with Killian?' Gerd asked.

Sten was immediately wary. 'What about him?'

'How is he feeling?'

'Fine, I think. Given the circumstances. You've spoken with him, haven't you?'

'Yes. That's a nice cabin he's got.'

'It turned out really well.' Sten took another cookie. 'I just wish . . . You know, in a different world I would have been the one to help him build it. But that's not how it turned out.'

'Such is life, sometimes.'

'Yes, I guess so.'

Gerd and Siri waited.

'So,' Gerd said, when nothing happened.

'Well.' Sten dipped his gingerbread pig into his coffee, ate it, and warmed his hands on the mug. 'Tonight I felt like there was something I should tell you.' He looked at Gerd. 'I saw you today, you know.'

'You did?'

'When I was at Madeleine's. Or I suppose I saw you see us. But I want to make sure you know we were just having coffee.'

'And that was all I saw,' Gerd said, flashing an innocent smile and throwing up her hands.

'Do you know each other well? You and Madeleine?' Siri asked.

The question seemed to come as a surprise.

'I guess we used to, back in school and so forth. We were good friends back then.' He looked at Gerd. 'As you know.'

Gerd nodded. 'But were you *just* friends?'

Gerd asked the question as though it weren't dangerous at all. Sten took a sip of coffee, set his mug down, and leaned back. The chair creaked alarmingly.

'I suppose I wondered if it could have turned into something more. But it never did. Madeleine met Göran, and I met Linda. I liked Göran. A lot. He was a good guy. It was a hell of a sad day when he died a few years back. By that point, Linda and I had gone our separate ways, and when Madeleine's grief started to pass, I started courting her a little bit, again. Or whatever the word is. Nothing major, of course.'

'What did you do, for instance?' Siri asked.

'Nothing out of the ordinary. Gave her a ride to Oskarström, helped in the vegetable garden, had a cup of coffee in her kitchen afterwards, like today, or a beer or two. No one else knows, not Killian and definitely not Linda. They would be hurt. If something had happened between us, I would have told them, obviously, but since it didn't, I didn't tell anyone. Madeleine didn't either.'

Sten turned to Gerd again. 'You know how it was when Göran died, how Madeleine and Felicia had to move. Right?'

'Yes,' Gerd said. 'But it would probably be a good idea for you to tell us anyway, if only to catch Siri up.'

'They couldn't afford to stay in their house without him, the bills were too much. They actually didn't have anywhere to go until Karl-Henrik, as they say, reached out a helping hand. Doesn't that sound nice?'

He scoffed.

'They moved into that old house on the other side of the field. Karl-Henrik's grandparents used to live there, before they ended up in the nursing home, so it had been empty for years. And sure enough, they had an affair there after that, Karl-Henrik and Madeleine. Madeleine, as gullible as she is, I'm sure she was still wracked with grief over Göran and probably wasn't thinking clearly, but still – she believed Karl-Henrik was going to leave Lillemor for her. That's when it all started, when he let them move into that house. In fact, for all I know, it might still be going on.'

Sten let out a mirthless laugh, but it was cut off when he got some cookie down the wrong pipe.

'You're laughing,' said Siri. 'May I ask why?'

'Well, because it's all so absurd. To think that Karl-Henrik would get a divorce. It's only in the city that men get divorced for their mistresses. Out here, you get divorced so you don't kill each other. I mean,' he added, 'Linda and I had some great years together too. It was only towards the end that everything fell apart.'

'What about you?' Siri asked.

'Hmm?'

'When you heard about Karl-Henrik and Madeleine, what was that like for you?'

'It just was. Nothing I could do about it.'

'But would you have wanted to do something, if you could?'

'Like what? I tried to talk to Madeleine. He's no good for her, I've always felt that way, and anyone can see it. And,' he went on, 'she's actually not so good for him either. Madeleine seems to arouse something inside him, the way women sometimes do to men.' He paused. 'What?'

'It just seemed like there was more you wanted to say,' Siri said gently.

He squirmed in his seat. Considered another cookie, but decided against it.

'I mean, I don't know. But . . . well, like I said, I don't know if their affair is over, and maybe they aren't really sure either; do you always know something like that? Sometimes you think something is over, and then you meet and it flares right up again.'

He spoke as if this had recently happened to him.

'But,' he went on, 'whatever's between them, it's changed now.'

'How so?'

'Well, he violates her. Sometimes.'

Violates. The word fell from his lips, sharp and hot like a poker.

Maybe it had been about love, once. Who could say, really, what love looked like? But it wasn't the same anymore. As far as he could tell, Sten said, Karl-Henrik came to Madeleine to take something from her. Always late at night, when Felicia wasn't home, after Lillemor and the kids were in bed and the lights were out in the big house. That's when he came.

'Apparently, Lillemor can't anymore. She's getting past her prime. But that's no excuse for what he does. Or did. He's taking advantage of his power over them.'

Siri got up and went to the next room, where she picked

up a printout of the police report from last autumn. She placed it in front of Sten.

'What is this all about?'

Sten read it in silence.

'Ah. Right.' He looked up. 'Well. It was all of this. I had just found out about it. We had a go at each other that night, I confronted him and told him to lay off.' Sten suddenly looked uncertain. 'But I don't want to take it any further, or anything.'

'We understand,' Gerd said. 'But we might talk to other people about it, and that might mean we have to bring up this incident.'

'Do whatever you damn well please,' he said. 'Just solve this.'

'Do you think,' Siri said, 'that Karl-Henrik really did lay off? I mean, after this?' She nodded at the report. 'Has he left Madeleine alone since?'

Sten blinked.

'I doubt it,' he said, and stood up to leave.

33

Evil bastards. They were out to get him, he could feel it.

Karl-Henrik Söderström stepped back from the window and stared at the scrawny Chinese cop's uniform-clad back until she was gone.

The day before Christmas Eve.

It was the day before Christmas Eve, and she had the nerve to come to his house and ring the doorbell Mikael helped him install less than a year ago. It took them all day to mount it correctly, get it to ring the way it was supposed to. That was one of Karl-Henrik's favorite things, just working on a project with his older son. Mikael was good with electronics. He understood how things worked.

And then she shows up, that cop, and presses her bony thumb right to that button. Who did she think she was? He couldn't believe it.

This was *his* home, *he* controlled its sounds and signals. Now his and Mikael's doorbell rang in the front hall every day as people stopped by with flowers, questions, offers:

We just wanted...

How are you holding up?

Is there anything we can do? We'll be home all through Christmas, just come on over if...

If what? If he happened to suddenly get over his son's death?

My son's death. He had no problem thinking those words, or even saying them out loud.

He looked around for his coffee cup. Only one last mouthful

left. He went down to the basement, found the bottle, and poured a refill, then headed back upstairs.

The house was quiet. The patrol car that had been parked outside was gone. He saw tracks in the snow, from vehicles and animals. *Work*, he thought, *try to get some work done, even though there's no point anymore, except to pass the time.* All this time, what was he supposed to do with it? Maybe he should be like his wife and just sit up there on the sofa, listening as it passed in the loud tick-tock of the wall clock.

Once, when Mikael was little, he'd said it sounded like that clock was counting down to something.

'It's counting down to your tenth birthday,' Karl-Henrik had said. 'When you turn double digits. That's a big day, when you get to add another number to your age. It won't happen again until you turn a hundred and can add a third.'

The boy's eyes opened wide. A hundred. Did people get that old?

'You will,' Karl-Henrik had assured him, tousling his hair.

The family photographs on the walls; Mikael's Christmas presents, all wrapped; the door of his room ajar. The mess on his desk, math book and graph paper on top, the bed sloppily made. Only days ago he was moving around this room; making a racket and eating breakfast and showering; getting dressed and shouting goodbye when he left; breathing and laughing and being alive. Sounds, all those sounds, endless sounds, there had been so many different ones, and he couldn't bear that they were gone. So many moments, details, tiny everyday routines that passed through this house, and now they would never happen again.

He brought the cup to his mouth and drank half of its contents. The liquor burned, a pleasant stinging in his throat and down to his stomach, radiating out to his chest, shoulders, heart. Slowly, he grew numb.

What had she wanted, that puny cop? For a moment, his memory was a blank. This had happened more than once in recent days – he couldn't recall something that had happened just minutes earlier.

'Is it true that you and Madeleine Grenberg had an affair?'

Right. That was it. He had cursed at her, obviously, to defend himself, but then he went on the attack: 'I thought you came here to tell me who killed my son, not to catch up on gossip.'

She was unfazed, or at least she appeared to be. 'That's why I'm asking. So that I will be able to tell you as soon as possible.'

'So you don't know.'

'Not yet. Did you? Have an affair?'

Yes? Of course. Of course they had. He had nothing to hide anymore. The only reason to hide things was to protect yourself. For Karl-Henrik, that time was over.

Madeleine. It had never been about him, not really. If it hadn't been him, she would have found someone else. She needed security, after Göran. If he had taken advantage of that, it wasn't intentional. He had found work on the farm for her out of sheer goodwill.

He didn't like the way this cop with the narrow, dark eyes was watching him.

'You don't think Madeleine might have felt, I don't know, obligated to see you?'

Now he roved about the house, cup in hand. He'd downed the first half in one gulp; the rest he drank in smaller mouthfuls. He let the liquor sit on his tongue so long that his saliva thickened it, and then he could swallow and start all over. As long as he had something in his mouth, he would be okay.

Obligated.

What a word.

What did his relationship with Madeleine have to do with Mikael? Nothing. But they didn't get it. They didn't understand a damn thing, those fucking cops.

They ought to talk to Sten Persson instead. That untrustworthy bastard. He had come up to Karl-Henrik once, looked at him with his vacant, pale eyes and told him to leave Madeleine alone, claiming that Karl-Henrik had forced himself on her. He'd threatened to go to the police.

Vacant and pale, that was the perfect description. When Sten looked at you, the lights were on but no one was home. They'd been at the bar and Karl-Henrik had brushed him off, shoving that idiot away from him. He and Madeleine had nothing to do with one another, he said. Sure, it was a lie, but why bother to be truthful with someone like Sten?

Forced himself on her? Where the hell did people come up with this stuff?

The shove had knocked Sten off balance, but he caught himself and stayed upright. Karl-Henrik tried to whack him one, not that he'd planned it, the urge just came to him in the moment. Controlled by their urges — that's people for you. Like animals.

Sten darted out of the way and responded by elbowing Karl-Henrik in the jaw. It hurt like hell and the walls began to spin. Karl-Henrik tried to hit back, but something caught him in the cheek and he fell to the floor. When he came to his senses, Sten was gone and he was sitting in a corner of the bar with no idea how he'd gotten there.

He didn't mention any of this to the cop.

On a table of their own in a corner of the hall were flowers. They had flooded in, bouquets with those little cards, so many that they formed colorful islands in every room of the whole house. They were the only thing Lillemor seemed to care about. As soon as a new one arrived, she came down from upstairs, meticulously snipped their stems, and scoured the cabinets for a vase. Once a day, always in the morning while he was in the basement, she made sure the flowers were happy and had plenty of water.

He heard her footsteps through the floor, moving above him. Sometimes it sounded like she was talking to someone. It took a few days for him to realize she was talking to the bouquets.

At some point in all the years that had passed in this house, it had become a labyrinth of passages, of nooks and crannies, and those who lived in it wandered alone along different paths until they suddenly ran into each other. He had still known Mikael, he was sure of it, but Filip? It was like he couldn't talk to his younger son.

And then there was Lillemor. The moment he tried to touch her she recoiled, as if he were a creepy stranger. Maybe that's what he had become. How anyone could live a life as incomplete as his had been these past years, like a person with no heart or lungs, was beyond Karl-Henrik.

And then something remarkable happened.

The cop asked about Jakob Lindell.

34

Karl-Henrik had heard about the break-in, but he couldn't say how or from whom. It was just something that registered with him but didn't prompt a reaction. Like the weather. Had it been when Bengt called to offer his condolences? No, probably not. Not even Bengt Lindell was that tactless. Bengt was just like everyone else out here: green with envy. No surprise, really. Whoever had the most money attracted not only the most respect, but the most disdain. You couldn't have one without the other, Karl-Henrik knew, and he had lived his life without bothering to care.

But Bengt hadn't mentioned the burglary. He was probably ashamed – who wouldn't be? He had only himself to blame, withdrawing his savings from the bank and stashing it in the kitchen bench.

'Apparently it came up during the party,' Siri said. 'The money, that is. Jakob and Mikael had a fight. Do you know if they fought often?'

'About money?'

'No, in general.'

'No. No, Mikael, he was . . .'

'Yes,' Siri said. 'I know. But could it have happened even so?'

'Yes,' said Karl-Henrik, suddenly helpless. He was only in control of insignificant things now. The important stuff had slipped from his grasp without his even noticing. 'Yes, I guess it could have. But Jakob and Mikael got along. All the boys out here are friends. They like each other, and they like their parents.'

It sounded simpler than it was, but it felt true.

'Speaking of,' said Siri. 'Do you think Mikael looked up to you?'

Karl-Henrik would have liked to reach for his cup, but he couldn't. The question had made his arms go limp.

'Yes. He did. I know he did.'

Mikael never said so. As a father, you just know.

'And he liked Felicia a little extra, didn't he? In fact,' she added, 'that was what you were trying to say after the Advent service.'

Felicia. The other Grenberg. All these goddamn Grenberg women, as if they were the answer to the riddle, the solution to everything.

'Yes,' he managed to say. 'He sure did.'

It was true. No doubt about it. Each time Felicia's name came up recently, Mikael had gone all quiet and red in the face. Again: as a father, there are some things you just know.

Siri shared her theory: Mikael had called Felicia from Pierre's house, maybe to see how she was doing, maybe to convince her to come to the party.

'When she said she was going to stay home, Mikael went to her place instead, after the party,' the policewoman continued.

'Do you know this, or are you guessing?'

'I'm trying to understand. I'm sure Mikael was eager to see her.'

The words burned inside Karl-Henrik, acid in his blood. When he thought about Mikael, what his boy wanted and wished for and dreamed of, all the things he wanted Mikael to experience. The world was his oyster, just out there waiting for him. He remembered what it was like to be eighteen and in love, that ache in your body and your heart when you were apart. He'd felt that way about Lillemor once upon a time.

That was how Mikael felt about Felicia. What was so strange about that?

Then Karl-Henrik thought about Mikael's hands, how soft and small they had once been, and how deft and capable they'd become as they held the Nintendo controller a few years later; how rough they had started to get in recent times. It had been years since those hands were soft now, but it didn't feel like it. He could still feel that little hand in his own, dimpled knuckles and tiny fingers. He missed Mikael's hair, how it smelled when he was warm and how he laughed too loud when he was on the phone, until Karl-Henrik and Lillemor had to turn up the TV to hear the news. It was almost unbearable, and he wanted to shout in Siri's face, but he couldn't. So he just sat quietly.

Karl-Henrik realized he wouldn't be able to go on. An endpoint was approaching, when everything would stop. He couldn't see it yet, didn't know where it lurked, or when it would happen, but it was there and it was close.

He had a box of dynamite in the basement. The boys had brought it home last fall to blow up a boulder so they could expand the west pasture a little more. They'd only needed a fraction of the supply; most of it was still downstairs. He thought of it more and more often these days, that dynamite – every time he went to the basement. One fantasy that he'd begun to entertain was to walk down there with a lit match. Drop it, or maybe just fumble it by accident, and watch as the fire caught and grew, then close the door and go back upstairs. He would sit in the kitchen with one last cup and smell the smoke rising from the basement, yes, just smoke at first. Then the heat. And finally – it probably wouldn't take long – the explosion beneath him as the dynamite ignited.

He went to the basement for more liquor. There was the dynamite, in its box.

'Are you getting any sleep, Karl-Henrik?'

It was Siri again. Was she back? He looked around when he reached the top of the stairs. No, it was just his memory. What a traitor, the mind; he could no longer be sure what was real. He drank more.

'I'm not sleeping at all.'

'I thought as much. How do you spend your nights?'

'Driving around.'

Siri had turned her head to nod toward the door. The shotgun stood there as testimony.

'Do you take that with you?'

'Yes.'

'Who are you looking for?'

The question, which must be perfectly reasonable in her mind, seemed foreign to him. He didn't know who had killed Mikael, but he knew that the rumors of his nightly drives would spread and reach the culprit. Whoever it was, he would know Karl-Henrik was looking for him. But no matter how he tried, he couldn't explain this to the cop.

He slurped from his cup. Still small mouthfuls, although they were greedier. Something was creeping up behind Karl-Henrik, a shadow that threatened to grow if he didn't hold it back.

'Are you planning to bring anyone in?'

'We're working pretty intensely right now,' was all Siri said.

She stood up to go.

The simplest way people in Skavböke know to describe what it means to be human: to search for meaning in another person. And when that's no longer possible, if someone disappears, or is taken away from you, it's easy to become lost.

*

There it was again, the doorbell. No one was waiting outside, but Karl-Henrik heard the tones anyway, heard them clanging through the hall and into his heart. And there sat his older son, crouching beside a crate full of cords and pliers again, so patient as he installed the doorbell and tested it to see if it worked.

Karl-Henrik drained his cup. He went to the toolbox, got out a pair of pliers, and went to the front hall, where he clipped the wire to the doorbell.

35

A note about the dynamite. Lots of people knew about it, and this was originally thanks to Karl-Henrik, no matter what actually happened later on.

Sometime in late fall, Sander and Killian were walking home from the bus stop when they spotted two figures approaching in the distance. It was Mikael and Filip. Together they were carrying something heavy, but Sander couldn't tell what.

The first frosty nights had arrived. The brothers were wearing heavy fall coats and gloves, and their ears were red with cold. They walked under an overcast sky, hauling a wooden box the size of a milk crate, and they each held one handle while sticking the other arm out for balance.

'Hello,' Sander said when they met. 'What are you two up to?'

Mikael and Filip's faces were pale as a sheet. Then it began to dawn on Sander what they had.

'We're going to blow up a boulder on the farm,' Mikael said. 'We picked this up from Frans's.'

'Can you manage that?'

'It's not very far. It's just heavy.'

Killian and Sander joined them and soon the group reached Killian's house. There stood his mother's old Saab.

'We can borrow the car,' Killian suggested. 'It'll be better. It's still a ways to go.'

Mikael seemed relieved, but not Filip. He looked anxious. With Sander's and Killian's help, they gingerly loaded the crate into the cargo area of the old Saab.

'It must be a big boulder,' Killian said.

'We only need a couple of these guys,' Filip said, 'and we'll save the rest.'

Killian got behind the wheel while Sander sank into the passenger seat and the brothers hopped in back. They cautiously took off for the big farm.

'Why didn't you drive in the first place, though?' Sander asked. 'You've got a bunch of cars.'

'Dad thought we should walk,' Filip said, and then, to Killian: 'We have to park a ways away, so we can walk the last stretch.'

'Not while carrying dynamite,' Mikael said grimly.

Filip snapped at him: 'He's going to say it was my fault, that it was my idea to take the car. Because he thinks I'm the lazy one. Don't you get it?'

Mikael didn't respond. Filip heaved a loud sigh and gazed out the window. After a moment, he yanked his headphones from his coat pocket and put them on. The music, fast and harsh, leaked into the rest of the car.

They inched down the county road. Sander tried to meet Mikael's gaze in the rearview mirror.

'Is it always like that?' he asked. 'With your dad, I mean. Like the time we were sitting on the log to pick off the wild boar.'

'He means well. He's preparing us to take over the farm. It's been in our family for so long, all the way back to my great-great-grandfather. But times are hard now. He doesn't want it to fail. So when *I* fail . . .'

'But you're not a failure!'

'That's not how he sees it.'

'Why does he want you two to haul a crate of dynamite through the whole village, though? It's so dangerous!'

Mikael shrugged. 'To toughen us up, I guess. He does this stuff sometimes. And it's not *that* dangerous.'

Killian swerved slightly toward the center line to avoid a pothole the size of a serving platter, deeper than a bucket. Sander's father had called in to report it, but no one had come out yet. That was how it went out here. Things in town were important; Skavböke wasn't. No surprise there.

Filip had to listen to rants about how he wasn't more like Mikael; Mikael had to hear that he was useless. That he needed to be tougher. Which meant nothing could be good enough, everything was a vicious cycle of disappointment, and maybe that wasn't much of a surprise either. It was like a pothole in the road. It just was.

They could see a glimpse of the Grenbergs' house on the other side of a field. Mikael's eyes followed it, like he was searching for something, almost longingly, but he didn't say anything.

'Do you even want to take over the farm?' Sander asked.

Mikael laughed. 'It's better than nothing, at least.'

'Is that the alternative? Nothing?'

'Yeah. Isn't it?' He gazed dejectedly at the road again and placed a hand on Killian's shoulder. 'You can stop over here, and we'll walk the last bit, like Filip said. That probably is the best plan after all.'

36

Christmas in Skavböke was usually a very special time for Sander. The comforting peace of the holiday arrived gently, tenderly, like a wave of calm over the countryside on the afternoon of December twenty-third. Cars returned home and fell silent; the last school day of the year was over, and everything lit up. It brought a remarkable sense of belonging, to know that everyone else in the village, and maybe the whole country, was doing exactly the same thing and feeling the same way as he did.

But something happened when they lost Mikael. Death extended its rays like a dark sun and Sander had started to think strange thoughts.

Almost nothing was more important than words, in his view; words not only described the world but shaped it, created it, and therefore they could also change it.

But words weren't enough. He was beginning to understand that now.

The word *fear* must have been invented by someone who didn't know what it was to be afraid; *rage* by someone who had never been angry. It's the same with the word *love*. It's just something you can use to fill an empty space in your mouth, a silent maw that needs to be plugged. Sander, as it would turn out, was not the only one who felt this way; it was as if the whole village had begun to lose faith.

He wondered what caused all of this, why it happened at all and why it was happening to him in particular, at this particular moment in time, but he couldn't come up with any explanation.

Maybe that was why he finally said it out loud, at the dinner table:

'I'm going to apply to Stockholm University for this fall. My grades are good enough.'

They were shocked into silence, both his dad and mom. But he didn't wait for them to catch up. Instead he told them about the department head from Juridicum, Magnus Ardelius, and as he spoke it felt more and more unnatural, almost cruel. Mean. As though his longing to get away was a violation of an agreement he hadn't previously been aware of, but which was now becoming painfully clear.

'I think that's wonderful,' his father said at last, his voice subdued. 'That's great news, in the midst of all this awful stuff. Isn't it, Eva?'

Sander's mom was staring vacantly at nothing. She had put down her silverware. 'What do you want us to say? Thanks for telling us?'

'You don't have to say anything.'

'This is all great to hear, Sander.' His dad smiled, but only his lips moved. The rest of his face was stiff and firm. 'I'm sure we're just a little surprised, is all.'

'You don't have to help me,' Sander said.

'But we want to, of course. When will you leave, if you get in?'

'I don't know, exactly, yet. In August, I assume, but I suppose it depends on housing and stuff. We don't know anyone in Stockholm, do we?'

'We hardly know anyone outside Skavböke,' his mom said helplessly, and the words landed nowhere, not with anyone.

*

Afterward, he tried to assess how it had gone. About as he'd expected, he decided, and he felt the walls of the house starting to move, pulling closer to him. *Away*, he thought once more. *I have to get away.*

37

Passing through Oskarström, you will see signs showing the way to Halmstad. Once you reach the city, there are similar signs but with an even bigger destination: Gothenburg. Few of the kids had gone that far north up the E6 highway unless it was for a school field trip, but one time, when Sander's class visited Gothenburg to enjoy a day at the amusement park Liseberg, he had seen even more new signs pointing hopefully toward Stockholm. From Stockholm, a brand-new train would take you to the airport in just twenty minutes. Twenty minutes to get to the rest of the world. There was always something bigger out there. To Sander, at the end of 1999, the world outside felt remarkably close and infinitely far away at the same time.

When he walked into the hall, his mom asked if he wanted to help decorate the Christmas tree.

'Yes, join us,' his dad said from the kitchen. 'We're just about to start.'

'I'm going out,' Sander said.

All movement in the kitchen ceased.

'Now?'

'I just want to take a walk.'

'On the night before Christmas Eve?' Eva said. 'Can't you stay home? Considering everything that's happened? And next Christmas won't be the same.'

'But I'll be back in a little bit.'

'Where are you going?' Erik said.

Sander opened the front door and let in the cold. 'Just out.'

The evening fell around him in heavy curtains, and all at once he was far away from all of them. He had nothing more to say, nothing in common with them, aside from the house he lived in and the place where he'd grown up. It was an unfamiliar thought: here were the people closest to him, the only ones he really belonged with, yet it felt like they were on the other side of a wall he couldn't pass over again. Or didn't want to.

Deep down, in the part of himself Sander seldom let anyone reach, he had begun to crackle and spark. The world was his. It was waiting for him. He was ready. Not tomorrow, not in a week – Sander was ready to get away. *Now*.

This was how it had to be. As he turned his back on his parents and walked out into the dark, he felt his ferocity like a huge black bird clinging to his back.

Ice-cold. The moon was ice-cold, and it shone like a single spotlight across forests and fields. It reached all the way to the outskirts of Skavböke, to the old spruce forest that strove dense and tall for the sky. Not far into this forest was an odd clearing, a place where the trees seemed to have shifted over to make way for grass and rocks, like a half-finished soccer field. Surely more was supposed to have happened there, but what? No one knew. Some things were bigger than humankind.

The single lightbulb hanging from the ceiling in Killian's cabin emitted a pale-yellow glow that made the small window shimmer as Sander approached. It looked warm and welcoming.

It took only a second to make sense of what he was seeing. But it would take a very long time, maybe almost the rest of his life, before he could form an overview of the consequences it would bring.

A blanket was spread out on the floor, and Killian was on

his knees atop it. He was buck naked, his blond hair mussed like someone had just had their hands in it. His back was covered in sweat and Sander could see the well-defined muscles in his shoulders tensing and releasing. One hand was stroking his cock. It was long and thick and glistening with saliva, or something else, and it was a lot bigger than Sander's. In Killian's hand, it looked almost threatening, like a weapon.

On her back before him lay Felicia; at first holding ridiculously still, but then her hips rose as if they were searching for something in the air, and she grabbed for Killian's free hand and he squeezed it hard. When he pressed into her, her gaze was steady on him and her expression didn't change. As though what they were doing absorbed all their focus.

He could never tell anyone about this. What he'd witnessed, everything that had happened recently, and was happening right now, in front of him, was the sort of thing he had no choice but to carry alone. Sooner or later, that's all you are. Alone.

He felt so stupid, so childish. And Killian – he'd tried to convince Sander to take a step back. So he wouldn't get hurt. How long had his best friend been lying to him?

As he stood by the window outside the cabin he'd helped his best friend build, emotions stirred in his blood, winding around each other, becoming hard to pick apart: humiliation over having been betrayed and duped; grief over seeing them like this, like a peeping Tom; shame, as if he had done something wrong. And also a peculiar, reluctant heat that seeped through his thighs and into his belly, an excitement that grew as he stood there watching Felicia take Killian into her body, all of him, as though he were witnessing Fate itself.

Something in the distance tore his attention away from what was going on inside the cabin.

A car was coming.

38

'Goodness, you're still here?'

Gerd stood in the doorway, a thick envelope in her hand.

'I had a supervisor during training who could do that,' Siri said.

'Do what?'

'Sneak up on folks without making a sound.'

'I'm not sneaking.' Gerd stepped into the room. 'You just weren't listening. What are you doing here?'

'I'm working. Isn't that enough?'

'On the night before Christmas Eve?' Gerd looked at the empty chair on the other side of the desk. 'Would you like some glögg?'

It wasn't long before Gerd had set her envelope on the table, pushed the chair back, and crossed one leg over the other with a steaming glass in hand. The scent of the alcohol-free mulled wine spread through the room, spicy and strong. A lull came over them, a pleasant stillness.

'It's pretty nice out here,' Siri said at last. 'The nature, and everything, the houses. They're small, and old, but lovely.'

'Yes,' said Gerd. 'I don't think I always notice anymore, myself.'

'Are you from here?'

'From Åled,' Gerd said. 'You?'

'From town.'

'I mean, originally. Or whatever the word is.'

Siri paused as she drank.

'Indonesia,' she said eventually.

'Can I say that? "Originally," I mean.'

'You can. But I'm guessing it's not a question *you* get very often. And I've been in Sweden for almost as much of my life as you have.'

'You know, out here, for us — it's not easy for people to navigate the right words. Swedish has become a minefield in recent years. Anything can suddenly be wrong. But I didn't mean any offense, if that's how you took it.'

Siri didn't respond. Her eyes on the envelope, she asked instead, 'What have you got there?'

'Photographs from the party. There weren't as many as I thought, actually. Maybe people don't bring cameras to parties anymore.'

They had, after considerable effort and some help, managed to locate three disposable cameras. Gerd had shown her badge and had the film developed at Göte Karlsson's Photos on Viktoriagatan in town, while she enjoyed a schnitzelburger from the station canteen a few blocks away. When she returned to Göte Karlsson's Photos, a large stack of photographs was waiting for her in an envelope on the counter. She thanked Göte, told him to send the bill to the Halmstad police, and took off.

Gerd pulled the photos from the envelope.

'As I expected. The unvarnished truth of a house party. Kids taking pictures of each other chugging drinks. Pissing in the bathtub. Throwing up in the sink, falling down stairs, breaking things. Beer cans, liquor bottles.' She held up a close-up. 'Someone who sneezed and wanted the results documented for posterity before he wiped his face.'

Siri raised an eyebrow. 'Is that Filip Söderström?'

'It is.' Gerd rolled her eyes. 'My God. We sure as hell didn't act like this when I was a teenager.'

'Of course you did. It's just that no one had a camera with them to document it.'

Gerd muttered and flipped through the pictures, stopping when she came to another of Filip. 'I wonder how he's doing. He's always been a little sensitive, you might say.'

Siri looked through the photos several times. She saw Mikael and Filip, Jakob, Pierre, Sander and Killian, Alice and Isabelle. Pictures taken early in the evening: a sea of shoes and jackets in the hall. Beer cans and plastic bottles on a table. Drinks being mixed in the kitchen; the digital oven clock in the background: 7:47.

These were followed by more chaotic, blurry shots from later, but none of them, as far as Siri could tell, gave any hint of what was to come. Pictures from upstairs showed Isabelle mixing liquor in some sort of plastic bowl, while the background revealed a picture that had been pulled from the wall and a porcelain bowl that had shattered, likely during Mikael and Jakob's scuffle. Pictures from the living room showed that Alice had napped on the couch for a while, and out in the hall you could see Sander and Killian approaching the front door, about to leave. The clock on the wall read a few minutes before one.

Gerd and Siri added the photographs to the case materials.

'If anything,' Siri said, 'I think the pictures seem to corroborate what they've told us. What do you think?'

'I'm afraid I agree,' Gerd said glumly, raising her glass. 'But cheers to kids telling the truth to the police once in a while. There is hope.'

Siri raised her glass as well. 'But someone isn't. I've tried to make up my mind who I believe, whether Jakob or Killian is the liar here.'

They each took a sip of glögg.

'We should be able to find out, we just have to be a little creative.' Gerd looked at the clock on the wall. 'I'd like to take a little field trip.'

Siri put down her glass. 'Now?'

'Yes siree.'

39

It was getting hotter in the cabin. They needed so few words, Killian and Felicia, hardly any at all, maybe because there weren't any words to describe what had befallen them.

That was how Killian thought of it sometimes. It was as if his tongue didn't know what to do, nor the rest of his body. As if she had poisoned him. He couldn't tell her so, but that's what it felt like – she was moving inside him like a foreign substance in his heart, his head, in between his legs. He could feel himself transforming, or splitting. Cleaving. Maybe that's what love does to you. Cleaves you in two.

She was lying quietly beside him now, and with her eyes closed as if he'd drained her. The lightbulb flickered overhead. With her eyes still closed, she said:

'I might love you, Killian.'

His body went perfectly still and he felt absolutely nothing in his chest, nothing but a peace like unrippled waters.

He would build her a house with his own two hands. A house with a garden. That's what he dreamed of. It would be a simple house, which pained him, but he would make it work. Even if he had to force the state of everything to fall into line, he would do it.

'Same, about you,' he said.

She opened her eyes. 'Have you told him?'

'Not yet.'

'When are you going to? It's better he hears it from you than finds out some other way.'

'He's going to leave this summer anyway,' said Killian. 'It doesn't matter.'

Felicia stroked his back. Killian saw shadows on the walls; everything that had happened had struck fear in him. Down to the bone.

'Then you might as well get it over with. It's better that way. What are you afraid of?'

'Nothing.'

Felicia was smart, not at all like Killian. More like Sander, really, but without the need for books. Sander'd always had books to help; she never had.

Maybe Sander was the one who deserved her, but she chose Killian. If it was a choice – he wasn't sure, because of the way he thought about it: that this had befallen them. Like a force greater than either of them. Whatever it was, it had started one afternoon at school.

He had just found out that Lundström had given her a VG – the second-best grade you could get – on her essay about Ellen Key, and she wanted to celebrate. She loved to celebrate things, she told Killian. In fact, you could celebrate anything, especially life's everyday moments: your last day at a summer job, a successful driving lesson, that you had sex or got your period, that fall break had begun. People didn't celebrate enough, was Felicia's firm view.

'Okay,' Killian said hesitantly, gazing around. 'But what does that have to do with me?'

'I'm happy I got a good grade and you're the person sitting closest to me right now.' She looked around the empty common room. 'I mean, sort of. I guess we're the only ones here.'

He considered this. 'So now you're going to celebrate your grade?'

'Yes, of course.'

That same night, they ran into each other in Oskarström, at the store. They were each holding a bag in front of the bulk candy.

'Celebrating, huh?' Killian asked.

She grinned and plunged the scoop into the bin of gummy Ferraris. 'I'm going to a movie with Alice and Isabelle. They asked me to pick up some candy.'

Killian peered into the bag and recoiled. 'What kind of sicko are you?'

'What?'

'You don't have any chocolate! Only sour binkies and crap, that's grandma candy. I'll have to help you out.'

'Girls can't eat chocolate; it gives us zits.'

Killian stared at her, trying to make sense of what he'd just heard.

'What,' she continued. 'You didn't know that?'

'But you don't have any zits.'

Felicia regarded him with something like pity, as if she was astounded that he didn't understand how the world worked.

'Because I don't eat chocolate, duh,' she said slowly.

Killian didn't say anything for a moment; he seemed lost in thought. 'But you've tried it before, right?'

And that's how he made her laugh for the very first time.

Now she was lying there beside him; she was his, and she was still all warm. He gently rested a hand on her belly.

'You have to tell him,' she said again. 'Or do you want me to?'

'No. No, I'll do it. But, you know, he likes you . . . or, I mean, all guys like you, basically. Even Jakob.'

She was so frail, so vulnerable, in all her strength. He watched her rib cage rise and fall.

'Isn't that weird?' she said.

'Not really,' Killian said, feeling his hunger for her awaken again, deep in his belly. 'Mikael liked you too.'

When Killian said his name, she stiffened. She sat up, gazed down at him. 'Why would you say that?'

'I don't know.' He cast his gaze down. 'I . . .'

Just then they both heard a noise outside. They looked at the window. Someone was coming.

40

'We don't use these very often,' Gerd said as she unlocked the cabinet. 'Mostly for drug testing, those rare times we find someone who seems high. It's faster to take the sample out here than to drive people in. Oftentimes it keeps things from escalating as much too.'

In the bag: disinfectant, test tubes, needle kit, Band-Aids, labels, the obligatory form to fill out. Everything you needed.

Siri stood behind her, hesitant. 'But we don't have a warrant.'

'That's a good point.'

Gerd looked around and her eyes lit on the bulletin board, full of old fliers and reminders. *New emergency number: 112! Lock the door when you leave! Updated routines for processing suspected sexual offenses.* A pun someone had clipped from a newspaper: *It's hard to explain things to kleptomaniacs. They take everything, literally.*

'Here.' She pulled down the routines for processing sexual offenses and folded the paper in thirds. 'This will do. Now we have a piece of paper to wave around. Do you want to collect the sample? I've noticed you're good with your hands. Nimble fingers.'

'No, I'm fine.'

Siri didn't say more. What was about to happen didn't sit right with her. Not only was it against protocol, this kid was only eighteen.

They drove through the dark and up to Skavböke, where they parked on the road. Siri turned and saw a shadow in the darkness, crossing one of the fields.

It looked like Sander, but she wasn't sure and didn't mention it to Gerd.

The house was dark and quiet. Linda Persson's car was in the driveway. The light was on in Killian's cabin, dangling there lonely but warm.

'Hey,' Gerd said, the collection kit in her hand. 'I don't think he's alone.'

They caught a glimpse of a dark mane of hair inside. Someone pulled on a shirt. Gerd raised a curious eyebrow and approached, knocked gently on the door. When it swung open, he stood there looking sheepish, with no shirt and jeans that hung from his hips.

'Good evening, Killian. We need to talk to you.'

Behind him, Felicia Grenberg, wearing only a sweatshirt and panties, was trying to find something.

'Hello there,' Gerd said cheerfully.

Felicia stopped mid-motion and smiled self-consciously. 'I was just about to go.'

'We can wait,' said Gerd. 'No rush.'

They stepped into the cabin. The heavy scent of bodies struck them. There could be no doubt about what had been going on in here. There was still a blanket on the floor, rumpled and warm.

On the floor, aside from the blanket, a rug had appeared since Siri's last visit. It was a rough black tongue stretching across the pale wooden boards.

Felicia found her white jeans but lost her balance as she put them on. Killian reached out to keep her from falling over. The two teenagers exchanged glances, and Killian couldn't help but laugh.

Once Felicia left, Killian seemed unsure of what to do. He had put on a T-shirt.

'Hardly anyone knows,' were the first words to come out

of his mouth. 'We want to keep it a secret. For as long as we can. We both feel that way.' Killian noticed the sample-collection kit in Siri's hand. 'Is that why you're here, though?'

'I'm afraid not,' said Gerd, as though this errand were a burden on her. 'I'm sorry to show up unannounced like this, but it really couldn't wait. We need a blood sample from you.'

'Why?'

She looked at the spartan furnishings and sat down in a chair after testing it for stability.

'You could use some cushions,' Gerd said. 'How's that nose of yours?'

Killian blinked. 'Fine.'

The wound had started to heal.

'Here's the thing,' Gerd said, with the ease that comes from a lot of experience in the field. 'We're here because you have a cut on your nose. It's the kind of cut we often see after car accidents. The driver hits the steering wheel. In the car where we found Mikael, we also found blood on the wheel. That's why we need a sample from you, so we can rule you out as the driver, rule out your blood. I've got a piece of paper here somewhere . . .' she said, starting to pat her pockets, 'that proves two things: we have the right to take a blood sample, and you're not the only person whose blood we're taking. Where the hell did I – Here.' She held up the folded page of new protocols. 'As soon as we're done with that, we'll leave. Is that okay?'

Gerd put the paper back in her pocket. Siri didn't say anything. She thought of Felicia and Killian, of Madeleine and Sten. The heart is a fickle thing. This would change everything.

Wouldn't it?

Killian sat down on one of the chairs and offered his arm, just as if he were visiting the school nurse. Gerd opened the bag and took out the disinfectant, wetted a cotton ball, and carefully rubbed down the inside of Killian's elbow.

Siri watched him.

'Is it going to be your blood, Killian, that we found on the steering wheel?'

He shook his head. 'It has to be from someone else.'

'Here's a little poke,' Gerd said.

Killian didn't react. He watched the tube fill with thick, dark blood.

'Someone else,' Siri repeated. 'Are you sure of that? You could help us out, here. Your blood could have ended up there anyway. I understand not wanting to tell the police the whole story – you didn't tell us about you and Felicia, for instance. That's no big deal. We're all human, even us cops, we realize maybe you don't want to... Well, anyway, we believe you know more than you're letting on. And if you tell us what you actually know, it might help us catch the person who killed your friend.'

Killian didn't say anything for a long time. His gaze was oddly vacant. Another cotton ball.

'Hold that.' Gerd took out a Band-Aid and stuck it on. 'All done.'

When Killian finally spoke, he said:

'The reason we didn't tell anyone, about me and Felicia, I mean, it's because of Sander. He likes Felicia. But you must have known that already.'

'No,' Siri said. 'No, we weren't aware of that.'

'He's going to move away after graduation. So we thought we would just wait until then. I don't want to hurt him or anything. Felicia doesn't either.'

'That's six months away. Do you really think you can keep this a secret for that long?'

Killian smiled wanly. 'It's already been months.'

41

One early spring, when they were all out skating on Lake Galta, Killian fell through the ice. They must have been around eleven then, maybe only ten. Pierre had brought hockey sticks, Jakob a puck, and Mikael two small goals.

One second, Killian was there with the hockey stick in his hand; the next there was a sharp crack and water cold enough to paralyze muscles splashed up across the ice. Killian didn't even make a sound; his mouth was a black hole and his eyes were wide with shock.

The sight was petrifying; they couldn't move. But Sander bolted into action: he got down on his belly and extended his stick to Killian, but Killian couldn't get a grip on it. Killian's face was turning blue; he was hardly moving. He stopped shivering.

'Help me!' Sander shouted. 'Come on, help!'

But they couldn't. Sander tossed the stick away, tore off his gloves, and army-crawled forward. The ice beneath him creaked and popped forebodingly.

And he thought about how lonely everything would be in Skavböke if he couldn't reach Killian, thought of how the soccer goal would be empty, how Killian's shoes would never again sit beside his outside their classroom, how he would never hear Killian knock on his window, see his face outside; and soon he could already feel his grief throbbing, tearing in his chest, as though he were the one fighting for his life in the icy water.

Sander had reached the hole. He grabbed his friend by the

shoulders and strained harder than he was capable of, and then he pulled.

Afterward, Sander's throat hurt, although no one could recall hearing him scream.

He hauled Killian out of the water, impossible though it seemed given his large frame and heavy, waterlogged clothes and skates, and dragged him across the ice to the safety of land. He collapsed at his friend's side and they lay there staring at the milky-white sky. Only then did shock loosen its grip on the other boys, and they rushed over.

'I thought you were going to die,' Sander managed to say, patting Killian awkwardly on the shoulder, like he'd seen older men in the village do after they all pitched in to free a mired thresher.

These were simple memories. He didn't see any complexity in those emotions, none at all, just the horrid feeling of almost losing your best friend, and the absolute determination that Killian must be saved.

As children, Sander and Killian had birthday parties together, shared a desk in the classroom, played war in the forest, and chased each other through fields. They stood outside the school nurse's door, waiting in terror for Helena Johansson to call them in, stick her hand into their pants, and make sure they had two testicles, both in the right place. They rode mopeds together, got drunk together, and talked about girls. If one had a secret, so did the other.

They shared something no one else could be part of. Perhaps that was the crux of the dizzying experience that was having a best friend, a terrible intimacy you couldn't free yourself from.

On the morning of Christmas Eve, Sander lay on his bed and stared at the ceiling.

When he summoned the memories now, it was like they became physical beings that sucked all the energy from him. The treachery in Killian's cabin felt calculated and ancient, as though it had roots so far back in history that he was brushing up against millennia of betrayal. It all choked the air above him, memories from the past and recent moments too. Killian and Felicia, naked in the cabin.

You know how getting out of here is like your dream. Isn't it? This is mine.

Killian's words.

All those words were dead now, dead as rocks, nothing but a burden and no help at all.

From his back pocket he took the page he'd torn from Filip's notebooks.

He read: *snow is falling, let it fall, my brother is dead and the snow is falling, let it fall, i'll make it through this too, with explosions and drugs, who has drugs, who has something for me, or for all of Skavböke, something, i miss him so much, what am i going to do if this doesn't pass, i want to light myself on fire, the explosion awaits, the snow is falling*

Dangerous words, as though the paper might burst into flames any second. That was why he had torn the page out.

He fingered the paper.

Maybe not all words were dead.

Sander considered Filip's words again and thought: Yes. That's exactly it.

Out of nothing, in life, you cultivate what you believe are trusty companions, and then you hurt them until they begin to pull away, until they leave completely. The circle is complete: life is as lonesome as it was when it began.

He understood that things would never be the same, and that, in this particular moment, he wished his best friend were dead.

*

Killian called around lunchtime. It had begun to snow.

'Hi,' he said. 'Can we meet up?'

Moments darted through Sander's mind, cold and quick: stepping into the night with a ferocious bird perched on his back, heading for Killian's. That crafty cop Siri Bengtsson's flashing brown eyes, her hand holding the pen, the glow of the word POLIS on her shoulder as she stood outside the door minutes earlier, Killian sinking into Felicia, sinking into her and vanishing, the pleasure on Felicia's face, Mikael at the party. Filip rewinding the videotape and Karl-Henrik being led out of the chapel by the two cops. Killian and Sander leaving the party and walking home, Felicia and Killian again, once more, again, Felicia turning around to puke during their kiss, Sander tearing a page from Filip's notebook, Killian and Felicia again. They swirled around him, all of these, brushing against his skin like apparitions.

'Hello?' Killian said. 'Are you there?'

It sounded like something was stuck in Killian's throat. Something had happened. But what? Did he know Sander had seen them?

'Yes,' Sander said icily. 'I'm here.'

'Can we meet up?' Killian repeated.

'We can.'

He hated Killian, hated Felicia, loathed them both the way an invalid loathes the healthy.

42

It was only for a day, but it felt strange to have time off. Siri prepared the boiled potatoes, Christmas sausage, and creamed kale; she sliced the Christmas ham in her parents' kitchen simply to have something to do with her hands, to fend off the feeling that she was wasting time.

Otherwise, the holiday was peaceful and followed the same pattern it had since she left home: Mom and Dad hosted lunch; her aunt arrived around two, the cousins – both accompanied by their families these days – a little while later. Then they prepared for Christmas Day after Donald Duck and his friends wished them a merry Christmas and a happy New Year during the Christmas special everyone watched each year.

Snow was falling. It would be a cold night. She went for a walk with her father. The city was so quiet now, wrapped up in a warm, thick blanket of tradition. Windows glowed and Siri thought of all the human lives in there, all gathering together. She liked being part of something that wasn't about work, yet on this particular Christmas Eve, her thoughts were drawn back to Skavböke time and again.

They talked about last fall's hunt, how she had missed it for the first time in years.

'Yes,' she said, 'but I have a job now. That's just how it is.'

'Maybe next year you can at least come along for one day, though?'

It was true. She could do that.

'I don't want to guilt trip you,' her father said. 'You know that.'

'I know, Dad.'

'Then again,' he went on, 'if you have to hunt down people for work, maybe you don't want to hunt animals in your free time.'

'No, I'd really like to come if I can.'

From the pocket of his coat he produced a package. He smiled and handed it to her.

'I was thinking...' he began, then laughed. 'Oh, I don't know what. Merry Christmas.'

She opened it with stiff, frozen fingers. When she saw what it was, she laughed too. *Book of Enigmas*, a collection of puzzles and riddles from all over the world, old and new.

'I know things are a little hectic out there in Oskarström right now,' he said. 'There are all sorts of problems to solve, but all of them are good for the mind.'

'Thanks, Dad.'

It was lovely, in the end, that some things never changed.

When they went back up, returned to the warm and the chaos, Siri's mother told her someone had called to ask for her while they were out.

'I took down the number,' her mother said. 'I almost didn't hear the phone ringing for all the commotion in here. I'd call from the bedroom if I were you.'

In the living room, the children were arguing about where they should sit while the presents were handed out, and the adults watched the drama with small glasses of mulled wine.

'Sorry to bother you,' Gerd said. 'I just wanted to see how things were going.'

'I'm great,' Siri said. 'How are you?'

There was no background noise. Gerd wasn't all by herself, was she?

'I was at Isidor and Margareta's,' Gerd said, as though she

knew it needed to be said. 'And I'll be heading over to my sister's, soon, up in Varberg.'

'You have a sister?'

'She's a banker. It's exactly as boring as it sounds, but she's my sister, so what can you do.'

'I can imagine,' said Siri, who didn't even know if she had any biological siblings in the world.

'Are you managing to keep your brain in check?' Gerd said.

'And not think about work, you mean? Not exactly.'

'Same here.'

Gerd sounded gloomy. Siri opened her mouth to say something but didn't quite know how to put it.

'So, listen,' Gerd said instead. 'Now I'm thinking Killian Persson has a motive, after what we saw yesterday. If he's with Felicia, and Mikael forced himself on her, then . . .'

Gerd didn't finish her sentence. Siri tried to find the right words, but nothing useful came to her. She looked at the *Book of Enigmas*, which she was still holding.

'Yeah,' she said. 'Exactly.'

'Maybe we should bring him in. When we get the test results.'

The words stung. 'I just want you to know that, I mean, what we did yesterday, and the way we did it, I'm not going to go along with something like that again.'

Silence. A grunt. 'But we got the sample. That's how we've done it forever.'

'It doesn't matter. It wasn't okay, and you know it. We had no legal right to take that sample.'

'Who cares?' Gerd scoffed. 'As long as we move the case forward? We needed to do it. We can't just stand around twiddling our thumbs.'

'Halmstad's going to be furious. After all, when it comes down to it, this is their investigation.'

'Halmstad is always furious,' said Gerd. 'Goes with the territory.'

Long seconds passed.

'I just needed to say that,' Siri said.

'And now you have.'

A click. Siri sat there on her parents' bed.

Out in the living room, something broke and one of the kids started crying, a loud and pitiful wail.

43

The swelling on Killian's nose had subsided. All that was left was a scab of dried blood. He was wearing jeans and a T-shirt under his unzipped winter jacket. The path to the cabin had been shoveled after the day's snowfall. As the cold swept in, the ground turned to ice.

On the table in the cabin was a wrapped present. The paper was red with silver curlicues and said 'Merry Xmas' in English. The ribbon had spirals of white.

He picked it up and held it out to Sander.

'Merry Christmas.'

Sander stared at the present, feeling feverish. Killian clearly hadn't wrapped it himself; his packages always looked like someone had sat down on them by mistake. He wondered if Felicia had done it.

'But I don't have anything for you,' Sander said without taking it.

'That's okay.' Killian smiled uncertainly. 'Here. Merry Christmas.'

Sander hesitantly accepted the gift but didn't say anything. It wasn't very heavy. He considered throwing it at the wall.

'What did you want?'

He had been blinded to all but his own feelings until now, but Sander was starting to realize that something really was wrong. Even so, he found himself unable to care.

'The cops were here yesterday, late last night, and they took a sample of my blood. They're going to compare it to the blood on the steering wheel in the car.'

He fell silent, as if trying to read what this might mean in his friend's face. But Sander revealed nothing.

'Okay,' he said, with neither judgment nor sympathy – just as a statement.

'I'm screwed, aren't I.'

'Tough to say,' Sander said bluntly.

Killian seemed to be waiting for Sander to say more. He didn't. Instead he fiddled with the present and wondered what was inside, finally set free from everything around him. This was what he had needed, he realized now. The wedge that would break him away wasn't between him and his dreams of Felicia, or between him and his parents. The real parting was with Killian.

'Tough to say? What's that supposed to mean?' Killian said. 'What is going on with you? Is something wrong?'

'No. Nothing's wrong.'

'I don't know what to do,' Killian said.

'Well, for starters, you should chill out,' Sander said flatly.

'I have to get out of here.'

'Where to?'

It was like a fresh brand of panic was taking hold of him. 'I don't know. Just, take off. Take Mom's car.'

'Okay,' Sander said, as dully as before. 'So do it.'

Killian's eyes went wide. 'Is that all you have to say?'

'Yeah. Just go. It's just as well.'

As if it was my fault, Sander thought, and then he said it aloud, in a voice that rose, surged up like a wave he couldn't hold back. The words fell from his lips even as his eyes began to sting.

'As if this was *my fault*. This is exactly what always happens, I'm the one who has to clean up your mess, because you're so stupid and thoughtless that you can't even predict the consequences of your actions.'

'But Sander, I –'

'No, listen to me,' Sander snapped, because along with his rage came sudden clarity, banishing everything that wasn't significant now. 'So you've come to me again. Me. When everything catches up with you and you're about to go down for it, what do you do?' He weighed the Christmas present in his hand, small and dainty. He squeezed it hard. The paper rustled. 'I thought you were my best friend.'

'I am.'

'How can you be? You call me. Me! And meanwhile you've been lying to me for ages. Haven't you? So what are you going to do now, when I refuse to help you?'

'But you *are* my best friend.' Killian froze. 'Is this about Felicia?'

The name was a needle in Sander's heart, but he didn't let it show.

'Felicia?' He said her name like it was an insect he wanted to squash. 'Do you think I care about Felicia? I'm getting out of here, Killian! I'm going to Stockholm, because I'm going to study the fucking *law*. You know, *law and order*. I don't give a shit what goes on around here, because *that's* the work I want to do. I'm not about to get involved; this could ruin everything for me. What the fuck am I supposed to say when they come to me, huh?'

'But you said –'

'You only ever think of yourself, Killian. Always, nonstop. You always have. You don't give a single shit about me. Don't you get that?'

Killian looked stupider than ever, his arms hanging slack at his sides.

'You know he was all over her, right?' he said.

'What? Who?'

'Mikael. Felicia. He raped her. Or he tried, at least.'

'When?'

'Like around St Lucia Day. She told me, she didn't know what to do.'

'What the hell does that have to do with this?'

'I mean . . . everything.'

Sander stared at him, far too upset to absorb what Killian was saying. Or was that exactly what he was doing? Taking it in, feeling how this knowledge changed shape and turned into fury and jealousy: Of course Killian knew, while he didn't. Of course he and Felicia had conspired to hide it from him, from everyone.

Sander's eyes widened. '*Was* it you?'

Killian looked surprised. 'Who did what?'

'Uh, Mikael! What the hell do you think?'

Killian averted his eyes.

'Just answer me!'

Killian gave up. 'I guess maybe I should just leave right now.'

Sander sensed something new inside himself, a dark seed that had been planted within him long ago and was finally beginning to sprout. With all his might, he hurled the present against the wall. It made a dull thud and fell to the floor. Killian gazed sadly at the package but didn't say a word.

'Because what else can you do, Killian? When you come to me, and I don't help you, what do you do? Just run away. Go ahead, because you never could solve anything on your own. Don't just stand there like a fucking idiot, *leave*, for Christ's sake!'

Without a word, Killian glanced toward the car, his mother's Saab, and all at once Sander could sense that everything around him was decaying, falling apart; how finally, now, his fate had turned as he stood with an adamant finger pointed straight at Killian's chest, a command.

44

When Christmas Day dawned, it brought a tentative kind of sunlight that filtered gently through the trees.

Siri was standing next to Gerd out in Esmared, almost thirty kilometers from Skavböke, observing the wreck from a distance. She hadn't gotten much sleep.

The resigned paramedics and firefighters took notes, filled out forms, and performed a few last routine measures. Slender tendrils of smoke were still rising from what had once been an old Saab.

'Merry Christmas, or whatever, although I hadn't expected to see you again so soon.' Gerd stomped in place on the asphalt to keep her feet warm. 'You were right. Yesterday. About the blood sample.'

'I just felt like I needed to speak up. Hope you understand.'

Gerd nodded. 'I'm sorry.'

'It's okay.'

And it's a little late now, Siri thought.

Gerd made a face. 'What a terrible smell.'

'Is it him, do you think?' Siri could hear how weak her voice was.

'The smell?'

'In the car. Do you think it's him?'

'I hope not.'

Many rumors circulated, in the following days, about Killian's death.

That he'd been drunk or that he'd had some sort of

breakdown; that the accident outside of Esmared, right where Halland became Småland, was caused by some problem with the car. Or that fate had simply caught up with him at last, and that was that. The darkest theory said it wasn't an accident at all, really, because someone had drained the brake fluid earlier that evening and turned Linda Persson's old Saab into a death trap. Frans Ljunggren had noticed suspicious stains on the gravel road outside Linda's house the next morning, perhaps from a leak.

Whatever the case, Killian had been spotted on the night between Christmas Eve and Christmas Day. He was behind the wheel of his mother's Saab, speeding out of Skavböke. It was obviously Killian: he was recognizable by his blond hair and the scab like a thick, black swipe of marker over his nose. He seemed to be heading south, according to Isidor Enoksson, who had just finished talking to his sister on the phone and had gone out to throw away the trash from the Christmas smorgasbord. It was a few minutes before twelve thirty when he saw the car, which had taken a left after passing through Årnilt and headed down the old road toward Råmebo and Breared, and on toward Simlångsdalen.

Half an hour later, someone called the emergency number to report a car fire out in Esmared.

The technical investigation determined that Killian must have been driving at high speeds. He had likely gone into a skid on the ice and tried to brake, and, when that didn't work, pulled the hand brake to correct. But that only made it worse. The car overturned, flipped onto its roof, and slid across the road and into the rock wall near the shoulder. The gas tank burst and in an instant the car was engulfed in flames. Traces of the accident would still be visible years later, dark spots on the scorched asphalt.

It burned for quite some time before anyone happened by.

Killian, or what was left of him, was still behind the wheel. The damage to the car had been so severe he couldn't escape.

As Siri stood out in Esmared, observing the remains of the car and its driver, she thought: We didn't do this, did we? Or was it us? Did he take off because of us?

45

The news of Killian's death reached Sander a few hours later. When the phone rang in his house in Skavböke, he was the only one available to pick up. His parents were out on the property chopping wood; Dad with the ax and Mom stacking, as always, while they chatted. A pleasant moment for them both; they often found themselves chuckling together. This was something he would miss when he was gone – seeing his parents interact this way.

A cop whose voice he recognized was waiting on the other end of the line.

'This is Siri Bengtsson. We met last week. I'm calling about your friend,' she said. 'Killian.'

'Okay?' Sander managed to say, when she didn't continue right away. 'What is it, what about him?'

A protracted silence. 'I have some really bad news, Sander.'

Right and wrong. They don't fall from the sky; the concepts are created on Earth to stave off catastrophe. It's as simple as that. Inevitably, and just as simply, those very same catastrophes are only to be expected when someone breaks the rules.

Later on, Sander's memories of the time just after he learned of Killian's death were awfully fuzzy. It was as if his head were gone too. He couldn't make any decisions, could hardly register where he was. At the height of this blur, he put one foot in front of the other, stepped into the bathtub, showered. Stuck first one arm into a shirt someone (his mother?) was dressing him in, then the other.

But there was one thing he knew for sure: somewhere in this void that surrounded him for those first few days was the crematorium in Halmstad. Lundström had taken them there, the whole class, for a religious studies field trip early last fall.

The sun still beamed with the warmth of summer up in the sky as they gathered outside, Sander and Killian, Alice and Isabelle, Mikael, Pierre, and all the others; a softspoken man with glasses, wearing jeans and a long-sleeved shirt, came out to greet them. His head was shaved bald.

'Maybe he accidentally stuck his head in the oven for too long,' Killian whispered, making Sander giggle.

Felicia was behind them. Sander turned to her and smiled. She smiled back, but she was looking at Killian.

The operator spoke as though he were addressing someone right next to him rather than a group spread in a semicircle around him; it was very difficult to make out his words.

When the cremation begins, he told them, the body is in a casket that is conveyed into a large oven.

'We'll visit that room at the very end.'

Disposal of a body by cremation had once been called 'committing to fire'. The body is simply burned into ash. The crematory oven reaches temperatures of between eight hundred to one thousand degrees Celsius, and the process takes about eighty minutes. It's a very environmentally friendly method, almost perfectly clean, because the temperature is so high. Under optimal conditions the oven is even exothermic. The operator asked if anyone knew what that meant.

When no one said anything, Sander raised his hand.

'It means that the process creates more energy than it uses, or something like that.'

'That's basically it. Although we say *release* and *absorb* energy. The exhaust gases that arise during the cremation can contain particles, which must then be filtered out. The energy from those gases goes to the district heating plant to heat buildings, and metal from titanium implants and so forth is gathered and sent for recycling.' Here, the operator paused. 'You may have heard,' he added, as if this was a matter of great sorrow and distress, 'the myth that gold teeth go to the staff who work at the crematorium. This is not true, and in fact it is chemically impossible. At a thousand degrees, everything melts. There are other myths, such as the rumor that the person screams or even moves during the cremation process. That is not true either. In death, everything is peaceful and quiet.'

They had all moved into the building by now. Sander had imagined the crematorium as a factory, vast and industrial, all brick or stone, heavy machinery, men in sooty work clothes. As if the dead were blocks of coal being shoveled into a boiler.

Instead, it looked a lot like their school, the area by the main office: big windows and pine furniture, brochures with titles like 'All About Cremation' and 'For the Bereaved'.

'We are the last stop,' the operator said. 'Life has reached its endpoint, but the person still has value; the body still has rights. Even in death, we are very careful to protect these rights.'

The last stop. He spoke so oddly, as though he were both a priest and a bureaucrat. He described what happened before a body arrived, which forms were filled out and by whom, how the next of kin chose an urn for the ashes and how the urn arrived at the crematorium; how each casket was given a fireproof identification tile. He showed them the room where they stored the caskets before they were taken to the oven.

'When it's all over,' he said, 'we keep the urns in this room, which is always locked and alarmed. We take them out on the day the ashes will be spread or buried.'

Sander leaned toward Killian. 'Do you want to be cremated?'

'I think so. It sounds pretty easy on the survivors, I think. Do you?'

'I don't know,' Sander said. 'It feels so violent somehow. Despite what he says.'

'Sander,' Lundström said softly; he was leaning against the wall behind his students, his arms crossed. 'Killian. Quiet down and pay attention.'

Something had changed during this past half hour. A tranquil mood enveloped them, as if it had been summoned by the operator's words. As if the solemnity of the moment had gradually settled inside them. As though he had been waiting for this change, the operator nodded and said:

'I think we can go in now.'

Sander ended up behind Killian and Felicia.

It was a large room. The ceiling was high, and the space was very clean; everything was bright and cool. The crematoria hardly looked like ovens at all. Their shape reminded Sander of playhouses; they were angular, with sloping roofs, made of shiny metal. A large hatch with a small window. The primary and secondary chambers.

'Here we go,' the operator said in a composed voice, still as if it were of no concern to him whether anyone could hear him. 'Here's one now.'

Behind them, two technicians pushed a casket along.

The oven door opened. A smell filtered out, dark and rich. The casket was placed on a lift and raised. The operator kept talking, but Sander could no longer hear him; he was staring into the vast, black chamber of the oven.

Soon they saw the casket devoured by flames, and Sander

thought of the person inside, who had once been a living, breathing human, had perhaps had a soul, and was now a piece of meat rapidly turning to ash.

Outside the crematorium, he'd seen an aged wooden sign, with a verse from the Bible carved into it: *I am the resurrection and the life. Whoever believes in me, though he die, yet shall he live.*

46

On that Christmas Day, Sten Persson went to see the Söderströms. Exactly what happened between Sten and Karl-Henrik never became clear, although both of them came out of it unscathed – at least outwardly.

Sten rang the doorbell unannounced. When no one answered, he walked around the house and down the cellar stairs. That door was closed but unlocked. From upstairs, Lillemor could hear the two men's voices, agitated but muffled. She couldn't make out any words. After a while, they stopped.

According to Karl-Henrik, Sten accused him of causing Killian's death. Everyone knew that what had happened to Killian had to do with the Söderström family, that it was because of the tension between Karl-Henrik and Madeleine, and the way Mikael looked up to his father. Jesus Christ, he was crazy, Karl-Henrik said, so angry that he almost went at Sten with his fists. Like Karl-Henrik wasn't grieving too? Like he wasn't grieving? For fuck's sake, *his* son was the one who was murdered. Killian, Sten's stupid fucking boy, had gotten in that car of his own free will and sped off on the icy roads.

None of this was true, according to Sten. Sten claimed that he had come to the Söderströms' because he was seeking reconciliation. He had found Karl-Henrik down in the basement, so drunk he had to hold on to a shelf to stay upright. He patted the dynamite and said, 'If worse comes to worst.'

If worse came to worst, what?

They talked about what had happened over the past few days, and Sten, still in shock over losing Killian, said he didn't know what to do with himself. He wanted support, he said. But Karl-Henrik fended him off, accused Sten of trying to interfere in Mikael's murder investigation.

Interfere? How the hell did he mean?

By running his mouth about things that had nothing to do with Sten, things Sten didn't even have a clue about.

'My son is not a fucking murderer,' Sten said.

'Well, he's dead, in any case. Same as mine,' was Karl-Henrik's response.

This retort was the one thing they agreed happened. That, and the fact that upon hearing it, Sten had stormed out in fury.

A curse. That's what some people figured.

The previous year, an old woman in the village had died smack-dab on Christmas Eve. She had grown roses, the most beautiful roses in the area, and each summer they bloomed bright red and thriving all around her house. People said the death of the gardener would turn the roses white, and certainly no one really believed this — until last summer when astonished neighbors flocked to the garden. You could see it with your own eyes as you walked by: the crisp petals gleamed white as snow in the sun.

Maybe it was a sign, or a warning that greater and more incomprehensible events waited in the wings. A year to the day later, the woman's daughter visited the cemetery to light a candle and leave a frozen Christmas flower next to the gravestone. While she was there, she noticed that the lawn and the paths seemed neglected, uneven and covered in footprints. She complained to the caretaker, who shook his head.

'We do upkeep here every week. But it's like the dead walk around out there at night. Restless, I imagine. It's understandable.'

He said it with warmth, as though he were more fond of the dead than the living.

The thought of village ghosts roving above ground at night was both frightening and fascinating. And then there was Mikael, the will-o'-the-wisp in the dark when people talked about him, like a sudden mirage. Just a flash, then it was gone.

That was the kind of thing that came to mind upon hearing the news of Killian Persson's death. Curses, roses, the dead returning at night; visions and reflections in the dark. You couldn't be sure of anything anymore.

'Someone is trying to kill the boys of Skavböke.'

So people said that Christmas. Little did they know the worst was yet to come.

The worst? If it's even possible to rank such tragedies.

Well, but it is.

Day had slowly given way to night, and Christmas dinners were over. While the rest of the country made their way to pubs and bars to get drunk now that they'd fulfilled their holiday obligations, a heavy pall lay over Skavböke.

'No parties for you,' terrified parents told their kids, 'given what happened out there, what might still be happening. You are staying home.'

The adults claimed it was for their own good, but the affected teens hardly saw it that way. Instead they considered this a punishment of sorts, and maybe it was; maybe what had happened to Mikael and Killian was everyone's fault, in some regard. Sander felt unfairly linked to violence and death, even though it was true that these were what occupied his thoughts more than anything for the moment.

His parents thought he had finally dozed off. They'd heard him milling and crashing about upstairs, but now, at last, the noise had ceased. He must have been so exhausted after everything that had happened.

They held each other on the sofa and spoke softly. Erik placed his lips to his wife's hair. She closed her eyes.

'It's so awful,' Eva whispered. 'Have you talked to him?'

'I tried. But he doesn't want to talk.'

'We need to keep an eye on him. You know, I've almost been thinking maybe he should talk to someone.'

'What? How do you mean?'

'You know, a psychologist or something. Just so he has someone to turn to in case he needs it. I don't know.'

'Yes,' Erik said. 'Yeah, maybe. Have you checked in with Linda, by the way? And Sten?'

She had talked to both of them. Linda was completely beside herself and couldn't say a word; all she did was scream and cry. Sten, though, had been numb and cold. He had gone over to see Karl-Henrik Söderström.

'He did?'

'Yes, apparently.'

'Why the hell would he do that?'

Eva looked at her husband and shook her head.

'I don't know. But I guess it didn't end very well. I told them they need each other now, him and Linda. They should take care of each other. After all, Killian was both of theirs. I asked what Killian was doing in the car, but Linda didn't know.' A shiver ran through Eva's body. '"I just don't know what Killian was up to recently. Something was going on with him." That's what she told me.'

'Well, yeah, he killed Karl-Henrik's boy,' Erik said.

He felt Eva stiffen. 'You think he did it?'

'Everyone's been saying so. It'll be good for Sander to get out of here, to get away from all this.'

Eva nodded slowly. 'We'll have to keep an extra eye on him from now on. He's had his dark moments. This could . . . well, I don't know what.'

And up in his bed, wide-awake, lay Sander.

He picked up the phone and dialed a number he knew by heart, even though he'd never called it before. It rang on the other end.

'Hello?' said a soft voice.

'Hi. It's Sander.'

'Sander,' said Felicia. 'Hi.'

He had no words. None at all. 'I just wanted to hear someone's voice. Is this a bad time?'

He must have sounded as lost as he felt.

'No, it's fine.'

Too many questions inside – they got stuck. He wanted to cross them out and come up with a new one, the right one. He tried, but it didn't work, so he just lay there breathing. In the end, Felicia was the one who spoke:

'He stopped by and said he had to go away for a while. But that he would come back. Killian, I mean. I tried to get him to stay but he wouldn't listen.' She exhaled. 'He said you had a fight.'

The guilt was a tremendous wooden cross on his shoulders.

They came back to him now, all those words inside him that hadn't stayed where they belonged, deep down in his body and his soul; they had flown from his mouth and driven Killian to take off, to flee. They had driven him to death. He said it aloud now, for the first time:

'It's my fault.'

'No it isn't.'

But she didn't totally believe her own words. He could tell.

'You and Mikael,' he said. 'Killian said you . . . that he had forced himself on you. Is that true?'

'Does it matter?'

No, maybe not. That didn't matter anymore either.

Except, yes. It did.

'I just want to know,' he said. 'Did he?'

Felicia didn't say anything for a long time. 'What do you think?'

'But . . . when? Where? How . . . I mean, why didn't you say anything?'

'Who would I tell?'

She fell silent again. Sander could hear her sniffling.

'I'm sorry,' he said. 'I . . .'

'Killian was the only one who knew.'

'Is he the one that did it?'

'Did what?'

'Mikael.'

A long silence, more profound this time. 'What do *you* think?'

Sander had no idea anymore.

Lots of people said: Killian was probably trying to flee. Guilt can do strange things to a person. But that didn't make it any easier to come to terms with.

Even so, that Christmas folks tried to distill the truth, what it all meant, because what else could anyone do? They all lay awake in their beds: Sander, his parents, Karl-Henrik, Lillemor, Filip, Kjell Östholm and Frans Ljunggren, Linda and Sten Persson, the Lindells, everyone. Eventually most of them fell asleep and straight into dreams, and who can say what they dreamed about, really — and what if it was the same dream? It could have been, why not, a single, collective dream, just like on the night Mikael died and it all started.

A dream that grew out of the community itself, out of the land and the soil. A dream about cruelty that hadn't yet taken on a permanent shape, because it was still just a dream, but soon, very soon, it would . . .

Well.

Here, like a pry bar under the world itself.

Here it came.

47

Some people, those who still lay awake in their beds, heard it. Like thunder, they said, it was like being on the coast as a storm blows in from the sea.

Gerd was listening to the comms radio, to her colleagues in Halmstad, where, as usual, the Christmas revelers were moving through the streets like one big steamroller of drunken fights and festivities. Out here, all was quiet and still.

Siri said her name. Gerd rose from her chair, a half-eaten Lucia bun in her hand, and went to see what was up. It was just past eleven thirty at night on the twenty-fifth of December.

'Frans Ljunggren in Skavböke called,' Siri said. 'He said Kjell Östholm's farm has disappeared.'

'What did you say? Kjell Östholm disappeared?'

Siri glanced down at her notepad, as though she had to double-check her own notes.

'The *farm* disappeared. That's what he said. I asked him to repeat himself twice.'

They headed for Skavböke without lights and sirens. Siri drove, while Gerd finished her Lucia bun. It was nice not to have to chat.

'Listen, how are you doing?' Gerd asked at last.

'I've just been thinking about Killian Persson. I'm having a hard time letting it go.'

'The way he died?'

'Yes, but that's only part of it.'

And that it might have been our fault, Siri thought. *If what we did in his cabin drove him to flee.*

Once they were out of range of the streetlights, Siri turned on the high beams. The white headlights shone into the forest and over the fields and a call came over the radio. Gerd reached out to answer it, her mouth still full of saffron bun.

'We're getting a whole lot of calls from Skavböke,' the bewildered operator said. 'We don't know what's going on. I wanted to let you know we're sending more cars, so you know to expect them.'

Siri, grim, sped up.

But then she hit the brakes as hard as she could. Something in the car frame cracked loudly and the car swerved and nearly went into a skid. When they jerked to a stop, Gerd's Lucia bun got caught in her throat and she coughed violently.

'Well done,' Gerd said. 'You've got a lead foot when the situation demands.'

Siri gulped, as though she could swallow down the shock.

They shakily got out. Siri found a flashlight. From this vantage point they should have been able to make out the farm, the stable, and the house, the old barn. She should be able to see all of that from here. But she didn't.

Siri lowered the beam of the flashlight. It was like a plug had been pulled from the earth. The beam caught the asphalt rubble way down in the ravine, no telling how deep it had gone. The road was missing.

The cold December wind carried a peculiar smell: sour old earth and cropland, strange metals. In the distance, a dog was barking furiously, but suddenly it stopped, as though it had been frightened or silenced by force.

The car was perched at the very edge of the brand-new cliff. Siri grabbed the hot engine hood for support and aimed the trembling beam of the flashlight out beyond.

'Oh my God,' Siri said. 'Everything's gone.'

48

Whatever happens, morning will always dawn, but a morning like this would probably never happen again. That's what people said after the fact, as though the night had been a crime against previous nights, a jag in time.

For Sander, it would always be different: what happened that night was not something he could separate from all the rest. It was simply the next stage, or maybe the end, the brink of the cliff. He had reached the precipice that had begun to take shape on the night Mikael was murdered.

The earth could no longer hold him. Without Mikael and Killian, it couldn't bear him, so it buckled.

That must have been what happened.

For many people, it began not with thunder but with a dull rush that sounded almost like the sea. It increased in strength and shook the walls, knocked pictures down, broke dishes. People in the area were roused from bed, sleepy and confused, with an icy knot of fear in their chests.

Sander's parents came upstairs and opened the door to their son's room. When he wasn't there, they turned to look at each other, fearing the worst. They put on coats and shoes and ran out to look for him.

'What are you doing out here?' his mother exclaimed when she almost collided with him on the front steps. He was fully dressed, gazing down toward the village.

'I woke up and came out,' he said vacantly.

'Are you okay?'

He didn't respond. Around his wrist was a bracelet he'd

never worn before, a thin band of leather wound several times around and fastened with a small clasp. He touched it over and over.

Those who lived a little higher up could look down over Skavböke, but in the dark of night it was hard to make out the change until your eyes adjusted. At first it merely seemed like a larger, deeper blackness, far below.

And that — the fact that you couldn't see what had happened, only hear it — was almost even more dreadful.

Animals bellowed and howled so loudly that you would have thought they were being pursued. And then there was the field. Once your eyes adjusted, you could see that it was moving in the quiet moonlight, and not the way it usually moved in the window, when the fallow fields stooped in waves of wind. On this night, it looked as though something were tearing at the very ground.

Östholm's old combine was still standing in one of the fields, its reel broken. In the clutches of the landslide, it was nothing more than a toy. The ground opened up, an enormous maw expanding with a roar. It swallowed the combine and their neighbors' houses, their farms and property. Its hunger knew no bounds.

Erik squinted. 'I think there's a fire over by the Söderströms'.'

Unaware of what he was doing, Sander had taken his mother's hand.

'Fire!' Sander's mother shouted at her family. 'Down there. Jesus, it's on fire!'

The flames awakened slowly, like sleepy animals. Soon they were lapping eagerly at the house. Surrounded by their glow, the walls fell in and the roof collapsed; it took only a few minutes. Those who had set off to help had to turn back. They came upon a vast hole, a bottomless chasm that would get even bigger if you came too close.

'We have to go around, I think,' said Bengt Lindell, who was coming back uphill, out of breath as he passed Sander's house. 'But I don't know how far that goddamn hole goes, I can't see a thing. I think that's where it started.'

'At Söderström's?'

'Yes, exactly. Did you hear the explosion?'

'No,' Eva said. 'At least, I don't think so.'

'I woke up,' Sander said. 'I don't know why, maybe it was the explosion.'

As they waited for ambulances and fire trucks to arrive, people dug out flashlights, cars and trucks started up and got as close to the edge as they dared, their high beams aimed at the wreckage to try to make sense of what had happened. The rubble of the Söderströms' house was burning like a torch.

Life — sometimes it's exactly like a story. If it had been in this instance, Sander would have already known as he stood there, could have counted the dead. It would have been simple. But of course it wasn't. Who had been home? Who was somewhere else? Where had they been?

Knowing that they must have lost someone, but not who, wondering who was gone, never to return to the group gathered on the hill, was a state of being without a name. Sander stood alongside his parents, frightened and grim. He thought of Killian, Felicia, Mikael; he thought of the boy on the bridge. Where was he, when he jumped? He touched the bracelet on his wrist again.

Wherever that boy was, Sander was in the same place right now. Maybe he'd been there for days.

In the distance he could make out the chapel. It stood there in the cold, under a vast sky on the other side of the maw, clean and white and untouched as though it were protected by the Lord himself. The cross reached for the sky.

49

The landslide, when it finally stopped moving, was the size of eight soccer fields and as deep as a lake. Siri stood in mud and brush up to her knees. It felt like the ground was trying to suck her into the depths. Later on they brought in boards and baffles to walk on, but not enough of them. They had to be moved around, and it took an unreasonable amount of time to search every square meter.

Helicopters hung in the air like insects. There was no parking lot around here big enough for the many vehicles that arrived, so they were all over the place. Police dogs barked and the area filled with people slowly picking through the rubble.

One second you might be walking by the remains of a splintered house, only to find yourself moments later in front of a garage that had fared so well the paint cans were still lined up on the shelves and tools were still hanging from their nails. Inside the houses, demolished bathrooms shared space with kitchens where late-night sandwiches still lay on plates, uneaten.

Siri stopped.

'Gerd!' she called

A foot was sticking out from under debris. It wore a thick, handknitted sock that was now rusty brown with blood. From the toes hung a slipper.

Gerd and Siri began to dig with their hands, tearing at rubble and pieces of house, helping each other lift it away, but the house seemed to sink farther and farther into the muck the harder they fought to free the body.

'It's impossible,' an exhausted Gerd said at last. 'We need help.'

When they finally got her out, she could hardly speak. Hours spent stuck there, pressed into the mud, had brought on hypothermia. The internal bleeding was only discovered later, at the hospital.

'Felicia,' Siri said, crouching at her side. 'We're here now. We're going to help you.'

'You have to . . .' Felicia said. 'We're . . . I'm having a baby.'

Gerd froze.

'We'll do everything we can,' she said. 'I promise. How far along are you?'

'I don't know, exactly. Six weeks, I think. At the most.'

Felicia grabbed for Gerd's hand and she took it, squeezed it gently. Sudden sorrow took hold of Siri's heart and squeezed.

'Felicia, stay here with me. Look at me. Felicia. Felicia!'

50

Fresh snow fell between Christmas and New Year's, settling like fine dust over everything. It hampered the search for the missing. Helicopters were still hovering; emergency vehicles and trucks were lined up just outside the cordoned area. Volunteers from the community turned up but couldn't do much; it was still too risky. The media flocked nearby like they were up against the barricades at a concert.

The radio on Gerd's shoulder crackled. It was one of the patrols on the other side of the crater.

'He's back,' the crackle said. 'Same question.'

'Next time, don't answer him,' Gerd snapped. 'Just let it be. I told him we'll be in touch as soon as we know.'

Bill, Kjell Östholm's new hunting dog, had been home alone on the farm. Kjell himself had survived; he had been spending Christmas Day with Frans and was on his way home when it all started. Thank goodness Frans had convinced him to stay for coffee, too, so he hadn't gotten far. Now he was going around demanding information about the dog from every police officer, firefighter, and ambulance driver he saw.

'I never should have left him home alone,' he said. 'I knew it. I knew it. But I've always let my dogs do whatever they please, and he didn't want to come along to Frans's place.'

'We'll find him,' Vidar Jörgensson assured him, although he didn't seem to believe his own words. 'Don't worry.'

Vidar was one of the many officers who'd been called out from Halmstad. When he first arrived at the site of the collapse, he was dumbfounded by the destruction. But shortly thereafter, he got hold of himself and began to pitch in, just like everyone else. So many people arrived during those days in Skavböke, so many people gritting their teeth and lending a hand. The community would remember that.

A little while later, Siri's radio crackled. A discovery.

She and Gerd moved cautiously toward the spot; it wasn't far.

He lay on his side, his eyes closed. One leg was at a funny angle, but that was the only sign that he wasn't just asleep.

'He was under that,' Vidar said, pointing at a large machine. 'We didn't see him until we moved it away.'

'What is that?' Siri asked.

'A lathe. We think it was in the basement.'

'The Söderströms' basement?'

'Yes, could be. I don't know their name – the big house that was here. It took moving straps and four men to lift it away.'

Gerd crouched down to study the body.

'What the hell was he doing so far from the farm?'

'He's totally stiff,' Vidar said. 'Poor bastard.'

His fur was dirty and dusty, the fine strands swaying gently in the breeze. Great splinters of wood had drilled into his body, leaving deep wounds.

Gerd looked at Vidar.

'Call up Kjell and tell him –'

'Gerd, there's something in his mouth,' Siri interrupted.

Something was wedged between his teeth.

Getting the dog's mouth open was no easy task. It took all three of them to pry his jaws apart. When they finally gave way, there was a harsh, dry snap, like a branch breaking.

'Damn, they were stuck,' said Siri.

She reached inside and got hold of a scrap of fabric, the size of a napkin but jagged. She held it up in front of Gerd.

Someone in the area, dead or alive, owned a flannel shirt that was missing a bite. It was dark green, with pale yellow and blue stripes.

They heard a phone ringing loudly somewhere.

'Where the hell is that ringing coming from?' Gerd bellowed.

A patrolman they didn't know waved apologetically, a receiver in hand.

'It's for you,' he said, offering it to them. 'You're from here, right?'

Gerd nodded at Siri.

'Take it.'

She gripped the phone. 'Hello?'

'Hi, I'm calling from forensics.' The man cleared his throat, as though ashamed of calling in the midst of events like those he had seen on TV about Skavböke. 'About the blood sample you took from Killian Persson on December twenty-third. It's a match for the blood we found on the steering wheel in the Volvo. He was driving.'

'Thank you,' Siri said wearily.

51

Information about a landslide in Skavböke had first reached the overnight editorial crew at *Hallandsposten*. Soon thereafter, it spread to the evening papers and national media. For the first few days, helicopter footage of the disaster was broadcast on TV. The video was slowed down, stretching the images out, making them thinner, like pulling on a rubber band.

Quick clay. A type of marine clay that's very stable in solid form and can support houses, farms, and roads, even though it's mostly made up of water. The solid structure of this clay is maintained by salts, which help it hold together. If it's suddenly disturbed, it can quickly become a liquid sludge. Since quick clay is covered by topsoil, it can only be discovered by way of geotechnical sampling, and that, as far as anyone knew, had never been done in Skavböke.

The cause of the disturbance to the ground was a box of dynamite in the Söderströms' basement. It had been ignited.

This was how the incident was described – in passive terms, as though it had simply happened. No reason to lay the blame on anyone. The detonation had caused the landslide and the fire that consumed the remains of the Söderströms' house.

When Siri gazed out over what was left of the village she had been getting to know, her eyes grew moist.

'If only we'd been a little . . .' she said, then shook her head. 'Shit. If we'd just gotten a little further, maybe we could have prevented it.'

'How so?' Gerd asked.

'It's all connected, right? Mikael, Killian, the explosion – all of it. It has to be.'

'Hmm,' said Gerd. 'Yes, maybe. In which case, the question is how?'

And whether we're up to the task of figuring it out, Siri thought. *We might not be.*

They were still searching the area and had arrived at the wreckage of Killian's cabin.

'What's that?'

Something was peeking out of the rubble like a white brick. When they got closer, they could see what it was: a white plastic bag with the logo of Sennan Carpentry AB, identical to the bag Bengt Lindell had used to wrap up the family's savings after withdrawing it from the bank the week before.

They gingerly opened it and found a thick bundle of bills inside.

'Oh my,' said Gerd, and went to secure the discovery.

As it turned out when they got it back from forensic analysis, the bag was covered in Killian Persson's fingerprints. It seemed to have been hidden under some sort of hatch in the floor.

Siri's phone rang. It was Sander Eriksson.

52

Mikael Söderström's poor little brother sat before them, wearing guilt around his neck like a pendant. The room was comfortably cool but, considering the task that awaited, this was of little import. His mother was in the intensive care unit, and it was unclear whether she would survive; his father was a few units away waiting for the alcohol to release its hold on his body and withdrawal symptoms to abate. And his brother was in the morgue.

'How are you doing, Filip?'

'Okay.'

They'd been in touch with social services, since neither of his guardians could be present. A tiny sparrow of a woman carrying a folder full of forms was waiting in the lobby looking anxious when they came down.

Filip had refused to say a word in her presence. Eventually Siri had asked her to wait outside, and now she was standing on the other side of the door and picking at her cuticles.

'We'll make sure Helén talks to you afterwards. She's here to help you.'

'I don't want to talk to anyone. Especially not a soc lady.'

'It might still be a good idea.'

'What?'

'Talking to someone, even if you don't want to.'

'Really?'

'Yes, definitely.'

Filip stubbornly crossed his arms.

'Either way, we need to talk to you about this,' Gerd said,

taking out a piece of paper that had been hastily torn from a notebook by Sander Eriksson just a few days ago.

It was no longer folded up; now it was neatly tucked into a sheet protector, marked with a sticker in the margin; on it was an evidence number.

'Do you recognize this?'

Filip leaned forward, glanced at the paper, and leaned back again.

'No.'

'You don't? Take another look.'

'Why would I? I didn't write that.'

'Are you sure about that?' Gerd turned the document around and read from it: '*I want to light myself on fire, the explosion awaits.*' She tried to make eye contact with Filip. 'There was a box of dynamite in your basement at home, and you knew it was there.'

'No, I didn't. I had no idea.'

'You and your brother carried it home last fall, isn't that true?'

'No.'

Gerd sighed. 'If you didn't write this, I would say someone went to great lengths to make it seem like you did.'

Filip shrugged. 'So?'

'Who might that be?' Gerd asked.

'How should I know? Did Sander or Killian give you that?'

'Why do you ask?'

'I know it was one of them.'

'How do you know that, if you didn't write it?'

'I'm missing a page in my notebook. They brought my backpack to my house when I forgot it at school.' He nodded at the paper. 'One of them must have written that to screw with me.'

'Why would they do that?'

'Guess you'd have to ask them.'

'Can you tell me what you were doing on Christmas Day, in the evening?'

'Yes. But I don't want to.'

'It would really help us out. And you, too, of course. And your mom and dad.'

When Filip didn't respond, and simply stared at Gerd instead, Siri cleared her throat and offered a matter-of-fact explanation.

'Filip. If we assume you *aren't* the one who blew up the dynamite, it had to have been someone else. That person destroyed your entire farm. They could have killed you and both your parents. Don't you want to help us find out who did it?'

'It was Sten.'

Gerd and Siri exchanged glances.

'Sten Persson?' Siri asked.

'Yes.'

'You sound pretty sure of that. How come?'

'Sten never liked Dad. I don't know why. But I'm pretty sure Sten would love for terrible things to happen to us. And now they have. Wouldn't you say?'

Siri considered this. Two sets of rivals, Sten and Karl-Henrik; Killian and Mikael.

That was how it seemed to her now, in light of the past few days.

'Besides,' Filip continued, when no one else spoke, 'Sten came around our place on Christmas. He was poking around the basement. I saw him.'

In the ensuing silence, Siri leaned closer. 'Can you tell us more about that?'

'He wanted to talk to Dad. I guess you'll have to ask Sten if you want to know more. Or Dad.' Filip gave a laugh. 'If you even can. He's probably still too drunk.'

'We'll do that, Filip. But,' Siri added, 'doesn't this all make you pretty mad? It would be no wonder. You know, Helén, right outside, she –'

'How about you just find the guy who killed my brother? Oh, oops, that's right, you can't, because he crashed his car before you got your heads out of your asses and arrested him.' Filip suddenly stood up. 'I'm done now.'

'No, you're not.'

'Yes, I am!' he bellowed, as though it were his turn to detonate. 'I'm finished with you.'

Siri was shaken by his outburst. She struggled not to let it show.

'Filip,' she said calmly. 'Why are you so angry?'

'Why the fuck do you think?' he shouted.

Eyes blazing, he looked at the door as Helén from social services hurried in, alarm all over her face, and that was the end of the interview.

53

One Sunday, years ago, Isidor Enoksson had stood before everyone in the chapel and described existence in all its plainness: how the world, as it truly is, is immense. 'Close,' that's what we can reach out and touch. That's all we mean by the word *close*.

But even the parts we cannot reach are created with wisdom and intelligence. The Earth is full of natural laws, and everything has its place. The grass grows for the creatures and the grain for man, so that the farmers can work until night falls. People are reliant on – or maybe he said at the mercy of – one another, just as birds are to the air. Peace and order sprout from the soil and flow over man like rain.

Sander had, as usual, been dragged to church by his parents. It was a duty he had to suffer during the year of his confirmation. But after Isidor's sermon, he, too, felt a strange warmth in his body. Whatever awaited him, it would be suffused with meaning.

Close, Sander thought now, *is what we can reach out and touch*. He was only a body now, a body that had given what it could.

On the way to the hospital, Sander saw the newspapers. They featured a new young face today, a teenager who had vanished over the Christmas holiday. It didn't even have to do with the landslide. An intense search was under way. Killian had been supplanted by yet another tragedy, and Sander felt robbed, somehow.

He went through the main entrance and to the reception desk, hesitation seeping through his bones.

When he spoke, he heard the hollowness in his voice. 'I'm here to visit Felicia Grenberg.'

The receptionist consulted the clock on the wall behind her, then looked at her computer. She typed in *Grenberg* with her index fingers.

'All right.' She pointed at a long corridor. 'Take a right at the end of this hallway. Then it will be the first door on your left.'

The hospital windows looked onto a dark sky. December was the strangest month; soon it would be over, and with it an entire millennium, but it didn't feel that way.

Sander had heard from Felicia's mother that she was still in the hospital. On the morning she was supposed to be discharged, they had discovered an infection and she had to stay.

He walked to the end of the corridor. Nurses and doctors passed him, glancing discreetly his way. He found the room and peered inside. Felicia was lying on her back in bed, dressed and under a blanket. A TV droned at low volume.

When she saw him, she reached for the remote and muted the show.

Next to the bed was a chair. Sander tentatively sat down.

'Hi. How are you feeling?'

'My fever is gone. It doesn't hurt all that much either. I think I'll get to go home tomorrow.'

'Where will you go? When you leave here?'

'To an apartment here in town, over by Nyhem. We'll have to see what happens after that. I don't know if there's any saving it.' Her voice sounded strange, as though she were talking about a lost jacket rather than an entire home. 'How about you?'

'Our house is higher up. So it survived. We're staying in Andersberg right now, but I think they'll let us move back home soon.'

He'd prepared so many words, but none of them would come to him in the moment. His head was full of fog.

'Killian . . .' he began.

'I know.'

Everything became blunted. Sander was nothing but the sound a hand makes against a brick wall, a sack of dirt landing on a lawn.

'I've been lying here for so long,' Felicia said, 'with so much time to think, watching the fucking news over and over again. And all I can come up with is . . . part of me is so glad I lost the baby, because that way I won't have to explain to him that his father is dead.'

This didn't hit Sander the way one might have expected. There was no shock, no physical sensation of a slap or a bang. It reached him like a piece of information he already knew.

Of course. His best friend was going to be a dad.

Sander looked down. 'Did he know?'

'Who?'

'Killian. Did he know he . . .'

Felicia shook her head.

Did he know. Past tense. That was the first time. Until now he had persisted in using the present tense, as though language were a tool with which he could force reality to conform. As long as he spoke about Killian as though he were alive, it was possible to imagine that he really was. Even so, Sander knew: this bluntness inside him was the confirmation that his best friend was gone.

'Do you know how his mom and dad are doing?'

Sander shook his head. He couldn't bear to think about it. Instead, he saw his hand move as though controlled by someone else. He placed it gently atop Felicia's. It was strange – he'd spent a lot of time imagining what her palm would be like, in so many different ways. How it would feel against his skin, how it would smell and taste. But he had never imagined it like this. Dry and rough, just skin and bone.

She took his hand and squeezed it the way a sister hugs a brother, then let go of him and placed her hand on her belly again, over the emptiness inside, as though that were where it still belonged.

She observed his hand, the bracelet.

'That's nice,' she said. 'Is it new?'

He didn't reply. He thought about telling her about the page of Filip's notebook, what it had said, how he had handed it over to the police. But why would he? What did it matter now?

He wanted to ask Felicia if she had liked him the way he had liked her. Back before Killian came into her life, had she felt anything when they kissed, the way Sander had? But he didn't dare. He could guess what the answer would be, so why bother? Anyway, that didn't matter anymore either.

'It's so insane,' he said, 'that I'm still here and he's gone. It was supposed to be the other way around.'

There was a glass of water on the table next to the bed. Half-full. He looked at it and didn't understand. It was so simple to keep on living, to simply take the glass in hand. Clasp it gently and pick it up. Bring it to your mouth. Drink in the water and swallow. *Swallow*.

From a distance it would probably look like he was drinking, and that was accurate. He had just broken it up into tiny steps. Life was a series of steps, jags in a stream. Anything can be divided up that way. You just tackle one thing at a time, and if it's still too big you can divide it into smaller parts. Is there a limit to how small? If there was, Sander hadn't found it yet. Incredible to think that it was so simple.

'Was it really an explosion?' she asked.

'The dynamite at the Söderströms' place ignited. Or that's what they think, anyway.'

'It's so crazy. I'm sure they told me that, I just don't remember. That fever I had, it made me so loopy for a while. Who set off the dynamite?'

'No one knows. But I heard the police think it was Sten.'

'Killian's dad?' She looked surprised. 'Why would he do that?'

Sander hesitated. 'I actually don't know. But they had a fight, him and Karl-Henrik. I guess he was at Linda's house for a few hours after that. But he took off that night. No one knows where to. He says he went home, but no one can confirm that. Did you see him?'

Felicia shook her head.

Mikael had forced himself on her. He had hurt her. Knowing this had burned inside Sander before, but for some strange reason it didn't now. Mikael was dead. His father, who had perhaps made Mikael the person he was, had lost his house and his life was ruined; he probably wouldn't recover. He couldn't cause any more harm to anyone. Sander didn't know how it had come about, but when he thought about it he could see a greater, deeper sort of justice in the situation as it stood now. Like the murals in the chapel: being forced to see the whole picture at last. That was justice. This time, it had struck the Söderströms.

'Have you been back?' she asked. 'After what happened, I mean? Have you seen it?'

'Only the pictures on TV, in the paper.' And only then, as the words were coming out, did he realize what he was about to say, realize it was true: 'I don't think I'm going to go back.'

'Me neither.'

But she wasn't as certain. Sander could tell. As though it mattered now, who was certain of what, who wanted or did what, who would stay and who would leave.

He thought of the brilliant white chapel, the dark wooden

bell tower. He could hear the bells ringing in his mind. Something inside him had become distorted.

He reached out again and placed his hand near her side. Sander started it, but there was no choice, really. At last she placed her hand in his, more purposefully this time. There was no one else there, they were in the middle of a frigid winter, and she probably needed someone to hold on to.

54

New Year's came and went, the old millennium was left behind and the new one began, apparently without any major incidents or crises. The banks kept earning money, and so did companies; by all appearances, satellites stayed up in space. The cows were milked, the tractors all started, and life went on.

Sander's suit hadn't been washed, just the shirt, and it stayed out rather than being hung up in his wardrobe. First Mikael, then Killian. Frans Ljunggren observed all the tealights and candles on the graves, all the lanterns and flowers, and said: 'Maybe someone should open a store around here.'

Killian was laid to rest on a Sunday five weeks after the landslide, on the twenty-ninth day of the new millennium, under a bright-blue January sky. A cold, white sun shone down on the chapel, making the frost that had settled onto the village overnight sparkle.

Sander's best friend lay in an ash-colored casket adorned with a lush bouquet of white roses. Sten and Linda had chosen the flowers. When the congregants arrived, Killian's parents were already seated in the front pew, as though they had rooted there, staring at the roses like they might become brittle and dry, might crumble at any moment. No one could imagine how they could possibly be coping.

Just for today, people were trying to look beyond the rumors of Sten's role in the landslide that had caused so much destruction. He denied having started it, of course, but few believed him.

Today, though, was all about his son. Oddly enough, this brought a sort of temporary détente for the whole village as they were finally allowed to experience a single, straightforward emotion: they could simply grieve. Maybe. They had all seen the wreck, what was left of the car, but no one had witnessed the fireball itself. In his final moments, Killian had been alone at the brink of the cliff.

Inside the chapel, everyone was looking around for Felicia, but she arrived so late that many began to wonder if she was coming at all. In the end, though, there she was, with Madeleine at her side.

The news that she had been pregnant but lost the baby in the landslide had begun to spread. Many people questioned whether Killian could really have been the baby's father. Some insisted it had to be Sander, and others even suspected Mikael. Some spoke in a mildly insinuating tone, as if the lack of clarity they all felt surrounding the identity of the father were Felicia's own fault.

Isidor Enoksson was speaking up by the casket now. His words slipped away through the air, out over the congregation and through the small cracks in the chapel doors, off toward the ruined village. Or perhaps they seeped into the ground and vanished, burrowing all the way to the dead. If words could reach that far. Surely they could, if they were the right words.

'*We believe*, we say in the Apostles' Creed. But we don't say so to account for our understanding of faith. We do this – we all recite the same words at the same time – to remind ourselves that we are not alone, that there's something we all share: the remarkable thing that is faith. As high as heaven is over the Earth, so great is His mercy to those who fear Him, who believe in Him.'

It was hard to look at the casket. Killian shouldn't be here, locked up in a big, sealed wooden box; he should be somewhere else. Sander pictured a car driving off into the night on Christmas Eve, wild and careless, over and over again. He couldn't get rid of the image. He didn't know where Killian had been trying to go, and when he tried to imagine a place where his best friend would be happy, it was difficult; the only place Sander could imagine was here in Skavböke.

He closed his eyes. Voices echoed like ghosts.

We believe in God, the Father Almighty, Creator of heaven and earth. We believe in Jesus Christ, his only Son, our Lord, conceived by the power of the Holy Spirit, born of the Virgin Mary. He suffered under Pontius Pilate, was crucified, died, and was buried. He descended to the dead. On the third day he rose again. He ascended into heaven and is seated at the right hand of the Father. He will come again to judge the living and the dead.

PART THREE

By the Cemetery Where Killian Persson from Skavböke Is Buried

55

When he returned one July day, many years later, no one had seen him for a long time. But there he came, as though emerging from a different world, sailing through the summer in a car that looked brand-new.

He arrived at the parking lot of the chapel, stepped out onto the gravel, and looked around. Perhaps he was trying to determine which of his old selves was waiting.

Over the years, the ranks had grown smaller in their village. But those who remained, and who saw Sander Eriksson when he came, thought he looked the same. He was over forty now, but he was still slim and gangly, although perhaps his posture, which people recalled as having been very upright, was a bit more slumped. It must have been the endless hours he spent at the lectern in front of his pupils each day. Silver strands threaded the dark hair at his temples.

Isidor Enoksson was standing near the steps outside the chapel doors. He was over eighty now, but his eyes were still lively; he was holding a hymnal and seemed unbothered by the summer heat. When he saw Sander, his face lit up.

Inside the chapel, the windows were open. A white casket stood at the front, surrounded by floral wreaths with white ribbons, memorial phrases. A portrait sat on a small easel. It must have been taken before the illness struck. The face in the portrait was furrowed but warm, hopeful; a sharp and curious gaze meeting the lens of the camera.

Sander took a seat behind a woman with dark hair. Was that Felicia? Yes, it was. Or maybe not.

Isidor had left his spot by the front steps. The doors shut behind him, and he slowly closed window after window in the chapel. After exchanging a few words with those in the front row, he left the last two windows open. The scent of aftershave lingered in his wake. Bells rang out.

When the doors of the chapel opened again, Isidor was startled and turned around. He seemed surprised, as though he'd been expecting someone else, but he offered a kind nod and a big smile. There weren't a lot of people who could smile that way at a funeral without raising some eyebrows, but Isidor had the knack.

It was Filip Söderström. He stepped in wearing snow-white sneakers, black suit trousers, and a short-sleeved black linen shirt. As old as he was now, the years were visible on his face.

Now someone else arrived; maybe this was the person Isidor had been waiting for. She wasn't alone. Two helpers propped open the doors, adjusted the ramp, and helped get the emerald-green mobility scooter through so Filip's mother, Lillemor, could steer into the chapel. Frail and white-haired, skin and bones. There was no trace of the beauty she had undeniably been. A few people turned to look, but most didn't bother. Filip was among them. He didn't move from his spot in the pew until his mother was parked next to him. Then he reached out one hand and mechanically placed it on top of hers.

What were they doing here? Some said it was reconciliation. Some said duty. Maybe it was both.

No one bothered to close the doors again, and the sun shone in on the chapel floor, bright and strong. Hymnals were opened in silence. Place-keeping ribbons adjusted. *Beautiful nature, beautiful pilgrimage of the souls*, they sang.

Sten Persson had lived the last season of his life in Åled,

not far from here, in a small house with stone steps leading to the front door, and a driveway where he could park the car. He had come to the brink of self-destruction more than once over the years. A few years after Killian's death, he and Linda tried to live together again, but it was hard. Sten had been too far gone, and maybe the same went for Linda. Then she suddenly got sick and died. That was ten years ago now. Following Linda's death, many people had noticed the marks on Sten's forearms and feared that there were more to come, that it would happen on a day when no one dropped by for a visit or had time to call an ambulance. Sooner or later, they said, because that was so often how it went.

In recent years, though, he seemed to have come to terms with what had happened, or maybe just with himself. Was that possible, to come to terms with yourself? Yes, presumably it was. Maybe that's what everyone was doing all the time.

And if anyone needed to do it, it was Sten.

The cancer was in his pancreas. Sten got the diagnosis only last winter and now, just six months later, he was gone too. Almost exactly the same course of events as Linda.

The bells faded, but hardly anyone noticed.

Sander sang along with the rest of the congregation. His voice was smooth and gentle and seemed to come from a lonely place inside his skinny chest. Suddenly he was distracted. The shapes of the shadows on the chapel floor transformed, as if something outside the chapel doors were blocking the sun. Sander glanced at the entrance for a third time.

It was as if he wasn't entirely alone after all, but it was hard to describe exactly how. No one had accompanied him to the chapel. At least, no one visible.

The last notes of the hymn lingered in the chapel, as though they didn't want to let go, and then Isidor began to speak. In time, he mentioned both Linda and Killian.

It was almost eerie to hear their names after so long. Thinking the names was one thing, but listening to them come out of someone's mouth – it stung.

Sander sat perfectly still. His face was under control. Only his hands needed to twist and clasp each other, as though the pain dwelled inside his skin.

In the summer of 2022, it sometimes felt like everyone had lost the ability to remember places and people and things, and most of all, who they had once been. Events in life happen once, they're not repeated, they never return. Except in memories, and without memories it's hard to make it all fit together.

When they were little, they heard that the coffin maker made the lids thinner than the rest of the casket so it would be easier to rise again when the time came. Sometimes, for children, he didn't make a proper lid at all, just a flimsy slab. He didn't want to cause himself a fright if he could avoid it.

The question was, what would have happened in their case, those who had been lying in the ground at the cemetery in Oskarström for over twenty years? Were they children or not? How old were they, really? It seemed unthinkable that they could have been as old as eighteen, yet so young.

By the time Sten Persson was buried, a few years after his ex-wife and over twenty years after his son, a lot had changed. The young people of Skavböke had grown up, gotten married, and become parents, and, all things considered, had turned out okay – most of them, at least. But for an instant there in the chapel, it didn't feel that way at all. As if time were something other people could take hold of and bend violently to their will, could use as a weapon.

56

An hour later, it was over. As the congregation filed out of the chapel, God felt far away. Voices spoke, low and tense and restrained. For some, the heat was a heavier burden than the grief. Men stood with their hands in their pockets; women held their small clutches.

'It was a nice service,' said Sander's mother, Eva.

'If only it weren't so damned hot.'

'Shh, Erik. Don't swear. The priest.'

'He swears, too, you know.'

Sander went over and gave each of them a tentative hug. His mother smiled weakly. 'Good to see you. We were hoping you would come, that it wouldn't be like with Linda.'

When Killian's mother died, they let Sander know, of course, and wondered if he would come to her funeral. He had said he would, but later, suddenly, he was unable to make it.

'We're heading home now,' she went on, 'but you'll drop by, won't you, before you leave?'

'Well, I'm heading straight back.'

'Oh, you are. I see.' She looked disappointed but embraced him again. 'But we'll see you in August, right, when you're back with the kids?'

Sander nodded. Olivia, her name was. She and Sander had two children, a boy and a girl. They lived on Backavägen in Snöstorp, a sleepy residential neighborhood on the east side of Halmstad. It was the kind of place you dreamed of: a classic wood-frame house with a big lawn, flowerbeds, and a small pool in the back. There he lived a calm and quiet life, at an appropriate distance from his childhood.

His father patted him on the shoulder and hobbled after his wife. He really should have had his cane. Last winter he'd taken a bad fall and his broken leg hadn't healed properly. He only used the cane when he was at home, since he didn't like the way he looked when he tried to walk with it.

Sander looked over at one of the fields of grass swaying gently in the summer breeze and gazed thoughtfully at the edge where the forest took over and the shadows began. He gently turned the worn leather bracelet on his wrist as though it were on wrong and he wanted to adjust it.

Jakob Lindell came out of the chapel to stand beside Alice, but then he excused himself and slowly came Sander's way.

'It's been ages. How are you?'

'I could use a drink. But I suppose that would just be adding fuel to the fire.'

They remained a few meters apart as though it would be risky to get too close. Over the years, Jakob had grown broader shoulders, a barrel chest, and a little round belly. For an instant they could see their teenage selves again, and they smiled faintly in mutual understanding. The moment for a longer conversation came and went.

'I'm heading back again,' Sander said. 'But it was nice to see you. Say hello to Pierre. And Alice.'

'You're not coming to the reception?'

Sander couldn't tell if Jakob was relieved or disappointed. 'I only came for the service, wasn't planning to stay long.'

'Did the two of you keep in touch, you and Sten?'

Sander shook his head. 'We stopped to say hello if we passed on the street, of course. But it was rare. And that was all.'

Jakob scratched an unshaven cheek. 'Sure you don't want

to come along after all? I'm sure I'm not the only one who'd like to see you.'

A memory returned to Sander, swift and hot like a spark in a darkened room. An image, was all, and when it faded again it left old feelings behind.

'What do you say?' Jakob asked. 'Just for a little bit?'

Sander looked puzzled.

'To the village hall,' Jakob clarified.

57

Everything was unfamiliar somehow, as if it weren't Sander himself but some other person who had once been here, grown up here, lived here. At the same time: the smells rising from the road and the bushes, the trees and the ground, everything he could see was already inside him, somewhere, deep down.

The mourners moved on foot down the gravel path, scattered groups dressed in dark clothing. It took some time to get to the village hall; it was a few kilometers away. They sweated in the heat.

It was picturesque, the hall, resplendent in classic red siding with white trim and windows that had been fashioned by real carpenters a long time ago. Inside, savory sandwich cakes and sweet princess cakes waited on a long table, tastefully decorated. Folks wondered who had arranged it all, but no one asked. A fan hummed in one corner.

The congregation entered in small groups, all these people who hadn't gathered under the same roof for so long. They chatted and enjoyed coffee and treats. Isidor moved slowly from table to table. He stopped next to Filip, placing a hand on his shoulder and speaking softly to him before moving on to kneel laboriously in front of Lillemor. He took her hand between his own and patted it gently.

Soon they were all together, the boys from Skavböke – or what was left of them. The glances they exchanged said more than an outsider would realize. Sander got up to refill his coffee. He was just about to set the pot back down when someone next to him stuck out a cup and said, as if in an astonished greeting:

'Sander?'

Sander turned his head. 'Oh, hello, Filip. It's been ages. Milk?'

'No thanks, I take it black.'

'It's nice to see you. I wasn't really sure you'd be here.'

'I felt like I needed to come. For my own sake, mostly.'

'I can understand that.'

'I don't know if you can. But thank you.' For a moment he was silent, as though there were more words to be said but maybe not to Sander. Then he added: 'It's always sad when someone dies. But I'm not exactly mourning him.'

'That makes sense,' Sander said. He was still holding the pot of coffee, like he was a server. 'How are things?'

'Oh, under control, I suppose. Just working, soldiering on.'

'Where are you living these days?'

'In Frans Ljunggren's old house. I bought it from him a year or so before he died.'

'When did Frans die?'

'Last winter. It was his heart.'

Frans too, Sander thought. Old man Östholm, Sten, Linda, Karl-Henrik, Mikael, Killian. So many people gone.

'Sorry to hear it.'

'Yes, but it was his time. He was over ninety, after all.'

Frans had left most of his belongings in the house after the sale, Filip told him. Furniture, curtains, the tools and equipment in the garage, even the silverware in the kitchen drawers.

'But I ended up throwing those out,' he said. 'They were all pretty rusted through.'

He'd gotten the household goods in exchange for a bottle of liquor he supplied to Frans, who planned to smuggle it into Patrikshill, the nursing home he had just moved into. That got a chuckle out of Sander. He remembered the old mechanic and was about to recount a sudden memory of him when Filip put down his undrunk cup of coffee and looked at his phone.

'I've got work this afternoon. I have to get going. But it was nice to see you again.'

'It was,' Sander agreed, and returned to his table.

The others fell silent as he sat down.

'What happened to Filip?' Jakob asked.

'I guess he had to go to work.'

'Can't have been easy for him. Coming here, I mean.'

'No,' Sander said. 'I was thinking the same thing. What would I have done?'

If he'd been the one to lose a brother, if it had been his home, if he'd been convinced Killian's father had destroyed it.

Jakob lowered his voice. 'You know, I've actually spent a lot of time thinking about that.'

'What you would have done in Filip's situation?'

'Yes. Or no, not really.' Jakob shook his head. 'Fuck it.'

They sipped their coffee. Sander waited, but Jakob didn't elaborate.

'He told me about the house, anyway,' Sander said. 'Funny story.'

Jakob raised an eyebrow, and Sander recounted what Filip had said. When he was done, Jakob shook his head.

'It's a wonder he's still alive, Filip. You know, that Frans Ljunggren was always so sly. He had quite a few demands for that bottle of liquor. Nothing homemade, he said, it had to be real, boughten liquor, so of course that meant Filip had to go to Systemet to buy it. And once Filip got himself clean, I don't think he was as scared of anything else as he was Systemet. As I'm sure you recall, Frans Ljunggren wasn't what you'd call a generous soul. He liked that house and wasn't about to give it to just anyone. So he wanted to see if Filip could go in the liquor store and buy Frans a bottle without falling off the wagon. If he could do it, Frans would sell. I'm sure it wasn't easy for the poor bastard, but Filip did what it took.'

Sander's phone buzzed. A text from Olivia, wondering how it had gone, if everything was okay at the house on Backavägen, how much farther he had to drive.

She thought he was on his way back. He probably should have been.

It was high time to leave.

He tried to catch Felicia's eye. She didn't look up; she was sitting with her mother, Alice, and a man Sander didn't recognize.

Sander left the village hall and went back to his car, and just like that he was gone again, almost as if he'd never returned.

58

He pulled up at the house in Snöstorp. All he was supposed to do was make sure it was still standing, go through the mail, and make sure the timed sprinkler system was worth the outrageous price they'd paid for it earlier in the summer. Then: on the road again.

Hardly anyone was home on Backavägen. When Midsummer arrived, everyone on the street had loaded their lives into SUVs and RVs and headed off on vacation.

Well, almost. The Johanssons were back. The house across the street had a trampoline in the yard, with a safety net. When Sander stood on the lawn, he could see the neighbor girl's head bouncing up and down, her hair following. From a distance she looked a little like Josefin, his daughter. They played together on occasion.

Symbols: pale skin, a lull, a casket, a gravestone. An empty hook in the hall where a coat used to hang. That was all. Those were the kinds of images people had of death. When was the last time he'd attended a funeral? January, in the year 2000. Over twenty years ago. Was that unusual? What was the average interval between funerals for a man of his age?

He went back inside, inhaled the scent of his own home, his own life. It was another hot day. He wanted to take off his suit jacket but decided not to. He went into the bedroom he and Olivia shared and sat down on the bed, thinking about how lucky he was to have Olivia and the kids in his life, to have people to miss and long to see, people who missed him and wanted to see him too. He wondered if Sten Persson had had that.

That summer turned out to be a very tough one, as he would recall later. A heat wave settled over the country like a threat; people couldn't handle it. For days there wasn't a hint of a cloud in the Halland sky. Only nights brought relief.

That was also the summer his dream came back.

Sander was eighteen and back out in Skavböke, picking his way through ruins. It hurt to breathe, as though the very air were dangerous. He looked around, searching for some sort of answer. There was a hint of the unfinished here, an action waiting to be taken. Then he lowered his gaze to the ground.

He realized he was supposed to dig. He stuck his hands in the earth and clawed up soil, grass, and scrub. He dug down as deep as a grave, and soon his shoulders, back, and fingers were aching; a pang appeared dreadfully close to his heart. At last he touched something.

For a moment, Sander took in the face that had emerged. Pale violet and stiff, more a mask than a face, but then its eyelids fluttered and the face was staring back. Sander's scream was so loud he woke himself up.

They say everything you encounter in a dream is a shard of yourself, like pieces of a shattered reflection. In that way, dreams are an enigmatic sojourn.

But if this dream was an answer, what was the question?

The tall trees swayed gently in the summer breeze, and above them, in the bright blue sky, curly little wisps of clouds drifted by like cotton candy, and as he focused on those, he thought, *Yes, concentrate on those, like cotton candy, it's simpler that way, everything will be so much simpler if you just let everything be as it is.*

He held tight to that thought the way the victim of a fall grabs frantically for the railing.

59

Sander was sitting at the kitchen table and going through the mail when he heard something dripping. It's strange; sometimes sounds are there the whole time but you don't notice them. Then, suddenly, they pierce the fog.

He turned his head. Not in here.

The bathroom faucet. It was leaking, even though it was off.

His phone vibrated in his pocket. A video call from Olivia. In the background, waves crashed as loud and clear as a highway.

'Hi. Hello there. How are you all?'

The phone was shaky in Olivia's hand. She was newly tanned and wearing her black bikini.

'We're still on the beach here.' She aimed the phone at Josefin and Albin, who were packing sand into a bucket. 'Say hi to Dad.'

'*Hi to Dad,*' the children chorused.

'Well, as you can see we're just fine.' Olivia laughed. 'You're not on your way yet, though?'

'I went to the reception at the village hall for a bit, and when I got here I decided to tackle the pile of mail. And just now I realized that the bathroom faucet is dripping. But yes, I'm on my way. I wish I were there going for a swim with you all instead.'

'How was the funeral?'

'Mostly it was hot. But it felt good to be there, at least. Can you believe it was the same priest? Isidor. He's still alive. He has to be a hundred years old.'

'Some people are like that,' Olivia said. 'They don't stop until they drop, because if they stop . . .'

'They drop,' Sander supplied.

'And your back was okay?'

'Sitting in a pew isn't that hard. But that reminds me, I haven't done my exercises today.'

Olivia turned away.

'Hey, Dad's going to play worm again! Want to watch?'

The children hurried to the phone. Their little faces, sun-drenched and curious, filled the screen.

Sander smiled wearily.

'Otherwise you won't do them,' Olivia pointed out.

Last spring, when the doctor explained what to do, Sander thought it sounded simple. You stand facing a wall, no more than a foot away. Then you stick out your neck like a vulture until the tip of your nose touches the wall. Then you sink down a little and look up at the ceiling, so your chin is touching the wall instead. Then you stick out your chest and keep moving, until your chest is the only part touching the wall.

It was harder than it looked.

Delighted, the kids threw themselves onto the sand and tried to imitate their father. Olivia showed him. He caught a glimpse of her feet, toes burrowed into the warm sand, the gold chain heavy and expensive around her ankle.

'It's chaos here. So many people. But still one too few. We miss you.'

'I'm just going to grab a bite to eat and try to fix this faucet.'

'You're not going to call a plumber?'

'If I do that, I'll be here until school starts again. I'll try to get this taken care of and then hit the road. Tell the beach I'll see it soon.'

After they hung up, he walked through the house and into the bright living room, where the afternoon sun streamed across the floor. He opened the door and stepped onto the patio to take a lap of the yard.

Skavböke lingered inside Sander but it was here, in this house, with Olivia and his kids, where he belonged. That's what he thought.

He worked on the stack of mail, bills and documents, forms that needed filling in. Then he dealt with the bathroom faucet. Sweaty, bent double in front of the sink, his back aching for real now, he took apart the handle. After quite some time he figured out that one of the rubber gaskets was cracked. He didn't have a spare on hand and had to drive to Biltema out in Stenalyckan to buy a new one.

It was late by the time he finally finished and headed out the door. He had the car keys in hand when his phone rang again.

That's when it happened.

'This is Jakob,' a voice said. Over the phone he sounded just like he had when he was eighteen. 'Listen, I don't know if you heard, but . . .'

It seemed Jakob didn't quite know where to go from there.

'But what?'

'Sorry. We, Alice and me, were out shopping this evening. Then – um, I don't quite know how to say this.'

Jakob's voice sounded strange. Sander pressed the phone tight to his ear.

'What?'

'Are you still home, or did you leave already?' Jakob asked, as though he hadn't heard Sander's question. 'There's something I have to show you.'

60

Brothers, Vidar Jörgensson thought as he stood next to a field in Skavböke and gazed out at a region that was just settling down for the night after another hot day. *Two dead brothers.*

It was past nine. Behind him, men and women with cameras and notepads in hand milled around gravely. They methodically noted what they found, took photographs, and spoke in subdued voices. Vidar took out his phone, dialed a number, and waited as it rang on the other end.

'Okay,' Markus Danielsson said, his mouth full of food. He swallowed. The tinkle of silverware. In the background was the soothing hum of a restaurant's patio seating. 'Let's hear it.'

'So,' said Vidar. 'Blunt trauma to the head. Two or three blows.'

Vidar heard his former colleague and current boss let out a deep sigh as he stood up and wandered away from his table to continue this conversation in private. Vidar remained at the edge of the field, waiting.

'What are you eating?'

'A ribeye.'

'That would hit the spot right about now.'

'Has it been confirmed that it's him?' Markus said, his voice lower.

'Yes, it's Filip Söderström. According to the ME, it happened a few hours ago. Toward late afternoon, early evening.'

Seconds of silence.

'Well, listen,' Markus said then, sounding apologetic. 'I

had hoped you'd get to enjoy a nice, calm summer, but this is going to be yours, I fear.'

'Right,' Vidar said. 'Fair enough. I'm going to get back to it here, but I just wanted to let you know. Phones are going to start ringing.'

'How does it look on the scene?'

'I don't know yet. Too early to say.'

'Well, how does it feel?'

Vidar turned his head. Filip was lying on his back in the grass, well hidden. Only one shoe was visible. The teens who'd found him, a couple who had been sneaking off to canoodle in the summer night, had thought someone was sleeping there. Maybe a drunk. At first they shouted at the shoe, expecting its wearer to wake up and move. When nothing happened, they approached.

'Skinny,' Vidar said. 'We'll have our work cut out for us.'

'I'll see if I can free up some people for you,' Markus said.

Vidar observed the surroundings a little while longer, as if something he was looking at wasn't quite as it should be. Only the crime-scene techs and a coordinator were inside the police tape; the officers stayed outside the blue-and-white barrier.

'Does anyone here know this area?' he asked, glancing around. 'Anyone live nearby?'

A young officer with long, dark hair tucked under his cap raised a hand and approached Vidar at the edge of the cordoned area.

'I'm from Åled,' he said. 'I'm Adrian. Adrian al-Hadid.'

He offered his hand and Vidar shook it.

'Great. Where are we?'

Adrian looked puzzled. 'In Skavböke?'

'I mean the landslide.' Vidar pointed at the field. 'The foliage is different here; it runs along the edge of this field almost like a ribbon. What was here before the landslide?'

Adrian scratched the back of his head. 'I was three years old back then, in 1999. I don't know. But I can find out.'

The young man hurried off toward one of the patrol cars. Taking care not to make a wrong step, Vidar ducked under the blue-and-white tape and picked his way to the body.

He was a slender man, Filip Söderström, skinny and sinewy, with pronounced shoulders. He hadn't even made it to forty, but his face looked like the far side of fifty. A shadow of stubble covered his chin and cheeks. The blow to his head had cracked his skull, and his head rested in a sludge of blood and broken soil.

The hands of a tradesman, with black rinds under the nails, dirty fingers, veins standing out on his forearms. No marks in the bend of his elbow – not anymore, but they'd been there once; as Vidar knew, old tracks went deep into the skin. Jeans and a T-shirt; in his pockets they'd found a wallet, a lighter, keys to his house and a company van that was sitting silent and unlocked out on the road.

It was cool outside now. Lovely – you could breathe again. Vidar crouched down. No doubt this was the scene of the crime. Tracks in the grass and dirt; footprints. Vidar squinted and studied the ground at such close range that he could smell it.

Blood. Spatter on the little green blades.

'Hello,' someone said. 'Hey.'

Vidar stood up and turned his head. The young officer was back. Adrian something. He was holding his phone. Then he realized where he was standing and looked at his shoes as if he'd destroyed a very important piece of evidence.

'Shit.'

'It's fine. Just watch where you step on your way back. What is it?'

'Well, I found an old map; it was faster that way. There was a farm right here, as you can see. Several buildings.'

He held the screen toward Vidar.

'Find out who it belonged to,' he said, turning back to the body. 'And,' he added, 'find the names of the people who worked on the investigation back then.'

The response was immediate.

'The farm was theirs.'

'Whose?'

The officer nodded at Filip Söderström.

'The farm – it belonged to the Söderströms. I sent a picture to my dad and asked him. He drives a truck and used to have deliveries out here sometimes, so I took the chance. Their house was right here.'

Vidar raised an eyebrow. Only now did he realize his young colleague was shaken up by the sight of the body.

'Well done,' he said to Adrian. Curious onlookers were starting to gather around the police tape, in the warm night. 'So he was killed on what used to be his own family farm.'

'Sure is *kymig*,' Adrian said tentatively. 'Right? It is, isn't it?'

Brothers, Vidar thought again. *Two dead brothers.*

'Yes,' he said. '*Kymig* indeed.'

61

Jakob Lindell climbed out of his car in front of the house on Backavägen. He was wearing worn jeans and an oil-stained T-shirt, and he took in his surroundings as though he'd stepped into a completely unfamiliar world.

'I don't think I've ever been here before,' he said. 'Damn, it's lovely. Everything is so . . . neat, somehow.'

'Yes, it's nice,' said Sander, who had come to meet him at the gate. 'We like it here.'

He had left his old life behind in some ways, but even so, Snöstorp was no more than half an hour from Skavböke. The trip took longer than it seemed, though. He who manages to escape his past gets to live twice.

And now this.

Filip is dead.

Sander paused and lowered his gaze to Jakob's hand. He was holding tight to a plastic bag.

'Would you like anything?'

'Yes, but I guess it should be an NA beer. I'm driving, after all. If you have some? But you go ahead and have something stronger, if you'd rather.'

'Like I said before, that would be fuel for the fire today. I think I have some NA around here somewhere.'

Sander went to the kitchen and found two glass bottles in the door of the fridge; he opened both and handed one to Jakob, who took a big gulp and set his plastic bag on the table.

'Christ, what a day,' he said.

After supper that evening, Jakob and Alice had headed to Oskarström to go grocery shopping on Blåklintsvägen, where once a week he dropped off his horse-racing bets and lost money. Of all the things she tried to love about her husband, Alice liked to say, this was one of the hardest to accept.

No one had ever expected she should need to love him at all, really, but one summer night after graduation, plans changed. A few weeks later, Alice's period was late. They got married that winter, and Lisa arrived in April. By that point, they had moved into the house over by Öjasjön, an old two-story house with a two-car garage and a piece of land that turned out to be too acidic to cultivate.

Tonight, the road to Oskarström was blocked off with blue-and-white tape, and police kept watch, eyeing the cars that came by, stopping them. In the distance, a glimpse of a white van on the side of the road.

Jakob, pensive, turned his bottle in his hands.

'Both of us recognized the van, so when it was our turn to talk to them we told them what we knew. Which wasn't much, really, just that he'd been at the funeral and was heading off to work. Or at least that's what he said. I mentioned who had been there, including you, of course. Have they contacted you?'

'Not yet. But sounds like it's only a matter of time.'

Jakob took a sip.

'So someone killed him,' Sander said, staring at the floor.

'Seemed so, anyway. Who the hell knows. But he did have a rough time of it for a while there. Maybe some old grudge caught up with him.'

'I guess we'll find out.'

'It's too bad. He really had straightened himself out. At least, it seemed like he had.'

It was almost ten. The kids must be asleep by now. Even if Sander left this minute, he wouldn't reach Kivik until long after Olivia went to bed. Even so, he wanted nothing more than to take off, just get in the car and go.

Sander tried to absorb what Jakob had told him, take in the implications, but it was hard. Everything that had been confined to the past was creeping closer. Filip, beaten to death. Two brothers killed over twenty years apart, brothers he used to know.

His eyes went to the bag on the kitchen table.

'Was there something in the bag?'

'Oh, right.' Jakob put down his bottle and peeked inside the bag, as if to make sure its contents were still inside. 'I don't fucking know, it was so long ago, but I've always thought this was strange.'

What Jakob told Sander then wasn't really strange at all, and didn't take very long to explain. Even so, for Sander, by the time Jakob was finished, everything had changed.

62

During Christmas of 1999, area teenagers were nearly universally forbidden by their parents from going out, and silence lay over Skavböke like a membrane. Jakob hung out in his room, where he talked to friends on the phone, read old comic books, and watched a movie to distract himself and keep from overthinking things.

'*The Empire Strikes Back*, as I recall. That new edition, with the special effects.' Jakob kept sipping his beer. 'Afterwards I went out to the yard, I don't know what time it was exactly, but it was right before the landslide. Maybe fifteen minutes before? I was going to put more wood in the stove out in the garage. That's when I saw someone run past, not too far off. He was coming from over by Söderström's, you know, along that trail that used to be there. I didn't think much of it, but a minute or two later, while I was still messing with the woodstove, a dog started barking like mad. Then I heard a boom. A huge boom, deep and muffled, like something had exploded, but what could be exploding in Skavböke, you know? I went to see what it was, but I didn't get very far before the ground started to feel... I don't know, it just felt wrong. Do you remember that?'

'No,' Sander said. 'But I was indoors. I was sleeping.'

Jakob glanced down and nodded thoughtfully.

'Anyway, I hightailed it inside and ran into my parents in the door – they'd heard the boom too and were on their way out to see what was going on.'

'You were okay,' Sander said tentatively, trying to recall a fuzzy memory. 'Right? Your house survived?'

'We were lucky. It ended just a couple hundred yards from us.'

Jakob stared at the checkered kitchen floor. It had cost Sander and Olivia fifty thousand kronor to install, all in all, and almost as much to tear up and replace after a water leak six months later. Beneath those tiles they'd found hints of the original flooring, an old beige linoleum identical to what had been in Sander's student apartment during his year with Felicia.

'Dad ran out to see if he could help, and he was gone for a really long time. So long that I was afraid he wasn't coming back, that something had happened. Then I ran out, too, after him. I didn't get far before I tripped over something, I don't know exactly where.' He took a large piece of fabric from the plastic bag and held it out. 'It was this.'

It was a flannel shirt. Dark green with pale yellow and blue stripes, threadbare and old.

Jakob held out the bottom hem of the shirt. It was torn; it looked like something had ripped off a piece or taken a big bite out of the fabric.

'They said Kjell's dog had something in its mouth, do you remember that? A piece of a green shirt. They thought it belonged to whoever set off the dynamite, that the dog had chased him, tried to catch him or something. It has to be the same shirt.'

'Yes,' Sander said. 'It definitely looks that way.'

'I knew it at the time, when I found it.' Jakob rubbed the fabric contemplatively between his thumb and index finger. 'He was wearing this, the guy I saw, the one who ran by on the trail. I saw the pale stripes. I could see them even though it was dark.'

'But you don't have any idea who it was?'

'No, I do,' Jakob said, looking at Sander with concern in his eyes, as though he wished he didn't have to say more. 'I do have an idea.'

63

In time, a truth took shape about the landslide, and it revolved around Sten Persson, Killian's father. Just about everyone knew he was behind the sudden explosion in the night, and the resulting disaster.

There were also other hypotheses, if that was the right word. One of them had to do with Filip, but Sander had always struggled to believe it, even though he had personally handed that piece of paper over to the cops.

'But Filip was at a party in Årnilt when it happened,' he said to Jakob, who was currently sitting in his wife's dedicated seat at the kitchen table.

Jakob was still holding the shirt. Now that he'd revealed its existence to his childhood friend, he seemed unsure of what to do next.

'But he couldn't have been there all night. I saw him.'
'Are you sure it was him?'
'Well, no, not one hundred percent.'
'You think he would have tried to kill his own parents? Why?'
Jakob shrugged.
'Maybe something went wrong, it didn't go the way he planned. Or maybe he didn't know they were at home. I tried to ask his dad about it, maybe a year before he died, and I showed him the shirt, but it was no use. The booze ruined Karl-Henrik, he didn't even recognize me. He thought I was some con man who wanted to steal his farm, which he didn't even own anymore. Totally out of it.'

'So it's true that he drank himself to death?'

'He had a heart attack. Untreated diabetes, but of course that was because he hit the bottle so hard.'

'Damn.'

'I know.' Jakob shook his head. 'A whole family, just wiped out. Well, of course Lillemor is still alive, but, you know . . . I'm guessing you saw her at the funeral.'

'He didn't say anything at all that time, though? Karl-Henrik, I mean.'

'He was absolutely convinced it was Sten.'

Sander's gaze was firm and direct. 'And it was, wasn't it?'

'Yeah,' Jakob said, folding the shirt gently. 'Maybe this doesn't mean anything.'

'Have you had it this whole time?'

'I didn't know what else to do with it. For years I forgot I even had it.'

'You never considered turning it over to the police?'

'No, I did – years ago, when Alice and I were getting ready to move to our current place. I found it in a box and thought, well, what the hell, maybe I should give it to the police. Better for them to have it. But then I heard the Oskarström station had closed and Gerd Pettersson was retired. Siri, if you remember her, she didn't stay. I didn't know who else to turn to, so I just never got around to doing anything. I didn't think about it much either, it was so long ago. And everyone agreed Sten did it. But now that Filip . . . oh, I don't know. I just happened to think of it tonight. You know, out there, everyone, I know it's not a fresh wound or anything, like people sometimes say. But it still hurts. So I just wanted to take care with this.'

It still hurts. The words flew past Sander like sparks. If he reached out to touch them, his hand would be singed.

'Why didn't you hand it over when you found it, though?'

'Everything was chaos after the landslide. I just never got around to it. Everyone wanted to move on.'

Sander watched him dubiously. Was that true? A thought flared inside him, a possibility he hadn't recognized before.

'You should turn it over now,' Sander said. 'There might still be traces on it.'

Jakob picked at the label on his bottle.

'Maybe that's why I came here. To hear you say that.' He seemed to be considering his words carefully before he spoke again. 'Didn't Filip write something about blowing his house sky-high?'

'Kind of, but not in so many words. The police questioned Filip, I know, and after that they were pretty sure it was Sten.'

'Oh. Okay then. It's a goddamn mess, in any case.' Jakob finished his beer and exhaled loudly, as if trying to expel something. 'By the way, is it true you still haven't been to his grave? Killian's?'

'No. I've been there.'

'Good. That's good for you, I imagine.'

'That's what my therapist says too.'

'You go to therapy?'

'My wife thought we needed to. Apparently I have a hard time opening up about certain things.'

'That's understandable, after everything you went through. Isn't it?'

'Sure, but it doesn't help. Understanding why you have problems doesn't make those problems go away. At least, not always.' He considered something, glanced at the bundle Jakob had placed on the table between them. 'That looks kind of large to me. Filip was pretty slight. Didn't you have a shirt like that?'

Jakob was taken aback.

'No, no. Filip did.'

'I seem to recall you did.'

'No, I didn't.'

Outside the kitchen window, the light was finally fading. Twilight over Halland.

Jakob had said something more, but his words were far off, muffled.

'What was that?'

'Oh, I was just saying, Filip too now. Almost makes you wonder who's next. Or maybe you don't think that way? Like it's not actually over yet?'

Sander turned to face him. 'Are you afraid?'

Jakob looked down. 'I'm thinking about Alice and the children and so on. I'm not afraid, but . . . well, I guess I am a little. Aren't you?'

He had survived once. Those few times an invisible hand had been about to suffocate him, he'd gasped for air and tried to make it look like he was breathing normally.

Survival: the most basic instinct. To think that it could bring about such a deep sense of guilt.

64

As the evening and night wore on, the picture began to take shape. A certain Sten Persson had been buried earlier that day, Vidar learned. Killian Persson's father.

Filip had attended both the service in the chapel and a portion of the reception at the village hall. Then he left to go to work. But he never turned up there. Instead, it seemed, he had stopped his company van along the road where his childhood home used to be, stepped into the young, green foliage, and was beaten to death.

Vidar clicked his pen, crossing out names of witnesses and tipsters. Some had nothing of value to share, while others he hadn't been able to reach yet because it had gotten too late.

He yawned as he sat in the car. He bought new washer fluid and a to-go cup of coffee from the twenty-four-hour gas station in Sånnarp. The digital clock in his car said it was seven minutes past one in the morning. Eighteen degrees Celsius outside. He watched cars pull into and out of the station. Men and women climbed out, filled up, purchased midnight snacks.

He leaned against the headrest and drank his coffee, closed his eyes. He'd been thirty years old back then, in 1999, still in uniform as a patrol officer. He remembered the landslide – he'd been there as a small cog in the great relief effort over the following days. It looked as if a bomb had gone off, he recalled. All that was left of the area was a crater. Now the main suspect, Sten Persson, was deceased.

He thought about Filip Söderström and the rap sheet he'd read through this evening: assault and intimidation, possession and larceny, often all at once; the most recent was from five years ago. Filip was kicked out of Billiards & Bowling in town any number of times, drunk and irate after a fight not even the instigators could come up with a reason for. He drove under the influence, crashed, was taken to the station in a patrol car. He threatened his father, tried to steal cash from his mother, fell asleep on a park bench and had to be woken by a security guard at dawn. He had spent time renting a room from a known addict on Maratonvägen and later lived with women considerably older or alarmingly younger than him. Eventually he gained firsthand experience of several prisons in southern Sweden, then spent a long time at Rasmusgården, a rehab facility outside Falkenberg. The signs were crystal clear: he was going downhill fast.

But then, clearly, something changed. For the last few years his record was a blank where you expected to see another page or two. Change took time, but there must have been a catalyst somewhere. Vidar underlined Rasmusgården and added a question mark next to it.

Four years ago, Filip was listed as 'gainfully employed', and the house in Skavböke became his official address last winter. Often there was a woman to thank when a man suddenly shaped up, but Vidar didn't see anything to indicate he had a partner; there was nothing about that in his interviews or the database. No signs in his home, either, according to the initial report from the officers on scene there.

They should be getting in touch again soon, incidentally. Unless they decided to wait until morning.

Vidar opened his eyes, bolted down the rest of the piping-hot coffee, and brought his phone to his ear.

'I'm calling about an old case,' he said when someone picked up. 'A homicide in Skavböke, 1999.'

The detective on duty yawned and hit some keys. 'Okay, here it is.'

'Can you give me the names of the investigators?'

The man on the other end muttered and clicked at his computer. 'There were quite a few, both out in Oskarström and here in town.'

'Who was it in Oskarström?'

'Gerd Pettersson, she died a few years ago. And Siri Bengtsson.'

Vidar jotted down the names. 'No perpetrator apprehended,' he said, 'if I recall correctly.'

'Suspect deceased, it says here.' He clicked again. 'Killian Persson. But it seems to be an open case, still.'

'Can you check if it's been digitized?'

A pause. An old American car rumbled into the station. The driver, a young man, got out to adjust the tire pressure. A couple was entwined in the back seat; Vidar could see their silhouettes in the glow of the station lights.

'No, it hasn't. It's still in the boxes.'

Boxes, Vidar thought. *Dusty old boxes, yet again.* 'Can you have them sent up?'

'Consider it done.'

Vidar's phone beeped as a call came in. For a moment he considered ignoring it and simply going home to see Patricia instead. They were supposed to split a bottle of wine on the patio eight hours ago.

He accepted the call.

'Oh, hello,' came a familiar voice that was much less frenzied than last time. 'This is Adrian al-Hadid from patrol. We're still out here, my shift is almost over, but I wanted to stick around until you arrived.'

'Go home and get some sleep. I won't be there until tomorrow anyway.'

'No,' Adrian said with an unexpected air of authority, as though he had grown ten feet taller out there in Skavböke. 'I really think you'd better come now.'

65

As it turned out, it wasn't quite true that Filip Söderström had moved into Frans Ljunggren's house and left everything where it was. He had discarded quite a bit of old furniture and bought some new pieces and even repainted the bedroom.

The patrol officers kept watch by the police tape while the technicians found evidence of a bachelor's simple life: dirty laundry in a faded blue IKEA bag, an unopened package of condoms in the nightstand, and half a six-pack of near-beer in the fridge.

But that wasn't all. They also found signs of a structured daily life, like a trash-sorting system under the sink and thriving houseplants. You got the impression Filip had honestly done the best he could with what he had.

Vidar advanced slowly through the creaky old house. Wide floorboards, a low ceiling. Cramped rooms. A wardrobe with wrinkled shirts on a row of identical hangers. He gently ran a hand along them.

The techs were still going from room to room. Cameras clicked. Low voices conversed.

'We're almost done,' one of them said. 'But there's not much to write home about in here. Just the stuff you'd expect to find. Well, that and his planner.' The tech handed over an ordinary daily planner with a blue plastic cover. 'It was on the dresser.'

Vidar tentatively picked it up and paged through it. Few notes, most of them work-related, it seemed. On the day of Filip's death, the entry read *Funeral SC 12:00 Work 1:30*.

SC. Skavböke Chapel, presumably.

'Nothing to suggest anyone else has been here recently?'

'Not in here, at least. I don't know how it's going out in the garage.'

The garage had once been a workshop. Filip had moved all of Frans's old junk to one side to make room for his car. A workbench with too many little drawers to count and a cabinet full of tools and equipment crowded alongside barrels, lumber, and what seemed to be the remains of a car engine on four pallets. It smelled like wood and metal, like an old construction site. Vidar studied the cluttered tool bench, wondering what had belonged to the old man and what was Filip's.

'Over here,' Adrian said dully.

The young officer was so exhausted that he drooped like a dried flower. He nodded at the other tech, who was crouching down, holding a few cotton swabs in her gloved hands. Her attention was on the gardening tools that leaned against the wall like a giant, sprawling bouquet: crowbars, spades, hoes, shovels, and rakes.

The tech ran a swab along an old-fashioned spade, a heavy one. It had a well-worn wooden shaft, an iron handle, and a blade flaking with rust and age.

'Blood,' she said. 'Human. I'm no expert when it comes to blood, but I'd say there's some old and some fresh. And fingerprints as well, along the shaft.'

'Recent ones?' Vidar asked.

'Recent and old, I think. Both.'

'Is it the murder weapon?'

The technician had been having a hectic morning even before the call came from Skavböke. By the time Vidar arrived, she'd been on duty for twenty hours. She blinked, feeling the lack of sleep.

'The blade matches the wounds on his head, in any case.'

'Who found the spade?'

The technician nodded at Adrian, who blushed.

'I noticed there was something on it and spoke up, that's all. He seems to have wiped the blade farther down, but not very carefully. He must have been in a hurry, because he didn't even notice these tiny spatters higher up. Or maybe he didn't care. See for yourself.'

Vidar leaned over and saw the streaks at the bottom, and dark-red freckles closer to the top.

'Wonder what he used to clean it.'

'We haven't found anything yet,' Adrian said. 'But the garage door was unlocked when we got here. According to the people we spoke to, Filip only locked it when the car was parked inside. Otherwise he left it open.' Adrian looked like this was the craziest thing he'd ever heard. 'Apparently that's common out here.'

'Was it open,' Vidar said, 'or unlocked?'

Adrian consulted his notes. 'Unlocked. That's how I interpreted it. Closed, but unlocked. So he must have come here afterwards to leave the spade here.'

'Leave it,' Vidar said, 'or put it back.'

Adrian opened his mouth but didn't say anything.

'There.' The tech stood up. She handed four test tubes to Adrian. 'Take these in right away. Tell them to start processing them immediately.'

'Did you see his planner, by the way?' Adrian asked. 'I had a minute to take a quick look on my break.'

'You're supposed to rest during breaks.'

Adrian ignored this.

'There's nothing remarkable in it, as far as I can tell. Work, parties, birthdays, stuff like that. But I did notice a day in June was labeled with a number one. People with drinking problems do that sometimes, mark their first day of sobriety. I mean, that's not necessarily what it was for, but considering his history. I didn't see any signs of hard drinking here in the house – kind of the opposite, in fact. Maybe he just had a short relapse, and whether that's of any significance, I have no idea.'

'The samples,' the tech barked. 'Now. Get going.'

Adrian gave a curt nod and left the garage. Outside, morning rose with a yawn.

'We'll be getting the new machines this fall,' the tech said, making sure her vinyl gloves were still intact. 'Then we'll be able to do rapid testing in the van and get an answer right away. This is how we have to do it until then, but we're pretty fast. You should have an answer by the time you get to work tomorrow. The fingerprints will take a day or two, though.'

Vidar examined the workbench again, the walls covered in tools and equipment. The perpetrator had been here. After the fact. He looked around, breathing slowly. There was a noise. It took a moment for him to realize it was his phone. Who the hell was calling at this hour?

'Hi there, little old me again,' came the duty detective's happy-go-lucky greeting. 'Sorry to be calling so late – or maybe it's early. Anyway, I figured you were still at it. Two things. The boxes are outside your office as we speak. I went down to get them myself; it was faster that way. You've got quite the stack waiting for you.'

'Nice.' Vidar sent up a grateful thought to the worker bees on call. 'What was the second thing?'

'Someone's here asking for you.'

'Right now? Who is it?'

'A . . .' the man said, reading from a piece of paper, 'Sander Eriksson. Seems pretty urgent. And he's a bit agitated, if you ask me, he hasn't gotten a lot of sleep. So it must be important.'

66

Bizarre, Vidar thought later, as he stood on the street and watched the slim man vanish slowly into what was left of the Halland summer night. Light had long since begun to return, and the birds were up and bursting with song.

Vidar went up to his office and found four boxes outside the door. Inside them, it was December of 1999. He ran his hand over them, too exhausted to work but far too curious to leave the boxes be.

Bizarre. Was that ever the right word.

It had still been stuffy, the air stale, in the lobby where Sander Eriksson was waiting for him.

'Can we sit outside?' Sander wondered. 'It's cooled off now. Somewhere nearby?'

They left the building in silence and settled on a bench in Norre Katts Park. The rotunda up on the hill was closed, but faintly illuminated. Colorful garlands hung from the trees. A group of young people were still hanging around on the small stage, holding cans and bottles. Some sort of banner had fallen to the ground.

'I'm not quite sure what was going on up there,' Vidar remarked, mostly just to have something to say.

'I read in the paper that it was supposed to be an evening of poetry.'

'Nice,' Vidar said, as though he didn't understand what that entailed.

'Not a poetry fan?' Sander said.

'Oh, I am.' Vidar smiled. 'I'm just not so sure poetry likes me back.'

'Same here. My wife is the one who got me to appreciate it. It took a while.'

'I had actually been planning to get in touch with you tomorrow. But this is fine, too, of course. I heard from my colleague that you wanted to talk to us.'

Sander looked at his hands like something might be written there, some instructions.

'My family's in Kivik on vacation, and I was supposed to head back there right after the funeral service. I only came here for the day. But then I ended up stuck in the house for a bit. And then Jakob Lindell dropped by. You guys had talked to him.'

'He came to see you in Skavböke?'

'No, in Snöstorp. That's where I live. And I . . . I don't know, he brought this shirt with him. Did he give it to you?'

'Why would he give us a shirt?'

'Because I told him he should.'

'No, he didn't. What about it?'

Vidar posed the question as though it were no big deal, but Sander's face was pale and when he opened his mouth to speak, he didn't seem to know what words might come out.

'I thought maybe you knew.'

As best he could, Sander recounted what Jakob had told him about the night of Christmas Eve in 1999: the wood in the stove, the figure running by, and the shirt he'd found in the dark. According to Jakob it had belonged to Filip, and a scrap of it had been recovered from a dead dog's mouth. This last detail rang a bell for Vidar. He remembered that. He remembered the rubble, and standing down there with two officers from Oskarström, helping them pry open the dog's jaws. The cracking sound as they gave way.

Beyond that, Sander's story jumped back and forth in fragments, and Vidar had a hard time piecing them into a whole.

By now Sander had his elbows propped on his knees, like he was trying to control an increasing wave of nausea.

That's when Vidar realized what was plaguing Sander. He should have waited for Sander to say it himself, but the long workday and its many conversations had worn down his patience. He slipped:

'You don't believe it's entirely true. What Jakob Lindell claims.'

'No, I think he's lying.'

'How come?'

'I don't know how much you know about what happened that Christmas.'

'Not much, so far,' Vidar admitted. 'I know people say Sten Persson caused the landslide, but the police never had the evidence. He'd been at odds with Karl-Henrik Söderström.'

'There were rumors about Filip too,' Sander said.

'Right, some sort of threatening letter?'

'He was sixteen and he had just lost his brother. He was in crisis. It wasn't a threatening letter, not really, and teenagers write all sorts of shit anyway. I should know – I'm a teacher. For one thing, Filip was at a party on the other side of our community when it happened. The only reason to think Jakob saw Filip is that Jakob himself is so sure it was him. No one else saw Filip at all that night. For another thing, Jakob said he found the shirt when he tripped over it. But how the hell do you trip over a shirt? It just falls to the ground. You don't trip over a shirt, you step on it. Besides, why didn't he hand the shirt over to the police? He must have known it was significant. And another thing – I knew Filip back then. He never wore a flannel like that, only T-shirts and hoodies. I don't even know if he owned that kind of shirt. Jakob, on the other hand,' he continued, 'wore flannels a lot.'

Vidar began to ask some gently probing questions: So Jakob had brought the shirt with him to Sander's house? How was he storing it? What did it look like? What did he do with it after showing it to Sander?

The kids up by the rotunda were starting to trickle back home. One of them seemed to have fallen asleep, to the others' annoyance. They tried to wake him up by aiming the stage lights in his face, but it didn't work. They ended up throwing the banner over him like a blanket, until he began to squirm and bat his hands in irritation.

'So,' Vidar said, having finally arrived at the simplest yet perhaps most important question of all, 'what do you think? Why did Jakob tell you this, if it was all lies? And why now?'

Sander didn't say anything for a long time.

'People always said it was one of my close friends who killed Mikael.'

'Killian,' Vidar supplied.

As though he were putting his thumb on a nasty bruise and pressing down.

'I never wanted to believe it was him. Or maybe it's more like I had trouble believing it was him. I think it was someone else.'

'No one wants to think their friend could do a thing like that. Wasn't it true that they had a fight at that party, Mikael and your friend?'

Sander shook his head.

'Mikael and *Jakob* had a fight. And there was a burglary too,' Sander went on, 'that same night. Fifty thousand kronor went missing from Jakob's family's house. After the landslide, the money was found at Killian's place. But if it was Killian, why didn't he take it with him when he left? He could have used it.'

'You mean someone might have put the money there after the fact?'

'It's just never made any sense to me. What if it wasn't Killian, but . . . well, what if it was Jakob who killed Mikael, what if he's the one who set off the dynamite at the Söderströms' and caused the landslide? What if the dog took a bite out of his shirt? He might have realized it would get out eventually, so he held on to the shirt to frame someone else – someone who can no longer defend themselves.'

'Sounds pretty convoluted,' Vidar said. 'Why would he do that?'

'For the money? I don't know. For Felicia, maybe?'

'Felicia?'

But Sander didn't say more; instead he gazed at the park, toward the Nissan and its still, cool waters, past the bike trail.

'Is that the sun coming up?'

'Yes,' Vidar said. 'It is.'

They got up and walked back toward the station.

'By the way,' Vidar said, before they parted ways. 'What did you wear?'

Sander stared at him, puzzled. 'What?'

'Did you used to wear flannels back then?'

Sander regarded him for a long time. 'Yes, on occasion.'

'On occasion,' Vidar repeated, like he was testing the truth content in his mouth.

'But never one like that.'

'Good to know.'

67

He drove home to Marbäck, got a few hours' sleep, then woke up and kissed Patricia, who was dozing in one of the loungers in the yard. They had met when they were young and had one child, Amadia, who had moved out several years ago now and would be starting an architecture program at the university down in Lund in the fall. Until then, she was living in town, which meant Vidar and Patricia had their big house in Marbäck all to themselves. Most of the time it was cozy and quiet there, but Vidar would have loved to start days like this one by hugging his daughter.

Instead, he sat down on the lounger next to Patricia's and spent some time just relaxing in the sunshine.

'How'd it go yesterday?' she asked.

'Iffy. We're going to have our work cut out for us.'

She reached out and stroked his cheek with a gentle smile. 'You'll figure it out. You always do.'

He smiled back and took her hand.

'Yeah, maybe. But I don't really feel like it.' He took a good look at his wife, who was stretched out in a bikini and sunglasses, bearing an astonishing likeness to her twenty-five-year-old self. 'You look outrageously hot.'

'I know. I love you too.'

'I love vacation,' Vidar muttered, bending over her for another kiss before he took off with exhaustion hanging like shadows under his eyes.

*

When Vidar pulled into the farmyard, it was lunchtime. Someone, maybe a customer, was just taking off in an old Volvo station wagon with rusty spots all over its grille and hood. At the wheel, a glimpse of an elderly man with a furrowed face; Vidar thought for a moment he looked familiar, but the context escaped him.

The house was in Nydala, near the nature reserve in Fäberga. It was a two-story building made of weather-beaten wood that had turned gray over the years. Vidar passed a black mailbox and parked next to a big white Mercedes SUV. A gravel path led to a small studio in a remodeled old barn, where, according to her minimalist website, the woman he was looking for did all her work. The barn was trimmed with white and the double doors were heavy and black but currently open. In one corner of the vast yard was a swing set, and colorful outdoor toys were scattered on the lawn.

The sun burned the back of his neck, warmed the ground. Gravel crunched beneath his shoes. He yawned and heard dull thuds coming from the studio, rhythmic and somehow pleasant. A radio blared summery music. All manner of wooden furniture crowded alongside raw materials and workbenches inside.

Vidar stepped into the studio. Patches of sun on the concrete floor led him to a tiny woman crouching in front of a bureau. In her hand was a hammer the size of her forearm, and she turned her head when she noticed him. Vidar had expected her to be alarmed, or at least surprised, but she simply put down the hammer and came to greet him with a cool distance, as though Vidar were just another customer, one she didn't really have time to deal with.

'I apologize for showing up unannounced,' he said, offering his free hand. 'I'm Vidar Jörgensson.'

Her eyes dropped quickly to the binder in Vidar's other hand before she accepted the greeting.

'Siri Bengtsson,' she said, gazing steadily at him with clear brown eyes.

She was about his age, he knew that much. They'd met in the rubble out in Skavböke. Her thick, dark hair was streaked with gray these days, and time had left its mark at the corners of her eyes, but that was all. She was tough and tenacious, he could tell from her shoulders and arms. She was wearing a sleeveless top and work overalls, clogs.

'Nice studio. Did he buy anything?'

'Who?'

'The man who was just here.'

'Oh. No, he was just looking. Most of them are.'

She went back to the bureau, bent down, and gently ran her hand over the wood as if to examine it.

'Studio,' she echoed. 'That's a nice way of putting it. But it's really just a barn.'

The ceiling was open to the roof and the walls were lined with well-maintained tools that Vidar recognized from the barns of his childhood in Marbäck.

'I don't have a barn, but my dad did. I have to say, it didn't look like this. Aside from the tools. You're a cop, right?'

'Definitely not.'

He could tell that Siri Bengtsson had guessed from the start that he had come to talk about that portion of her life.

'But you used to be.'

'A long time ago, and it was a very short stint. I'm betting you want to talk about Filip Söderström. I'll warn you right now that I've forgotten most of the details.'

Vidar gave her a long stare. 'We haven't released his name to the public.'

'What you did release was plenty.'

They'd tried to anonymize the information, but it was hard. Modern media was a lot faster than the old kind. A middle-aged man, originally from the area in which he had been found, background of petty crime and drug abuse. And Skavböke. His name and photo had already popped up in the murkier corners of the internet, alongside details of the misfortunes that had befallen his family once upon a time and wild speculation about what was going on now.

'Actually, it's Filip's brother I most want to talk to you about. Or hear you talk about, rather.'

Something new appeared in Siri's gaze, what was it, pain of some kind? A distasteful memory returning back to her? Maybe he was seeing things. It disappeared just as swiftly, a spark of something he couldn't identify.

Siri's phone was on the bureau. She picked it up and checked something. 'You think the murders are related.'

'I think they might be.'

'You quit the force too, I heard,' she said.

'That's right.'

'But then you came back.'

As if the man in front of her were a riddle she wanted to solve.

'Yes. Which I regret, on days like these.'

She tilted her head and smiled for the first time since his arrival.

'No, you don't.' She looked around like she might see something in the barn that could help her make up her mind. 'What I'd really like is for you to leave, but I realize you're not going to. If I answer your questions as honestly and thoroughly as I can, will you be satisfied?'

'Honestly and thoroughly. Then I'll leave. Agreed.'

She nodded.

'Go ahead.'

68

They sat in wicker chairs in one corner of the barn. A flourishing plant sat on the table between them. Vidar recognized it as elephant's ear, one of the few plants he could name. Next to the pot were magazines about carpentry and interior design, all cheerful, hopeful cover photos. Vidar placed his black binder on top of them.

'I haven't sat in a chair this comfortable in a while,' Vidar said.

'There's no need to flatter me.'

'How did you come to be a carpenter?'

'It's a long story. Or maybe not. The station in Oskarström closed in January of 2005, after a decision was handed down from Halmstad. I'm sure you knew that. I had already quit by then, must have been, what, two years before that? But right around the time it closed I ran into Gerd. She was packing boxes at the station and asked if we could grab coffee. Sure, okay, I said, but I was kind of reluctant.'

'What did she want?'

'Just to visit. Nothing in particular.' Siri's gaze darted, just for a second. 'I didn't know what I wanted to do with my life, really, all I knew was I never wanted to work for the police again. This was before I met my husband, before the kids. Authority-style work in general – I didn't really like it. Gerd said I was good with my hands, she had noticed that somehow, don't ask me why. She suggested I try to take up some kind of craft. Weave rugs or whatever. That's actually how it started. But I like a little noise too. Weaving was too quiet. Cabinet-making and furniture restoration is a good fit.'

Vidar felt the chair with one hand. Stable, hardy. As though time would only make it stronger.

'I imagine you charge good money.'

'Very good money. But I'm also really good at what I do.'

'I can imagine that too. Speaking of boxes...' Vidar knocked on his binder. 'That stuff Gerd was packing up, I think I've unpacked it again. And unfortunately, Gerd isn't around to talk to me.'

'So you want to ask me about them.'

Vidar couldn't tell if this was a question or a statement. 'What do you think happened?'

'When?'

'On the night Mikael Söderström was killed.'

A fragile silence. 'What do you think?'

A good question. He'd been expecting it.

'It's remarkable you two got as far as you did, given your limited resources. The way I see it, most of the evidence suggests you were right. Killian Persson was the killer.'

Siri crossed her legs and leaned back. Maybe she was wondering if this was his real opinion or just something he was saying to mollify her.

'Most of the evidence,' she repeated. 'But not all of it.'

'That's not unusual. In fact, my first question has to do with exactly that. Suspect deceased, it says somewhere in here. But even so, you didn't close the case.'

Siri shook her head and looked at him, perhaps hesitating one last time. Then she began to think, fumbling way back in her memory.

'The prosecutor agreed to keep it open. Gerd and I both felt there was good reason to, partly on account of the landslide. I seem to recall some information came to light, something relevant to the sequence of events.'

'Like what?'

It wasn't easy to remember. Vidar could see it on her face.

'The money, for instance. We only found it after the fact. And even though it strengthened our suspicions against Persson rather than pointing to a different perpetrator, we didn't know if more information would turn up, new circumstantial evidence. But there were other uncertainties too. There was . . . shit, I don't remember.'

'I know this isn't easy,' Vidar said gently. 'But you know how it goes, I have to ask.'

'Well, take the phone call, are you aware of that? Placed from the party Mikael was at. Someone called, what was their name, the family with the teen daughter – right, the Grenbergs. The phone rang late at night, from the party. Maybe it's just a random detail, but both Gerd and I felt that call was important.'

'Why?'

'No one at the party admitted to making any phone calls.' The memories seemed to be slowly returning to Siri. 'Neither the mother nor the daughter reported that they'd answered one. Someone was lying.'

'That was your conclusion, that someone was lying?'

'Can you think of any other explanation?'

Vidar smiled mildly and waited.

'The footprints in the snow around the car – we identified two sets, one from Killian Persson and one from Sander Eriksson – even though we were never able to prove they were theirs. But there was a third pair as well, from what we interpreted as a witness. And the money, the family who put their life savings in the kitchen bench. Persson took it, clearly. But why? And why didn't he take it when he left?' A pause. Siri leaned back in the wicker chair. 'You know, it was that kind of stuff that motivated us to keep the case open.'

'Did you get any answers? Some material was still being

logged in the months following the landslide, but after that there's less and less. By that summer, new information had dried up completely.'

'Other cases with better prospects for being solved had to come first. We weren't making any progress. Shocking, isn't it?'

'Not really.'

'Exactly.' Siri studied him. 'So why did you come back?'

He realized he was going to have to respond, but he took his time, as if he had to formulate his answer in his own mind first. Maybe he really did need to.

'I had a thorny path through my career, too, you might say.'

'Yes, so I heard.'

'But I think in the end I realized I needed this. My life was worse when I wasn't on the force.'

Siri seemed to find this answer satisfactory.

'Sander Eriksson,' Vidar said. 'What was he like?'

She considered this.

'Smart. Really smart. Does he still live there?'

'Not in Skavböke, but he lives in Snöstorp.'

'He was planning to go to Stockholm, as I recall. To the university. But sure, maybe it makes sense that he ended up staying. He'd just lost his best friend.'

'And you don't think he had anything to do with the murder of Mikael Söderström? After all, if that shoeprint was his, that places him on the scene. Or with Killian's death?'

She jiggled her foot while she thought.

'In Mikael's case, I honestly don't know. But Killian's? No. He did seem to blame himself pretty harshly the few times I talked to him afterwards, though. I think something happened between them toward the end, but I don't know what it was.'

'Is it true he got together with Felicia Grenberg? Someone mentioned that.'

'Oh, yes, right. He did. They even lived together for a year or two. Haven't you talked to him?'

'Yes – last night, in fact.'

He rested a hand on the binder. At the back was his summary of the conversation with Sander.

'I can guess what you've got there, and I don't want to see it. That wasn't part of our agreement. You were going to leave once you'd asked your questions, and it seems like you've asked. And I answered.' She rose from her chair. 'So if you *are* done, I have work to do.'

Vidar stood up as well, his chair creaking pleasantly. He held out the binder.

'I assumed it would be easier to drop this off rather than convince you to come pick it up. I'll come back tomorrow, if we don't talk in the meantime. You don't have to take a look, but you're welcome to do so and let me know what you think.'

She stared at the binder like it was a threat. Vidar set it down on her chair.

'Was it Skavböke that made you quit?' he asked without looking at her.

'No. I just couldn't handle it anymore. It was time for something new.'

She said this so frankly and simply that at first glance it had to be true. But no. He didn't think this was quite accurate. Vidar could tell there was more to it, but he feared it was buried too deep to uncover.

'Please go now,' she said. 'My husband will be home with the kids in about an hour, and I need to get some work done.'

69

Isidor had just stopped by the independent-living complex in Oskarström to see Hasse Ek. The old man still ranted about shadowy figures who showed up to irradiate him, but after a bad fall on the stairs a couple years ago, he could no longer take care of himself. In the co-op where he lived now, staff were just a corridor away, twenty-four hours a day. It wasn't so bad, Hasse said, since he had a lovely window in his room, the food was good, and his bed was comfortable. Besides, he claimed there was less radiation here. To be sure, a summer temp once tried to install a microwave oven, but Hasse put a stop to it right quick. And it was nice that the priest himself dropped by once in a while.

Filip Söderström's mother, Lillemor, had a room just a few doors down in the same co-op. As Isidor passed it today, the door was ajar and he glimpsed a woman by her side. Felicia Grenberg.

How peculiar, that the body sometimes ceases to understand, that it no longer remembers how to function. Lillemor had a very hard time moving her body; some days she couldn't speak, either. Her eyes were clear and she was obviously conscious, but it was hard to hear what she said. As if the words were too big for her mouth, demanding of her lips and tongue effort they could no longer manage.

Isidor stopped by the door and cleared his throat. Felicia turned around.

'Hello,' Isidor said kindly. 'I just wanted to see how you're both doing.'

'It's . . .' Felicia said slowly, turning to Lillemor. 'It is what it is.'

Isidor nodded. He'd already been by to offer his condolences to Lillemor once, and he didn't know what to say next.

'Just let me know if there's anything I can do.'

That would have to suffice. Neither of the women responded.

Felicia went back to the crossword she was holding: '"Vegas landmark that doesn't exist?" One, two, three . . . six letters. The next-to-last letter is a *g*.'

Lillemor blinked. Made a sound.

'What was that?'

Lillemor repeated herself, louder this time.

'Right. Of course. *Mirage*. Let's see now, "Swede at the dinner table?" eight letters. The first one is the *r* in "mirage."'

It was hard to say what Felicia got out of this. Maybe women needed to stick together because they were the survivors. In Skavböke, it was the men who died. Or maybe she felt guilty about what had happened, for some reason.

Just like me, Isidor thought, and silently went on his way.

It must have been sometime in 2004 when he received a call from Rasmusgården. Isidor hadn't been in the office at the time; as the priest in Oskarström he seldom was. The works of the church are performed among the people, he liked to say, and not in an office. It was arduous work, of course, and he was getting on in years even then, but no one ever said faith would be easy. In fact, not having faith is the much easier way to go. But Isidor was a believer ever so, almost resigned to his status as one.

The woman at Rasmusgården left a message but didn't say why she was calling. Treatment centers seldom did, as eager as they were to protect their patients. If 'patients' was the right word in this context. It probably was.

Isidor called back and was informed that a resident there had been asking for him, time after time. When Isidor heard the resident's name, he jumped in his car and got on the E6 highway heading north toward Rasmusgården.

It was in Skrea, just outside of Falkenberg. Filip Söderström would be turning twenty in less than a month, and he was sitting alone on some patio furniture without cushions, a cup of coffee in front of him. It was him – Isidor recognized him, but barely. All sinewy joints and knobbly bones, cheekbones sharp and protruding like the corners of a triangle, and skin so pale it had taken on a bluish tone. His hair was longer and his features stiffer, grown considerably more weathered and rough in just a few years. His voice was different too – it had lost its verve and, seemingly, its presence. The boy Isidor remembered now sounded dull, slow, and absent.

'I didn't think you'd come,' Filip said, addressing the air in front of him.

Isidor took a seat beside him. 'How are you, Filip?'

'Things haven't been great. But now, here, this is better.' Filip squinted in the sunshine. 'This morning I saw a deer give birth to a baby, what are they called . . . fawn. Nature recreating itself. Just like at home. It's nice.' He lifted his coffee cup in a toast. 'I've discovered I like coffee too.'

Was a confession close at hand? That was all Isidor could imagine, that Filip was about to tell him what had happened during those days and nights in December five years before.

'They said you wanted to see me.'

'They're always saying I need to talk to someone. They suggested you, since you're from home. I guess I wanted to talk to someone who was there.'

'There for what?'

'You know, when everything happened. Back then.'

Isidor cleared his throat. It sounded rather more ceremonious than he'd meant it to. 'Did you play a part in it, Filip?'

'I would like to . . .' Filip began, seemingly ignoring Isidor's question. 'I would like to start over. I don't know if that's possible, but that's what I want. I can't live like this. You know, I spend so much time thinking about everyone who was around back then. About all the stuff that happened. But it's like no one gets it. No one gets that my *brother* was murdered and he was the only brother I had, and he's never coming back. And Mom and Dad, you know, how can I possibly start over? When the very basis of my life just isn't there anymore?'

'That must be incredibly painful,' Isidor said. 'That, and everything that happened after.' He paused. 'Have you thought about writing it down?'

'What do you mean?'

'You could just write about what happened that day. When Mikael died. It might help you process it.'

'But I can't write.'

'You don't have to show it to anyone if you don't want to. It would just be for you, to work through it.'

Isidor waited for a long time, but Filip said no more. He gently placed a hand on the boy's shoulder. He felt the bones there under his shirt, fragile but hard. Filip looked surprised. He touched his chest as though something were growing inside, something he didn't recognize.

Isidor couldn't say how long he sat with his hand on Filip's shoulder. But he believed in forgiveness and mercy, and in letting them develop in their own time.

'I'll be back tomorrow, Filip.'

Stupid, he thought as he walked home from the co-op. *So stupid of me, I never should have gone up there that time. Should have just let him sit at Rasmusgården.* That would have been better. Maybe he'd still be alive today. But how could he say so to someone else? Some burdens had to be carried alone.

And all around Isidor, the merciless summer went on.

70

'Sorry to bother you. The staff said it would be okay.'

A woman turned around to look at him.

Vidar took a step forward.

'Felicia Grenberg, right?' He offered his hand. 'My name is Vidar.'

They shook. Her palm was rough and warm.

'The older man who was just here,' Vidar said. 'I ran into him on the way out. Who was he?'

'Must have been the priest,' Felicia said. 'Isidor Enoksson.'

'That's right. I thought he looked familiar.'

He was the man Vidar had seen leaving Siri Bengtsson's farm in a Volvo.

'Could I talk to you for a bit, Lillemor?'

Lillemor gazed at him blankly. Felicia set her crossword on a table next to the old woman's bed, on top of a stack of books and photo albums. Then she left the room, reluctant as a parent leaving a child alone with a stranger.

Lillemor had been notified of her son's death. It was one of the first actions the investigative team took, and Vidar had been the messenger.

'It'd be good if she likes you,' Markus had said.

'She's about to be told for the second time in her life that her son is dead,' Vidar said. 'There are better ways to make a first impression.'

'Just do your best.'

When he gave her the news, she didn't say or do anything for a long time. As Vidar finally placed his big hand over her frail one, though, and put an arm around her shoulders, she looked at him with what might have been surprise, as if it had been so long since someone touched her she'd forgotten how it felt.

'Lillemor,' he said now. 'It's me, Vidar. From the police. I'm back, just like I said.'

'Yes,' she said.

Vidar looked at the crossword Felicia had left behind.

'"Swede at the dinner table." What do we think?'

Lillemor produced a word. It sounded a little like 'roo bake.'

'Totally agree. Want me to put it down?'

He picked up the crossword and took out his pen, wrote in *rutabaga*. Lillemor's eyes followed. There was nothing the matter with her mind.

'Well,' he said, 'I have some information for you, as I promised, and one question. Let's take care of the information first.'

Lillemor made a noise like 'mm'.

'We're still trying to figure out what happened and why. My colleagues only just finished with Filip's house this morning, so it's still very early in the investigation. We know more now than we did before, but not by much. As soon as I have anything else to share, I'll come visit again. That's a promise.'

He paused. She waited.

'So,' Vidar said, after a silence that felt longer than it was. 'To my question. Filip moved into an old house up in Skavböke.'

'*Flonk Yungerns.*'

'Frans Ljunggren's, exactly. Were you ever there? In Filip's house?'

It took a long time for her to express herself. 'Once or twice. Hard for me.'

'Hard how?'

'Physically. But memories too.'

'Of course. I understand. Were you ever out in the garage? Do you remember what it looked like?'

'A little.'

'He had tools there. You know, shovels and rakes and so on. Do you remember that?'

'Yes.'

'What I'm wondering,' Vidar said, taking out a folder that held a photograph, 'is if you recognize this.'

She looked at the picture. 'House.'

'Yes, that's right. We took this picture at Filip's house.'

'Spade.'

'Yes.'

She didn't say anything for a long time, only speaking up again just as Vidar was about to move on.

'Garage?'

'Yes, it was in the garage.'

'Never sawt.'

That didn't mean much. The spade had been in plain sight, but it was just one of many tools. Nothing that would catch the eye.

'Now I have another question. It's about Filip and your husband, Karl-Henrik.'

He thought he saw Lillemor move suddenly. He couldn't say if it had really happened or was just a flicker of his eye.

'Did the two of them ever discuss the landslide together?'

A sound like a strangled cough came from Lillemor's mouth. She tried to say 'Sten Persson.'

'It was Sten Persson,' Vidar said slowly. 'That's what they said?'

'Mm.'

'And do you think so too?'

A growing silence. Vidar waited.

'Who else?' she said at last – a good question, and it was his job to answer it.

At the tip of Vidar's tongue was another name. Jakob Lindell. He wanted to float it as a question, to test the idea. But he couldn't, it would be too risky, so he said nothing.

Vidar had accomplished all he came for. He looked at the crossword again.

'Free of clocks,' he said, counting. 'Eight letters.'

After pondering for a moment, Lillemor replied, 'Timeless.'

Vidar picked up the crossword and entered it.

That was when he noticed something under the newspaper. A thick photo album bound in burgundy velvet. It looked full. Vidar tentatively picked it up. 'Is this yours?'

'Yes.'

'Do you look at it often? You and Felicia?'

'She shows me.'

'May I have a peek?'

Lillemor nodded weakly, and when Vidar opened the album he found scenes from the past, moments from a life that no longer existed. Dinners, parties, holidays. In one of the pictures, someone, probably Karl-Henrik, was dressed up as Santa Claus.

He stopped on one page and paused for a second, perhaps a fraction too long.

'What beautiful pictures,' he managed to say, his voice quaking. 'Could I borrow this?'

Long seconds passed. Lillemor's eyes grew oddly blank. When she finally spoke, her voice was thick.

'Take good care of it. It's all I have left.'

71

If you asked Felicia about her life in the first few years after the landslide, you would get a peculiar comparison in response.

'It was like being shipwrecked,' she liked to say. 'That's what it was like.'

Shipwrecked. It wasn't her usual manner of speaking. The description must have come from someone else, maybe one of the many psychologists or doctors she'd encountered over the years. Or one of the men? If it even mattered. One way or another, the word had been offered to her and she had accepted it the way the injured accept painkillers.

'Hi,' she said bluntly when Sander appeared at her door.

No surprise or curiosity, almost as if she had expected him.

Felicia was wearing denim shorts and a T-shirt with a large bird printed across the chest, the kind of shirt you would buy at the market out by the shore at Östra Stranden. One second passed, then two more, as they simply stared at each other. Then, as if on a signal heard only by them, they smiled and met in a stiff but friendly embrace.

Her body, in his arms, was both foreign and familiar. When they let go of each other, the scent of her hair lingered and he resisted the urge to hug her again.

'I figured you would be showing up. That's why I held off on my walk.'

The air was still comfortable, the worst of the heat yet to gather, and birds whose names he no longer knew soared across the sky. Soon Felicia and Sander were strolling down the gravel path, the mood between them tense and a bit uneasy at first. Although they lived only half an hour apart, on different outskirts of the same small city, they hadn't seen each other in twenty years.

When they did begin to speak, the words were strained. But after a while, the conversation flowed more smoothly; they relaxed and realized, with some relief, that they seemed to get along. They shared a very particular sense of humor, which was perhaps not unusual for two people who also had a tragedy in common.

'You usually take walks,' he said; he meant it as a question but it didn't sound like one.

'Yes, that's my alone time, you know? Good for my well-being.'

He knew she worked at some store in town these days. For a while she had been employed by the clinic as a nurse, until she quit. She'd gotten married, eventually. Sander didn't know the guy, but he'd heard from his parents that the two of them had gotten a divorce a few years back. By that time, they had two kids.

'They're up in Falkenberg with him now. We share custody. It works out pretty well. He's got a new partner up there. Jonathan likes her, Majken doesn't. I guess that's how it goes.'

'Jonathan and Majken. Nice names.'

'You didn't know their names? They'll be fifteen and seventeen this year. Fall babies, both.'

Children, marriage, divorce. Work. All of this – how had it happened? He understood it determined who she was today, and he couldn't connect with it except in a general, abstract sort of way. Their story had begun and ended much earlier.

'It's weird,' she said, 'having kids. Don't you think? You've only just made it through your own childhood, and suddenly you're responsible for someone else's.'

'Yeah.'

He missed Albin and Josefin the minute he was away from them for more than a few hours. He always had, and he wondered if it would ever stop. Parents of adult children often said you never got used to it, you always missed your kids. It was just that the way you missed them changed. Or maybe that was only something they said, and you really did get used to it?

A person can get used to just about anything. He'd learned that much.

Now he remembered. Their life together was coming back to him. Both of them had studied at the college; teacher education for him and nursing for her. They saw each other every morning and evening, spending nights together in their student apartment on Bolmengatan. Hours of desperate intimacy, as if they were trying to free themselves from chains neither understood, followed by arguments and silence, absence.

She took a part-time job at Hemköp, working the cash register, ringing up groceries. She found it pleasant, only having to say one thing, and saying it over and over.

They had been bound together, Sander and Felicia; when Killian died, Sander made a promise to himself always to stay by her side. It was a salve for his conscience; he could pay off his survivor's guilt by filling the hole left by the dead. No one else knew about this promise, perhaps not even Felicia. He'd never mentioned it, after all. The most fervent and significant promises are seldom spoken aloud. But he figured she knew anyway.

She glanced at his wrist.

'You kept that. The bracelet. I can't believe it's held up.'

'It's pretty worn by now, but it would feel strange to take it off.'

'He's the one who made it, right? For a Christmas present?'
'Yes.'
'He told me you threw the package at the wall. You must have changed your mind.'

Twenty years, he thought. Twenty years since they'd last walked side by side. So bizarre. His arm naturally brushed against hers now and then.

'I don't blame you for how things turned out,' she said. 'I used to, of course, but not anymore.'

'You mean . . .'

'Olivia. You don't even have to say anything.' She laughed as though an absurd thought had come to her. 'Oh my God, what were we? Nineteen? Twenty? We were doing the best we could. How long does it take to cheat on someone, a second? Two? And it's done. But the path there, leading up to that moment, it's a lot longer. I was angry because you didn't mention anything during that time. I was wrecked. But after a while, I realized it was about me too. About us. How we couldn't talk about the important stuff.'

Words she got from someone else, Sander thought.

'I suppose that's true,' he said.

He had other memories as well. They showed up like phantom pains.

And then he thought of his recurring dream. It must mean something: the landslide debris, the pressure in his chest, something unfinished. The sound of his own voice as he called out for his dead friend. Then the impulse to dig, all the dirt and muck coming up, the pain in his hands, and he finds something. The shirt Kjell Östholm's dog took a bite out of. He stares at a mask of a face, but not a real face. Suddenly the eyes fly open, and he recoils under Killian's terrified gaze.

'You're at Vallås School, I heard,' Felicia said.

'Yes. I ended up staying. Where do you work again?'

'Åhléns.'

'That's right. I think I heard that somewhere.'

They were walking along the edge of the old landslide. If you forgot about it for a moment, you could see it in the foliage, the growth younger and more tender. Like a scar.

'I thought you were supposed to head back yesterday,' she said then.

'Right after the funeral, was the plan. But . . . now Filip, you know? I had to call Olivia this morning to tell her I have to stay another day, to talk to the police and stuff. It's just weird that it's happening all over again, somehow.'

He was walking around with a feeling in his chest, a sense of something unfinished. He couldn't quite grasp where it came from, but he knew he didn't want to subject Olivia to it, much less the kids.

'That's why I quit nursing, I think. I wanted to help people, thought I would be good at it. And I probably was. But I couldn't handle it.'

'I never believed it was him.'

Felicia looked at him. 'What do you mean?'

'That Killian killed Mikael. For a while I told myself it was him, because it was easier. But really . . . do you think he did it?'

Felicia's voice was suddenly weary, like before.

'We went over this so many times. We can't – does it matter? Like, maybe? Back then, I really didn't think he did it, but then again, I was so in love with him. The kind of love that only happens when you're a teenager. I don't know. If it wasn't him, then who was it?'

That question had nagged at Sander for so many years now. Who had killed Mikael, if not Killian? He had never found an answer, really, and maybe that was an answer in itself. The only option left was Killian.

Right?'

'Jakob came to see me last night,' Sander said.

'Did he?'

'He brought a shirt.'

Felicia listened. When Sander finished his story, he looked at his hands, flexing them as though they were brand-new, or had just been holding some foreign object. Was it going to feel like this every time?

She placed a gentle hand between Sander's shoulder blades and stroked his back slowly. In that moment, he understood why he'd once fallen so hard for Felicia Grenberg.

'I don't know what to say,' she said. 'Are you going to tell the police?'

'I already did.'

'But, what, you think he also killed Mikael?'

'I don't know. Maybe.'

During their time together, Sander had tried to bring up the topic of Mikael on several occasions. How he'd treated Felicia, the assault. She never wanted to talk about it. But it linked Killian to Mikael, it gave him a motive. And Killian had been driving the car that night; the blood on the steering wheel was his. Sander knew that.

'You know,' Felicia said slowly. 'I don't really blame Mikael either. I mean, for what he did to me. Not anymore. He was only doing what Karl-Henrik did to my mom. That was how he was raised to treat women. It took becoming a mother myself to realize that. Isn't that strange too? It's like you become more forgiving when you have your own kids. Killian was the one who realized it, that it all started with Karl-Henrik. Well, and you did too, of course. You were always so clear-sighted when it came to all that.'

Sander didn't respond, didn't know what to say.

'But still, I regret . . . I mean, I never should have let Killian go,' he said, all in the same breath, as though he were both confessing to and denying a serious crime. 'That night, when I was at his house. I should have stopped him.'

'Sander, you can't put that on yourself.'

'I know that. Everyone says so, they always have.'

'Then what's the matter?'

He opened his mouth but found, to his surprise, that he didn't know what to say.

72

Killian was dead. Sander had personally witnessed the urn containing his ashes being lowered into the ground. But the soul is a stubborn being, much more so than the body. It can linger for a long time.

Killian's soul likely did just that, because Sander and Felicia were never really alone on Bolmengatan. Maybe they could have behaved in a different way. Sander knew that; they could have talked about Killian, his life, the kind of person he'd been. That was how folks treated the dead back home in Skavböke, and that was how they remembered Killian's father, Sten, that summer so many years later. They kept him alive, even though he was gone, by talking about him.

The dead can often help the living in that way. Like an invisible ribbon in the air, they encircle those who are left behind and pull them together. But they can also drive a wedge between the living.

So Sander and Felicia could have tried harder to avoid what happened. Or could they? Maybe it only seemed that way. Sander wasn't sure.

Maybe, in fact, the way it went was the way it had to go.

He wondered so many times why he couldn't be happy with Felicia. What he was missing or longed to find. Back home in Skavböke, all he dreamed about was leaving, and, barring that, being anywhere at all with Felicia. The tragedies in Skavböke, not least Killian's death, had brought them together and, sure, their prospects could have been better.

But time healed most wounds, and what couldn't be healed could be endured.

That was the kind of thing love could do. As powerful as death, it is. Wasn't that true of love? And if it wasn't, what was love for?

'You don't want to?' she asked one night.

'No, I do. I don't know what's going on,' he said.

'Do you want to try again?'

He was afraid of failing again, because he wouldn't be able to cope. 'Not tonight. Is that okay?'

'Of course. Hey. It's no big deal.'

His shortcomings. He didn't know why they tormented him so, but they did. She would beg him to go deeper inside her, to the point where her eyes lost focus and her body began to quake seconds before she opened her mouth to scream. But he could only get that deep with his hand. It sounded vulgar when he put it into words, in his mind, but it was like he knew he couldn't go as deep as Killian had. He pictured a hollow space inside Felicia that would forever remain untouched, longing for something she couldn't have.

Sander had tried to accept the responsibility imposed upon him; he wanted to be the man he needed to be, but he no longer knew how. He had no language for it, and without language you become paralyzed. Everything becomes either/or, no conclusion, you come to a standstill.

Silence piled up between Sander and Felicia, sometimes temporarily dissolved by sharp words, bitter fights. He feared they would begin to hate each other, and eventually it felt like they did. Hatred, that was a strong word, but if that wasn't what he was feeling, why was he thinking it?

It came out in the little things: Sander couldn't stand her bad sense of humor and Felicia couldn't stand the way he never wanted to listen to music at home. Sander was tired of how she could never make up her mind about what to wear anytime they left the house, and Felicia was sick of his refusal to wear anything but comfortable everyday clothes. He was annoyed at her new habit of gabbing to her classmates on the phone until late at night, a never-ending chatter, and she was irritated that he wouldn't leave the bedroom lamp on until she had come to bed, too, and that he never wanted to talk when they were lying in bed, only read or have sex. Sander hated that Felicia went out some nights, without telling him where she was going or when she planned to be back; Felicia hated that Sander never talked about his real feelings, would only say everything was fine, as usual, it's fine.

'Some words don't mean a damn thing,' she snapped one night.

'Believe me,' Sander said. 'I know.'

She couldn't stand how self-absorbed he was, stuck so deep inside himself; he couldn't stand how quick she was to burst into tears. He couldn't abide by how impossible it was to satisfy her, and she found it unbearable that he tried so hard. He hated that she was such a terrible liar, and she hated that he forced her to lie. Sander was uncomfortable with how much Felicia talked to her mother, and Felicia despised Sander for being unable to stop talking about the past.

All of this — where did it come from? He suspected she knew the answer as well as he did. Killian remained a silent and invisible presence, as the dead tend to do, and at the same time he swelled like a boil between them. Sander wanted to be free, going so far as to wait at the bus stop in town, on the verge of taking the bus to Oskarström to visit the cemetery and the gravestone that waited in the lush green foliage there. But he couldn't do it.

Or did he, perhaps, not want to be free at all? Was freedom in fact what he feared most of all?

He often saw the chapel in Skavböke in his mind's eye at night, just as he'd seen it on the night of the landslide. Unnaturally large and white, it towered against a clear sky.

'Do you wish you hadn't stayed?' she asked him once.

'Why do you ask?'

'Because of . . . like, this. You seem so . . . you're the one who chose to stay with me, I know that you've said so. But do you regret it?'

'No.'

He no longer knew if he was lying. But he felt that familiar feeling in his body, the urge to flee rising like a fever in the summer night.

73

In the summer of 2002, the search for a missing young man resumed after the police raided an encampment. Sander read about it in the paper and saw a picture of Siri Bengtsson's grim face.

This was also the summer he spent many days at Billiards & Bowling. It was in the basement of a parking garage in town, a building with thick brick walls, countless nooks and crannies. On weekend nights, the line to get in was all the way down the street, but it was a decently comfortable place during the day. Sander would sit down there by himself, with a cup of coffee and his textbooks. When it got late enough, he might have a beer or two.

But tonight he was alone with a book when he heard a voice he recognized.

'Don't get up, I just need to take a leak.'

Sander turned around in time to see the back of someone vanishing into the culvert that led to the restrooms. He was sharing a table with four other young men, empty glasses and packs of cigarettes on the table.

'He's a cagey one, that guy,' one said.

'Yeah. What an odd duck. Can't fucking hold his liquor, either. He pukes every time.'

'He brought a flask, did you see?'

'I bet he can't afford to buy any when he's out. Or maybe there's rat poison inside.'

Then he returned, Filip Söderström, skinny and rangy like

a bag of bones in clothing; he looked beyond unsteady as he sat back down in the booth.

Sander heard Filip guffaw loudly, a drunken racket that made the others urge him to calm down.

'Whaddaya mean, calm down?'

'You're being so fucking loud.'

'Aw. Shut up.'

'What did you just say?'

Filip cocked his head. 'I said, *shut up*. Can you do that?'

A crash, the clatter of tables and chairs. That was how violence began, like a tiny explosion in the dark, out of nowhere. One second everything is still; the next, it's simply there.

One of the men grabbed Filip by the collar and was about to haul him across the table, but it was difficult since Filip was windmilling into the man's face.

'For fuck's sake,' one of the other guys said wearily, trying to protect his bottle of beer from the scuffle. 'Can you just –'

Filip's elbow caught his jaw and cut him off. The man grabbed his face, set his bottle down at a safe distance, and swung a fist at Filip's head.

Filip sagged over the table, still trying to strike back, but he was slower now. He took a blow to the mouth and red droplets flew out. They yanked him out of the booth and Filip's feet slipped around on the floor, his feet scrabbling for balance.

The man holding Filip by the collar was getting ready for a punch or a kick. Then something happened. His grip on Filip's jacket loosened and suddenly the man was down on his back. Filip collapsed too, but he quickly looked up, trying to figure out what was going on.

Next to him stood Sander. He'd jabbed his foot into the back of the man's knee. The man tried to crawl back up, but

Sander grabbed him by the hair, a thin brown mop, made a fist with his free hand, and struck the man in the cheek so hard it made his knuckles crack. Something in the man's face broke, and he began to let out a shrill howl as he fell back to the floor.

Everything stopped. Now that it was over, the staff approached. Filip gaped at Sander, blood trickling from his lip.

'Sander?'

'Hi,' Sander said hoarsely. His hand ached and throbbed.

'You're bleeding.'

Filip gingerly brushed the back of his hand over his mouth and observed the man, who was still lying on the floor and panting.

'I'm fine. Thanks for the help.'

So strange to see him like this, in the dim lighting. Filip asked if he wanted a cigarette, and Sander said no.

'Some fresh air, then?'

'That sounds good. I'll just grab my stuff and pay.'

They emerged into a warm, clear July evening. Filip's cigarette was stained with blood from his lip.

'Good to see you.' He blew out smoke, unbothered by the blood, and looked at the book in Sander's hand. 'What are you reading?'

Sander showed him the cover.

'*The Heart Is a Lonely Hunter*,' Filip read. 'Speaking of, weren't you supposed to go to Stockholm? Please, have a seat.'

He said it as though they were in his kitchen. Sander sank onto the curb next to him. The odor of alcohol was stale but sharp; it mixed with the cigarette smoke.

'Yeah,' Sander said. 'I was supposed to go. But it didn't work out.'

'Why not?'

Each time he met someone he hadn't seen in a long time, the same question: *Weren't you supposed to . . . ?*

'I needed to stay,' he said simply. 'I'm studying to become a teacher.'

'Do you like it?'

'Yeah, I guess.'

Filip offered him a drag of his cigarette. Sander took a look at the bloody filter and declined once more.

'How have you been?'

Sander was asking out of concern, or at least he tried to make it sound that way. Filip chuckled like it was a bad joke.

'You're looking at it. But don't worry about me.' He raised his head to look at Sander. 'You live with Felicia, right?'

'Yeah.'

'But I saw you last week, with a blond girl. Out in Tylösand.'

74

He had told himself that the throngs on the beach at Tylösand would render them invisible. But Halmstad was a small city, in the end, and no affair could go on unnoticed forever. The only question was who would find them out first, and what would happen next.

'What's her name?' Filip asked.

'Felicia and I . . . we've been having a rough time.'

'You don't have to explain yourself to me, I don't care. Anyway, we're all made of the same stuff.'

Stuff, Sander would think later on, or could he actually have said *dust*?

'I've cheated in every single relationship I've had.' Tendrils of bluish smoke rose from Filip's lips. 'If you can call them relationships. But what's her name?'

'Olivia.'

Like he was confessing a sin. That was how her name sounded.

Could it be, Sander had begun to wonder, that sometimes you get so used to living with guilt that when it finally begins to fade, you have to replace it with a fresh source? Even in the gloomier emotions there can be a certain amount of security, and Sander had lived with his guilt about Killian's death for so long that it was as familiar to him as hunger or exhaustion. But without it, he didn't know who he would be, what would happen. Maybe that was why he cheated.

'What were you doing in Tylösand, though?' he asked Filip.

'Swimming, obviously, like everyone else.' Filip laughed at

himself. 'No, I had an errand to run out there. You know how they do an "after beach" there, do you ever go?'

'Sometimes.'

'Some poor bastard sits on a stool playing "Wonderwall" while people get drunk in the sunshine. Sometimes they want to top it off with something a little stronger than alcohol, you know.'

'Good business, I take it?'

'Crazy good. That sheet you tore out of my notebook, remember that? Christ were they ever gunning for me after the landslide, those two cops. Fuck. Hey, I know it was you. It's okay, I'm not angry. Not right now, anyway.'

Sander found Filip's hopscotching between different parts of their past disorienting.

'I never thought you were the one who caused the landslide,' Sander said tentatively, as though he were trying to defend himself against the next accusation. 'Everyone knows it was Sten.'

'Mm.' Filip didn't say anything more for a long time. 'Then why did you give them that piece of paper, you bastard, if you didn't even think it was me?'

'I guess I just wanted to do the right thing. Or I don't know. I just did it. But it would have seemed weird if I hadn't too. Like I was trying to hide something, to protect myself. Or you.'

Filip raised an eyebrow, as if this were a scenario he hadn't imagined. He seemed to be considering what it meant as he finished his cigarette. 'Are you sure you don't want any?'

'I'm fine, thanks.'

'You know Rasmusgården? There's a spot there for me, if I want it; it would probably be good for me.'

'Where is that?'

'Near Falkenberg, I think. You get to spend a lot of time

outside, like on the grounds, I mean. Did you hear about the guy who disappeared, by the way?'

'Who?'

'That guy they're looking for, Hampus Olsson, he went to our school. I saw it in the paper last week.'

'Oh. Yeah, I read something about that. Did you know each other?'

Filip shook his head.

'Not really, it was more like he was just there. But it's *kymig* as hell, isn't it? When people disappear. Maybe it's actually better to know that they're dead.'

Sander realized he was bracing himself. As if his body needed to make him say something before he figured out what it was.

'I'm sorry,' Sander said. 'About what happened, with Mikael and all. I don't think I ever offered my condolences before.'

Filip took one last drag of his cigarette and stubbed it out with his shoe. Exhaled smoke. Blinked, then touched his lip again. He stood up, still unsteady. 'I think I'll go back down again.'

'With those guys? Why?'

'Gotta do something. I'm thirsty. Take care of yourself, Sander.'

'You too, Filip.'

Sander was reeling when he got back to the student apartment. As soon as he took off his shoes and greeted Felicia, he went to the bathroom and took a long shower. The water washed away not only the physical traces of his encounter with Filip but also, he told himself, the remains of something more difficult to articulate.

75

Olivia was – for lack of a better word – different. She had grown up in one of the fancy houses on the hill by the hospital, and when Sander began to chat with her one night when he was out, he realized there was something inside him that had never been fulfilled. For the first time in a long time, he thought about the departure that had never come to pass, the person he could have become. Maybe he could still change his life; after all, he was barely twenty. The idea took root in him, and in Olivia's presence everything seemed new, everything was politics and literature and art, a glimpse of a world he wondered if he would one day be able to make his own. Maybe.

The temptation proved too great. That was perhaps an odd way to put it, but that was how it felt.

In any case, the consequences were perfectly clear, and cold as ice: he began to cheat on Felicia.

Yet he was crushed when his unfaithfulness came to light and Felicia left him.

The hatred, if that's what it had really been, vanished and was replaced by something deeper, murkier. Perhaps it wasn't until that point that he understood it was real, what he'd done, and that he was about to lose her. In its early stages, infidelity takes place within a fragile membrane, in a space the everyday world can't reach. What happens in there will never get out, you tell yourself. Maybe it wasn't even Sander himself in there with Olivia, just someone very much like him. He often thought so after the fact, when he looked at his reflection and wondered who he was seeing.

'I don't want you to go,' he said on the day Felicia moved out, back home to her mother.

Tears in her eyes, she laughed in resignation, apparently amazed at what an idiot he was. 'Sander, it's not just that you slept with someone else. You lied about it for months. I can't stay.'

In that moment, he hated her. Not Felicia – he loved her more than ever – but Olivia. Suddenly she was distorted, a symbol of everything that had gone wrong, all the twisted parts inside him. For a while he avoided her, stopped answering when she called, and stayed away from places she frequented.

Killian was dead; Felicia was gone. Sander entered adult life all on his own, and slowly he sank through the darkness toward the bottom.

When he heard, two months on, that Felicia had started seeing someone else, jealousy began to eat at him, moving through his blood like poison. But it was never pure jealousy; it was always mixed with guilt. This was his fault, all of it. If you traced the events far enough back in time, you would never find any other origin.

His nights were sleepless and his days endless. Everything was falling apart. He loved Felicia. He told himself that his love for her was one of the few constants he'd ever had in life. His happiest moments had been shared with her. How could she not feel the same, despite what he'd done?

He'd had years to prove how much he loved her. Now, without warning, it was too late.

So he sank.

76

Five years went by. Five Midsummers, Christmases, New Years, birthdays; five years of weekdays linked together like the cars of a train. He graduated, got a job, and gained weight. Went to the new gym in Sannarp and lost it again, tried to go on dates and have relationships but found he was always happier on his own.

This was what those five years did to Sander: transformed him into the person he had, perhaps, been all along.

Then came something he didn't expect. It was as if he found a previously undiscovered hatch inside himself. A new portal opened. He tried to take possession of it bit by bit, until his old self let go.

A conquering of sorts.

Then he unexpectedly saw her again, one Thursday at the Coop. Sander had stopped to buy laundry detergent and a new dish brush on his way home from the library. She didn't see him. He had time to notice that there was no ring on her left hand. Which didn't mean much, really. But maybe it was something.

When he picked up the phone that evening, he wasn't sure if she'd even answer.

'Hello?' came a clear, soft voice in his ear.

'Hi. This is Sander Eriksson.'

'Sander Eriksson,' said Olivia. 'It's been ages.'

'Yeah, I know.' He laughed without knowing why. 'I saw you today. At the Coop on Gamletull.'

'You did? But you didn't say hi?'

'I didn't know if I . . . Should I have?'

'Did you want to?'

Seconds ticked by. His heart began to pound.

'Yes,' he said.

'Then I guess you should try again,' she said. 'Next time you see me. At the Coop on Gamletull.'

'On Saturday, maybe?'

She didn't respond for a long time – was she waiting for him to retract the question? When he didn't, she said: 'At seven?'

'At Coop?'

Sander heard her smile.

'We can grab a drink somewhere.'

Olivia was still angry at him. During the awkward period when Sander was still trying to convince Felicia to stay, his guilt wore Olivia's face. He grew cold and dismissive toward her. Nothing fair about that. But does fairness have any place in love? He doubted it. Now, five years on, he felt changed. She noticed it. And he suspected she understood, too, even if she had been hurt.

Perhaps it was impossible to fix everything that had once broken. But in time, they found their way back to each other.

Two years after he saw her at the Gamletull Coop, he proposed. They bought the house on Backavägen three years later, and soon Albin and Josefin arrived. How lovely to find that people could bond over welcome changes, too, he thought. He was so happy, perhaps for the first time.

77

One autumn morning in 2017, Sander was sitting on the terrace his wife thought should be glassed in, reading in the newspaper about a lecture that was planned at the college that same night. 'Law for a New Era' was the headline. Olivia was in the bathroom, and the kids were still asleep. He sat there in the chilly sunshine with no one to turn to.

By this point in their marriage, problems had arisen. Or rather, reappeared. Perhaps that was the right word. He and Olivia had started going to couples' therapy, and the previous day's session was still on his mind. In front of their therapist, a very likable man in his sixties who always wore clogs, Olivia had blurted a frustrated heap of words:

'He closes himself off, he doesn't share his feelings. He doesn't talk. I think it has to do with all the stuff that happened when he was young. It's a trauma he hasn't processed. I've tried to help, but he can't do it.'

'Trauma,' the therapist repeated, as though the word were a stone you could hold up to the light and inspect from many angles.

'His best friend died. It was an accident, but –'

'Sander,' the therapist interrupted in his practiced way. 'What do you think about what Olivia is saying?'

He was silent for a long time.

'Olivia's mom – I mean, your mom, Olivia – is a psychologist. Your father is a principal. You come from a family that talks about everything. You have vocabulary for all the ways you feel. That's one thing I love about you, that it's so simple for you.'

'It's not simple.'

'But you have the language. I don't.'

'You are a Swedish teacher,' Olivia said evenly.

'There are different kinds of languages,' the therapist gently interjected.

'And it's not easy for me to open up like that. I understand that it's expected of me both at home and here, in front of both of you. That's what you two do, Olivia, that's what we're supposed to do in this room, I'm not stupid, I know that.' He took a breath. 'I just can't, I think, even if I want to. For you.'

'For *us*,' Olivia corrected. 'For the *kids*. So they learn that it's good to talk about things. God, sometimes I think you don't even understand that you're a parent. With everything that entails. It's like you're still a teenager, like you got stuck back there.'

But he hadn't. She was wrong.

He wasn't stuck, hadn't been for a long time, and maybe this was what confused him most of all. That it had been possible to move on. You can get used to anything, or endure it for as long as you must.

The words lingered in his mind as he read that page of the newspaper. He recognized the lecturer's name: Ardelius, now Professor Emeritus. The man from Stockholm.

That evening, he holed up in his office and read student papers.

Then he got in the car and went to the college.

The lecture was held in one of the auditoriums he remembered; he'd been here often in the parenthetical era his college years now felt like. Sander felt both very young and much older than he was as he took a seat in the back. True to form, he'd brought a notebook; he opened it to a blank page and clicked his pen. Ardelius was sitting in the front row, paging through his papers. Sander stared at the back of the old man's graying head as if he hoped the professor would feel it.

'Well, let's see if this is worth a listen,' a familiar voice said.

He turned. Indeed, it was him. Older and grayer, of course, just like Sander himself, as though time had brought them closer in more ways than just career-wise.

'Yes, I've heard this speaker is an interesting one,' Sander said with a smile.

Lundström laughed. What followed was a silence between them. His former teacher was the first to break it. 'So you ended up staying.'

There it was again. This time, it was given as a fact.

'Yes, that's how it turned out.'

'Does it feel right?'

'For the most part.'

Lundström nodded as if a hunch had been confirmed. Then they both turned to the retired professor who walked spryly to the podium and adjusted the microphone. The room fell silent.

'Is it true that you became a teacher?' Lundström whispered.

'Yes. Swedish and English.'

'Why?'

'I'm not really sure. It just happened.'

The professor's talk went on for forty-five minutes. Then he stopped abruptly – perhaps he'd been living according to the university timetable up in Stockholm for so long that it was part of his internal clock now.

'Right,' he said. 'That's that. Thank you.'

Now and again, Ardelius had looked up from his notes to

search the sea of faces. He'd squinted up at the corner where Lundström sat and seemed to nod in recognition. Sander couldn't tell if the professor recognized him too.

There was a Q&A period. By the time that was over, it was almost eight thirty and the audience was quick to exit the auditorium. Sander hovered behind Lundström, who walked down the steps and approached the podium. A bright gleam in those cool, intelligent eyes.

'John,' Ardelius said. 'Good evening. I'm so glad to see you.'

Lundström offered his hand. The old man took it warmly between his own.

'It's been ages.'

'Yes, perhaps it has. Time is strange, when you're old.'

While they chatted, Sander lingered nearby, waiting. After a moment, the professor turned to look straight at him. Sander stepped forward.

'I just wanted to say hello. I don't know if you remember me.'

Ardelius squinted behind thick glasses. 'No, I'm afraid I don't. I'm sorry.'

'Eriksson,' he said hesitantly. 'Sander.'

The old man took him in, his face unchanging. Sander wanted to vanish from sight, hide his blazing cheeks and his darting gaze.

'Did you study with me?'

'I never got the chance. But I was going to, it was my plan to.'

'I see,' the professor said uncertainly. 'Oh, of course, that's right.' He smiled faintly. 'Now I remember.' Whether he was just saying it or whether he truly remembered Sander was impossible to say. He smiled wearily and all at once he seemed to long for his hotel bed. 'Have a good evening. Thanks for coming, both of you.'

Sander went home to Snöstorp and Backavägen, Olivia and the children, his mind somehow at ease, relieved of a burden he hadn't even known he was carrying. No one missed him out there in the great big world. Maybe it was just as well that he had stayed.

78

Two dead Söderström brothers and their equally dead friend Killian Persson, in the midst of a tough summer that never seemed to end. More than twenty years had passed – it was such a long time, and even so it took nothing more than death to bring all three together again. That was how Vidar saw them: three coins tossed into a vast darkness.

He sat in his office with Lillemor Söderström's photo album on the desk before him. Pages of milestones and rites of passage: birthdays, last days of school, holidays, dinners. Ordinary moments. A boy, probably Mikael, beaming proudly atop a small motocross bike.

Another picture was labeled 'Inga-Lill, 42!' Jakob Lindell's mother's birthday. It must have been a lovely autumn day. The sun was shining. The photograph showed a long table outdoors, set with a white tablecloth, plates and glasses, yet-unopened bottles. A salad covered in aluminum foil waited on the table. Two women were just bringing out a platter of meat.

As he turned the page, his phone vibrated in his pocket. When he saw the name on the screen, he realized he hadn't expected to hear from her.

'Hello there.'

'I'm calling about your binder,' said Siri's cool voice in his ear, skipping the pleasantries. 'I was just browsing through it. There should be documents from the investigation into the burglary at the Lindells', but maybe you just haven't gotten that far yet?'

Vidar went over to the boxes. 'I don't know, I didn't see any.'

'They might be in a separate binder. Gerd and I combined the investigations, as I recall, because we suspected they were related, the homicide and the break-in. That's all I wanted to ask. You can pick up your binder whenever, I –'

'Hold on.'

Vidar lifted a box onto the desk and began to search through it. Nothing in the first box.

Somewhere nearby, a truck engine revved to life. Siri was outdoors. The vehicle accelerated, coughing and loud, and slowly faded into the distance.

'Could you come get it today, do you think? Or should I bring it in?'

'They're not here.' He turned to the next box. 'Have you spoken to Isidor Enoksson recently, by the way?'

'Why do you ask?'

'I just wondered.'

'I haven't seen him in years.'

Vidar was nonplussed.

'He didn't visit you the other day?'

'No,' she said. It sounded genuine. 'What's up?'

The cogs turned slowly behind Vidar's temples. He had stopped mid-motion and was staring at the material concerning the burglary.

'Here it is.'

The binder was labeled 'Miscellaneous Investigation Documents' and contained transcripts from supplemental interviews and witness statements, random tips that had been received in the days following the murder. Ideas that led nowhere. Some of the names he recognized; others he didn't know.

'Okay, here it is,' he said again. 'Here we go.'

The burglary files were in a separate folder at the back of the binder.

'Look at the photographs. The ones Gerd and I took of the scene, after the burglary.'

There. He was looking at the Lindell family's house in the winter of 1999, in a backwater part of Skavböke. It needed a fresh coat of paint; there were patches of snow on the ground and the trees were bare. He saw a life that reminded him of his own life, around the same time, back home in Marbäck.

'There's no spade hanging from the siding, is there?' Siri said. 'You know, the way folks do, between two nails.'

'I don't see one, anyway.' He turned the page. More photographs. A close-up of the broken glass, a smeared shoe print. 'No. No, I see the nails, but no spade.'

Another prolonged silence.

'Listen,' Siri said. 'I can't . . .'

'It's all right. I can pick up the binder later. But you need to tell me what I'm looking for.'

'A spade was hanging there just a few weeks earlier, according to Gerd. She was sure of it, although I don't quite know how.'

Vidar didn't respond. He was sweaty. Summer blazed mercilessly outside.

'Did she ever visit Lillemor Söderström?'

'Oh yes, she did. I think Gerd felt sorry for her. Filip hardly ever visited her during those rough years he had, if he came at all.'

Vidar went back to Lillemor Söderström's album. Inga-Lill Lindell's birthday celebration in the foreground, the platter of meat arriving at the set table. And there it was, the spade he recognized from Filip Söderström's garage. If it was possible to recognize a spade, that is – but it seemed like the same one. It hung against the siding as though it was commonly used for work around the house, in the yard. He pulled over the burglary report again, found Inga-Lill's government identity number. Its digits told him she was born in October of 1957. She had turned forty-two in 1999. Just two months before the murder, the spade was there.

A knock at his door. Waiting outside he found Adrian al-Hadid in uniform, his cap in one hand and a piece of paper in the other, his eyes shining.

'What is it?'

'The spade,' he said, holding the paper out to Vidar, who read it as he stood with his phone still in hand.

'Siri, can you hold on quick?'

'I'd rather not.'

'Just for a second.'

The results had come in less than fifteen minutes ago. The fresh blood on the spade belonged to Filip Söderström. The older blood had come from his brother, Mikael.

'They were killed with the same tool,' Adrian said.

Siri said something in Vidar's ear, but he couldn't hear what. Adrian cleared his throat.

'What are you thinking?' he asked.

'That we don't have much time.'

Adrian folded the paper in half. 'Why is that?'

Exhaustion crept through Vidar's head, making his thoughts sluggish.

'Filip spent time at Rasmusgården, I saw somewhere in the files. Get in touch with them and see if they'll give you any material. When he was there, for how long, what he got up to, staff notes, all that.' He went back to his phone call. 'Siri?'

But she had hung up.

A scenario: Jakob kills Mikael with the spade, likely for some reason connected to the fight at the party, or maybe the burglary that happened later that night. Maybe both. Filip knows, and tries to confront Jakob after Sten's funeral. Jakob kills Filip to suppress the secret. Or maybe not? The spade is found at Filip's place. How long had it been there?

Or maybe: Filip kills his brother. After the funeral years later, he's the one who is confronted by Jakob, not the other way around. Filip reacts as before, with violence, and Jakob is forced to defend himself. He kills Filip and thinks he needs to lie about it afterward.

Yes, that could be it.

But something chafed.

And then there was Isidor Enoksson. Why was Siri hiding the fact that he'd visited her? Because Vidar hadn't been mistaken, right? No, he'd seen the priest at her place. Hadn't he?

There was still so much he didn't know.

And the storm cloud hovering above it all: if Vidar was right, Killian Persson was perfectly innocent.

79

Word had it that the Lord had revealed to them a spade. Isidor Enoksson didn't doubt for a second that this was so. Strange things, really, spades. No matter how deep man digs, God's works are always greater. Isidor had spoken these words during a service once, but he no longer recalled the context. It slipped away like so many things did.

Seeing the miracle in the individual.

Sometimes it was very simple; other times, very hard.

What had happened once upon a time out there in Skavböke, were there visible traces? Perhaps in the people, yes, but not in the land. The land had healed. The young trees reached for the sky in groves and the fields were arable again. New farms had arisen where the old ones had collapsed.

Even so, it was as though the community, at least part of it, wanted the truth to come out. That spade was probably the clearest sign.

Things seemed to emerge from the land. At first you didn't even know what you were looking at. You thought it might be a piece of trash, or an object someone had dropped. Then you realized: Didn't that belong to . . . ? Didn't that used to be hanging on the wall at . . . ?

Tools, construction material, old junk, the kind of stuff it was common to run across out in the countryside, but unusual objects as well: a dish brush, unused coffee filters, a hockey stick, a headband. Artifacts or clues. Years later, and it could still happen; you'd be walking by a grove of trees or cut across a field, and there they were. As if the earth were spitting back out what it had once swallowed.

Some objects found were recognized.

Not all of them, but some.

One of the found objects was, yes, a spade, and the one who discovered it was Frans Ljunggren. He didn't recognize it. According to Frans, it had been peeking up out of Östholm's old field like a rusty metal tongue one morning. Frans had pulled it out and looked around, unsure whether anyone had noticed him.

Then he took it home, pleased to have gained a new tool, and stashed it with the others; he bragged about the discovery to those around him. Not least Filip Söderström, who was given a tour of the house and workshop before it became his.

'This here, why, I found it for free out in the field. Well, no one's going to miss this, I said, so I brought it home with me.'

When Filip told Isidor about this, the old priest mused about spades, what strange things they are.

'Whose do you think it was, originally?' Isidor said.

'I think I recognize it,' Filip said. 'I think it's the one that used to hang on the wall outside Jakob Lindell's house.'

80

'I would like,' Vidar said calmly, 'for you to explain to me in as much detail as possible what you did after the funeral.'

The interrogation room was small, the air cool. They were alone with only the computer for company. Vidar hadn't even glanced at it so far. Instead, he was ready with a pen and notepad.

Jakob waited, his hands resting on his knees, anxiously eyeing Vidar from across the table.

'What did you say?'

'The funeral,' Vidar repeated patiently. 'What did you do after the service? Be as specific as you can.'

Jakob launched into his account, though he was hesitant at first. Then he gathered momentum as if someone had shaken him and the words couldn't rattle out fast enough.

'Thank you.' Vidar gestured discreetly with his hand, asking Jakob to pause as he finished jotting a note. 'There was coffee at the village hall. Then what happened?'

'Then it was over.'

'And what did you do after?'

'We just went home. Me and Alice.'

'Right. But be as detailed as you can, Jakob. What time was it when you left?'

'Gosh.' Jakob made a face. 'I don't know, maybe two thirty or three? I dropped Alice off at home, and then I ran some errands.'

'How come you dropped Alice off first?'

'Our youngest was with a babysitter while we were at the funeral. Tora – that's the babysitter – had to get home.'

'How old are your kids?'

'Eight and fourteen. And Lisa's twenty-one, she lives in town. We' – Jakob realized more explanation would be required – 'Alice and I went grocery shopping later that night, but by then the fourteen-year-old was back home and could keep an eye on her little sister.'

'So you were alone?'

'When?'

'When you ran errands after dropping Alice off. You did them alone?'

'Yes.'

'Did Alice know you had errands to run even before the funeral service?'

'Uh, yeah, I had mentioned it. She knew I was probably going to get a few things taken care of afterwards, if I had the energy. It depended on how taxing the funeral ended up being.'

'What kind of errands?'

'I . . .' Jakob began, but then he didn't say anything for a long time.

He looked guilty, slumped in the chair like that, but guilty of what, Vidar didn't know. He put down his pen and set his notepad aside, a tried-and-true maneuver.

'What is it, Jakob? Something is weighing on you, I can tell.'

'Well, it's just . . . you know, I . . . I only had one errand to do and that was checking the oil in my car, at a garage in Oskarström. And I could just as easily have done that on my own at home. I guess I just wanted some time to myself after the funeral. I needed it. You know, actual time alone. Away from my wife and kids, shopping lists and laundry and . . .'

'From life,' Vidar said.

Jakob laughed in shame, like he was admitting a shortcoming. 'Basically.'

'I'm sorry,' Vidar said, picking up his pen again. 'But did you mention this when you spoke to us yesterday?'

'No, Alice was with me. I couldn't say it in front of her, and I didn't think it was even that important. I was gone during the time I said I was gone.'

'And when was that?'

'Oh, between three thirty and seven, maybe? Something like that.'

'Did you see anyone during that time? Or did you speak with anyone, on the phone, for instance?'

'No – I wanted to be alone.'

Vidar gazed at him for a long time.

'So what were you doing between three thirty and seven?'

'Like I said, I went and got the oil checked in my car, that was the first thing – there's a garage behind the Preem station in Oskarström. Then I went to the cemetery. I do that sometimes when I need to think. I sat in my car in the parking lot, is all, and . . . you know, just thought about stuff. I thought about how another one of us would be lying there soon. Sten, I mean,' Jakob added. 'After that, I went back to Skavböke. I didn't exactly have anywhere else to go. That must have been around six, and I stopped at a place where we used to grill out in the summer.'

'And by "we", you mean . . .'

'Me and my friends. Sander, Killian, Alice, Felicia, everyone from back then.'

'Right. And Mikael.'

'And Mikael. Yes, of course.'

'How long did you stay there?'

'Oh, until I went home again. An hour, maybe. We still had to get groceries.'

'And what did you do? While you were there, I mean.'

'Like I said. I just sat in the car, thinking. I smoked – I keep a pack of cigarettes in the glove box. It all came back, all of it. I think because it wasn't just that it was Sten's funeral, it was, like, that everyone was there. Everyone that's left.'

'Did you get out of the car at all? Take a walk?'

'No, I just sat there. That's what I usually do.'

'And you didn't call anybody either?'

Jakob looked like he'd been caught red-handed. 'I actually didn't have my phone with me.'

'How come? I mean, it's pretty common to take your phone when you go out.'

Jakob ran a hand through his hair. Vidar could tell that it was trembling. When Jakob replied, he sounded almost frightened.

'I just didn't want anyone to bother me. Like I said, I wanted to be by myself.'

'Do you leave your phone at home often?'

'Sometimes. Not often, I guess, but sure.'

'Did Alice know you didn't have it with you?'

Jakob didn't say anything. He shook his head. 'I left it in the garage.'

'So if she asked, when you got home,' Vidar said, 'say, if she'd called you and you didn't pick up, you could tell her you'd forgotten it.'

'Yes,' he admitted, perhaps relieved that Vidar had said it for him. 'That's about it.'

Vidar waited, looking almost bored, like he wanted to get this over with so he could go home. He studied Jakob's hands. Hands almost always revealed more than a face. Did Jakob have it in him?

Yes, he probably did. But why?

'I'd like to ask you about that evening too. After Filip was found and you spoke to us. What did you do after that?'

Don't say it, Vidar thought. *Lie to me.*

Lie to me, and I've got you.

81

'Nothing,' Jakob said. 'We were just at home. Trying to make sense of what had happened. The kids wondered, too, they knew something was up.'

'Did you talk about it?'

'Not in detail. The fourteen-year-old got it all anyway, of course, just like us when we were that age.'

'So you didn't make any calls or anything?'

'We talked to Alice's parents. Or, you know, Alice did.'

'And you stayed in Skavböke all that evening and night?'

'Yes.'

Vidar clicked his pen and jotted something down before placing it aside again.

'Thank you, Jakob. That's good.'

Jakob exhaled and leaned back. Vidar had placed a binder on the floor earlier. Now he put it on the table and paged through to the right sheet protector, turned it around to face Jakob.

'You recognize this,' Vidar said, 'don't you?'

It was the scrap of fabric, dark green with lighter stripes, the one Siri and Gerd had once extracted from the jaws of a dead dog.

'I've been given to understand,' Vidar continued, when Jakob didn't answer, 'that you know where the rest of this is. Is that true?'

Jakob stared at Vidar. He opened his mouth, but nothing came out.

Instead, Vidar spoke: 'How come you didn't tell the truth from the start?'

'I . . . just didn't know.'

'But you talked to someone about the shirt.'

Jakob nodded again, but this time he looked grim, as if Vidar's question confirmed that a betrayal had taken place.

'Who?'

'Sander.'

'And what did he recommend you do?'

'Go to you. To the police.'

'But you didn't.'

Vidar's questions were becoming statements.

'No,' Jakob said, his voice as flimsy as a whisper. 'I didn't.'

'Why not?'

'I didn't know what to say.'

'What were you doing on Christmas Day in 1999? In the evening?'

'I was at home.'

'You spent quite a bit of time outside, didn't you? Stacking firewood and so on.'

'Yes, I did.'

'Alone that time too, is that right?'

'I think so. But everyone else was right inside.'

'But you were alone outside. No one saw you.'

'No, yes, I guess I was alone.'

Jakob was starting to sweat.

'I know how it is with firewood. It takes a long time. You must have been out for half an hour, at least?'

Jakob shifted in his chair. 'I don't remember. But something like that, sure.'

'So you see, Jakob, how this looks and why I'm being so persistent. You don't tell the truth the first time we speak to you after Filip Söderström's murder. You don't tell your wife the truth about where you are or what you do that afternoon. By your own account, you don't see anyone or speak to anyone. In other words, you have no alibi. Nor do you have your cell phone with you, which can be read as premeditation: you don't want anyone to see where you are or have gone during that time period. And now it turns out that you have also lied to me during this conversation.'

Vidar watched for a reaction on Jakob's face before he went on, but Jakob's gaze was blank.

'Not to mention all the uncertainty concerning your actions surrounding the burglary and the theft of your family's money after Pierre's party. You have been hiding things from us for a long, long time, things with a direct connection to what happened in Skavböke in 1999. You can't quite account for your whereabouts at the time of the landslide, and there's even a motive to explain why you might have been so upset with the Söderström family. The fight with Mikael, and the money.'

Vidar placed a gentle finger against the scrap of fabric behind its plastic sheet.

'It appears you won't reveal anything until you are confronted with information that renders your story impossible. Then you revise it. This is a strategy of sorts, conscious or not, that we often see in interviews like this one, and it's never a good sign.'

Jakob sat very still. Dark circles were appearing under his arms.

'What's more,' Vidar said, turning the page of the binder, 'we've got this.' He pointed at a photograph of the spade they'd found in Filip's garage. 'You recognize it, I believe.'

Jakob stared at the picture without saying anything.

'Do you recognize this, Jakob?'

He shook his head. Vidar turned the page again. Another photograph, this time the one from Lillemor Söderström's photo album.

'Here it is, just two months before Mikael was murdered, at your house. That's the same spade, isn't it? It was used in not one but two homicides. So I have to ask, Jakob. Did you kill Filip Söderström?'

'No.'

'Did you kill his brother, Mikael Söderström?'

'No.'

'Did you cause the landslide on Christmas Day of 1999?'

'Christ! No!' Jakob was breathing hard. 'No,' he said again, his voice fainter this time.

'So what is going on here? If you want to go home,' he added, more as a statement of fact than part of any particular strategy, 'you need to help me out first.'

Jakob looked helpless.

'It wasn't me. None of that was me. I haven't seen that spade in, I don't know, ages. I didn't even recognize it at first, that it used to belong to us. And as for the shirt,' he continued, 'I just didn't know what to do with it.'

'Why didn't you hand it over to us?'

'Because I didn't know what to say. That I found it? And what would have happened if you didn't believe me? Everyone knows Killian killed Mikael. The landslide, that was Sten. I thought that was all pretty well settled. So what did the shirt matter? It was all so chaotic afterwards, it took a long time before I even thought about it again.'

'What?'

Jakob looked confused. 'What, which part?'

'It took a long time before you thought about what again?'

'The shirt. It was like everything else blocked it out.'

'But you still had it?'

'I found it in the basement. So, yeah, I still had it.'

'I've been told that Filip didn't wear flannels very often,' Vidar said slowly. 'Isn't that true?'

'I don't remember.'

'But if it is true, then isn't it unlikely for the shirt to be his?'

Jakob shrugged. 'I don't know. Maybe he borrowed it from someone.'

'But you wore flannels like this one. Right?'

Jakob sat up straighter.

'Sometimes,' he said, and then, each word growing heavier, as if he wanted to make them mean more than they did: 'And so did tons of other people.'

'But this one's not yours?'

Jakob's eyes bored into him. 'No. It's not mine.'

Vidar observed him for a long moment.

'I'm going to ask a colleague to go home with you and pick up the shirt.'

For the first time, Vidar's voice was cold as ice.

82

After his walk with Felicia, Sander visited his parents. They were old now, over seventy, and they'd been retired for several years. They still lived in his childhood home.

'So you stopped off in old Skavböke after all?' his father said as he stepped into the front hall.

'As it turns out.'

'Because of this terrible situation with Filip?'

'Yes.' He closed the door behind him to keep the heat out. 'Mostly that.'

His father nodded and tapped his cane on the floor.

'It's so terrible,' his mother said, shaking her head.

'Yes, almost like before,' said his dad. 'Let's talk about something else instead.'

They talked about something else instead. But eventually, conversation petered out.

'You've always said it was your fault,' said his mom. 'Killian. But it wasn't – no one else thought it was. What do you have to feel guilty about?'

There it was again. Like a shadow behind him in the forest, a figure following him, moving from tree to tree. Hands preparing to grab or attack.

'I survived, Killian didn't. I got to get married, have a job, house, kids, everything. I got a whole life. He got nothing.'

'But that's not your fault.'

Old words writhed inside Sander, echoing and banging and crawling to the surface from a deep, dark place inside him.

I guess maybe I should just leave right now.

Sander had thrown the present at the wall. He could still hear the thud.

Because what else can you do, Killian? When you come to me, and I don't help you, what do you do? Just run away. Go ahead, because you never could solve anything on your own. Don't just stand there like a fucking idiot, leave, *for Christ's sake!*

His words had driven Killian off and caused his death, and Sander couldn't even be punished for what he'd done. In some ways, it would have been easier if he could have faced judgment, first judgment and then sentencing, and then a period of suffering inflicted upon him from the outside. Then, perhaps, penance. That way he could have moved on. Mercy?

His mother asked after Olivia and the kids. Maybe they were the mercy, in the middle of all this: his children.

'What luck,' she liked to say, 'that you stayed. Otherwise we never would have had such a close relationship with our grandchildren.'

She was right. And that probably wasn't such a small thing, either.

That you stayed. Yes, in some sense he had; in some ways not. It was half an hour from Skavböke to Halmstad, a little more from Skavböke to Snöstorp. Sander had left and had also stayed, an ambivalent state that might have left more of a mark on him than he wanted to acknowledge. When his parents saw the kids it was always at their place in Snöstorp, never out here in Skavböke. The kids had asked, of course, why they never went to see Grandma and Grandpa Eriksson. They visited their other set of grandparents almost every week. Sander had always come up with excuses, explanations: it's so far away, it's more fun here, Grandma and Grandpa like to get out of the house. He could make up a lot of reasons, but one day he would run out, and the kids were getting older. He wouldn't be able to rely on this evasiveness for much longer.

When he left Skavböke that afternoon, the fields were shimmering and the sun warmed the ground.

The late-afternoon light was tender; a great, kindhearted hand warming everything it touched, and since it was said to be God's hand, it reached every last corner, made the world shine.

He parked his car by the cemetery in Oskarström and found himself lingering behind the wheel for a moment, but eventually he got out and stood at the edge of the parking lot to gaze down at the spot where his friend was buried.

It probably looked like he was getting ready. As if he would take a step forward any moment now, start walking down there. But Sander didn't move.

There was a slight breeze up here. It was pleasant. He told himself that was why he was staying put.

He thought of Sten Persson's funeral, his dream about Killian that was stronger than Sander and had dragged him here. Maybe that's so: everything alive is drawn toward death, and Sander was drawn to Skavböke, to Killian.

He gazed at the headstones and wondered which of them belonged to his friend. Something shifted in his chest. His eyes fell on the trees, the paths, the fields. Almost everything was the same here. The map of his childhood.

A sprinkler moved rhythmically back and forth. Its jets billowed over the green grass like a fan. He returned to the car. Behind him, the dead tried to penetrate the veil, as they always did; they wanted to come through, but no one noticed.

83

Vidar spent the day alone with only the investigation material for company. He read it all from the start, every last bit, reports and logs and interviews; he studied photographs from the scene of the crime and the party, he read documentation concerning the landslide, the accident that had taken Killian Persson's life, the few advances in the case that had been made on this side of the millennium. At last he turned to the whiteboard and uncapped a marker.

Skavböke, December 1999

A car, its back gate open in the dawn light. A big, blond eighteen-year-old holding secrets in his heart. A third pair of footprints; a witness who never came forward. Why not? An abyss. Over twenty years later, a dead younger brother. Once a little brother, always a little brother, even if you're the only one still alive. Siri's notes from that first, crucial interview: *lying* for Sander Eriksson. *hiding something* for Killian Persson.

Vidar drew it all out. House by house, the community spread across the whiteboard. Söderströms', Ljunggrens', Östholms'; there were the Lindells' and Grenbergs' places, Erikssons', Perssons'.

He made a red *X* where Mikael Söderström had been found in Madeleine Grenberg's Volvo, and another for the detonation of Söderström's dynamite, ground zero for the great landslide. He hesitated for a moment but then added one last *X* to mark the spot where Filip Söderström was killed.

There were some parts way back in the investigation he couldn't make sense of. 'Miscellaneous investigation material' was a hodgepodge of dead ends and sidetracks, the final measures taken before the case seemed to fade away for good. He knew Gerd Pettersson and Siri Bengtsson had needed to move on, deal with other cases. But even so, something chafed at him. Here were new details, names that weren't linked to the rest of the material. He thought of Siri Bengtsson and wondered what she had been working on in her final days on the force, before she quit.

He doggedly kept at it, just like a jigsaw puzzle he couldn't tear himself away from. Now and then, someone from the investigation team would drop off a report or an interview transcript. To a man they described Vidar as absent-minded and worn out and thought he ought to go home and get some sleep. These days, police work was all about conserving energy for the long haul – didn't the old-timers know that?

After a while, Adrian al-Hadid turned up holding a bag.

'One shirt, just for you,' he said. 'Jakob Lindell was happy to hand it over.'

Vidar shot a quick glance at it. 'He was?'

'Not exactly.'

'Send it for testing, please. How are things going with Rasmusgården?'

'They're supposed to get back to me.'

'Head over there if you don't hear from them today.'

Adrian nodded.

'Right,' he said. 'One other thing. Jakob Lindell. He wanted you to call him.'

'What for?'

'He didn't say.'

Vidar went back to the whiteboard and observed it, hands on his hips. Adrian did the same.

'What do you think?' he said.

Vidar turned his head wearily. 'That I think better when I'm alone.'

Adrian trudged off with blazing cheeks. After a while, he came back, his footsteps even more hesitant.

'Yes?' Vidar said coolly, before Adrian could speak. 'What is it now?'

'I'm sorry to bother you, but, uh, there's someone downstairs who wants to talk to you.'

'To me?' Vidar reached for his coffee. 'Who is it?'

He followed Adrian down. The heat dissipated. 'How the hell can it be cooler down here than up in our offices?'

'Something about the AC up on your floor, I think.' They arrived in the lobby and Adrian glanced uncertainly from Vidar to the visitor. 'Is this okay, or . . . ?'

84

'Is he any good, that one?' Siri asked, watching the young man as he walked off.

'Just a little clingy.' Vidar held out his hand to take the binder. 'I apologize. I should have come by, but I got stuck here.'

Siri looked relieved to be rid of the burden.

Vidar's phone rang. He answered and heard the technician's voice, but the line was staticky and jerky, cutting off her words. It took a lot of concentration to understand her. Even so, he thought her tone sounded strange.

'Hold on,' he said. 'One more time.'

'We got the results,' she enunciated.

The forensics unit had just completed their analysis of the fingerprints from the spade that had been used to kill both Söderström brothers. Those prints had been run through the national fingerprint and description databases several times.

'We got a very likely match to an old print,' she said. 'One taken from the shift stick of Madeleine Grenberg's car on the morning of December 18, 1999, during the investigation of Mikael Söderström's murder.'

Vidar took a breath in the sudden silence. 'And the one from the spade is not an old print.'

'No, it's not. It's a new one. That's why the results took so long. They wanted to be sure.'

'That makes sense,' he said, holding his breath.

'I agree, that makes sense. But it's basically the only thing that does.'

'I need to make a call. Thank you.'

For the first time since the investigation landed on his table, his voice was strained.

'What is it?' Siri asked.

Vidar looked at her as if he'd forgotten she was there. 'Wait here for a minute, can you do that for me?'

The phone rang and rang before Jakob Lindell picked up, almost whispering, as though he were hiding the conversation from someone else.

'Thanks for calling,' he said quietly. 'An officer stopped by to pick up the shirt.'

'I know, we got it, thanks.'

Jakob took a breath. 'I don't think it was Filip I saw that night.'

'What?'

'The night of the landslide. It wasn't Filip.'

Vidar didn't know what to say. 'No?'

'No, it all turned out wrong, everything, I –'

'But you saw someone.'

'Yeah, definitely.'

'So who do you think it was?'

Silence on the other end. Siri was standing across the lobby with her arms crossed.

'Jakob,' Vidar said. 'Who do you think you saw?'

'I . . .'

More silence. Jakob cleared his throat.

'Who,' Vidar said, emphasizing every word this time, 'did you see?'

85

There was something new in the air when Sander returned to Backavägen. The street was hushed, not just deserted for the summer but quiet, as if some invisible force had cleared all life out of it ahead of an oncoming disaster. Or maybe his visit to the cemetery and its dead was just sticking with him.

He stood with car keys in hand in the driveway. All he had to do was go inside, gather some things, drink a glass of water — his mouth was dry. Lock the door and arm the alarm and head out. He looked at his watch and wished he had a cigarette.

Then he found himself standing in the kitchen. He had gone inside and was holding a glass in his hand. It was empty. He hadn't filled it. Or had he drunk it already? Where had this gap in his memory come from?

A dull vibration ran through Sander's body, electricity rising and fading in slow waves.

He had gone back out to the driveway, into the warm evening. No more glass in hand. Or had he never even gone inside? No, he had — behind him, the door was open. He must have gone in.

This disorientation was making him feel nauseated, and the edges of his vision started to go black.

Someone was coming, way down on Backavägen. Sander staggered backward and nearly fell. In the nick of time, he regained his balance and made it into the house, where he closed the door and turned the lock.

He and Olivia had replaced the front door, must have

been about three years ago. They'd chosen one with frosted glass, to let the light in. Albin and Josefin liked to stand there and make faces at their parents, because their features were hidden by the frost.

He stared at the windowpane and waited. Steps right outside, heavy and purposeful.

The outline of a massive figure on the glass.

Teeth. Teeth in a mouth without a face, they came for him, gaping in the summer stillness. A man.

The handle moved down, then up again. Locked. Sander waited, but nothing happened. The visitor simply stood there.

Sander knew he had to open the door.

Dangers from below ground. Old portals open once more. The man outside stared at Sander as the door swung open, as though he didn't expect to be welcomed in. At his feet was a threadbare backpack.

'Hi,' the visitor said at last. 'Long time no see.'

86

Hard to say where Sander was, other than right here, right now. Everything around him, all the familiar everyday objects, the kids' jackets and shoes, the hat rack, Olivia's coats, the umbrella, the rug on the floor – all of it had become astonishingly foreign.

'Could I . . .' the man in the doorway began, 'it's so hot. Could I come in and have a glass of water?'

He picked up his backpack. Sander held his breath and stepped aside, let him in, whatever he was. The man glanced around the front hall with curiosity, at the hooks for adults and children.

With a start, Sander reached out and grabbed the man's forearm. The man laughed uncertainly.

Wrinkles around his eyes, crows' feet. He was very tanned. Sander was still grasping the man's arm, but then an icy gust came between them and he dropped it abruptly as if his grip frightened him.

The man looked over Sander's shoulder, at the kitchen.

'Could I just have a little water, please? I'm so thirsty.'

Sander turned around, looking away from the visitor for the first time. He slowly went to the sink and filled the glass he had just been drinking from; he turned his head. The man was still there. Sander held out the glass and watched it be swallowed by a hand meatier than his own, veinier, browner. The skin tougher.

'Thank you, Sander.'

The man drank greedily as he eyed the bracelet around

Sander's wrist. Rays of sun fell through the picture windows in the living room, warming the ash-gray herringbone parquet.

The man sat down on the kitchen bench and exhaled. One of the cushions slipped out of place and he straightened it, a movement so ordinary that it appeared even more surreal to Sander. He pulled out a chair and sat down too.

'Killian?'

'Been ages since I heard anyone say that name out loud. It feels kind of weird.'

He looked out the window at the driveway, Sander's car gleaming in the sun.

'Nice to have a car. Walking everywhere really takes a toll. Especially with this heat. But at least there are sidewalks here. It's nice.'

Something shifted in Sander's throat, something that wanted out. He was afraid it was a scream, but it didn't quite feel like one. He didn't know what it would be until he opened his mouth.

Sander began to laugh. Killian just stared at him.

'Are you okay?'

'Okay,' said Sander. '*Okay.*'

Sander's laughter grew louder. He made a face. The man at his kitchen table began to laugh, too, at first in a terse, bursting sort of way, like he was trying to suppress it, but then noisily and warmly as it tumbled all through his big body. Wave after wave passed through them. The sound ricocheted and echoed through the empty house. They sat there like two friends who had pulled off a massive con.

'It was you I saw,' Sander said, 'wasn't it?'

Killian stiffened. Were the words more dangerous than Sander thought? When he relaxed again, it seemed like it took a lot of effort. 'Where?'

'Outside the chapel. And after the funeral. Across the field, over by the bushes where the Söderströms' house used to be.'

'Oh.' His shoulders slumped. 'It probably was. I couldn't miss it, you know? He was my dad.' He had grown solemn, the last words sounding awfully thick as they came out. 'Yours are both still alive, aren't they? I thought I saw them. How are they?'

Questions for an old friend you run into at the grocery store. As if the events of the past had suddenly become insignificant.

'They're getting old. Dad uses a cane. But they're good.'

Killian, if it really was him, didn't respond. Maybe he was thinking of his own parents. One hand tapped lightly at his glass.

'What is going on?' Sander said, but it wasn't entirely clear who he was addressing.

'Can we just . . .' Killian began, but then he hesitated, as if he, too, were beginning to realize how bizarre this was. 'Can we just hang out for a little bit? You know, like we always used to. Is that okay?'

An odor rose from Killian when he moved, maybe it was his clothing. Sander inhaled it. All the other senses can fool a person, but not smell.

It was really him.

'What do you mean, what do you want to do?' was all that came out.

'Do you have any beer?'

'No.'

Killian glanced at his backpack. 'Good thing I do.'

His eyes sparkled. Then he stopped to consider something and quirked his lips.

'I understand I have a grave. I'd like to see it.'

87

Siri was unprepared for this, Vidar could tell. As she walked by his side through the leafy dark shadows of Norre Katt Park, she didn't speak for a long time, perhaps trying to get her memories in order before she fixed them into words. She was the one who had suggested they take a walk; she said she did her best thinking when she was moving her body.

'It really didn't start with Hampus Olsson,' she said now. 'I guess Hampus Olsson has probably never been a significant factor, at least in this case. Or – who knows. All I know is, this whole mess started with a raid we did in August 2002. My last big one, before I quit.'

'A raid on a homeless encampment,' Vidar said.

'Yes, near Fegen. When we arrived, I saw someone lurking around the edges of the encampment, and he seemed out of place somehow. Or maybe he was just a newcomer. But he seemed familiar, and I wondered if he could be Hampus Olsson, who ran away from home at Christmas in 1999. I started looking for him, and eventually, mostly thanks to sheer luck, I ended up in possession of the cap he must have been wearing. After that, we started to search the area, with human chains.' Her voice was restrained, as though each word was full of pain. 'Eventually I ended up talking to a farmer out in Mjäla.'

'I saw that. But what happened next? There's no follow-up in the material.'

'Nothing,' Siri said curtly. 'Nothing happened after that.'

Which was perfectly true, but it wasn't the whole story.

88

As they drove through Halmstad, everything seemed distorted. Killian was in the passenger seat with a can of beer in his hand, watching the edge of the road. He leaned against the headrest and said, more to himself than to Sander:

'Oh, so this is how it looks now. It's all so different.' He frowned as if this were an important realization. 'At least, I think it is. I don't actually remember what it used to look like. It feels weird to come home.'

He turned away again, as though the sight made him feel dejected. They sailed across Wrangelsleden and onto Highway 26 toward Oskarström.

'Quite a bit has changed,' Sander confirmed, mostly just for something to say.

'Home,' Killian went on, as if pondering the word itself. 'When we were eighteen, it was such a simple word. Wasn't it? Not for you, maybe, since all you wanted was to leave.'

He said it without accusation, just a statement of fact.

'But I stayed,' Sander said softly.

'You did.' Killian took a sip of beer. 'It's nice, though. Seeing you, I mean.'

'Same to you.'

Sander didn't know if he meant it.

'Do you have kids?'

'The jackets you saw in the hall are a little too small for me,' Sander said, but when Killian didn't seem to catch on, he clarified: 'I've got two.'

'Wow.'

'Are you surprised?'

'I don't know. Maybe. I didn't picture you with kids.'

'Me neither, but then I grew up.'

They were approaching Oskarström. The sun was slowly sinking, but dusk was still hours away. The drive leading to the cemetery parking lot was narrow, and Sander slowed down. No cars here now. Killian straightened up in his seat, preparing himself.

'Have you seen it?' Killian asked as they climbed out of the car. 'The headstone.'

'Many times.'

'So you know the way?'

Sander hesitated. 'I mean, I haven't been here in real life.'

'So you haven't seen the stone?'

'Not for real, no.'

Sander squinted at the sun and drank his beer. It was lukewarm by this point. He'd drunk alcohol and driven his car, and now he was drinking again. He would never drink and drive otherwise, but it was like he was underwater, or in a fog, and everything was dreamy and slightly distorted by waves and white veils. Maybe that was why he wasn't afraid of being caught, wasn't scanning for police cars or other people who might spot them, recognize them, break the two of them apart again.

They stepped down into the cemetery and began to walk among the gravestones. Sander read: *Rest in peace. We miss you. Beloved grandmother, mother, sister. Beloved son, father, grandfather. Beloved grandma and mom. Beloved wife. Beloved husband and father. Beloved son. Beloved papa and brother. Beloved father and grandfather. Beloved mother and friend.* No beloved soul got out of this place alive.

After searching for a while, Killian looked up and said: 'That must be it. My stone.'

'Killian, are you sure you . . . you don't have to . . .'

'I am.' He looked at Sander and, as if to reassure him, reached out and touched his friend's arm. 'It's okay. I think I need this.'

He rested alone here, not far from his mother. *Killian Persson, 1981–1999*, in a long line going back through generations.

'Weird,' he said simply. 'Soon Dad will be lying around here somewhere too.'

So many times Sander had imagined this: standing before the grave and reading his friend's name. He had always held off, as if he weren't quite ready yet but would be someday. Now he was here, but it didn't feel real. These were circumstances that didn't belong to any reality he recognized.

He understood it was a lovely headstone, but he couldn't see it that way. Instead, he was about to be overcome by a sudden, burning fury. What he read on that stone was a mistake, and he didn't understand how it could have come to be, whose fault it was. He twisted the leather bracelet like it was chafing him.

Killian sank down on the grass in front of the gravestone tailor-style, his sturdy long legs surprisingly flexible.

'I just need to sit down for a minute. Want another beer?'

Killian had a few more in a bag. Sander sat down next to his friend and was given a can. They drank and stared at the grave without saying anything.

In his mind, Sander returned to the short stretch of county highway that wound through Esmared. He had thought of it often, how it lay there smooth and slippery on that Christmas Eve night. The flames blazing forth and the moaning, solitary wreck of the car. More than once, years later, he had almost gotten in his own car and driven to that spot, just so he could say he had been there, to the place where his friend met death. But what would he do there?

'I just don't understand how the fuck you can be sitting here,' Sander said at last. 'We buried you. You died.'

Killian chuckled, a sound void of happiness. 'I sure did.'

89

Farmer Jansson was chipper and pleasant when Siri paid him a visit during the human-chain search for Hampus Olsson in 2002; he was well over sixty but still active and able-bodied. He had twinkling eyes and was never far from a genuine, loud laugh. Siri spoke with him as they stood in a bright old entryway with hand-stitched embroidered art on the walls.

He'd had his suspicions, he said. He'd hung out a Help Wanted sign months earlier without much hope. In late 1999, no one was particularly excited by the thought of farm labor. So when a young man came walking down the gravel road in late December, Jansson had the feeling something was off. When the young man said his name was Johan and he was willing to work in exchange for food and a place to stay, Jansson's misgivings only grew.

'He had to be running away from home, I figured. He couldn't produce identification either. When I asked what he was good at, he said he could do most anything. We'll see, I said. When can you start? Well, he said. Now? Or tomorrow? We happened to be in quite a pickle that day, because the ripsaw in the workshop was on the fritz and we needed it in the morning, for the firewood. So I told him, okay, the saw out there is broken. If you can fix it, get it to work, you can stay and work on trial starting tomorrow.' The farmer laughed, astonished. 'And wouldn't you know, that bastard fixed up the saw in under an hour? Anything else I can do? he asked, standing there in the doorway. So he started the next day, Johan did, although of course I realized that wasn't his real name. Lived in one of the farmhands' cottages.'

Even though the farmer didn't know who he was. Or, more accurately: even though the farmer knew he wasn't who he said he was.

'He was with us for almost two years. Never complained, never sick, always a hard worker. I don't know what he was running away from, but I knew he must not have had it easy. So I made sure he had a good life here, and I figured he had it better at my farm than wherever it was he'd come from. He wasn't much of a talker, that boy, but with a work ethic like that there's no need to be. I told him what to do, and he did it.'

'So he never mentioned anything about who he was or where he came from?'

'There's not much time for small talk out here. So, no, he never said, and I didn't ask. In any case, what happened later on had nothing to do with him.'

The farm was struck by hard times. It failed to recover, and the layer of 'surplus fat', as the farmer put it, had already been eaten up.

'He contributed a lot, Johan did. But I needed to rent out his quarters. That rendered him homeless, because I had nowhere else on the farm where he could stay. I couldn't exactly pay him a wage, either, aside from some small change here or there. So he didn't have any savings to rent a place of his own.' The farmer looked despondent. 'I told him he was welcome to keep working, but he would have to find his own place, and I told him I certainly understood if he wanted to find another job. But there was a farmer not far to the east, up toward Djuparp, who I thought could use some help. He took off that same day. I offered to drive him, but he said no, no, I ought to use these feet of mine for something. That was Johan for you. It was the last I saw of him.'

But he never arrived in Djuparp.

'Anyway, listen,' he said, 'that was all a long time ago, over a year ago now. But I called the farmer up there and told him a good worker was heading his way. He said he looked forward to meeting him and then I suppose a week or so passed. When no one showed up, he called me back and asked if I had been messing with him.'

No point in getting your hopes up, as Siri knew better than many. Hope made you stop thinking clearly, kept you from separating the facts from the wishes, made you see what you wanted to see. Even so, she felt a flutter inside her, a sudden warmth spreading to her stomach and up through her shoulders. She took out a picture of Hampus Olsson, the most recent of his school portraits, from the autumn of 1999. So many hands had held it by now that the edges were getting worn.

'Do you recognize this person?'

Standing in the hall, the farmer from Mjåla raised two bushy eyebrows, took the photograph between his thumb and index finger, and studied it closely.

'I'm afraid I don't.'

'Are you sure? This isn't the boy who stayed at your place? Johan.'

'Johan was blond, too, but he was a lot huskier, you know? Quite a bit bigger.'

Siri stepped out onto the stoop and felt the cold nip her cheeks; she began to trudge toward the others. Then she heard the farmer's voice calling out behind her.

'Hey. Hold up.'

She turned around. The farmer was on the steps, something in his hand.

'Yes?'

'I don't know if this will help, but this is Johan, during harvest time in 2000. We always try to take a picture on the last day, before we celebrate the harvest. I just thought, maybe you know what happened to him, or you could find out. Best farmhand I ever had. I hope everything worked out for that boy.'

It was a framed group picture taken in front of the barn. They were lined up like a motley soccer team, all of them: the farmer and his wife, their kids, the workers. Siri counted fourteen people in all. The farmer pointed to a young man crouching down and glancing at something off to the side, as if he hadn't expected to have his picture taken and couldn't think of an excuse to avoid it.

Siri stared at it.

'Are you sure this was taken in the year 2000?'

'Yes, of course. First harvest of the new millennium. Although it was a bad year, as I recall.'

'Could you remove it from the frame?'

The farmer freed the flimsy photograph with surprisingly nimble fingers.

'You can borrow it if you like. Does this mean you recognize him?'

'No, but I can pass the photo and your information along to my colleagues, and maybe they can track down Johan.'

Siri shrank into herself as she walked alongside Vidar through Norre Katt Park.

'I'm so ashamed,' she said. 'I don't know what to say, especially now, with Filip. It feels like it's all my fault. If only I'd said something, if I'd dared to speak up, maybe he'd be . . .'

'What?' Vidar said. 'Alive? Probably not.'

'But maybe he would.'

Siri stopped and took her hand from her back pocket. In her palm was a photograph, folded double.

90

'I stopped to take a leak around Esmared. I thought it was no big deal, it was Christmas Eve. It was dark and deserted. But I'm standing what, like three or four yards away with my johnson out, when I hear the car door slam and the engine start. The car takes off. Someone, no idea who, is behind the wheel. Never found out who it was either. He looked young. A junkie, maybe. Or, you know, the type who doesn't know the difference between "mine" and "yours". Hell if I know.'

It had been a chilly night, and Killian didn't have much with him. What few belongings he did have were in the car.

Then he heard a *whoomp*. He didn't understand what was going on until he saw an orange glow rising between the trees not far off.

'By the time I got there, the car was engulfed in flames. I saw the guy behind the wheel, he was stuck and couldn't get out.' Killian made a face. 'It was the worst thing I've ever seen. Goddamn. You know, this mental image of him burning to death, and I can still smell it. I wanted to help, but then there was another explosion and I hightailed it out of there. I might have passed out for a little bit, I don't know. When I climbed back up, it was still just blazing and I knew it was too late, he was dead. I thought of all my stuff in the car. But then it hit me.'

A young man in the car. Killian's ID and clothes in the passenger seat.

'I just left it there. And ran.'

A snap decision with consequences that would reach across half a lifetime.

'Where did you run to?'

'Just up into the forest. I slept in abandoned houses for a few nights. Then I came to a farm up north a ways. They had a Help Wanted sign. So I took the chance.'

'And you didn't come back?'

'I was terrified that the police would arrest me the minute they saw me. And they probably would have. They thought I did it. Everyone did.'

'Not me.'

Killian smiled sadly and looked like he wanted to touch Sander. 'But everyone else did. Except maybe Felicia.'

'So what are you going to do now?'

Killian took a deep breath.

'I don't know. I just wanted to see you. You're all I have left, or whatever.' He cast his gaze down, looking pensively at his hand around the beer can, and tapped it with the tip of his finger. 'It's strange, really, something that occurred to me as we were driving out here and I saw the traffic, the parking spots outside the stores, people eating ice cream outside Mack Inn. All these people who have to go to work, all the stuff they have to get through at their jobs. Then they sit in traffic on the way home and once they get there they have to deal with everything around the house too. Kids, relationships, bills, all sorts of stuff. It's like, I don't understand it. And still I'm always thinking about what it would have been like to live that way. I don't get it, but I still miss it. Maybe that's the craziest thing of all, longing for something you don't even understand.'

Sander leaned toward him.

'But you didn't do anything wrong. I know it. Maybe it's like you say, maybe it would have been pointless to try back then, but now? There has to be a way. You know, I'm heading back to Kivik. You can borrow my house for the night. If you want.'

'That's okay.' Killian smiled, took a drink from his beer, and stood up. 'I don't know where I'll go, exactly, but I'll be fine. I've been doing this for over twenty years now. What about you?'

'What? Like I said, I'm –'

Killian interrupted him impatiently. 'No, I mean, did you do anything wrong that time? Do you have any regrets?'

Sander took in the year on the gravestone. 1999. 'I have quite a few regrets.'

'Just wondering. You know, Sander, the stories I could tell, the life I've lived . . .'

'Do you want to tell me? So I understand?'

He looked down. 'I'm not sure it would make any difference.'

Killian was so much his old self, yet changed too. Both of them had undergone transformations that made their situation a lot murkier; it would take a long time to be able to see through it.

He who can move on from his past gets to live twice.

91

Siri had personally been to the scene of the accident, had witnessed the wreck and seen Killian Persson's fire-ravaged body behind the wheel. But after her visit to the farmer in Mjäla, after seeing the harvesttime photograph, doubt had begun to gnaw at her. She didn't mention it to anyone. What would she have said? That Killian had risen from his grave and walked off? They would have looked at her like she had a screw loose.

'Which,' she confided in Vidar, 'might have been true. I wasn't doing so hot.'

She was starting to reach her limits.

'But you looked into it?'

'His identity notwithstanding, I had received information about an unidentified man who left one farm and never arrived at his expected destination. That meant yet another possible disappearance. But also,' she added, her voice full of regret, 'I started to take a look at our investigation of the accident. If you can call it an investigation. I'm sure you've seen it.'

Vidar understood what she was getting at. It wasn't immediately noticeable; everything was in its proper place and procedures had been followed to the letter. But what had been done was flimsy. It was understandable: it had been Christmas, all the stations in the county were understaffed, people were enjoying time off. And what's more, the incident had not been remarkable, not from a law-enforcement perspective. A fatal crash on a deserted county road. Happens all the time. There was no reason to investigate any scenario other than the obvious one. Besides, the landslide in Skavböke happened less than twenty-four hours later. All resources were diverted to dealing with the aftermath of the disaster.

Vidar realized he probably would have done exactly what they did, prioritized the same things.

All that was left of the body in the car was bone and sinew; the fire had consumed the rest. DNA testing was still in its infancy back then. And even if they could have taken a sample from the remains, there wouldn't have been anything to compare it to, besides the small amount of blood that had been collected from the car in Skavböke, the blood believed to have come from Killian Persson. In this case, the use of dental records – a common method of identifying the deceased – had been made considerably more difficult because the driver hadn't been wearing a seat belt. The crash resulted in a fractured jaw and the loss of several teeth, many of which were never recovered. Accordingly, the results were based more on what was logical and probable than what was discovered during analysis. Vidar found this reasonable as well.

As he related these thoughts to Siri, she looked grim. They had stopped next to a bench along one of the park's gravel paths, protected under one of the big old trees. It smelled sharp and fresh, ancient.

'Right,' she said. 'But that doesn't actually change anything.'

'You didn't say anything to anyone? Not even Gerd?'

'What would I have said?' She sat down on the bench and slumped. 'That they buried the wrong person?' She shook her head. 'Yes, I probably should have. But I couldn't. I didn't know who I could talk to.'

Vidar waited. It was cool beneath the tree. He would be happy to stay here for a while, just for a chance to breathe.

'Then again,' she continued, 'the more I uncovered, the more convinced I became that it really could have been him at the farm. Killian, that is. And that he was the one I caught a glimpse of at the encampment, the guy who took off. I guess I just started to accept it, just to myself, that it could be true. That the body in the car belonged to someone else.'

Whoever it was she was searching for now, he remained in the shadows. Alive, perhaps, but at some point during her search Siri began to wonder what that really meant. *Alive*. Such a beautiful word, maybe the most beautiful of all. If you ignored what it could entail.

'Given the circumstances, I suppose we should have connected the accident with Hampus Olsson. But there was no reason to, really, not from what we could see. They were simply two separate incidents. By the time there was a link between them, it was too late.'

'Until you put the two together,' Vidar pointed out.

'And, like I said, it was too late.'

He supposed you could look at it that way, or at least tell yourself that was so if you had to.

'Then that's why you quit,' Vidar said, as though he had only just realized it. 'Because of Hampus Olsson and Killian Persson, right?'

She looked up at him. Her gaze was steady and warm but full of regret. She leaned forward, propping her elbows on her thighs and burying her face in her hands.

'All I wanted, once,' she said, 'was to understand stuff. Then, when I did understand, I couldn't handle it. And now Filip Söderström is dead. I don't know what to do. I'm so ashamed.'

Not so surprising, maybe.

Oftentimes, part of being human is living your life on the very edge of shame.

Vidar observed her hunched back and considered placing a hand there. She seemed to need it. Instead, he said: 'I have a proposal.'

92

When Siri finished speaking, Adrian al-Hadid glanced from her to Vidar and back again. His eyes wide, he picked up the old photograph from the harvest in Mjäla and studied it.

Vidar reached for the computer and stopped the recording. 'How do I save this?'

'It saves automatically,' Adrian replied, photograph in hand. 'Just wait a sec.'

Vidar muttered something unintelligible.

They were in his office. On the wall behind them was the big whiteboard with Vidar's hand-drawn map of Skavböke, now crowded with notes.

'So...' Adrian said, putting down the picture. 'Killian Persson is alive. Is that the conclusion?'

'It's a hypothesis,' Siri said reluctantly.

'I think we should assume that's the case,' Vidar added.

'And he killed Filip Söderström.'

'Maybe,' Siri said.

'There are many reasons to think so.' Vidar again. 'But it's a big... deal.'

Adrian snorted.

'What's that sound supposed to mean?' Siri asked icily.

'Nothing, just, a *big deal* – yeah, to put it mildly. I'm sorry, I don't mean any offense. It's just so crazy.'

The story Siri had shared was all she had, she said, as though in sharing it she had repaid a debt that had weighed on her for a very long time. Maybe that was so. Still, he had insisted on bringing her up here, like the tipster she now was, so that her story could be documented.

'He *might* be alive,' Siri said. 'You don't know any more than that.'

'For now, though,' Vidar said softly, 'we three are the only ones who are aware that this might be the case. We should probably keep it that way, for the time being. Markus is a good boss, but this might cause him a lot of headaches. What's more, there are family members to consider. Hampus Olsson's mother is still alive, for instance.'

Siri picked up a recent photograph of the murder weapon and studied the forensic report. Vidar wondered what she was thinking. She hadn't been this close to solving the puzzle for a long time – or maybe ever.

Also on the desk were copied pages from Filip Söderström's planner. Vidar considered them for the umpteenth time that day. *Funeral SC 12:00 Work 1:30*. The number one from June. What had he said about that, Adrian? First day sober. Had Filip started drinking again? Yes, maybe. But if so, shouldn't it have been noticeable?

Adrian sat up straight.

'What do we do? We can't label him a person of interest. A dead man. All hell would break loose.'

Vidar stood up and went to the whiteboard.

'Yeah . . .' he mused. 'So what do we do?'

'We might not have much time. If he only showed up because of his father's funeral, he'll drop off the radar again soon.'

Vidar studied the board.

'But why did he kill Filip?'

'He probably needed to dispose of a witness,' Adrian said.

'What?'

'Filip discovers Killian, likely around the time of the

funeral. Now Filip knows he's alive, that he's back. The only solution is to silence him.'

'Hmm.' Vidar blinked. 'Maybe. Nothing from Rasmusgården yet?'

'The material is on its way here by car. I got one of the summer interns to go pick it up.'

'Excellent.' Vidar ran a hand over his stubble. More to himself than to anyone else, he said, 'And where is he?' He placed a finger on the map. 'Here, more or less, this is where he kills Filip.'

'Hypothesis,' Siri reminded him, but Vidar ignored her.

'After that, if we assume Killian returns the spade, that puts him here, at Filip's house, not far from the scene. But then what?'

'He could be anywhere right now,' Adrian said. 'In forty-eight hours, you could walk all the way to Jönköping. If he got hold of a bicycle, he could be in Gävle for all we know.'

'I don't think he'll go that far now,' Vidar said. 'But we need more information.'

'Who should we ask, though?'

Vidar stared at the board, at the names. 'I have a suggestion.'

'Siri?' Adrian hissed. He had grabbed Vidar's arm to hold him back from leaving the room. 'You're taking *her*? She's a civilian.'

Vidar stared at Adrian's clasping hand in surprise.

'I don't really see any other option. You stay here and wait for the material from Rasmusgården in the meantime.'

Adrian's eyes grew wide. He let go of Vidar. 'Haven't you noticed what a state she's in? Depression is practically oozing out of her. You're looking at this as a chance for her to make peace with some shit from her past. That's nice, but it's not okay. That's not our job.'

Vidar looked at him in surprise again. 'We don't know what's going to happen next. Are more people going to die, in an hour, in a day? We need to know more. Siri saved Felicia's life once, and anyway, it was her idea to come along. Do you have a better suggestion?'

'So your only concern is the investigation?'

'Yes,' Vidar said.

'And you're prepared to risk Siri's safety for it? That's not okay either.'

This time, Vidar didn't respond.

93

It was a sultry evening, but heavy, dark clouds were closing in from the sea. The newscasters on the radio in Vidar's car warned of downpours. Nothing yet, in these parts. The village had settled in for the night. Livestock dozed out in the pastures, and insects chirped and buzzed loudly.

They almost missed it, an SUV half-hidden in a small grove of trees. Vidar stopped at the edge of the road and eyed the oversized vehicle as though it were a crime scene.

'Wait here,' he told Siri, and stepped into the humid, hot air.

Vidar approached with caution. He recognized the license plate. He rested a tentative hand on the hood. Still warm. He peered into the side window. Empty black beer cans on the passenger-side floor.

The car looked clean, although the roads got very dusty in this summer heat. He studied the door handle on the driver's side, then walked around the car to do the same with the passenger side.

He took out his phone and snapped a picture, then returned to his own car.

'You know who that belongs to, don't you?' Siri said.

'Yes. It's empty, aside from a few cans of Spendrups Premium Gold on the floor. Prints on both door handles too. Hard to say if they were fresh, but they looked it.'

They drove on, taking their time. Siri was quiet, looking out the window.

'You didn't even want to touch my binder at first,' Vidar

said. 'Now you want to come along. Talk about changing courses midstream.'

'Horses,' Siri said.

'Huh?'

'The expression is "changing horses midstream".' She turned her head slowly. 'Your colleague didn't want me to come, did he?'

'No. But he's young and idealistic, still.'

'More like he's a stickler for the rules.'

Vidar glanced her way.

'I know this is important to you, and it'll be great if you can get her to talk. But you have to follow my instructions.' He turned off the road, drove in among the trees, and parked in a small grove nearby, with a view of the house. 'Better if we approach on foot, I think.'

They looked around as they walked toward the house. Through the windows they caught glimpses of lamps, dim lighting, and movement. She was home.

A doorbell sounded loud and clear through the white wooden door. They took a step back and stood very still, listening for sounds.

A woman opened the door with an uncertain smile.

'Goodness,' she said when she saw Siri. 'It's been ages.'

Siri smiled in response. 'It's nice to see you, Felicia.'

They stepped into the front hall. Vidar introduced himself.

'If you think it's too quiet in here, that makes three of us. It's not the same when the kids aren't home. I always think it feels strange without them.'

'When will they be home?' Siri asked.

'Tomorrow. Then the battle will begin again.'

'Teenagers?'

'You bet. Do you have kids?'

'Two of them.'

'Teenagers?'

'Not yet, but I'm dreading it.'

'You'll miss them when they move out,' Vidar said. 'Believe me, I know.'

Felicia asked if they wanted tea. She rummaged in the cupboards and stood by the stove, waiting for a saucepan of water to boil. Steam rose toward the fan. On the kitchen table, in front of Vidar and Siri, she set cups and teabags, and an open jar of Halland Honey.

'I know something's going on,' she said once she'd poured the water and taken a seat at the table. 'I'm sure you're not here just for tea.'

'No, I'm afraid you're right,' Siri said.

Felicia dunked her teabag into the piping-hot water, avoiding their gazes. 'I don't know quite what to say. This is dredging up all that old stuff again, somehow. For a split second, you're eighteen again. And not in a good way.'

'I understand. I'm no longer a police officer – I want you to know that – but I thought I should be here anyway. If that's okay with you.'

Felicia nodded. Vidar had selected his tea. He watched dark ribbons swirl out of it like smoke, coloring the water golden brown. Felicia studied him, looking hesitant.

'We're trying to understand what's going on,' he said slowly. 'For that reason, I have some questions for you, and they might seem a little strange. But all you have to do is answer as straightforwardly and thoroughly as you can.'

Felicia crossed her legs and leaned forward, cupping her hand around her own mug of tea to warm it.

'When did you last see Killian Persson?' he asked.

'I thought you wanted to ask about Filip.'

'We'll get to him. When did you last see Killian?'

'Oh boy. Um, Christmas Eve of 1999. That evening.'

'And when did you last hear from him?'

'Well, that same night. That was it.' She blinked. 'Killian is dead. You know that, right?'

Vidar's tea was ready. He lifted the teabag out and wound it carefully around his spoon, squeezing out the last few drops and placing it aside.

'We have reason to believe,' he said, sounding apologetic, 'that Killian Persson might not be dead.'

'What?'

'We think Killian might be alive.'

She stared at them.

'Killian . . .' Vidar began, but Felicia beat him to it:

'What do you mean, *reason to believe*? What the hell kind of reason would that be? Are you completely –'

She leaned back against her chair. Her sudden rage evaporated.

'I know you were friends when you were young,' Vidar went on. 'That you were close. If he *is* alive, he might have contacted you, or tried to. That's why I'm here. I want to try to help him.'

'Help him.' She was breathing harder now, as if she needed air. 'I can show you his gravestone.'

'Felicia.' Siri took over now. 'We wouldn't be sitting here if it wasn't important.'

Vidar looked at Felicia's hands, quiet around her mug.

'What are these reasons you're talking about?' she said again, having collected herself.

'There is evidence that he may have been involved in Filip Söderström's death.'

94

In a small corner of Sander's mind, their reunion proceeded just as he'd imagined during all those desperate moments of fantasizing about it. Big smiles, laughter, hugs. Two cups of coffee on the table in his yard on Backavägen, or in town, all the questions that finally had answers.

Sander tried to ascertain whether the same thing was happening inside Killian as well, but it didn't seem like it. Instead, Killian's words echoed through him like a phantom bell. *The stories I could tell, the life I've lived.* More than twenty years had passed. How can you explain twenty years of events in a way that makes that length of time make any sense? It's impossible. All those little moments, occasions, emotions, the high resolution of the myriad experiences that leave their mark on every individual.

Killian simply sat with his backpack next to him on the floor of the basement, across from Sander, listening to the conversation Felicia was having with the police above their heads.

His expression was inscrutable.

They had lingered at the graveside for a long time. Sander watched the clouds gathering and asked for another beer. Killian handed one over.

'Felicia and I,' Sander tried, but he didn't know how to continue. It was like he was confessing to a great betrayal.

'I know,' Killian said bluntly.

'You do?'

'She told me.'

A cold flicker in his belly, an old tension returning.

'So you saw her?'

'After the funeral.'

The clouds moved in. A sudden chill made Sander shudder. He thought of Olivia and the kids.

'Maybe we should get going,' he said. 'I should be getting on the road to Kivik.'

Killian watched him with what looked like suspicion. 'So you're going?'

'I can drive you to her place first.'

He had, on Killian's request, parked in a nearby clearing and accompanied him the last little bit to Felicia's. She seemed relieved to see Killian, who gave her a quick hug but avoided eye contact.

Sander found himself in a house where whatever was going on was something he hadn't been aware of. He was on the outside of it, but even so he was compromised, involved in something he didn't understand. He looked at the two of them, standing by the kitchen table. As if Killian and Felicia were somehow back in the old days: they were young, in control of their own future, and nothing was going to happen to them.

The spell was broken when Felicia looked out the window with a start.

'What is it?' Killian asked.

'They're coming. The police are coming.'

95

Felicia didn't move as Vidar spoke. He avoided details, skipped specifics, never mentioned Jakob Lindell, or anyone else, by name. When he was finished, she began to ask questions: how many people knew about this, and for how long? Why hadn't anyone said anything? And how could they have been mistaken back then, when the accident happened, how was that even possible?

She came back around to that question over and over. Vidar tried to answer as truthfully as possible.

'So that's why,' Vidar said, 'we have to ask again. Have you been in touch with him? Has he tried to contact you?'

'Definitely not. Not that I know of.'

Felicia's voice sounded hollow. Maybe it was shock, only now taking hold of her.

'If he does try to contact you, we'd like you to let us know.' He took a notepad from his pocket, tore off a page, and jotted down his phone number. 'Can you do that?'

Absently, she took the piece of paper from him.

'Yes, of course. For sure.'

Meanwhile, Siri gathered their teabags and went to the sink to throw them in the garbage. Vidar tried to signal discreetly to her to come back to the table, but she didn't pay attention.

Instead, she gingerly closed the cabinet door, as if the slightest sound might shatter the conversation around the table, and took a lap through the house, her steps slow and light. She stopped in front of the basement door, as if something was happening there that only Siri noticed. Vidar, jaw clenched, stayed in his chair while Siri grasped the handle and slowly turned it.

96

Felicia's basement smelled like earth and paint and laundry detergent. They could hear the voices upstairs clearly; the walls were thin. Footsteps sounded sharp and decisive; furniture scraped loudly when they sat down at the table.

Killian had curled up in a corner as though trying to protect himself.

Felicia had told them that the slightest noise would carry up to the kitchen. Sander hunched and closed his eyes, felt exhaustion coming over him. It mixed with the mild intoxication that was rising into his head.

When he opened his eyes again, Killian was a silhouette of shadows and the occasional stripe of light. He had tucked his head between his knees and it sounded like he was snuffling. Sander saw his shoulders shaking.

'Killian. Killian,' Sander whispered softly, moving cautiously, silently to sit beside him. 'It's okay. Everything's going to work out fine.'

Killian didn't seem to hear him. The snuffling continued. Sander put an arm around his shoulders.

Killian seemed almost feverish. Sander told him again that everything was okay, even though it was starting to dawn on him that it wasn't; he told Killian things would work out even as he realized they wouldn't. He pulled Killian close and found him remarkably pliant, as if there was no will left in his large frame. Killian's head fell to Sander's chest and rested there.

This was just like the way Sander held Albin and Josefin

sometimes. When he thought of them, his heart lurched and he wished them all the good and beautiful things in the world, wanted them to be protected at any price. Hoped that any bad decisions they might be forced to make at the age of eighteen wouldn't haunt them for the rest of their lives.

Sander watched as Killian reached out a hand, searching for something to hold on to, and found Sander's upper arm.

They slowly sank farther onto the floor until they were nearly on their backs. Then it happened: for a brief moment, Killian's head weighed nothing against Sander's chest, as if he were merely vapor, or the chilly gust of wind that comes in when you open a window. Maybe he really *was* dead, after all. Then in a split second its weight returned, almost unnaturally great and deep, like everything Killian had gone through and still carried was present, but on a slight delay.

Gradually Killian grew still, and soon he was simply breathing. Above them, the police were still talking to Felicia.

Sander had spent so much time thinking about death over the years, Killian's death and his own, who he would be when the end came. Death was the greatest of all mysteries, he thought, and the answer would only come in the same instant it became too late to consider it. Now he realized he was wrong. Life was more profoundly mysterious than death could ever be.

He could smell Killian's hair. It smelled like the forest, earthy and fresh. Familiar and foreign all at once.

'I wonder what my real funeral will be like,' Killian whispered after a while.

'How would you like it to be?'

'I don't know. But if there's no alcohol, I'm not coming.'

'You're not going to attend your own funeral?'

'No. I mean, it wouldn't be the first time.'

An absurd laugh bubbled up in Sander's chest, but he swallowed it down.

'And,' Killian continued, 'I want them to play my playlist.'

'You have a playlist?'

'I have songs I like.'

Sander realized he didn't know what songs those were. He wished Killian could send them to him, but how? Did Killian have a cell phone, did he have social media profiles, did he subscribe to streaming services?

'And,' Killian went on again, 'whoever can't produce a picture of us together isn't allowed in.'

'What'll that be, then, like, three people?'

This time Killian was the one smothering his laughter. 'Plenty of alcohol for me, in that case.'

He didn't add up, Killian. It was like he was split in two, both markedly older and still eighteen. He spoke about death as they would have back then, in 1999, shallowly, fragmentally, uncoupled from reality. Death as nothing more than a fantasy, something you could easily keep at arm's length. Maybe that's what happens when you manage to fool death for so long.

'You always brought out the best in me,' Killian said. 'Do you know that?'

'I did?'

'Yes. That's how I felt, anyway. Most of the time, at least. Until... you know, that last night. But,' he added, when Sander opened his mouth, 'that doesn't matter now. I just wanted you to know that. That you saw me, somehow. In a way no one else did.'

'I never believed it was you.'

Seconds of silence from Killian, a few too many. 'What do you mean?'

'Mikael.'

When Killian finally spoke, he sounded different, like he had crept down into a tiny fissure inside himself. 'That night...'

Both of them fell silent as they registered Vidar Jörgensson's words on the top side of the floorboards.

There is evidence that he may have been involved in Filip Söderström's death.

Vidar's voice was deeper and more robust, clearer to make out than the other two. Killian didn't move. Sander kept listening, suddenly more attentive, but he tried to hide it.

They heard soft steps. Someone had stood up and was walking through the house. The footsteps approached the door to the basement. Killian slowly stood up and looked around in the darkness as if trying to locate something.

The steps stopped at the door. Sander held his breath.

'Killian,' he whispered. 'No.'

The handle turned with a creak. Killian thrust his hand into his backpack, and when it came back out his fingers were clutching the handle of a woodcarving knife.

'What the hell are you doing?' Sander hissed.

But this was a different Killian, unfamiliar, a stranger.

The handle jiggled. Someone was trying to open the door. Killian moved to the bottom of the stairs with his knife in the air. Sander followed him, very uneasy, and was just about to grab Killian by the arm when all the air was sucked out of the room.

Above them, the yanking on the handle grew more insistent.

'Don't say a word.'

Suddenly, Killian's free arm came out and his hand clamped around Sander's neck, firm and mechanical. The stranglehold was so unexpected that the shock didn't give way to pain until his head started pounding. His mouth and throat were producing sounds, but no words. Killian stared at Sander, his eyes blank.

Sander tried to call for help, but Killian's grip only grew more tenacious. He clawed at Killian's arm, but it wasn't enough. His friend was so much bigger, so much stronger. Killian looked toward the basement stairs again.

The yanking stopped. Steps again, steps retreating through the house.

Sander's vision was starting to go black. When Killian finally let go and lowered his knife hand, Sander felt the urge to cough and had to double over to stifle it, gasping for air. His fingertips were prickly, full of pins and needles. He slowly straightened up, feeling increasingly dizzy.

'I had to,' Killian rasped in a hollow tone, his voice vibrating with something Sander didn't recognize.

They stared at each other in the darkness.

97

As Vidar and Siri stepped into the yard after their visit to Felicia Grenberg, the clouds were forming towers and the day's heat gave way to a pale evening chill.

'I told you,' Vidar said as they returned to the car, 'to do as I said.'

'I did.'

'Did you go down in the basement?'

'No, the door was locked.'

'Good.'

'Someone's down there. All the doors in the house were open or unlocked, except that one. I'm pretty sure I heard something down there, like whispers. What brand were the empty cans in the SUV?'

'Spendrups Premium Gold.'

'There were some of those on top of the trash in the kitchen.'

'It's Sander's car. The SUV.' Vidar rested a hand on the wheel and gazed at the house. They had a good view from here. 'I don't believe her. She's a good actor, but not good enough.'

The darkness was coming their way; the wind intensified and trees began to sway.

Vidar took out his phone. Markus picked up on the second ring.

'How's it going?' he asked.

'Moving forward,' Vidar said. 'I think this might end tonight.'

'End?'

'I think we're going to solve it. I'm outside Felicia Grenberg's house. She's inside, and I suspect Sander Eriksson and Killian Persson are too.'

'Killian Persson? Isn't he dead?'

'Seems he isn't.'

Markus was always quick to rally in the most urgent situations. It was a skill he'd had since Vidar got to know him years and years ago.

'Have you seen him, were you able to identify him?'

'Not yet.'

A momentary silence. 'What do you need from me?'

'More people. A lot more. In case this all goes to hell.'

Markus was already up; Vidar could hear him moving around.

'Now?'

'If possible.'

'They'll be there. For now, just hold tight. Killian Persson – you really think it's him? For real?'

'Yes.'

'Jesus.'

Vidar didn't put the phone down after they hung up.

'I've known Markus since the academy. He's a good man. If there are officers available, he'll get them here. I just hope they make it in time.'

'Or what?'

'Or,' Vidar said, 'I'll have to manage on my own.'

98

When they came back upstairs, it felt to Sander like he was returning from another world. Felicia stood with her arms crossed, gazing anxiously at the driveway. Outside, the wind was blowing harder.

'I think that went well,' she said, as if to convince herself it was true.

It was so strange to see them together again, Felicia and Killian. Their contours had taken on a faint shimmer; both of them seemed like they might dissolve at any moment. So weird to feel the ache and sting in his throat, his tender skin. Killian had strangled him without an ounce of hesitation, and Sander had experienced the loneliest moment of his life.

'Was that true?'

Sander's voice was raspy, almost strained. He touched his throat. In the silent house, his question sounded harsher, more demanding than he'd meant it to.

Killian turned his head. 'Was what true?'

'What they said. About Filip.'

'What do you mean?'

It's so simple to love the dead as you remember them; it's much more difficult when they're standing in front of you, transformed by all the time they've spent underground.

'You should talk to the police, Killian.'

A shadow fell over Killian's face. Sander had tried to say it in a sensible tone, like he was simply giving his friend some advice, but his voice was stern.

'And what do you want me to tell them?'

'Just tell the truth. They'll understand.'

'I can't. They'll lock me up.'

Sander paused in the silence. 'Why?'

'You don't get it. You never did understand this stuff.'

'Killian. Why do they think you had something to do with Filip's death?'

Killian glanced at the kitchen table and the two chairs where the officers had sat. He put down his backpack, sat down stiffly, and rested his forearms on the tabletop. He raised his eyes to look at Sander. Felicia stayed by the kitchen window, watching the road.

'He saw me. After the funeral. Filip. I didn't know what to do. I couldn't let him . . .'

Sander quaked inside. 'You couldn't let him what? What happened?'

'I didn't quite give you the whole story, before. I didn't come straight to the funeral.'

99

'I needed . . .' Killian fumbled through his words, as though he'd kept quiet so long that they wouldn't simply come to him; rather, he had to actively search for them, test them out before he could say them aloud. 'I thought I could make my way to the chapel, no problem. For a long time I wondered if it was worth the risk, but it was . . . I didn't come when Mom died, even though I looked up when the funeral was. I've never been able to forget it, that I didn't go, that I never got to say goodbye, but I guess it was . . . you know, I was too scared to come. And afterwards, it was too late. So this time, with Dad, I felt like I had no choice. And I figured I would make it easy and quick. But when I got there, it was like something grabbed hold of me.'

He frowned, as if his story had already gone wrong.

'I don't know how to describe it.'

He came through the forest, avoiding roads and trails, but it was hard to figure out where to go. He knew about the landslide, of course, but he hadn't realized how much had been destroyed. Or had it always looked like this? He couldn't tell what was changed and what he had simply forgotten.

Between the trees he caught a glimpse of a woman working in a garden. She wore jeans and a T-shirt in the warm morning sun, and she was holding a big watering can. Killian stopped to watch her. He was close enough to hear the burbling of the water from the can, its gentle splatter on leaves and petals.

It was her. In the split second before she turned and looked straight at him, there at the forest's edge, he knew.

He couldn't simply pass by, avoid her. And when she touched his cheek, as if to make sure he was really there, something remarkable happened: she burst out laughing, just as Sander would do in a few days' time.

Felicia convinced him to come back to her house after the funeral. She needed to make an appearance at the reception at the village hall; she'd said she would be there, and if she didn't turn up people would wonder where she was. Then she had to go in to work for a while. But she asked him to stick around.

'Just so we can talk a little more,' she said. 'So I can understand. That's all. Just for a little while.'

So, after the funeral, he came back. She had left the front door unlocked.

Killian sat down at the kitchen table and hoped Felicia would arrive soon.

He couldn't think.

He had been spotted during the funeral, he was sure of it, but he told himself it was just the shock of being back, that and his grief over his father's death. It was *kymig*, he thought, how he'd stayed away so long to protect not just himself but others. Now he was completely unprotected, vulnerable.

Time passed. An hour, maybe two? He tentatively walked through Felicia's house, as if it might contain clues to the person she'd become. He pulled photo albums from the shelves and saw faces he didn't recognize, men and children, scenes from a life he had missed out on.

Someone arrived. He heard brisk steps in the yard and realized it wasn't Felicia. As if to confirm why his hands were trembling, Killian went to the door and opened it, and there he stood. He had changed into work clothes, like this was simply a brief stop on the way. Maybe it was.

There was a moment of absolute silence as they stood there, taking in what had become of one another. Killian was astonished. In Filip's face, he saw a life that reminded him of his own.

'I thought you might be here,' Filip said. 'I'm sorry for your loss. I have to go to work, but I thought we should talk.' He was holding a large, dark object in his hand. 'I have a feeling you recognize this.'

The spade. Everything surrounding Killian fell apart.

100

Filip didn't even seem surprised to see him. Killian wondered why but couldn't bring himself to ask. If one person knew, there must be more. Who? Would any of them call the police? He couldn't handle that, not now. For so long he'd gone to great lengths to keep from being noticed; he had given up so much. Was he about to learn that he had failed?

He recalled one of the few close calls: a homeless encampment one summer, long ago, where he ended up after spending some time with the farmer in Mjäla. The police had almost gotten him that time. He had dashed off through the trees.

They hadn't had time to see that it was him, he was sure of it. Or had they?

He never should have come back. He wondered if Filip understood the position of power he was in, if he knew how small Killian felt as he stood before him. How vulnerable he was. All it would take was one phone call, to just about anyone.

Killian looked at the road outside, noticed Filip's van. If anyone passed by, they would see him, recognize him. They would surely wonder what Filip Söderström was doing at Felicia Grenberg's house. Peril throbbed in his chest like a second pulse.

'I would really rather not stand so out in the open like this,' he told Filip. 'Can you come in?'

Filip hesitated, seemingly also uncertain about what was going to happen next.

'Let's take a drive and talk. You probably haven't seen what it looks like around here for a long time.'

Killian wasn't sure he wanted to find out, but he couldn't refuse. He climbed into the van, which smelled like smoke and old sweat, and settled into the passenger seat. He focused on breathing.

Filip got behind the wheel. He placed the spade between them and drove off slowly. The area looked so different. Killian could see the young forest, short and sparse compared to the older, lush growth. He sank deeper into the seat; he would be so easily spotted if they met any oncoming traffic. He glanced at the spade. Hadn't seen it for a long time, but he did recognize it.

'I know it was you,' Filip said after several minutes of driving in silence.

Filip's gaze flicked to Killian, or to the spade, before he went back to watching the road.

'My brother, I mean. That that's why you disappeared.'

Killian didn't say anything. He wanted to, but he couldn't.

'Okay.'

That was all he could manage.

'But I've never understood why,' Filip went on. 'I think that's what I want to know. That,' he added, 'and what happened to you. Clearly things didn't go well. When you've lived a hard life, you can tell when other people have too.'

Killian still didn't speak up. Filip seemed happy to wait, but they hadn't gotten very far when he abruptly pulled over. Killian didn't recognize the spot. Filip turned off the engine and set the hand brake, leaned back.

'Not a day goes by that I don't think about him,' he said. 'I don't visit his grave too often, that's not my thing, really. I have a hard time dealing with it.'

'Where are we?'

'We used to live here. Right there. The front door was there. It's crazy, isn't it? Like the house never even existed. I come here now and then to think. Used to do that quite a bit when I was in a treatment program years ago. It was... In the end I came here all the time, several days a week. I said so to Isidor Enoksson, actually – we sometimes talked about the old days. "What do *you* think you're doing when you go there?" he said. Priests.'

Filip chuckled wearily.

'What he eventually told me, as a kind of explanation, was that something went wrong here a long time ago. Something I haven't been able to make sense of, and the reason I keep coming back is to try to figure out what it was. As if I hadn't figured *that* out on my own.'

He looked serious now, as if Isidor's words had still meant something to him.

'I don't know if it's true, but it might be. I've never run into anyone else here. It's like people avoid this place. I just want to know why Mikael died. And what happened.' Filip nodded at the spade. 'I know this is what killed him. But that's all I know.'

Killian hesitated. 'I don't know what to tell you, Filip.'

'Just tell it like it was. Like it is. Just tell the truth, for once.'

He grabbed the spade and got out of the car, gesturing at Killian to follow him. Filip climbed down into the ditch, out into the grove of trees.

'Was it you,' Killian asked, 'who caused the landslide?'

He didn't respond. A sharp jab with his foot, and he thrust the spade into the ground.

101

Killian looked tormented as he sat at the kitchen table facing Sander and Felicia.

'I didn't know what to do,' he said. 'At first I didn't resist, but then he started to strangle me. I couldn't breathe. I managed to get around him somehow, and grab the spade... I just wanted him to stop, to let go. I panicked. That was all. I didn't want to leave the spade in his car after, so I tried to wipe it down and then I put it in his garage with all the rest of the tools. I didn't know what I was thinking. I panicked. I had to put it somewhere, I figured it would be worse if someone found it in the forest, and... I don't know.'

Sander couldn't move. He didn't know what to think anymore. It sounded true. Killian looked honest. But, he realized, there was nothing in Killian's story to prove that this was what had happened; there was only his own insistence it was so. Just like the story about the car accident out in Esmared. Maybe that was no accident at all, maybe Killian had killed Hampus Olsson in cold blood. Just like he could, in fact, have killed Filip, a calculated move, cold as ice.

Sander could still feel Killian's hand around his throat. All the guilt that had been piled on Killian might be deserved. And here Sander had defended him over the years, like an idiot.

The knife, Sander thought. *What did he do with the knife he had in the basement? Where is it now?*

'I don't understand how he could have known,' Killian went on. 'That I'm alive, I mean. He knew it even before he saw me at the chapel, I'm sure of it. He knew. But I don't get how.'

Sander stared at Killian. Felicia was still by the window, saying nothing.

'*That's* what you're worried about?'

'What? What's wrong?' Killian looked at him in genuine confusion.

'He's dead,' Sander said. His voice trembled. 'Filip is dead.'

'I know.'

'And you killed him. Do you understand what that means? Don't you even get the difference? Between life and death?'

A spark inside Sander, something old and grim for which he had no words. Maybe that was just as well. Life and death seemed to be nothing but words to Killian. It was like they had no counterpart in the real world, in his life, in his heart.

Sander's phone rang from his pocket. Everyone reacted as though an alarm had sounded.

'Don't answer it.'

Killian made it sound like a threat.

Sander stood with his phone in hand, gazing into those empty, pale eyes. Memories flashed through him. The voice was familiar, older but still Killian's, that burly figure, that face. Sander recognized everything that had been burned into his cells during a long-ago childhood, yet nothing was familiar at all.

'Is it the police?'

The question came from Felicia.

'It's Olivia. The kids. They're wondering where I am. I have to answer.'

'Don't answer it,' Killian repeated.

'Killian,' Felicia said softly. 'It's best if he takes it.'

Something snapped in Killian's eyes. He thrust his hand into his pocket, and out it came again.

'I'm not going to do anything. Just don't say anything about me. All I want is to get out of here.'

In Killian's hand was the knife, simple and ordinary, like a mechanic gesturing with his screwdriver. What had Sander expected, that more than twenty years could have passed unnoticed, without leaving impressions or scars? He knew better. The dead don't return for no reason, and when they do come back, they're no longer as they were in life.

The only problem was, Killian wasn't dead. Sander studied his friend's body, struck by how physical it was, flesh and blood and bone, organs working doggedly inside. He was alive, but Sander no longer knew him, and maybe he never had. A ratatat sounded, out of rhythm with the stubborn ringtone.

Raindrops the size of coins struck the window. Three or four, then more, and soon there were too many to count.

The sky was falling.

102

'Yes. No, everything's fine.'

Sander had set the phone on the table. Olivia's voice came from the speaker, blaring right into the kitchen in front of Felicia and Killian, and she had no idea.

'Are you sure?' she said. 'You were supposed to come back yesterday, and now you're not coming tonight either. Is everything really okay? Is there anything I should know?'

'I'm okay,' Sander said. 'It's just this thing with Filip. I promise, that's all. I have to talk to the police again.'

'What about?'

Killian stared at him.

'We can talk about it when I get there tomorrow. Because I will be there tomorrow, I promise.'

'Okay.' She sounded sad. 'The kids are asleep. Do you want to talk for a while? I miss you.'

He couldn't keep his voice from shaking. 'I think I'll try to get hold of the police now. I'll be there tomorrow. I miss you too. I miss all of you.'

'Okay. Good night.'

She sounded subdued, disappointed. A click.

'No,' Killian said, an icy veil draped over his voice. 'Leave it out.'

'Why?'

'Just do it.'

Sander left the phone on the table, and Killian pulled it his way. He placed the knife on the table, right next to Sander's phone.

'I'm not going to go to the police, Killian. I just needed something to tell her.'

'You think I believe you'd tell me the truth, over your wife?'

There was a sharp note to Killian's tone.

'I just fucking lied to her for your sake!' Sander exclaimed, his voice harsh and loud. 'Did I tell the truth? Did I say your name? Huh?'

'Sorry,' Killian said, his inner eighteen-year-old emerging again. 'No, you're right.' He reached out and touched Felicia's hip. It was a tender, passionate gesture. 'Could you walk around the house and see if there's anyone out there?'

It looked like she wanted to protest, but she didn't speak up. Just nodded slowly and went to the front hall, found an umbrella.

They were alone. His throat still aching, Sander stared at his friend as though gazing into a great cloud of fog.

'You choked me.'

'I had to.'

'You had to?' Sander was shocked at his words. 'Why?'

'I . . .' Killian trailed off.

'And now you're about to take off again.'

'I don't have a choice.'

'Where are you going to go?'

'I'll figure it out.'

'Killian, it was self-defense. Hey – you don't have to run away this time.'

Killian took a step toward Sander. 'You think I'm going to let them pin me to two murders? That's what would happen. You know it would.'

Everything around Sander had begun to quiver, as if reality were splitting at the seams.

Killian looked at Sander's wrist.

'I thought you threw that away.'

'I did.'

'Then you must have come back to get it. After I took off. Right?'

Sander didn't know what to say. All of a sudden Killian seemed insane again. He was impossible to follow, like an unpredictable pendulum.

Beyond the doorway, the hall. Sander could simply go, open the front door and head to his car, drive down to Kivik, out of this dream and back into real life, to Olivia and the children, all that was his. He didn't have to wait, to stay. There was no need to worry.

Even so, he knew it wouldn't be that simple. Killian stood in his way. He couldn't have imagined this until now, now that it was so very evident.

'Do you have any idea,' Sander said slowly, 'how much you meant to me? You let me believe you were dead. I could have helped you.'

The words came from way, way back in the past. Like he was calling up an image of an old monument, now crumbled.

Killian's face was expressionless.

'I didn't want your help,' Killian said. 'Then or now. I never wanted to see you again. I hated you. Don't you get it?'

Sander was taken aback. 'Why?'

Killian's gaze slid to the window. Rain beat against the pane. 'Where the hell is she?'

'What the hell happened to you, Killian?'

'That's what you think, isn't it. That something *happened* to me. That's how you see me. You know what? Everything that *happened* to me happened here, at home. And you had no fucking clue.'

Suddenly, Sander couldn't remember a thing. Not anymore. Hadn't Killian just said that Sander always saw the best in him? Maybe it wasn't so. Maybe Sander had been mistaken this whole time. Sander had been the greedy one. The one who wanted the whole world. That desire must have blinded him.

'I couldn't even come home for my mom's funeral! Do you know what that does to a person?'

'You could have come back.'

'To what?' Killian sounded almost sad now. 'What would I have been coming back to?'

'Come on! Me, Felicia, your family. Your parents. You know, Mikael, the money, even if it was you, you were only eighteen, you could have gotten help. You didn't have to throw your life away,' Sander tried, as a last resort. 'You don't have to this time either. You can't just keep running away over and over. Everything —'

'You'll go to the police. You even said so just now, right in front of me, to your wife.'

Sander stared at him. Killian was speaking and thinking like an eighteen-year-old again. As if he was stuck. Maybe he was.

'Yes, I'm going to go to the police. But everything will work itself out. As long as you stay.'

'And *you*!' As if Killian hadn't heard him, as if his rage had found another wave of strength, the accusation burst out and he grabbed the knife. 'What do you mean I threw away my life, what the fuck do you know? You got to live, and I didn't. You had everything, you had every opportunity, and this is what became of you? Tell me, what exactly have you done with your life? You didn't even leave town, for Christ's sake.'

'I stayed because I wanted to.'

'Why?'

'Because I felt guilty, obviously.'

'Guilty why?'

'I . . .' Sander began, but the words caught in his throat.

'Just say it.'

It came from Sander's lips in a whisper: 'What?'

'I know why you feel guilty.' Killian stepped closer to Sander again. 'Do you think she didn't tell me?'

'Felicia? What did she say?'

'Just tell me the truth.'

'I don't know what you mean. That is the truth. This is crazy, Killian.'

'Is that all you have to say? Are you that helpless? Huh?'

'But there's nothing more to say, Killian.'

Killian glanced down and adjusted his grip on the knife, looking at it as if it had only just appeared, placed in his hand by someone else.

'Go ahead, then, talk to the police,' he said. 'Go for it.'

Sander's mind ground to a halt.

There was violence here now.

103

It was pouring rain. From inside the car, Vidar and Siri watched the endless sweep of the windshield wipers. Constant little rivulets coursed down the edges.

Someone was walking through the downpour. Felicia. She looked around anxiously, under an umbrella, apparently trying to spot something. She went out to the road and scanned the area.

They had parked the car well into the grove; the old, gnarled trees shielded them from view, and the dim evening light and rain provided even more protection. Vidar put his hand on the door and prepared himself.

Just as Felicia seemed about to turn back toward the house, she saw them and froze. As Vidar climbed out, she backed away.

'Felicia,' he said in a low voice.

She hesitated. Vidar feared she would run, but when he opened the back door she quietly approached and got in, folding her umbrella and sitting down without a word. Vidar went back to the driver's seat and twisted around to look at her.

Rain dripped from her umbrella, forming little puddles on the seat.

'Felicia,' Vidar said calmly. 'We're going to help them, both of them. That's why we're here. But is there anyone else in the house, besides those two?'

She shook her head.

'Good. Are there any weapons in the house?'

She said something; Vidar leaned closer.

'I'm sorry,' he said. 'One more time. The rain – I couldn't hear.'

'He has a knife,' she said.

'Very good. Thank you, Felicia. Stay here.'

Vidar opened the door and stepped into the rain again. Siri placed a hand on Felicia's forearm. Her skin was bluish-gray; the evening had sucked all the color from the world.

He saw them through the kitchen window. They had turned on a light, and it lit up the room. There he was, Killian Persson – older now, of course, but just as big and blond, and there was Sander, who looked smaller next to his childhood friend. A strange shimmer hovered around them like a cold fog, everything easily distorted by waves and white veils. Maybe it was just the rain, but whatever it was Vidar was looking at, it seemed to be transpiring somewhere entirely different, in another time. If he squinted, it was like the image straightened out, the veils of fog and the water vanished, and Sander and Killian looked younger, maybe like they had in the past.

They were talking; their lips were moving. Then something happened. Sander shook his head. Killian stepped toward him in a threatening way. Sander didn't move. Instead, he looked directly out the window at Vidar.

Killian realized something was wrong and turned his head, his focus on Sander fizzling for a split second.

Vidar's and Killian's eyes locked. Killian seemed surprised, perplexed. Then Vidar saw the knife in Killian's hand.

Killian didn't waste any time. He tried to get past Sander, who snatched at him and caught hold of his shirt.

Vidar ran toward the house, but, slipping in the fresh mud, he wouldn't make it.

Through the pounding rain he heard Killian's voice: 'Fuck!

Let go of me. Just let me go!' Then, again, in a cry so loud his voice cracked: 'I gotta go! Let go of me!'

He tried to tear loose but Sander held on, and maybe it was this unnaturally firm grip that prompted Killian to raise the knife.

Sander tried to grab the knife, but it sliced his hand. Killian adjusted his grasp and punched Sander in the gut; he doubled over.

But he still didn't let go of Killian. Killian was struggling to get away, worm out of his shirt, but it didn't work despite his superior size. Instead, he yanked Sander up again, said something to him. Vidar couldn't tell what it was, but the knife was dangerously close to Sander's face.

Vidar had almost reached them. He heard a screech:

'Let go of me, for fuck's sake!'

Sander refused. He brought up his hand and whacked Killian in the cheek, hard. It looked like something might have broken. Killian's face contorted and he took a step back. Sander tried to swipe the knife, they fought over it, Sander with two hands and Killian with one. It was almost comical, like they were fighting over an invisible object.

Killian got a knee between Sander's legs. Sander coughed, went red in the face, and leaned so heavily on Killian that he lost his balance again. He staggered back, and Sander followed. When Killian regained his footing, something jerked between them and they froze.

PART FOUR

The Sign and the Rain

104

Blue lights flashed through the darkness and made time contract.

Isidor Enoksson sat at his kitchen table, watching them go by in the rain. A frightful mare, bringer of bad dreams, wrapped her wings around him.

He stared at his beer bottle. One sip left.

He drank it and eyed the label with disappointment, as though it had not delivered what it had promised.

Isidor suspected the worst.

Had to get over there, even though he'd been drinking.

He staggered to the garage, past his car to his bicycle. He walked it out to the driveway in the rain; it creaked loudly as he got on. Wobbly. Very wobbly, but it should work. Once, as legend had it, Isidor's predecessor, Hugo Edman, had made it all the way to Harplinge with the help of only a bicycle and two bottles of liquor.

Isidor placed his left shoe on the pedal and pushed. His foot slipped, and he nearly fell off but managed to catch himself in the nick of time. Would've been just fine to die there and then, he thought. But God hadn't sent him that sort of trial, not today.

Isidor climbed off the bicycle and tried to figure out what was wrong.

At last he realized the back tire was flat.

God da —

Isidor threw the bicycle down as though it had wronged him.

For I have sinned, the priest thought, gazing at the dark woods in the distance.

And then he began the walk to Skavböke.

105

It was all over, but it didn't feel that way.

Killian had fallen onto his back. The knife was stuck in his chest, and as he lay on the floor its handle pointed at the ceiling, standing straight and tall as a flagpole.

Vidar was out in his car, sitting very still. He had blood on his hands and three missed calls from Adrian al-Hadid. He ignored them, leaned his head against the headrest, and closed his eyes.

Living almost half your life in the shadow of a single incident, never understanding what had happened or how. That was what Sander Eriksson had done. Incredible, really. But sometimes you only understand something long after the fact. Killian had killed Mikael, Killian had killed Filip, and at last he had tried to kill Sander too. His best friend.

How had it all started?

At a party one night, a long time ago.

His phone rang again. Vidar opened his eyes and saw his boss's name. He brought the phone to his ear and closed his eyes again.

'What the hell happened?'

'They didn't make it in time.'

'Right, thank you, Vidar, I knew that much. An active lethal threat, and with a civilian right in the middle of it all.'

Markus was not very good at holding back his anger, never had been. Over the years, Vidar had come to appreciate this trait. An active lethal threat. Yes, that was what it had turned into. But he hadn't expected the situation to deteriorate so badly, despite Adrian's skepticism.

'Well, I did ask for backup,' Vidar said.

'It was on the way.'

'And she stayed in the car,' Vidar said. 'I couldn't just magically make her disappear, what was I supposed to do?'

Markus snorted with frustration into Vidar's ear.

'It is what it is,' he said at last. 'Screw it, I'll fix it somehow. What happened?'

Vidar didn't say anything for a long moment.

'I actually don't know. All I can tell you is what I believe happened.'

'Excellent.' He heard Markus sit down in a chair. It made a comfortable creak that seemed out of place in the moment. He was at home in Laholm. 'Go ahead, give it to me.'

'I think Sander Eriksson was trying to stop Killian Persson from taking off. That's what it looked like, anyway.'

'Start from the beginning, would you?' Markus said.

From the beginning? Vidar thought. *Where would I even start?*

The party? Maybe, but that really wasn't it.

'I think it's hard to understand what a bind Felicia and Madeleine Grenberg were in back then. They were dependent on Karl-Henrik Söderström; did you ever meet him? He owned that big farm in Skavböke.'

'No, I don't think so.'

'Me neither, at least not in his salad days, and I think I'm glad I didn't. Anyway, one night in December of 1999, there's a party outside Oskarström. Felicia isn't there, because Madeleine hurt her foot earlier that day so she stays home to help out. Around eleven, the phone rings and Felicia answers it. It's Killian Persson, and by this point she's been in a secret relationship with him for a few months. Killian heard that Jakob Lindell's father withdrew the family savings and has it stashed in their house. He says he's going to go take that money on his way home from the party.'

'Is this the fifty thousand kronor?'

'Exactly. Felicia and Madeleine need it, he says, that much money could free them from Karl-Henrik Söderström. Felicia probably tries to stop him, tell him no, it won't work, not like that, but the call ends.'

As if Killian Persson decided to cross a new line in the name of love. That's how Vidar thought of it.

'Fast forward to one o'clock. Half an hour before the murder. Killian leaves the party with Sander Eriksson. After a while, they part ways. Killian heads for the Lindells', thinking about how to get in. When he arrives, he sees the spade leaning against the house. Then . . .' Vidar said, hesitating, 'here's where it gets confusing.'

On the other end, Markus listened quietly. Vidar heard him breathing on the line.

'Mikael passes the house on his way home. Presumably he heard the glass pane break and stops to check it out. Tries to forcibly stop the break-in. Killian — maybe he's altered on beer and adrenaline, or who the hell knows, panic — hits him with the spade, once, twice. It's all over in a second, maybe two.'

So quickly fate can turn.

'So he's standing there in the dark. No going back. He needs help — what can he do? He runs to Felicia's. He takes their car and gets Mikael into the cargo area and drives off to dump the body. He manages to get away from the Lindells', but not much farther. When he loses control of the car and crashes, it's too far back to Felicia's place. He runs to Sander's instead.' Vidar opened his eyes. 'Something like that?'

'Something like that,' Markus repeated slowly. 'And this couldn't have been solved back then, back when it happened?'

Exactly. Could it have been? That was the question.

'Maybe. I don't know. I don't think so, given that Killian died and the landslide happened shortly thereafter. He looked to be the culprit, and when he died all the air went out of the investigation.'

'But he didn't die.'

'No,' Vidar said. 'He didn't.'

Markus let out what sounded like a hiss.

'Yeah,' Vidar said. 'I know. But this is where we're at. They did what they could back then, that's my sense.'

Now Vidar could hear that Markus was taking notes. 'What about Filip Söderström?'

'One thing leads to another. Unfortunately, Killian and Filip crossed paths after the funeral. Maybe Filip threatened to expose him? I don't know. We may never find out.'

'And the landslide,' Markus said.

Yes, Vidar thought. *The landslide.*

The blood had dried. If he rubbed his fingertips together, it flaked and fell away. It had been too late by the time Vidar knelt down beside Killian, but he'd still tried.

Vidar jumped as someone knocked on his window, frantic and loud.

'Hey,' Vidar said to Markus, 'I have to go.'

Outside, he saw the dripping face of Adrian al-Hadid.

106

Sander had Killian's blood on his hands. It mixed with his own blood, which slowly seeped from the wound in his hand. Before long, he couldn't tell which had come from his body and which was Killian's. He turned around to look at Killian's body over and over, convinced he would find it had vanished again, as though his friend were never more than a mirage.

Cameras flashed around him again and again like icy heartbeats. They had documented the blood and the bruises on his neck.

Sander sat on the floor in the kitchen and looked around for Felicia, but he couldn't find her.

Instead, there was Killian's backpack. No one had taken it. With care, he opened the bag.

Stuff. Just stuff. And yet: this was the worst part, as if its sole purpose were to torture him. Torture someone who could both remember and imagine. Were there more belongings of Killian's, somewhere? It seemed reasonable; this backpack was small and didn't hold much. Even so, he had his doubts.

This was what had belonged to Killian.

One pair of jeans, black. Lee. A hole in the left knee.

One T-shirt, dark gray. No, it had once been black but had faded badly. Traces of print across the chest: I JUST CAME FOR THE FOOD. Killian's sense of humor.

Two pairs of underwear. Björn Borg brand, threadbare. Holes in the crotch.

Socks.

A Nokia phone, an old model with buttons. Powered off, the battery dead. Slightly banged up at the edges and with a faded sticker on the back: a colorful mayflower, maybe put there by the phone's former owner. Or did Killian buy mayflowers for the annual fundraiser? Maybe he did.

A phone charger.

A bar of beige soap the size of a pack of cigarettes, wrapped up in a sticky plastic bag. Lemon-scented.

An unlabeled bottle. Sander unscrewed the cap. Acetone.

A brown comb with skinny, closely spaced teeth. Strands of blond hair were still stuck in it; it still had a smell. Killian's hair. Sander gently pulled one out and placed it in his palm. It was hardly visible, as fine and pale as it was.

A well-used wooden toothbrush. A tube of Colgate, half-full. How were Killian's teeth? He hadn't noticed.

A razor, Gillette. Pretty dull. Tiny grains of sand in the blades. No, hair. Killian's. Tiny, tiny bits of hair. The last time he shaved must have been just before the funeral.

A plastic bag containing one last, unopened beer, Spendrups Premium Gold. Where had the beer come from? Not the state liquor store.

An open, creased box of Beyond Thin condoms, the kind handed out for free by the Association for Sexual Education, sixteen out of thirty left. Could he have a child somewhere?

A bracelet made of light-brown leather, a little worse for wear. Soft from rubbing against his skin. *Like mine*, Sander thought, *only lighter brown*. The same clasp. They must have been made at the same time. *In the winter of 1999, he made one for each of us.*

No ID. No credit cards. No diary. Nothing. But: nine hundred and fifty kronor, cash, rolled up and secured with a purple rubber band. Hundred-kronor bills and smaller.

A hardcover book, Harper Lee's *To Kill a Mockingbird*, in

the new Swedish translation published just recently. It was heavily dog-eared up to page 218. Sander couldn't remember seeing Killian with a book, much less a hardcover one. A gift? Tucked in the middle of the book was a small bundle of papers and photographs.

In that bundle:

A piece of paper carefully torn out of a graph-paper notebook, much-thumbed; on the paper, an ink drawing of a cabin. The measurements carefully printed in Sander's handwriting. In the floor, a hatch with an arrow pointing to it, and a label: *Beer Bunker*. Killian's writing. They had made a blueprint? Yes, maybe. Way back in his memory, faintly, he could see their heads close together over a table, Killian propping his hand on his forehead. Yes. He remembered now.

Clippings of obituaries, several of them, Linda and Sten Persson's among them. Others, too, but with names Sander didn't recognize. From the years 2007, 2009, 2015.

A photograph: A vast sky. Treetops. It looks hot. They're all there, together. Down by the lake where they liked to grill. Mikael, Pierre, Jakob, Killian. And Sander. Smoke from the firepit. Killian isn't wearing a shirt, and he has an arm around Sander's shoulders. They're both smiling. Who took the picture? He doesn't recall.

A photograph: Felicia. A portrait, must be from the fall of 1999. She's wearing a T-shirt and an unzipped black down coat. He remembers that; it was the same coat she wore all that winter. Looks like it was taken in the forest somewhere. Maybe they were on a walk together. Killian is the photographer. She's beaming.

A photograph: Killian's mother and father, before the divorce. It was taken by a real photographer in town, maybe Göte Karlsson himself. They're kneeling, and between them, on a chair, Killian is a pink, round blob in pastel overalls. All three of them are laughing. Each parent is touching Killian. Rock-a-bye baby.

A photograph: A woman of around thirty, blond, unfamiliar. She's standing outside in a city. This picture looks more recent; that's all he can say about it.

A photograph: Killian and Sander. Eleven or twelve. They're outside the school, must have been school picture day. Killian is wearing a bow tie; Sander's hair has been wet-combed. Mom took this picture, Sander remembers. Killian is half a head taller than him. It's bright; they're squinting into the sun.

A photograph: Another one of the two of them, but they're older. Must have even turned eighteen already. On the road that runs through Skavböke, Killian in black jeans and a white T-shirt; Sander in pale blue jeans and a flannel. One blond head, one dark. They're walking side by side, laughing at something. What was it? No idea. Sander doesn't remember the occasion. Maybe Felicia was holding the camera? They look inseparable.

107

He couldn't see very well as he stood up, leaving the backpack on the floor. His vision was misty. He tucked the last photograph into his pocket.

Belongings. Maybe they don't say much about a person, really, not much and not the important stuff. Or at least, you can tell yourself that, if you need to.

Sander needed to. Because now he remembered.

He's back at ground zero. It's December of 1999. A party like so many others. He witnesses the instant before everything begins to distort. The needle of the compass still untouched. It's one o'clock when he and Killian leave the party.

Is it obvious, to look at Killian, what he's about to do? Maybe. Love is strange, and the heart is a fickle thing.

They go their separate ways in the night. Nothing hurts.

A bag of rice dropped onto the roof from up in the tall tree. That's what it sounds like.

You have to climb pretty high up the nearest tree, scoot as close to the end of a branch as you can get, and hang down from it. Then let go and land on the roof of the garage. From there, you can climb up to the roof ridge and boost yourself — this is the hardest part — over the edge and onto the ledge closest to Sander's window.

As a kid, Killian could do this almost silently. That was how he got into Sander's room unnoticed, so they could read comic books and play games long after the lights went out in

Mom and Dad's bedroom. But it's been a long time; he hasn't done it in years.

Probably never will do it again, a thought that dissolves and fades into memory: the sound of his friend, grown way too big and heavy for this, letting go of the branch and falling to the roof with a thud; Sander himself going to the window and unlatching it, opening it so Killian could climb in.

But it's happened again after all. It's nighttime, the same night as the party, but Sander is already home and in bed when a sound outside the window wakes him from a heavy, dreamless sleep.

He sees his friend dart by like a shadow on the roof.

On the other side of the windowpane, Killian's face is alight with terror. He's panting as though he's being chased, and streaks of blood on his face look almost black in the dark.

The Advent candelabra in the window tips as Sander opens the window.

'What —'

'I need you. Help.'

'But —'

'You have to help me, Sander.'

He follows his friend through the woods. The cold makes his lungs ache. Branches and brambles, icy and sharp, scratch at his arms. They come to a clearing in the black night, and the forest opens.

They're on a small hill. A narrow gravel road winds around the foot of it. On the other side is one of Skavböke's many vast crop fields. They're close to Östholm's place.

'Down there.' Killian catches his breath. 'See?'

Not far down the gravel road he can make out the shape of a car.

It's an old Volvo 240 with rusty fenders. The front has

run into something nasty and unyielding; the back hatch points to the sky. Smoke or steam hisses from the crumpled, busted hood.

'But . . .' Sander hears himself say. 'That's –'

'I know.'

Killian snuffles. His nose is bleeding badly as they start down to the car. The words trickle into silence, out into the night. He stands near the back of the Volvo and stares at Sander.

'It's . . . Sander, I . . .'

He was on his way home, he says, tired and drunk, and he saw a car on the side of the road. It was unlocked and the key was in the ignition. He didn't think about whose it was – cars all look the same in the dark. And, like he said, he was tired and drunk. So he got in and started for home, but then he lost control on the ice and drove straight into one of the big trees on the side of the road. He tried to keep going but couldn't; he'd hit his face really hard and he thought his nose was broken. His eyes kept tearing up too much. And besides, the car would only cough when he tried to start the engine again.

'When I got out, I saw that the back gate had flown open, I think it must have been because of the crash, because it was closed when I first saw the car.' He blinks. 'I think. I'm not sure, but . . . yeah, it had to have been. Anyway, I walked around and –'

'Where was the car when you found it?'

A sound nearby. A bird. It bursts into the night sky, like it just learned something important and needs to pass it along to the powers that be.

'I don't remember. Not at their house. I didn't get that far. It was on the side of the road somewhere.'

Sander walks around the car, comes to stand by Killian,

and bends down to see what's in the trunk. He smells something weird. Then he sees.

Something grows inside his chest. He doesn't know what it is, doesn't recognize it. A cloud of heat and smoke. It has to get out. Here it comes, a wave: Sander screams.

A single night, almost half a life.

He had trusted Killian, had even lived his life according to what Killian told him. Who killed Mikael? Sander didn't know; he only knew that it wasn't his best friend.

He'd been wrong all along.

As he stepped out of Felicia's house, the rain that fell over him felt fresh somehow, as if it would wash him clean of deeper things than blood.

108

Adrian al-Hadid was in Halmstad when he heard the call, and he hurried down to the garage as fast as he could, the binder from Rasmusgården in one hand and the bag containing Jakob Lindell's shirt in the other.

As he sped through Oskarström, he heard the voices of officers who'd beat him to the scene coming over the police radio: it was over. One dead, no other serious injuries. The ambulance, which was a mile ahead of Adrian, could stand down.

Adrian slowed down, too, as he saw a lone figure staggering through the rain. He was walking along the county road up toward Skavböke. A drunk?

Adrian stopped the car and got out.

'Hello,' Adrian said gently. 'How are we doing here?'

'I'm the one who says that stuff,' the old man barked, swaying on his feet. 'I'm the priest here, dammit.'

The heavy stench of alcohol rose off him.

'But what are you doing out here in the rain?'

'My bicycle was broken, what else was I supposed to do?'

Adrian raised an eyebrow.

'Where are you going?'

The old man nodded sadly into the dark, toward the flashing blue lights in the distance.

'To the emergency.'

109

'Is this all of it?'

Vidar weighed the binder in his hand.

'All but the medications list,' said Adrian, who was in the passenger seat next to him. 'But it doesn't really matter now. The shirt's in the bag, there. It's like you thought.' Adrian nodded at the house, which was teeming with intense activity around Killian Persson's body. 'It's his.'

Vidar paged through the binder. Intake paperwork, attachments from social services, notes for the medical record, a visitor log, some sort of diary describing his progress, a calendar of activities.

'Good, Adrian. Thanks. But no. It doesn't matter now.'

The emergency lights had attracted a small flock of onlookers from the village, those who lived nearby and had come out in the rain to see what had happened. Vidar saw Jakob Lindell among them.

'Interesting that he's here,' Adrian commented.

'Very,' Vidar muttered, his focus on the binder.

The diary entries weren't comprehensive, just undated pages from a plain old notebook, covered in Filip's scrawling, uneven handwriting. They were about the staff at Rasmusgården, his medication, how he felt. Vidar paged on and soon stopped at the visitor log.

Most were friends of Filip's, it seemed, but the visits were increasingly infrequent. His father had come once, his mother, too, along with two personal-care assistants. A couple of social workers, the occasional police officer. And then a name that showed up over and over, many times, every week.

'Hey, what was that you said before about Filip Söderström's planner?'

'What part?'

'Something about the number one?'

'Oh yeah, that he seemed to have had a relapse and marked his first day sober again. They do that a lot.'

'Do you remember what it looked like? The way he wrote the number one.'

'Sure, I guess.'

Vidar tapped the page.

The name that appeared in the visitor log over and over. The person who'd visited Siri the day after Filip was murdered.

'Could it have been a letter *I* rather than a number one?'

Adrian looked at the page. *I* as in Isidor.

I didn't know who I could talk to.

That's what Siri had said.

Suddenly it all clicked in Vidar's mind.

'That must be how he knew,' Vidar said slowly as the pieces fell into place.

'What?'

'Siri talked to Isidor Enoksson, who told Filip. That Killian Persson was alive.'

'He's over there in my car right now,' Adrian said.

Vidar turned to look at Adrian.

'What?'

'He was wandering around on the road, in the rain, drunk as hell, so I stuck him in my car.' He looked uncertain. 'Was that a bad idea?'

For the first time in what felt like ages, Vidar smiled.

110

It was Advent, after a church service. Siri had been waiting for Isidor by the entrance. She was there about a disappearance, she said. A teenager. His name was Hampus Olsson.

Isidor had heard the name; everyone had. The newspapers had run his picture on the front page for quite some time. But that was several years ago now.

Siri showed him pictures and asked questions. Had Isidor seen him? Heard anything about someone who looked like him? Would he be willing to keep these pictures and show them to colleagues and people who were active in the church's outreach programs? Maybe someone knew something, had seen or heard of a drifter like him.

The acoustics in the church brought a new ring to her voice.

A day or two later, she called the church office and said she wanted to visit again. Once she was facing Isidor in the room the congregation used for absolution and pastoral counseling, she didn't know what to do. She said she needed someone to confide in, but she wasn't sure who it should be. And then the words simply poured out of her, first the name, and then the astonishing notion.

I think Killian Persson is alive.

The words washed through Isidor like a chilly wave.

As if he had just helped her complete an arduous task, she sighed in relief.

An amazingly loud laugh burst out of her. In that bright,

quiet room, it echoed off the walls. She apologized immediately, said that she was just scared. Or confused.

Isidor remained very calm. At last he tentatively leaned toward her.

'How could anyone carry this all alone, for as long as you have, without breaking?' he said.

That was in fact exactly what someone couldn't do.

Together, Vidar and Adrian led Isidor into a corner of Felicia's house. Two forensic technicians had arrived and were moving meticulously from room to room. The house was very quiet now.

The rain was still falling in sheets outside, pattering loudly against the window.

'And you,' he said forcefully, 'told Filip.'

Isidor opened his mouth to respond. But then he shook his head one last time.

'I'm bound by confidentiality. I can't say.'

As though there could be no explaining it, what he had gone through.

'So you sit there with him at Rasmusgården,' Vidar said. 'Once a week, month after month. I've seen the documents, I know. Never in the capacity of a psychologist, and not even, really, as a priest – just as someone he can talk to. Someone with ties to the place where he grew up, who knew the people around him. It helped him. And there you sit, with reason to believe his brother's killer is alive.'

'But I didn't say anything!' Isidor exclaimed fiercely, as if an invisible pressure inside him had grown too strong.

Behind Vidar, a colleague had stopped short, reacting to Isidor's outburst.

'Is everything all right in here?'

Adrian raised a hand in reassurance. Isidor was breathing hard.

'For God's sake, I was the one who buried him! Can you imagine? The nightmares! Had the casket been empty? The ash at the interment – what was in that urn, dust? I know what I'm looking at when I look at the ashes of a human child. I buried someone, I know that much. But who?'

'So when,' Vidar repeated, 'did you tell him? Was it recently, this summer?'

'Filip had . . . he had matured. Become more grounded, somehow. He had gotten his life together, he had a job. Bought the house from Frans. He mentioned more than once that he wasn't as angry anymore, that he didn't . . . All he wanted was to find answers, so he could stop imagining what they might be. That was all. He needed to know, like one last step before he could move on to the rest of his life. And then, at that point, yes – back in June when we met for one last conversation, I suppose I said more than I should have.' A long, tense silence. 'What was I supposed to do?'

No one said anything. Maybe the question wasn't directed at them anyway.

'Thank you,' Vidar said at last. 'Now we know.'

'Is it true,' Isidor went on, 'that you have the material from Rasmusgården?'

'Why do you ask?'

Isidor nodded at Adrian. 'He said you did.'

Vidar stared at Adrian, who blushed.

'You should be able to find Filip's account in there,' Isidor said, 'of the night his brother died. I got him to write it down for his own sake, but I never read it. No one did.'

'When did he write that?'

'I don't remember, sometime while he was at the facility. I'm sure you know better than I do, incidentally, if you have the records. I want to go home now.' Isidor looked awfully sick. 'Can I please do that?'

III

Siri was standing in the rain when Vidar came out. She had stayed in his car with Felicia until they saw blue lights flashing among the trees. After seeing to it that Felicia received care from two police officers, she didn't know quite what to do and simply stayed out in the rain.

At last she crossed the road to the field, all a violet-tinged expanse in the dark. The night played tricks on her eyes and she couldn't see where the field ended; it seemed to stretch on and on, unending.

And there she stood, even now. She thought of the years gone by, how much she had forgotten, how much she remembered. All the time she had spent silently carrying what she suspected – no, knew – about Killian Persson. She should have called her husband, her children; they had tried to reach her multiple times. But she didn't know what to say.

Vidar came to stand beside her with an umbrella.

'Thank you,' she said stiffly.

Vidar held a thick binder in his other hand. She took note of it but avoided looking at him. Perhaps, at last, the truth had shown itself plainly: it wasn't always worth the price one might pay. Or it simply hurt too much. She didn't know anymore.

'I had to tell someone,' she said. 'But who could I turn to?'

Silence. The rain struck the earth so hard the drops splashed up.

'I brought you here because I thought you needed to come. And you lied to me.'

'I know. What can I say? I'm sorry.'

'I understand it must have been hard on you,' Vidar said, his voice restrained. 'But if you had told me the truth, that Isidor . . .'

'Don't you think I know that?' She struggled to speak. There was an ache in her throat and behind her eyes. 'That's all I can think about.'

In that moment, the downpour stopped as suddenly as if a hatch had closed. Vidar and Siri looked at the sky in surprise.

'Weird,' Vidar said, turning back toward the house.

They saw Isidor Enoksson being led to the road by Adrian.

'He came to my house,' Siri said.

'Yes, I ran into him.'

'You did?'

'The customer who didn't want to buy anything, is that right?'

'He asked if I knew what had happened. If Filip had come to me. No, I said, why on earth would he do that? Then I realized he'd told Filip that Killian Persson might be alive. That he . . . I'm sure that's what he really wanted – Isidor, that is. To confess he had violated our confidentiality.'

Adrian followed the unsteady priest for a bit, then stopped. Isidor didn't seem to notice, just kept walking off into the dark.

'He's going home on foot?' Siri said.

'For he has sinned, he said.'

'Maybe I should do the same.'

Vidar didn't say anything for a long time, as if he were considering a tough decision. Then he said:

'What time did Sander and Killian leave the party?'

'Why?'

'It was one o'clock, right?'

'I think so. Yes, one o'clock. We even had a picture of them, from one of the disposable cameras.'

Vidar nodded slowly and looked at the sky again, unsure if the rain would return. Then he opened the binder in his hand.

112

The account was near the back.

He told me to write to remember. I don't know if I want to, but at the same time it's all I ever do. Remember. I have nothing else left and soon I won't even have that, if things go on like this.

So it began.
Filip described the party, the last time he saw his brother, how and when he left. He was concise:

I leave at one with Elina, I know that much. The clock in the front hall shows one on the dot as we go. Elina is drunk and laughing, imitating the clock hands with her arms. Like a dance, she said, arms over her head. It's a position from ballet. I don't know if that's true or if she's just goofing around. But anyway, that's why I remember what time it is. My brother is still at the party somewhere. I don't say goodbye, because I'll see him at home.

'What are you thinking?'
Siri blinked. She couldn't think, so she just said what she felt:
'It's too specific.' She looked at Vidar. In the dark, his face was all angles and shadows, two glittering eyes. 'His memory. Elina's arms. It's too specific to be misremembered. But also, it has to be wrong.'
'It probably isn't.' Vidar tapped thoughtfully on Filip's words. 'Filip heads out with Elina. We know that. And it

happens at one o'clock. He writes as much himself, and he even explains how he knows. Or more accurately, it's one at the earliest, because the clock fell off the wall and stopped, we know that too. Pierre hasn't fixed it yet, he doesn't do that until he's alone. Which means they can't possibly have left any earlier than one. And Sander and Killian leave much later, all the witnesses agree. How long would it have taken to walk from the party to the place where you found the car?'

'At least half an hour,' Siri said.

'And Mikael was killed at one-thirty.'

Clocks spun before Siri's eyes.

'But,' she said, 'if Filip left with Elina at one o'clock at the earliest, and if we assume the clock has just fallen down, and Sander and Killian don't leave the party until sometime later on, then Killian can't be the one who . . .'

The timeline didn't match up. Sander and Killian wouldn't have made it to the scene of the murder.

'Killian didn't kill Mikael,' Vidar said. He looked up at the house again, toward the front hall and the dead body lying there, the physical remains of a human. 'And that only leaves one option.'

Vidar's gaze lingered on the house as Adrian went back inside, his stride purposeful. After a moment he came out again, with a tight grip on Felicia's arm. No handcuffs. He probably wanted to spare her.

Vidar studied her closely, as though her guilt should be visible in the shape of her.

'The witness,' Vidar said.

113

Vidar had warned Adrian to be cautious: Felicia had been carrying the truth about Mikael Söderström's death for over twenty years and had concealed it well. She had just hidden Killian Persson in her own basement. She had lost a pregnancy in the landslide. There was no telling what other surprises she might be capable of.

Adrian opened the door to his car and tried to get her to sit inside. Vidar and Siri watched from a distance.

Then Felicia said something that made Adrian stop short. He hesitated, just for a moment.

That was all it took. Felicia punched him in the face, tore herself loose, and ran for the forest.

Adrian looked surprised, then weary.

He ran after her, with Vidar a few steps behind.

She didn't get far. Just a short distance into the trees she was overpowered by Adrian, who pressed her into the muddy ground.

'She said she wanted to call her kids,' he grunted. 'What the hell was I supposed to say to that?'

Vidar looked at Felicia, lying there in the dark.

Sometimes, the eyes say nothing; other times, they say so much. Isn't that remarkable.

She had been hovering in the background of the investigation the whole time. When Vidar tried to talk to her, get her to confess, because it would make everything easier, she remained tight-lipped. Perhaps it was no wonder; she was probably trying to protect her family. And herself. Vidar had seen it happen before, more than once. And what would Felicia even have said? Still, he gave it a shot.

'Felicia,' he said, 'if you could tell me in your own words, how it happened.'

'Tell you about what?'

'The night Mikael died.'

'I don't know. I was at home.'

'I know that. But while you're home that night, Killian calls you from the party. Doesn't he? He tells you that the Lindells have withdrawn their savings from the bank.'

Vidar paused. This was a crucial moment. He hoped she would crack, that maybe this was going to work after all, because Vidar had seen that happen before too. Sometimes, something snapped loose inside them when the truth was laid out as fact, plainly and straightforwardly, and they capitulated.

But Felicia didn't react. She just sat there staring at her hands. Thin as a flickering flame. When she didn't say anything, he went on.

'Killian isn't the one who commits the burglary, you are. He isn't the one who gets caught by Mikael, you do. Isn't that so?'

'No.'

'But you see,' Vidar said, 'it couldn't have been Killian. He left the party too late. He couldn't have made it in time. And Sander was with him. Jakob wasn't there, neither was anyone else. Which only leaves you. And I'm guessing you didn't think anyone would get hurt, did you? All you cared about was the money, that's all you wanted, to help you and Madeleine.'

When Felicia heard her mother's name, a tremor ran through her.

'Here's what I think: When Mikael shows up, you get scared. He tries to stop you. What happened? Did he try to talk you out of it?' He leaned forward. 'Did he touch you? Did he try to hurt you?'

He waited again.

'I was at home' was all she would say.

'It would be no wonder,' Vidar said, as though he hadn't heard her, 'if you acted out. I mean, considering Mikael is the sort of guy he is, how he'd treated you before. You've got the spade you used to break the glass and get inside. You swing it at him twice. Then you run home to get the car, and that's when you see Killian. Because he's coming to your place after the party, as you had agreed, right? Is Madeleine awake at that point?'

He didn't think she had been, but he wanted to say her mother's name again. It made her quake.

Now she opened her mouth.

'Killian is dead,' she said.

'I'm very sorry,' Vidar said, because he was.

The next part of the tale hung in the air between them; Vidar could feel it. She was close to giving in.

'But in 1999, he's alive,' Vidar said. 'He tries to help you that night, when you tell him what happened. You aren't a witness to the accident, you're in the car when Killian drives off the road, but you take off before anyone can see you. We have footprints. Killian runs to Sander's for help, and you run home.'

That was all Vidar really had. He hoped she wouldn't realize that, that she would guess Vidar knew more about that night than he did.

He felt genuine sympathy when he looked at her. Eighteen years old. She must have felt so alone that night. Killian, too, presumably.

'That's about the size of it,' Vidar said, leaning back again, crossing one leg over the other. 'Does that sound familiar?'

A flicker in Felicia's eyes. She still didn't speak.

If there were any words left, after all these years, she was keeping them to herself.

'I wonder where she was going,' Vidar said to Siri afterward, when it was all over. 'Just now, when she tried to run away.'

There was probably an answer, there always was, just not the one you expected.

'Maybe just... away,' she said, a grim heaviness behind the words.

114

Whatever happens, morning will always come. A thought they turned to for comfort, the boys from Skavböke, when times were at their worst.

The night was cool and comfortable, and the first streak of light was just dawning low on the horizon as Sander stepped into the yard. Jakob was on his front steps, as though he'd been waiting for quite some time.

'I saw you over by Felicia's,' Sander said. 'I thought I would stop by first, before I took off. I wanted to apologize.'

'To me? What for?'

'For going to the police.'

'Oh.' Jakob cleared his throat, scuffing the gravel with his shoe. 'Well, it all worked out.'

'Yeah,' Sander said. 'I guess it did.'

Jakob nodded at a car parked under the big oak in the yard. Its hood was open and there was a neat row of tools laid out on a blanket draped over the bumper.

'I was out tinkering with the car, I like to do it after the kids go to bed. It's pretty well protected from the rain under there. Then I saw the flashing lights and wondered what had happened, so I followed them. When I got back, I just ended up out here.' Jakob was holding a bottle of beer. He took a sip and rubbed his fingers together like he wished he had a cigarette. 'Alice is asleep upstairs with the kids. She probably doesn't even know I was gone.'

Sander sat down next to him. Jakob noticed the bandage on his hand, but he didn't ask about it.

'Was Killian alive for real? Was that really him?'

Sander didn't respond right away.

'I think so. Or, it was him and it wasn't him.'

Jakob held out his beer, eyebrows raised. Sander shook his head. They sat in silence for a while.

'How are you doing?' Jakob asked at last. 'About Felicia, I mean. I saw them drive her off, so I basically figured it out.'

'Oh.' Sander blinked. 'I don't know.'

'You didn't know? That it was her?'

For an instant, despite all the time that had passed, he was ashamed. He should have known; they should have been close enough for her to tell him. But maybe they never were. He had only thought so – all the things he had confided in her. She was the only one who knew the truth about him. Sander felt his heart beating against his rib cage.

'She never said a word.'

'I guess it can't be easy to talk about something like that anyway.'

A brief silence.

'Nice car. What is it?'

'A 1969 Chevy. I found it in a barn down in Snapparp about a year ago. It's a 327 with Fuelie heads and a Hurst shifter. Put me back ten grand.'

'Nice,' Sander said again, since that was basically all he could say about cars.

Jakob gazed out at the yard and the land. For a moment they both watched the thin streak of warm light as it slowly grew on the horizon.

It had been such a very long night.

'You know,' Jakob said, as if something were weighing on him, 'I was so scared when the police came to talk to me. And your betrayal – I knew you were the one who told them about the shirt.'

'Again, I apologize. I felt like I didn't have any other choice. I've got too much to lose.'

'And I don't? Did you think about me at all? About Alice? Our kids?'

Sander didn't respond. He just squinted into the darkness.

Someone was heading their way on foot. A figure appeared. When Jakob spoke again, the words came out slowly and searchingly.

'So I had to tell the police the truth. I didn't have any other choice either. I'm sure you understand.'

A chill from the past heaved up through the years, rising through Sander's legs like water in a sinking ship. The figure grew, became clearer. It was Vidar Jörgensson.

'Good morning,' he said calmly, gazing at the sunrise. 'If that's the right phrase.'

The burly officer was holding a brown paper bag. He stuck a hand inside and pulled something out, held it up to Sander.

'I believe,' he said slowly, almost apologetically, 'this once belonged to you. Could that be true?'

He was holding the shirt. Sander studied it, then looked up to meet Vidar's gaze.

'What makes you think that? It's not mine, I've never worn that.'

Vidar didn't react, just stood there with the shirt in his outstretched hand.

Next to Sander, Jakob was stiff and silent, as if he were holding his breath. Sander had lied for so long, to so many people. It had come at a great cost. He had no qualms about continuing in the same vein. It was just that he had run out of lies.

'A shirt?' he said in a dead voice. 'That's not enough.'

Vidar smiled sadly.

'You're right, it's not. But I think part of you, deep down, wishes I had more. So this could all come to an end.'

He should have figured it out. She was the only one who knew. He had confessed to her as they were dividing up their belongings during the breakup; it just came out. Who would get the little chair? The sofa belonged to the apartment, so it would stay. Who had paid for the fancy dishes? Wall art – two each? I'm the one who caused the landslide.

He couldn't say how it had happened, why it had come out of his mouth just then, when it was already too late. Maybe that was exactly why. He'd almost killed her once. He'd killed the baby she was carrying. Now she was going to leave him, and he had nothing left to lose. That was probably why he said it.

When he cried, he did it quietly as she sat beside him on the sofa. Eventually she took his hand.

She had revealed Sander's secret to Killian. Killian the innocent. Killian the flight-prone. Killian, who became a shadow while Sander made it through without a scratch.

Maybe it was unavoidable.

The dead do not return, and if they do it creates a disturbance in the world. No matter the price, order must be restored.

115

When Vidar finally returned to his car, Sander watched him go, feeling pensive. Everything had that stillness that follows moments after a thunderstorm. After a while, Sander stood up and looked toward the forest, like he wondered if he should walk straight in and vanish too.

'Was he right?' Jakob asked.

'About what?'

'That you would have liked to go down for the landslide.'

Sander appeared to consider the question, but he didn't respond.

'Maybe you should tell her,' Jakob said. 'Olivia, I mean.' When Sander still didn't speak, Jakob went on: 'You're not a bad person, Sander.'

'I'm a person. Maybe that's enough. But why didn't you say anything back then, if you thought it was me all along?'

Jakob stood up to join Sander. It must have been a difficult question, because he didn't answer right away.

'I guess I couldn't really see the point. It was all over anyway. Mikael was dead, Killian too. I liked you, and I was pretty sure you got wrapped up in the whole thing by mistake, or maybe just because you wanted to help Killian. And in some ways I could understand, after I heard about how Mikael went after Felicia and what Karl-Henrik was up to with Madeleine. Or at least that's how I thought about it at the time, during all the chaos. It was extreme, though, what you did. I know you couldn't predict that the whole area was going to collapse, but you did knowingly risk hurting an awful lot of people.'

The moment when another person's image of you crumbles. Sander had experienced it many times now, but it still hurt.

'You're kind, Jakob. You always have been.'

'So they say. But I'm taking care of myself too. Alice says I'm not on my own side all too often. I didn't really understand what she meant until now.'

Moments slipped in and out of one another, borrowing features, taking on new faces deep inside Sander.

He threw Killian's Christmas present at the wall. The small package fell to the floor.

Then Killian died, and Sander lost his true north. That was how it felt, as if the very structure of his life had fallen to pieces. In the cover of darkness, he went back to retrieve the present late on Christmas Day, to have one last thing to remember his friend by. The package was just where they'd left it, as if it had been waiting for him.

In that moment, Sander found the money in the bag from the carpentry shop. Jakob's money. It was in the hatch he and Killian had built in the floor. The beer bunker.

Alone in the deserted cabin, a switch flipped inside him. Everything was already ruined, and he was going to go away. That was the fate he pictured. He wanted to wipe the slate even cleaner. Take off without leaving anything behind.

As though moral order must also be restored.

Suddenly he could see himself very clearly, as if he were looking at another person. Memory can create its own distance, a sort of separation in the soul. The light of the flash made him look colder than he felt.

The Söderströms' house symbolized everything he hated about Skavböke. Everything he wanted to get away from, everything that had hurt him and the people he loved. Killian, Felicia, Jakob, everyone. It wasn't death beaming like a dark sun over the village in that long-ago winter, but the dark cruelty of the Söderström family.

His hands, as they lit the dynamite, were steady and sure as a tailor's. His head was quiet and still.

Sander remembered a barking dog coming after him, jaws snapping at him. He wriggled out of his flannel and ran on. The shirt fell to the ground somewhere out there in the mud.

Then came the landslide.

He did it to free himself from this place, from what had once been. Instead, he became even more tightly bound to all of it.

He could have shared all of this with Jakob, and maybe it would have been true. But he didn't. Instead, he just said:

'See you around, Jakob. I hope.'

And he began to walk to his car, which wasn't far down the gravel road; he walked into the darkness and the slowly expanding dawn.

116

A memory, that was all Killian was now, once more, one of many.

That summer, Sander combed through every memory, one by one, as if he'd lost something and each memory was a box to search inside. No matter how hard he tried, he came right back around, in a vicious circle, to Isidor Enoksson's words: As high as heaven is over the earth, so great is His mercy to those who fear Him.

Mercy. Could it be?
Or maybe the operative word in that proverb, in Sander's case, was *fear*.
Was this a sign too?
All Sander had done was reunite with his friend after such a long time, and like a storm all the fear and brutality came crashing right back in.

One Friday evening in late August, he stepped onto the lawn at home on Backavägen. The house was quiet, the kids were asleep and Olivia was on the phone with a colleague, talking about a meeting scheduled for the next day. The sky was overcast. The day had been stuffy and humid and he'd had to suffer through the last few lessons of the week with a headache and very little patience. His back pain was starting to return.

Sander's face had hardened with the years, just as Siri had suspected long ago that it would. When he peered into the mirror, he sometimes felt he was looking at a face that wasn't his. Now it was starting to soften again.

Or maybe he was seeing it as it really was for the first time.

Another sign: he'd stopped having the dream.

The lawn had lost its color. Southern Sweden was suffering a drought, and on Backavägen they respected the watering restrictions. The news ran reports about forest fires in the nearby counties of Småland and Västergötland. He thought of those fires, picturing flames eating at trees and biting the ground, making all living things flee.

All living things flee. Yes, maybe for a while. But not forever.

Sooner or later, you have to turn back.

He went inside and up to the children's rooms to press his lips to their foreheads. They were fast asleep, tangled up in blankets and dreams. He hoped they would be able to stay there for a long time.

He kissed Olivia on the cheek and said he was going out for a while, would be back later.

'Everything okay?'

He smiled and nodded, although he wasn't entirely sure.

The right ashes were placed in the right grave. It had been an exhaustive task that ripped up more than just soil. Hampus Olsson's mother was still alive. The media ran sweeping, bombastic think pieces, demanding to find out who was responsible, interviewing locals. It was excruciating.

But in one sense, it was very simple. They changed the date of death on Killian's gravestone. They were all there to witness it together.

One year erased, another in its place. That was that.

Correction: everyone but Sander was there. But now, as he finally stepped into the cemetery in the twilight, he didn't hesitate, he had climbed out of the car and simply put one foot in front of the other. Simple as that.

He'd died, Killian, and he'd come back. And died again. It was confusing and left out a lot of important details, but that was the short version of the story.

Many things would continue to be left out of the story. No one knew what Killian experienced during his years of invisibility. There should be a word for that sort of thing, but there probably isn't.

Sander remembered the way to the grave. When he reached it, he simply stood there gazing down at it. If he was thinking any particular thoughts, he couldn't say what they were; he only remembered the words that came out of his mouth.

'I'm sorry.'

He wasn't expecting a response.

From the pocket of his jacket, he took a photograph. The last one he'd found in Killian's backpack, of the two of them, eighteen years old. Inseparable.

117

No dreams, just rain. He'd often mused, in recent days, that rain is forgiveness. A tiny piece of heaven falling to the earth.

He sat before the grave, breathing in and out. Thumbing the photograph of Killian in his white T-shirt and black jeans, Sander in his pale blue jeans and flannel button-up, green with pale stripes of blue and yellow.

He would linger here for some time, he knew.

He turned his gaze to the sky again. It would probably start to rain soon.

Not yet. But soon.

And in the very back of his mind, somewhere in the murky corners Sander seldom visited, it felt as though the truth had always shadowed him, ever since he'd lost his best friend one Christmas Eve over twenty years ago. A tattered figure moved from tree to tree, always edging closer, luring him in: *Turn around and follow me, come away into the darkness.* Into the unknown, with its unfamiliar paths.